ATLANTIS
Writhing

Highest Light Series

ATLANTIS

Writhing

Jean Brannon

Absolute Love Publishing

Absolute Love Publishing
Atlantis Writhing

Published by Absolute Love Publishing
USA

Illustration by Katerina Dotneboya
Cover design by Panagiotis Lampridis

ISBN-13: 978-0-9995773-5-6

United States of America

By Jean Brannon

Atlantis Writhing

Dedication

For Gregory Lawrence Hagin

Praise for *Atlantis Writhing*

"A captivating journey rich with visual splendor and anticipation woven into every page. *Atlantis Writhing* induces seeded memories to awaken the potential not only to heal on very deep levels, but to incite a return to natural harmony and inherent wholeness. As you're swept away in an incredible romance, you'll cultivate understanding and love for the sacred relationship with yourself and discover how true love versus mission may not be so different. Book 1 in Jean Brannon's Highest Light Trilogy will leave you yearning for more."
- Tania Marie, Author, Artist, and Reiki Master Teacher

"Journey with cosmic energy beings as they face the challenges of fighting for what they believe. Witness a romantic love affair filled with pure selflessness. Beautifully done."
- Ashley Ebba, Tantric priestess, yoga teacher, and model

ONE

Poseidia. Capital of Atlantis. 11,000 BCE.

My new green eyes startled open when we touched down, though the landing was as seamless as the hull of our starship, the Seraphinite. Somewhere along the 1.3 million light years between Ahlaiele and Atlantis, I must have dozed off. But I couldn't have slept long. We had been told the trip would take half an hour in Earth time. Not bad for covering 10 times the length of the Milky Way in less time than it takes most humans to bathe and dress.

"Elysia? Are you okay?"

At the sound of my Earth name, I smiled at Ava even as I struggled for breath. Stirring my freshly minted humanity, I swung one leg easily enough from the travel pod. The other limb prickled with a thousand pins I couldn't see so I dragged it to its mate. Glancing around, I couldn't help but wonder how my crewmates had mastered movement so quickly. My Ahlaielian companions (who I was still used to seeing as light, color, and vibration) were darting about in stunning, solid forms — bodies that required oxygen in regular, rhythmic doses. Gripping the pod's smooth lip, I willed air into my lungs.

"I ... I'm fine, Ava."

"You know what 'fine' means to the humans, right?" asked the Silver Ray as she gently sat next to me. She leaned closer, as if sharing a secret, her straight black hair falling forward to sweep my shoulder.

Among our crew, Ava was the only one who'd been embodied before. Multiple times through the centuries, in fact, but in an organically androgynous form. Because of the nature of this assignment and the resulting surgeries, this was her first tour of duty as a female and the first since the severing of her mesmerizing powers of persuasion.

"I'm sure it was in the manual." I looked at her sheepishly. "The one I never read."

"Oh, nobody read that thing!"

We giggled. From across the room, Captain Kendrick and his Gold Ray partner, Quenna, sent us curious glances.

Unlike Silvers, who on Ahlaiele are pure peacemakers, Golds are bold leaders, often called upon to guide civilizations in wise ways of abundance. They're capable of channeling any kingdom's currency, literally out of thin air. Or at least they can unless their souls have been split—as had Kendrick's and Quenna's—for the purpose of taking human form. The thought made my stomach turn.

I knew it shouldn't. We'd been assured wholeness would be restored once the assignment was over. Still, I found it hard to ignore my gut and the angst whispering to me that nothing would ever truly be made right again.

Ava draped an arm around my shoulders. With her shorter and slightly heavier frame, it felt every bit the security blanket she intended for me. "Well, you know how people will say they're fine when they're really anything but fine, right?" she asked.

"Sure. It's part of the vernacular. Or perhaps part of their charm."

"Exactly!" She patted my knee. "I think 'fine' really is an acronym meaning 'fragile, insecure, neurotic, and emotional'."

We snickered again, more softly but still loudly enough to draw stares. Across the room, Will (another of our crewmates) playfully tousled Quenna's hair until he'd teased a grin. Then he turned shiny black eyes upon Ava and me.

"Hey, y'all," he said in a raspy drawl. "I'll be damned if that rocket ride wasn't slicker than snot on a doorknob." Ava and I groaned as his lean frame eased behind the control desk.

"It didn't take him long to develop a way with words." Ava looked amused as Will's spidery fingers skittered across the keyboard.

For all his lightheartedness, Will carried warrior energy. Before the surgeries, he could summon any weapon as an instrument of Highest Light. Now he and Ava were ready to brave the dark regime Poseidia's new king was conjuring—without so much as a pocket knife or bargaining chip between them.

"Not long at all." For some reason, I was near tears. "So I really can mean it, then, when I say I'm fine?" I was feeling weak and nauseous and rather beyond human speech so I sent her a mind-message the old way—telepathically.

Mind-messaging was our only Light Ray gift we were told would even halfway translate into our new bodies. Although that, too, felt like energy moving through molasses. *Thank you for your calming presence, dear friend. It means more than I can say.*

"As long as we're here, I'll think there's something wrong with you if you don't mean it."

In my head I could hear her. Slightly fuzzy, like whispers beyond a door. But there was no mistaking that comforting tone. *I've got your back, my beloved. For as long as we are here. For as long as you need me. And then some.*

Those words had become our mantra once we were chosen for the mission. On Ahlaiele, loyalty and support are a given. But the thickness of Earth's third-dimensional reality creates the illusion of an impenetrable veil, a separation from Oneness for humans, and none of us knew for sure if we'd fall prey to this oppressed type of Lesser-Light thinking once we arrived. So we wanted to be ready to uplift and encourage each other whenever difficulties arose.

I worried that was what was happening to me. Had I somehow slipped behind the mantle already, only to be swathed in its gossamer shroud? I felt isolated, alone, and (as much as I hated to admit it) cloaked in death.

And then some, I messaged back as what felt like electricity surged through my body. I didn't need to turn my head to know who had arrived behind me.

"Ladies," he murmured, and I thought—not for the first time—that hearing his honeyed human voice was every bit as pleasant as his whale-like Ahlaielian tone.

"Hey, Hunter." Ava's grin reflected her happiness at seeing my Purple Ray companion. Purples envelop the energy of what we call "healing and feeling". Within our pairing, I was the psychic feeler (an empath) and Hunter was pure wizard, having performed both magic and miraculous healings. Before the crystal scalpel procedures, anyway. "You know, human doesn't look half bad on you."

"I guess I clean up okay." Hunter shrugged good-naturedly. "You're looking elegant as always, Ava." Skirting the travel pod, he kissed her golden-brown cheek. I watched as that simple action sent tawny bangs tumbling over his forehead, and I couldn't help but gawk. The psychic surgeons in charge of his physicality must have sculpted him from the depths of my most secret appetites, because his very presence quickened my pulse.

Hunter kept chatting with Ava, but I didn't hear a word. I was lost in my own reverie. Ever since I could remember—for countless centuries before being granted this human form—I'd fantasized about the flesh. And all too often I'd caught myself daydreaming about what it might be like to have a physical relationship with Hunter. We'd never discussed it, though. In fact, through all those eons I'd kept my yearnings to myself because the few times I'd felt brave enough to hint around, to see if any of my companion Rays had similar longings, I had discovered I was obviously the only Ahlaielian capable of lust. Of slipping from the virtuous thoughts that were supposed to be the only possible mindset in Ahlaiele's Highest Light frequencies.

Needless to say, I had long ago come to believe there was something wrong with me. Why else would I alone dwell on the vulgar vibrations we missionaries were always helping other worlds rise above? And with no physical body to boot? No flesh and blood capable of sharing the sensual delights I had all my life thought too much about?

No flesh until lately, anyway. Looking at Hunter, I trembled to think I finally had a physique ready for pleasures like holding hands. Or kissing. Or other desires I didn't dare name. The ones that singed my cheeks and made me crave them all the more. Skin on skin. Unhushed cries. Broken sighs in silky sheets. Hair and hands and lips and legs entangling. Touching and holding. Or writhing and releasing.

As my mind wandered further down that dangerous road, Hunter's gaze met mine. I could see as he crinkled one eye into a wink that he had an idea of where my shameful thoughts had been, and my face flushed. For some reason, the surgical team had made me a redhead. Not a bad thing at all, I'd thought, until I realized redheads seemed to blush more easily than other humans.

"Now, if this one could just get those long legs working," he kidded.

"Oh, uh, I'm fine, Hunter," I sputtered.

Ava burst out laughing, just as I realized what I'd said. I bloomed a deeper shade of rose, then tapped my feet as if to show them how strong I felt. In truth, I thought I might faint if I stood, yet I didn't understand why I was the only one struggling.

"You're not fooling anyone, El," Hunter replied, his voice kind yet firm. "Least of all me." His green eyes, mirrors of my own, surveyed my energy field as his hand hovered six inches from my body. Purple light waves crashed over me, and I found I could no longer sit up. Hunter caught me as I collapsed and helped me lay back in the travel pod.

"What is it, Hunter?" Ava's guarded tone drew Will across the chamber.

"She's too permeable," Hunter muttered as I shut my eyes, trying to still a runaway heartbeat.

"Too permeable?" Will asked.

"Yes," Hunter replied. "Her energetics have always been, shall we say, more sensitive than most. Even on Ahlaiele."

"I think we've all known that," Ava murmured.

"What happened?" Kendrick's commanding voice told me he was now standing to my right, but I dared not look. Keeping my eyes closed seemed to slow the vertigo spinning me around the ship.

"She's leaking energy," Hunter explained. "Too much, too fast. There are holes in her auric field."

"But why?" Quenna demanded.

"She's suffering the effects of being split off from half her essence." I felt Hunter studying me. "I mean, we all are, in our own ways. I know I could look around and tell each of you how your system is still reeling from the separation. But with El, the very sponge-like quality that allows her depth of feeling is being wrung out by Lesser Light.

So now she lacks enough male energy to hold her spirit inside her physical vessel. That's why the vibrations here are having such an easy time with her. Gui is already sucking and stealing. It will happen to all of us eventually, since every one of our natural defenses has been compromised. But it's worse for El."

"We need to move quickly, then, now that we're here on the ground." I could feel Quenna's growing impatience. "Get the balancing frequencies planted and get out. Before we all end up like El."

"Indeed," Kendrick sighed. "What I'd like to know is why we saw no evidence of this issue prior to leaving Ahlaiele."

"Even with all the days we spent in the third-dimension replicator, it wasn't enough," Hunter replied. "Especially since we had no way of duplicating what gui would do once it got its teeth into her."

"So what now, Hunter?" Ava asked.

"I need to take her into the Tranquility Room and see if I can still channel enough of the Purple Ray to seal and heal those gaps."

"All right. Do what you have to do." Kendrick's voice radiated its customary confidence. "Will, I'd like you to take charge of the reporting desk. Ava, I want you to remain on board, in case your assistance is needed. Quenna and I will disembark and deal with the Atlantean High Council. Agreed?"

"Agreed, Captain," they responded in unison.

I heard swift steps and hushed voices. Then Hunter's muscular arms gathered me from the travel pod.

"I've got you, El," he whispered, and I think I sighed as I curled into his chest. I vaguely thought if I died I would go pleasantly enough, cradled in those arms. As he carried me, I felt momentary warmth and vibration, and then I drifted into darkness.

TWO

For some time—I'm unsure how long—I floated in and out of awareness. I lay in the ship's chapel (the Tranquility Room) on one of its rounded couches. Downlights studded the ceiling's curved darkness like stars. Then there were Hunter's closed eyes, his lashes casting feathery shadows on cheeks as hard and smooth as stone. At some point, I watched him light candles with the wave of a hand. And at another, I felt his palms on either side of my head, and so much purple poured through my third eye I believe I fainted.

"Elysia," he whispered. From some deep stillness, my consciousness arose. I tried opening eyes too heavy to lift. As I sank again into the abyss, he rested his hand on my forehead.

"El, come back to me." Golden light flooded my mind. Suddenly, I was alert, staring into twinkling eyes. "Hey, you."

"Hey, yourself." My lips felt too thick, and when I tried to move I couldn't.

"Take it slow," he advised. "It's just the energy work. I can't channel efficiently here, so your body's still assimilating what I was able to do."

For precious moments, we gazed at one other. Hunter stroked my hair, and in the quiet I admired his strong chin and ridiculously straight posture. He'd been gifted with an athletic body that always observed proper carriage. Even though he sat beside me on a made-to-be-sunk-into couch, his spine was erect, his broad shoulders perfectly square.

"Where are the others?" I asked.

"Quenna and Kendrick are meeting with Poseidia's High Council still. Ava and Will are manning the control deck. They've been trying to update the Elders as I mind-messaged them about how you're doing, but the computer circuitry isn't responding, so they're on standby for now."

"So how am I doing?"

"Fair to middling is how I think Will would put it."

"Seriously, Hunter. Why was I so ill?"

"I think you've just taken 'homesick' to a new level is all."

I couldn't decide if I should allow him the white lie or not. He and I both knew my truth button was infallible. It scared me he would even think of fibbing. "Hunter—"

"It's not a lie, El," he countered, clearly reading my train of thought. "In some ways, your energy structure is longing for Ahlaiele's higher, cleaner vibration."

"And in others?"

"And in others, Lesser Light is longing for your higher, cleaner vibration. Your empath's sponge-like makeup is putting you in grave danger here."

"What does that mean to the mission?"

"The mission? Lords with Swords!"

"Hunter, please—"

"El, I'm talking about your life, your safety, our future—things that go well beyond the mission for me!"

"But we're here for a purpose—"

"Absolutely, we are. But not for long, if I can't find a way to protect you. And if I can't do that, the mission is lost. Perhaps even before it begins."

He caressed my cheek, and chills quivered me. It was a sensation I'd always yearned to feel. And though I feared I was falling prey to Lesser Light influences, right there in the chapel, I couldn't help wishing he would touch me elsewhere.

"What are you saying?" I asked.

"Somehow we underestimated the strength of their frequencies here."

"But you seem so ... unaffected."

"Not unaffected," he retorted. "Just not incapacitated. I do have concerns about Quenna; she's battling hard to adjust. But you ... let me put it bluntly: If I hadn't channeled enough of the Purple Ray to replenish your leaking life force, I believe you would be dead by now."

"For the love of Oneness," I sighed. "So I ... I'm not able to hold proper boundaries here, is that it?"

"That's the heart of it, yes."

"Hmmmm." Some piece of my mind was beginning to turn on his words. "Well, what if I made myself essentially invisible? In fact, what if we all did? So gui wouldn't notice us in the first place?"

"I'm listening."

"Okay. Look at this." Closing my eyes, I mind-messaged him. No words, just an image. "What do you see?"

"A perfect circle. Three equally spaced dots along its bottom circumference. With a break in the line—an opening—separating two of the dots."

"Yes."

"And this hieroglyph means ... what exactly?"

7

"Many things," I murmured. "I first saw the symbol right before we left Ahlaiele. When I traveled to the Outpost Library."

"I thought visiting was forbidden."

"I was only granted access because an Ahlaielian seer sought me out. She asked if I'd be open to deeper guidance for our mission and gave me the code to unlock the Manuscripts of Antiquity Chamber." I tried to lift my shoulders, and he helped me sit up. "I spent hours perusing the beautiful volumes without finding anything. Then, right when I was about to leave, a Lemurian text fell off the table and opened to a page on emotion and Lesser Light."

"And?" Hunter's clear eyes searched my own.

"It explained how like attracts like. We've known for all these centuries of ministering to other worlds how Lesser Light draws shadows to itself. How it lures the negative energies of others and pulls them into its collective consciousness like a magnet grabbing steel. But the text said our own combative efforts actually cause it to thrive, too. That our zeal to control feeds instead of curbs, just as surely as any of the lower emotional frequencies matching its own. I believe that was what I was meant to know. What the seer knew I needed to find."

Hunter's perfect brow furrowed. "I'm not sure I'm following," he said. "How does knowing that make you invisible? What are you suggesting?"

"We have to ignore gui," I explained, "so it weakens and starves. We can't nourish it with our fear, as so many humans do. Nor can we let it feast from our desire to fix it. Not here. Here we must act with indifference."

"But we're missionaries, El," he argued. "We've been trained to pay gui attention. To root it out in our humble attempts to rid the Universe of it. And it's always been our job to fix it. It kind of goes with the turf."

"I know. But we've never eliminated Lesser Light, have we? Not in a single galaxy where we've preached. And the trouble is, here in Earth's dense vibration — in these physical forms — we lack the supreme protection Highest Light has always afforded us. Our impenetrable shield is gone, because here we have access to much more than the unconditional love that's been our only vibration. Here we are privy to the whole realm of emotion, with its accompanying frailties and short-sighted impulses. We've only just arrived, and we're all feeling the change. It's not just me."

"Yes," he muttered in agreement. "And we've yet to leave the ship." He paused in thought and then nodded. "Okay. So how do we ignore it?"

"The symbol I showed you holds the key," I replied. "The Lemurians called it the Circle of Emotion, and it's a metaphor for all that is. Humans are like that middle dot on the forefront of all that is, deciding in each moment what's taken into experience, forming perceptions by which way they're looking. Either they're staring at the dot beside them on the unbroken line, which represents all that they love, or else they're watching the dot across the gap, which stands for all that they fear. And all they've not yet healed. "

"So they choose with a simple turn of their heads."

"Yes. Notice the three dots are equally spaced on the circle. It means humans are equally close to both love and shadow, equally in reach of what they desire and what they don't want. And most humans get conditioned early on to stare across the gap. To focus on all the things that feel wrong. But that type of thinking is what creates a break in the flow from Source, and through that breach gui creeps into their unguarded awareness."

"You're saying a human's fate on Earth depends on which way that head is turned?"

"Yes. Humans get so used to the sucking and starving, they think the mindset of 'there's never enough' is a normal way of being. Of course, in that weakened frame of mind, they're much easier to manipulate. Something Poseidia has used to its advantage for centuries."

"So we ignore the gui?"

"Yes. And heal our shadows."

"You know I'm used to healing anything, El. At least I was before the surgeries ..." He sighed. "But healing ourselves here — "

"All that's needed to heal here is to feel good," I interrupted. "To flood ourselves with positive emotions, with Highest Light. To focus on feeling the frequencies of love and gratitude in a type of Oneness Prayer to the self."

"You're kidding."

"No, I'm not."

"That's it?!"

"Hunter — "

He cut me off. "So let me get this straight. If I use us and our current situation as an example ..." His voice faded, and he shook his head.

"Go on. Please."

"I would be standing beside you on the unbroken side of the Circle of Emotion. As love." His eyes searched mine for confirmation.

"Yes, that's true."

"And on the other side of you, across the gap but equally as close to you as I am, would be a most vile and corrupt Atlantean. The most evil representative of Lesser Light I can imagine."

"That's also true."

"And so you're asking me to ignore my gut reaction, my training, my deeply entrenched judgments about how we need to outwit and outmaneuver gui and rescue all those serving Lesser Light from the error of their ways. In essence, pay no attention to the Atlantean. But instead focus my whole heart and soul on simply feeling good. And you're saying the way to feel good is by focusing on Highest Light — on feeling for the frequencies of love and gratitude — in spite of circumstances and surroundings."

"That's precisely what I'm asking of you."

"For the love of Oneness, El." He reached for my hand, and we sat for what seemed like an eternity. His warmth pulsed through my palm, comforting me like the heartbeat from home that it was.

"I know it's a tough concept to wrap your mind around," I said at last. "Especially since we come from a place where only Highest Light exists. And yet if we're to consider working with these natural laws and densities of Earth, this idea requires us to surrender. Into complete allowance of Lesser Light. To rest easily in her arms, becoming one with her darkness, so there's no boundary between. To accept evil without reaction, to refuse to look at where we ourselves are gouged and bleeding, and instead hold fast to the belief it's somehow all good. I think it's the only thing that will work." Tears misted my eyes. "I believe it's ultimately why no magic potion or mighty sword has yet helped Atlantis. Because gui has only continued to fatten herself off all the longing the witches and warriors have unknowingly fed her, in wanting so desperately to effect a change."

"Yes. I feel the truth in your words."

"But saying a Oneness Prayer — the act of conjuring feelings of love and gratitude — won't engage gui. There's no distress signal beckoning her. No crumbs for her to consume." I looked at him with all my heart's intensity. "I believe it's the only plan we can draw upon to stop feeding the dense collective consciousness. So we can do what we came to do. Plant the necessary balancing frequencies. And go home."

"It's not the idea that troubles me." He surveyed my hand's every contour. "It's how this would play out in real life, in real time. When we're the sheep among wolves. And we've ventured into their dens."

"Hunter —"

"And they're hungry."

"Look, I know this is challenging —"

"Challenging?!" Fire leapt from his eyes as he leaned closer. "Challenging was being able to channel enough energy into you with what's left of my healing abilities so you didn't die right in front of me. Okay? That was challenging!" Again he shook his head. "But this ... this is surely madness!"

"Is it?" I could feel an inner strength rising from within. "Is it really madness to try a radical approach? To allow what is simply to be? To surrender to something no one's yet been able to harness or tame, let alone destroy, in spite of any number of gifts and efforts?"

"But to surrender? When we've spent eternity as crusaders?"

"Yes."

"But how do we pull something like that off?" His question was directed as much to himself as it was to me. "Just the idea of holding the frequencies of love and gratitude, while plunked down in the midst of tension and tentacles, is enough to shiver my soul. Especially without our Light Ray endowments."

"I feel the same. But we will do it because we have to. Because I believe it can work. Because if anyone can get it close enough to perfect, we can. And because I don't see any other way. Do you?"

"You know I don't."

"Well?"

"Okay." He sighed, then looked deep into my eyes. "I'm in." He squeezed my hand gently with his and ran his thumb across mine.

"We'll have to get the others to agree."

"Let me handle that. Right now you just focus on putting two feet on the floor."

Shakily I stood, his arms steadying me. His hands made me feel so deliciously alive. I shoved aside guilty thoughts, the ones insisting gui had engulfed us. He bent toward me as I caught my breath. And then those lips skimmed my cheek before, all too soon, he withdrew.

"Hunter, please ..." I begged, looking up at his face that was still so close to mine. I felt dizzy and weak and elated all at the same time. And in spite of my shame, I didn't think I could bear it if he moved away. Disappointment and longing emanated equally from my fingertips as they twisted in his mane.

"Please you I will. And soon, as you've been desiring long before we had these supple bodies," he whispered. "And yet these feelings, this ... yearning — like the flesh — is new to me. So I wish to savor you, in small doses. A little ecstasy at a time."

"How very patient of you."

"I promise you'll not wait long." Tenderly — with such sensitivity it did, in fact, gentle my desires — he again kissed my cheek. "But now I'm supposed to return you to the control deck."

"Understood." I had no idea why, but in that moment I felt such crushing loneliness I wanted to sob. And yet I had to admire him for choosing restraint over indulgence. Of course, he was right. Why did he always have to be right?

"Okay, pretty human suit," he joked. "Let's go."

THREE

"I thought we'd lost you," Ava uttered through tears, embracing me as Hunter and I entered the control room. Before Will could hug me as well, a chime sounded and he slid back into his seat. As he typed, the rest of us slipped into the silver command chairs that formed a semi-circle with his.

"Love note from home?" Hunter asked, glancing at the screen hovering just beyond the reporting desk.

"Yup." Will frowned as he finished typing. "Our transmitter's down, and in spite of all the repair codes I've initiated, they still haven't gotten a damn one of my communications. But our receiver's good. This one says your mind-message was garbled, Hunter."

"Yeah, well ... I was a little distracted." Hunter winked at me. "Right, El?"

I smiled in response. He was flirting with me! I hoped it was dark enough so no one would notice my face had flowered another fantastic shade of scarlet. Being a redhead was fast becoming the bane of my earthly existence.

"Mind-messaging seems challenging to do with clarity here," Ava remarked. "So I can only imagine what it's like beaming a signal back home, across all those light years."

"Evidently, we all should have read that manual," Hunter quipped, which brought groans and more laughter.

Looking around at these souls seated next to me, my Ahlaielian companions, I felt overcome with gratitude. This family of mine, who was brave and loving enough to come here and help balance this unstable place without so much as a smidgen of their formidable talents, was a blessing. My greatest blessing.

Since being chosen for this mission, I'd been praying to be able to trust, to let go of the idea we'd have been better off venturing here with our souls intact. To have faced gui while standing in all our power. It was a true test of faith, of surrendering to Oneness and allowing ourselves to be used as Right Action dictated, knowing Highest Light would be guiding and directing. I only hoped Ava and Will would resonate with what I'd shared with Hunter. Try as I might to search and feel and allow some other idea to come, no other options had surfaced.

"Not that I want to change the subject, but there's a matter of business at hand," Hunter said at last. He filled the others in on what we'd talked about in the Tranquility Room.

"Lords with swords!" Will exclaimed. "Never dawned on me our feelings would be what pulls these bastards close."

I nodded in agreement. "This is much more complicated than I initially thought," I said. "I understood our mission as getting in, getting Highest Light energies planted, and then getting out before they realize what we've been up to." I took a deep breath. "But we have been programmed to react powerfully to gui, with all that data-dumping on how to defend and deflect and be on guard. If those are the very things attracting it, well, that makes things much more complicated."

"Wait," Ava interjected. "Certainly the Elders must have considered this? They must have known, right? Perhaps they thought they had no choice but to send us anyway?"

My stomach turned. "I'm afraid there's more," I said. Another wave of nausea hit, but I forced myself to keep speaking. They needed to hear the truth my emotional body was screaming at me. "Our predicament is no accident."

"What?" Ava's dark eyes widened. Before she could say more, Hunter was at my side, his hand between my shoulder blades. I could see and feel intense purple light radiating through and around me.

"It's happening again, El. You need to listen and do exactly as I say." Hunter's tone still held that softness I felt I would never tire of hearing, but there was no mistaking the stone-like strength of his intention. Feeling more and more lightheaded, I nodded.

"Close your eyes. Now breathe," he commanded. I did as he instructed.

"That's it. Breathe in the Oneness Prayer. No other thoughts, no other words, no other feelings." He placed one white-hot hand on my solar plexus and another over my forehead. In my mind's eye, I saw a mass of tangled thoughts and feelings writhing around my midsection. As I flooded myself with love and felt immense gratitude for Hunter's aid, the grip loosened. Little by little, the contortions eased. I floated in No-Mind, in the space filled only with the comforting purple light of home. And my beloved's hands.

I know not how long I drifted. But suddenly my eyes opened, and I found myself staring into Hunter's reassuring face.

"Hey, you," he whispered.

"Hey, yourself." I felt my deeper passions again stirring for the healing angel before me.

"No, you don't," Hunter cautioned. "No feelings right now. You are to remain in No-Mind. It makes it easier for the three of us to shield you. Which we need to do until we get you stabilized."

"I'll do as you say." My voice wavered in my ears. "And yet I have to share what happened. I was gifted with insight."

"All right," Hunter muttered. "But keep your eyes closed. And remember to remain in No-Mind."

Obediently I nodded, and then I told them how we'd all been deceived.

FOUR

"This is deeper and more far reaching than we ever would have considered," I began. As if preparing for a long story, Ava and Will retreated to the chairs on either side of me, while Hunter crouched at my feet. Even in that posture, he kept a straight spine. Looking around at their sober faces, I could feel them bracing for some brutal truths. And yet I knew there was no way they were prepared for what I was about to say.

"Go on, El. It's okay," Ava coaxed.

"I'm not sure exactly where to start."

"How about someplace near the beginning?" Hunter suggested.

"Okay." I closed my eyes and found it easier not only to find words, but to remain in No-Mind. "Ahlaiele has been breached. Lesser Light forces have infiltrated her highest quarters. And I'm uncertain, even if we complete this mission, that we'll have a home to which we can return. At least one we recognize."

"Well, kiss my go-to-hell," Will muttered. "Are you sure?"

"I wish I weren't." I squeezed my eyes together—hard—so no feelings or tears would come. "But I'm positive. While it's a fact my psychic gifts don't function fluidly here, the vibration of authenticity still runs through my core. Though, like with mind-messaging, information travels along my truth channel much more slowly in this dense atmosphere. But since Hunter's healing, a clear knowing of our circumstances has been welling to the surface. Just now it reached my consciousness. What I tell you is what has happened."

"How can this be?" Ava's whisper broke into jagged pieces, piercing my heart.

"The infiltration was carefully planned," I murmured. "Meticulously so. And by the best and brightest of the Atlantean elite, who have moved among us for a while now." Slowly I shook my head. "Their Lesser Light ways are so subtle. So seductive. The Atlanteans are masters of Dark Heart energy, the most addictive substance in the universe. Even the slightest taste can lower vibrations ever so slightly. Just enough to hook the most chaste heart's frequencies, opening the door to hunger.

Then need. Allowing the one who wields its power to gain access. And control."

"With the Elders?" Will exclaimed.

"Yes," I sighed. "With the Elders. That's why we were chosen for this mission. Not because of our wisdom or skills—as much as I liked hearing the Elders say that throughout our training—but because of our commitment to Highest Light." I swallowed hard. "They knew they'd risk everything by asking us to indulge in the tainted frequencies. And so they decided it was easier to destroy us, since we alone possess power enough to stop them and to keep them from poisoning the planet with the blight they now are. Or at least we did, before the surgeries." A shudder wracked me, as vivid imagery filled my mindscreen. "I can see Ahlaiele before me, how she appears from space. How her vibrant rainbow aura has darkened and grayed, as our fellow Light Rays succumb. As more and more of them writhe with desire for the Dark Heart's elixir."

"Highest Light, no!" Ava breathed. "And so all the preparation and training and data-dumping was just—"

"Smoke and mirrors," I whispered.

"And the fact we had our souls split?" Anger seethed between Will's clenched teeth.

"Insurance," Hunter replied.

"Yes," I said quietly. "The main reason for the surgeries was not to make us look like the Atlanteans, in the image of their idealized humans, as we were told. But to break our immortality codes."

"In the name of Oneness," Ava sighed.

"They had to ensure—as best they could—we were weakened," I continued. "Because we were never meant to make it to Atlantis alive. They inserted a computer code into our ship's programming, which was supposed to shut off life support soon after takeoff. Since the surgeries made us mortal, we should have died well before landing. Yet something must have malfunctioned. Maybe you'll want to check on that, Will."

"On it." Launching himself into one of the command chairs, his nimble fingers whizzed across the keyboard. "You're right, El. I found the code. And it's in plain sight. But only if you're looking. It seems a disruption in one of our ship's transmitters disabled it." He let out a low whistle, sinking back into his chair with folded arms. "So let me get this straight. Our home planet's been hijacked by none other than our most trusted teachers and mentors, who've become a bunch of Light-damned junkies. These scoundrels in turn weakened us, programmed the ship so we'd die obediently, and then fired us off to Atlantis. Am I missing anything?"

"That about sums it up." Hunter's voice was solemn.

"Perhaps it's because we were in a debilitated state and had been immersed in such intense training, but it's odd to me none of us saw this coming," Ava mused.

"I had no idea what was really going on." Hunter had taken to his feet pacing, his jaw hardening by the moment.

"It's like what Will said about the computer code," I explained. "We didn't see it because we weren't looking. We were coming from a place of complete trust and love. Never before had there been a reason to doubt or question. For me personally, any anxiety or misgivings I was experiencing, I attributed to the newness of having a human body. And the absence of half my essence."

"It's disturbing just how cunning their plan was." For a long moment, Ava watched her fingertips drum the control desk. "But that's neither here nor there. Right now we have to figure out what we're going to do moving forward."

"You're right, Ava. We need a plan," Hunter replied. "Will, do you have any idea when we should expect Kendrick and Quenna?"

"They were aiming to be back around dusk." He moved closer to the screen, his fingers once again dancing over the keys. "Seems the sun should be setting any minute now."

"That doesn't give us much time," Ava said. "But I know I'd feel more comfortable if we could pull something together before they return. At least, if we examine our options now, it should help us decide more quickly on a course of action once they've been briefed."

"I agree." Hunter stopped and stared at me, his eyes sharp. "El, what do Kendrick and Quenna know at this point? Anything?"

"Give me a minute." Closing my eyes, I sat up straight. I took several deep breaths, sinking ever deeper into my truth channel, which felt like a clean, hollow tube running the length of my body. I pulled my awareness as completely into the tunnel as I possibly could, feeling along its length and breadth for any information regarding Kendrick and Quenna. It wasn't the effortless flow of impressions my psychic gifts usually provided, but images, sounds, scents, feelings, and knowledge infiltrated me nonetheless. When I felt I had enough information, I opened my eyes. "They've been mind-messaging the Elders, so our betrayers know we're alive."

"Are they returning to the ship alone?" Ava asked.

"No."

"Lords with swords!" Will swore.

"Okay." Hunter's voice had never sounded more determined. "So we have to find a way to stay in the Oneness Prayer, in spite of all that's in front of us. And we have to do it quickly."

"Yes," I murmured. "By working together, it will be easier to stay grounded and focused."

"All right, so we set the intention to hold the Oneness Prayer. And if our minds stray? If we lose focus?" Ava's large eyes traveled from one of our faces to the next, looking for reassurance.

"Don't judge it. Just bring yourself back," I advised. "There are going to be distractions. The trick is not to have an emotional reaction, which creates the charge off of which gui feeds. And we can help each other with this as we go."

"Meaning?" Will's raised eyebrows for once made him look hopeful, and his expression fueled my faith.

"Meaning if one of us gets caught off guard, we still have three others holding the intention," I replied. "At any given time, by working together, we will be an unstoppable force of Right Action. One they can't see or feel, because we won't be engaging them. We'll only be vibrating love and gratitude, which are undetectable."

"And what if the enemy walks into this control room, crystal lasers drawn, and starts shooting? What if the sole intention in returning with Kendrick and Quenna is to kill us?" Will asked.

"Then I for one will be grateful, and I'll know as I die that while I lived I was an incorruptible force of Highest Light." I could feel Hunter's admiring gaze as I continued. "But I don't think it will come to that. Our training has taught us Atlantis is nothing if not an intellectually curious society. Our mere existence—when we should have long since been dead—will pique their leaders' interest, if they're true to their nature."

"All the Atlanteans I've ever met were ravenously curious. And our presence may actually plant a seed of doubt as to which Ahlaielian faction is truly in charge," Ava offered.

"That would be a mighty gift of grace," Will murmured.

"I'll be monitoring things energetically and should be able to offer anyone additional support as needed." Hunter surveyed each of our faces. "If you feel you're in trouble, look to me."

"Done." Will's countenance was the very picture of acceptance.

"I've got your back, my beloved," Ava whispered.

"For as long as we're here," Hunter added.

"For as long as you need me," I said.

"And then some," Will finished.

Together we breathed and prayed. I could feel us sinking deeper and deeper into a meditative state, where the Oneness Prayer's vibration wove together, like a hug. Such power I hadn't imagined experiencing while here on Earth. Then I realized I was sick to my stomach, and in that awareness I understood it kept happening because it meant gui was trying to gain access.

"They're here," I whispered.

"Let them come," Hunter replied. "We're just breathing in love. And exhaling gratitude."

Denser and denser the air became, as gui drew near. It was good practice, I thought, because even those few extra minutes allowed us to see what it was like holding the Oneness Prayer as we descended ever deeper into chaos.

FIVE

A strangling thickness descended as Lesser Light collective consciousness permeated the atmosphere. Only then, with gui literally in my face, did I recognize I'd been experiencing traces of it ever since we landed. As it wafted through the cabin, a hint of perfumed decay announced its presence, and my stomach heaved. Yet I knew there was no time or space for personal reactions then, as the shadows touched down. I needed to rest in the Oneness Prayer, in the unseen invocations of my dearest companions, and breathe, trusting Highest Light was watching over us.

Opening my eyes, I glanced at Hunter. I could feel him determining whether or not gui had engulfed me. I mind-messaged him reassurance, and he graced me with that dimpled grin. My stomach settled, and as Kendrick entered the room, I felt a level of preparedness I hadn't expected.

"Hunter. How is she doing?" Kendrick's sky-blue eyes held concern.

"She's good, Captain."

"Are you, dear one?" Kendrick knelt by my chair and placed a hand on my knee. I caught a whiff of tobacco and spirits and knew his returning in an altered state would make him less aware—and more vulnerable to the invisible influences infiltrating the ship. As well as those still waiting outside.

"I really am, Kendrick. Thank you for asking." I kissed his cheek, and he smiled before turning back to Hunter.

"I've been trying to contact you."

"We're having technical difficulties."

"Yes, I'm aware. We were able to get a mind-message through to the Elders, but only a brief one. And with much effort."

"Speaking of the Elders, there is much we need to discuss, Kendrick. The sooner the better."

"Of course." His wary eyes assessed Hunter. "Can it wait for now? Quenna is outside with an Atlantean delegation. They were hoping to come aboard to say 'hello' and to see to it our crew felt at home."

"It can wait," Hunter sighed. "For now."

"A delegation? Outside with Quenna?" Ava's dark eyes fretted as she rose from her chair. "We should have welcomed them immediately."

"I simply wanted to ensure Elysia was okay first." Kendrick peered at me. "Are you up for a short visit?"

"I am, Kendrick. I would be honored to meet the delegation."

"Then meet them you shall." He closed his eyes, and I could feel him mind-message Quenna. Moments later he looked up. "They're coming."

I sensed a tremor as the ship's door parted. Panic pounded my heart faster, and I took the deepest breath I could, willing myself back into No-Mind. In that deeper heart space, I was once again aware of the Oneness Prayer's comforting cadence. Through its support, I believed I could face what was ascending through the hallway.

Quenna was speaking with three towering beings as they emerged from the ship's entryway. She looked queenly, as usual, her blonde braids coiled into a bun. For the High Council meeting, she'd donned a floor-length gown, which matched her sapphire eyes. As we stood to greet them, Hunter stepped forward and kissed her pale cheek.

"My lady."

"Dear Hunter. It's good to see you. I'm glad all seems well."

"All is indeed well." He flashed his most irresistible grin, and I allowed my heart to soar momentarily.

"Everyone, I'd like you to welcome our three new friends," Quenna said, turning her attention to our crew. "Vicastus and Bellaeus are High Council members on Atlantis — very similar to the positions we hold on Ahlaiele. And Alaric is a visiting dignitary from our own Great Central Sun region."

Hunter again was first to offer greetings. Observing Atlantean custom, he locked forearms with Vicastus and then Alaric as Ava conversed with Bellaeus. Will strolled over beside Hunter, nodding and exchanging pleasantries. And I, pushing aside a rising feeling of inadequacy, met Vicastus' bold stare as he marched toward me.

"You must be Elysia." He held my hand before bringing it to his lips. "I am Vicastus, my lady." He was muscular, with dark blond hair, and wore a white tunic collared and belted with gold and rich gemstones. He looked every bit the warrior-ambassador I felt him to be.

"Yes, I am. It's a pleasure to meet you, Vicastus."

"On behalf of my people, I want to welcome you to Atlantis." His tone was kind, though it didn't resonate from his heart. And yet I understood how humans could be susceptible to his spell. "I do hope you'll be joining some of our representatives tomorrow morning for a Poseidian tour."

"Of course," I replied. "Ava has told me much about the markets by the sea. About the art and music and architecture, and I can honestly say I can't wait to see your lovely city."

"Ah, yes. Ava is an avid supporter. I would love nothing more than to see her join one of our governing boards. Now that she's in a suitable human body, of course." His eyes wandered to where Ava stood chatting with Bellaeus. There was no mistaking the lust in his face. "I think she'd be perfect."

"She would be ideal," I murmured, just as Alaric stepped forward.

"What woman could possibly be more ideal than this fair lady?" he asked in a voice like velvet. My eyes caught sight of Hunter laughing and gesturing with Bellaeus before resting on Alaric's face. He was strikingly good looking, with light bronze skin and full lips that for some reason kept drawing my gaze. Inwardly I laughed; I thought I'd geared myself up to meet all the clever ways of Lesser Light, but I was obviously not prepared for unadulterated desire. He was magnetically alluring.

He loomed over Vicastus, and his simple black uniform didn't begin to disguise his impossibly broad shoulders and rippling muscles. Vicastus—and even Hunter for that matter—was dwarfed next to him. In the dim light, Alaric's eyes emitted an exquisite gold-green beauty, yet there was an icy feel to him that radiated from his core.

"Alaric, this is—" Vicastus began.

"I know who she is," he replied coldly, glaring at me.

For some reason, I felt compelled to run my fingers through his sable and gold hair. High cheekbones only added to his appeal, an observation I felt uncomfortable making, as evidenced by my rapidly flushing face.

"I've waited a long time to see you, Elysia," he said in that same smooth tone.

My pulse quickened at his words, even as I felt unnerved by the harshness and ferocity that was coming off of him in waves.

"My dear, we all feel that way!" Vicastus interjected. "Our High Council and certain close friends like Alaric here have so eagerly awaited your arrival. It's been eons since a delegation has come from Ahlaiele, you know. So you're practically a legend among us!" Gently he squeezed my arm. "Would you please excuse me, though? I do wish to catch Ava before we adjourn for the evening."

"By all means, Vicastus. It's been a pleasure speaking with you."

"My lady." He bowed and then hastened to where Ava stood deep in discussion with Bellaeus and the others. I watched him go, taking the moment to collect my wits and my breath. Alaric and I were alone, and the sensual thrill I felt simply standing beside him made me fear gui was possessing what was left of my soul. How else to explain it? Taking a deep breath, I looked up to find gold-green eyes studying me.

"Quenna said you're from our own Great Central Sun region," I remarked as casually as I could, though there was nothing casual about the energy swirling between us. "Is your home far from Ahlaiele?"

"Most recently, I've been based out of one of the region's remote outposts, if that's what you're asking. Which isn't far from Ahlaiele." His tone was chilly and clipped, and though I waited for him to reach for my hand as a sign of respect, he remained bewilderingly still.

"And you've been waiting to see me?" I couldn't believe how uncomfortable I felt. And how aroused. It seemed strange how everyone else was talking together in a group, leaving us to ourselves. I kept my voice as calm as possible as I extended my hand in the customary greeting. "I must say I didn't know my reputation preceded me."

"More than you realize, my lady." Leisurely he bent to kiss my hand, his mesmerizing gaze locked onto my eyes. Had I tried to look away, I was sure I couldn't. So I surrendered as best as I could while those seductive lips neared my flesh.

The pleasurable electricity that shot through my body as his mouth made contact with my skin caused my breath to catch. Involuntarily I recoiled. Even then, Alaric didn't release my hand—or my eyes. Instead, he surveyed my agitation without emotion.

I felt at once breathless and weak. And shamefully elated. I felt my face blooming an ever deeper shade of red, and I began to wonder if my confusion might somehow serve as a mask for the guilty longing I could neither quell nor deny.

"Forgive me, Alaric," I stammered, "but I ... I wasn't anticipating ..." I felt a surge of anger in my field and sensed Hunter had just witnessed what had happened. Finally, I tore my eyes from Alaric's. Without speaking he released me.

"I'm still getting used to Atlantean custom," I mumbled, clawing my depths for composure.

"I'm no Atlantean. And I observe little custom, save what suits my very singular purpose." He glowered at me with an intensity I found overwhelming. I tried to think, to ground, to bring myself back to the Oneness Prayer, and instead found myself adrift in desires I knew I shouldn't feel.

"Pray tell what that purpose might be."

"You will learn. In time."

Questions bubbled to my lips, but I knew it was neither the time nor the place to engage him further. In spite of my need to know more. He made me want to feel his body against mine. It was inexplicable and utterly distracting. Frantically, I searched for something—anything— to say that might deflect his magnetism.

"I'm afraid your mysterious ways have rendered me a bit speechless," I finally managed.

"Words can only go so far, anyway," he murmured. "But feelings, well ... those are a different matter altogether."

"You ... know of the ways of emotion?"

"Yes."

"Of all the feeling realm's ... complexities?" Something made me again risk looking at him. Ice and fire in equal measure numbed and ignited his eyes. And though he shivered and seared my soul, I didn't wish to pull myself from those gold-green depths.

"Yes, my lady."

"Such pain," I whispered. I felt altered, utterly captivated. Transfixed by the spellbinding seduction of that ruthless scowl. I was no longer sure what I was sensing. But it seemed I'd stumbled into such an intricately layered energetic system that I'd become lost. "Eons of heartache. Of—"

"You're more like me than you may think, my dear Elysia," he interrupted. And though energetically he'd cut right through my words—effectively loosening any hold I may have been gaining on his inner world—I was still bound by his eyes. "I'm as much snake as human, for good or ill. And snakes are feelers."

"You'd call me a feeler, then?" My heart was hammering so hard I feared he'd see it through my uniform.

"Clearly, you are."

I didn't know if I was more petrified or pleased. In all my years as a missionary, no one—not a single soul—from any planet I'd visited had ever seen me for what I was. How had he known? Enchanted, I again lost myself in his eyes.

"I really didn't think—"

"Oh, I'm not asking you to think, my lady." Alaric's whisper was a slow hiss. He moved closer, as if to embrace me. "I'm asking you to feel."

Without another word, and without so much as a fluttery touch, Alaric peered into me with those unblinking eyes and energetically penetrated my emotional body. I felt overtaken simultaneously by the softest caresses and most urgent kisses, in all the places my body begged for such attention. Panting, I staggered back from him. Before I could find my breath, Hunter's arm was around my waist.

SIX

"Party's over." Hunter was firmly grounded in No-Mind, and I could feel the Oneness Prayer's rhythmic heartbeat deep in his core. His eyes held no emotion as he glanced first at Alaric and then at me. "Elysia, Bellaeus wants to meet you before the delegation departs."

"Certainly." I did my best to sink back into No-Mind. Admittedly, Hunter's presence made my task easier. "Until tomorrow, Alaric." I didn't trust myself to look at him, but my voice sounded calm, even to my own ears.

"Until tomorrow." His tone had once again iced over. In cold quietude, he crossed the room, the very picture of grace in motion. Moments later, the ship's hull sighed as it opened and closed. A hush fell over the group, and then all eyes descended on me.

"Alaric realized Elysia needed rest," Hunter called out so everyone would hear. "And so, as much as I know we've all enjoyed ourselves this evening, I believe it's wise to follow his example and retire."

"I so agree, Hunter." Bellaeus' elegant form seemed to float to where Hunter stood beside me. Her long white gown was accented with gemstones and precious metals, in a style similar to Vicastus' tunic. A mole rested just to the left of her lips, which only enhanced her sophistication. "Elysia, I did at least wish to make your acquaintance before we take our leave."

"Thank you, Bellaeus. It's an honor to meet you."

"The honor is mine," she replied. Her golden hair stretched into a bun, with ringlets framing her face. "On behalf of Poseidia, I want you to know how grateful we are you've come to honor King Gadeirus."

"Our crew feels it's an opportunity to serve, my lady." Floating in No-Mind, I met her gaze. "In the name of Oneness, we're happy to be supportive."

"Yes, of course." Distaste—so brief as to appear imaginary—flashed across her striking features at the mention of Oneness, and then she offered me her cheek. It felt cool and hard beneath my lips. "Tomorrow you'll be seeing the sights around Poseidia before the gathering, won't you?"

"I wouldn't miss it," I assured her. "I've long admired your city. Ava has told me of many happy adventures she's experienced here."

"Indeed." Bellaeus smiled at me, her slate blue eyes coldly beautiful. "Vicastus and I think she should move here. She's such a natural supporter of Poseidia."

"Ava really is at home here," Hunter interjected. "All she's been talking about is the food, and the markets, and the warm aqua sea. Oh, and the food, the culture, and the crystalline architecture. Did I mention the food?" Hunter's eyes crinkled as Bellaeus and I laughed.

"I do believe you mentioned the food, Hunter," she replied. "You'll see for yourself soon enough why it's so special."

"We're all looking forward to it, my lady," he said, taking her hand. "May I escort you out?"

"Thank you." She smiled at me. "Until tomorrow."

"Until tomorrow, my lady." I watched as they strolled toward the door, pausing to speak with Vicastus, who was arm in arm with Ava. Will stood with Kendrick and Quenna at the ship's hallway entrance. I walked over to Vicastus, who patted Ava's hand before turning toward me.

"We're taking our leave now," he said. His gray eyes radiated contentment, and I could tell he'd been enjoying Ava's company.

"Of course, Vicastus. It's been a pleasure meeting you." I offered him my hand, and he touched his lips ever so gently to the back of my fingers. I felt grateful there was no reminder of Alaric's earlier inappropriate behavior.

"The pleasure is mine, my lady. I look forward to seeing you again tomorrow." Then he turned, and together he and Ava walked with Hunter and Bellaeus toward the entrance. I heard laughter echoing as the ship's door hummed open and shut. For a long moment, there was silence. And then Kendrick smiled.

"Please. Let's sit for a bit." He gestured to the control desk chairs. Obediently, we took a seat. I found myself situated between Will and Quenna. "That went well. Don't you think?"

"Agreed, Captain," Will replied. I could feel the Oneness Prayer purring along deep beneath his relaxed expression. "They were pleasant enough."

"Indeed." Quenna's sharp eyes found mine. "What did you think, Elysia? Or perhaps I should ask instead what you felt?"

"I must say, overall, I agree with Will." There was my voice again, sounding so centered. But I knew I couldn't hide that something intense had happened. "I was taken aback by Alaric, though. He is quite ... unused to Atlantean manners."

"Alaric is a beast," she harrumphed, spitting the words out like bitter fruit. "He has no manners — Atlantean or otherwise. Perhaps the whispers are true."

"Whispers?"

"Yes." Revulsion contorted her features. "Alaric moves in Poseidia's highest circles of influence. And yet I heard mutterings today of how he curries favor through ... shameful means."

"Shameful?" I managed the barest murmur, praying no one heard the tremor I could not control.

"Yes," she replied. "Reportedly, he's a paid escort. One who sells pleasure for profit among the wealthy and powerful."

"Well I'll be Light damned!" Will exclaimed.

"Precisely," Quenna scowled. "Although he's so rude, I can't imagine how he could possibly muster enough ... charisma for these rumors to have any validity."

"Alaric is an unexpected twist, I'm afraid," Kendrick said. I was grateful for his words, which drew the others' attention. And which hopefully would allow me a moment to regroup. "From what I learned at the banquet, he showed up in recent weeks on a diplomatic mission — very much the way we just did. But what his true motivations are ... well, that remains to be seen."

"Rude or wicked or not, he impressed me as having a brilliant military mind," Will offered. He lounged in his chair, long legs splayed out in front of him. "He could quote from even the most obscure classical work I mentioned in passing. Books I wouldn't expect anyone but a dedicated warrior to have heard of."

"I had a similar experience with him this afternoon," Kendrick agreed. "Perhaps he is a warrior. Or one who's led battles. But he knew equally as much about leadership and kingly rights and rituals. In the short time we spoke, I became convinced he was a monarch."

"What do you make of him, Elysia?" Quenna asked.

"He's a being of many faces." That was true, and yet it was a downplaying of his darkness. "He is complex and multi-layered. And he seems to want to show us what we wish to see. Which makes him potentially dangerous. At least until we learn what his true motivations are."

"Yes." Kendrick appeared lost in thought. "He reminds me of tales I heard years ago, of the shape-shifters of old. Especially the lost king of Moldaaris."

"Certainly you don't believe those fairy tales!" Quenna scoffed. "Complete and utter nonsense."

"Some would say so," Kendrick replied. "But our own gifts are the stuff of rumor and legend across the galaxies, and yet we know they are real." He paused, and I felt him gathering his thoughts. "Have either of you heard of Moldaaris?" Will and I shook our heads in unison. "Well then. According to legend, it was when Lesser Light forces first began to overtake Poseidia— around a thousand years ago—when a large delegation from the planet Moldaaris came to Atlantis. Most of the crew were high-ranking officials, not unlike us. As you might imagine, it was considered an important and urgent mission, and was in fact the earliest known attempt to save humans from themselves."

"I swear this species is like a damned damsel in distress!" Will exclaimed. "Only she never actually gets saved. She just gets rescued in the nick of time from some immediate catastrophe and then throws herself right back into the arms of doom."

"So true," Quenna muttered. "I'm losing my patience with them already, and we barely got here."

"What were the beings of Moldaaris like?" I asked, redirecting the topic. I felt fascinated by Kendrick's words.

"An interesting and diverse lot, from what I understand," Kendrick replied. "There were no 'pure' bloodlines then, as are witnessed today on Earth, in which most Earthlings are 100 percent human. But all coexisted peacefully, honoring and respecting individuality as a rarified expression of the Divine. On Moldaaris, there was primarily a multitude of hybrid creatures such as half Moldaarin, which was very similar to a human, and half horse. Half Moldaarin and half dolphin was a common blending as well. Or half Moldaarin and half hawk. You get the picture."

"Or half Moldaarin and half reptile?" Will studied Kendrick's face. "I mean, that's what Alaric might be, right? With those eyes?"

"Yes, perhaps." Kendrick still had that dreamy look, as if he were a million light years from where we sat. "It was a known blending. In fact, snakes were revered on Moldaaris for their exceptional shape-shifting and leadership skills."

I erupted in gooseflesh. Alaric had told me he was half snake! "Honored even above dolphins?" I asked, incredulous a reptile could be cherished anywhere in the universe more than the gentle sea creatures. For some reason, ever since we began preparing for Earth, a fierce love of Poseidia's dolphins had welled within me. A feeling I could neither fathom nor explain.

"Yes," he answered. "Snakes have always been masters of enticement, of seduction through power. And the great snake king of Moldaaris reportedly saved his people from multiple wars and countless other disasters by mesmerizing an intergalactic community into peaceful coexistence when necessary." Kendrick paused, as if gathering his thoughts. "The legends say he was irresistible. Almost as if it were impossible to refuse him anything."

"Surely you must be mistaken about Alaric," Quenna griped. "I know I could refuse him anything and everything!"

"Well, I found him plumb fascinating," Will admitted.

I felt uneasy, wondering how effectively I would have been able to refuse him had Hunter not come to my aid.

"I'm quite sure he can be charming. Even hypnotic." Kendrick looked at me, and I felt myself blush. Again. I yearned to disappear. "Don't you agree, El?"

"Alaric embodies the ability to manipulate, which is one way of defining 'charming'," I said as casually as possible, doing my best to ground myself in No-Mind. I didn't want to talk about Alaric. "Kendrick, in your tale of the lost king of Moldaaris, I'm curious how he became 'lost' if he was so loved and received so much aid whenever his people were vulnerable."

"Just one of many avenues that lead back to Atlantis," Kendrick murmured. "Perhaps I'm telling you this now, on the eve before we journey together into Poseidia, because Moldaaris once sent an elite diplomatic mission to Earth. The old stories say they were invited by King Helionel, who ruled Atlantis at the time, so he might learn their ways and begin to quiet the growing unrest worldwide. Wars, poverty, famine. All the misery brought by Lesser Light."

"In essence, the same as we're aiming to fix now — only we're doing it energetically. And in secret," Will observed.

"Yes." Kendrick looked from one to the other of us as he continued. "The Moldaarin delegation was not operating covertly. They openly came in, assessed the situation, and laid out a blueprint for King Helionel to follow before they left. The only problem was the king didn't truly want to heal the world. He wished to dominate it. So he learned how to charm — not to synthesize, but to seduce. He learned how to mesmerize — not to unite and inspire the world's people, but to make them his puppets. And one by one, the kingdoms of Earth began to fall under his Lesser Light influence."

"The delegation must have been pretty upset once they discovered Helionel's true intentions," I remarked, leaning forward in my chair. I was eager to hear how this tale played out and at the same time wondered if its fate may be a predictor of our own.

"We'll never know the answer to that," Kendrick replied.

"How come?" Will's eyes narrowed as he stared at Kendrick.

"Because King Helionel ordered a military strike against Moldaaris as soon as the delegation departed." Kendrick's voice was somber. "Crystal-generated power beamed sonic and laser waves at the planet. In seconds, it exploded. And so, just like that, Moldaaris was no more."

"Just like that," Will whispered.

"Yes."

"And the Moldaarin king?" I asked.

"No one knows for sure," Kendrick answered. "Theories and speculation have filtered down through the centuries, but no one actually knows what happened. Some say the crew was killed as the crystalline-driven waves were projected along their path toward Moldaaris. Some say they re-routed their course once they witnessed what was happening, and it's rumored any number of the benevolent planets who'd helped their people in the past offered them sanctuary or safe passage to anywhere they wished to go to begin a new life."

"Kendrick, what makes you think Alaric could be the lost king?" Plainly, Quenna would prefer discussing most anything over and above the current topic. And yet I felt curiosity beneath her polished surface.

"Just a feeling, really," he answered. Once again he eyed me. "Which is why I've been so curious about your reaction to him, El. If you sense any truth to this legend."

"I think the metaphor of a 'lost king' describes his behavior and demeanor quite well," I replied, even as my mind screamed Alaric's similarity to the Moldaarin king must either be a coincidence or a clever manipulation. "He carries much personal power. But one who is lost can be quite hurt and thus feel justified lashing out at others, instead of using such tremendous charisma wisely."

"Perhaps you will feel into him more deeply tomorrow." Kendrick's voice was more command than question. "We need to know what—and who—we're dealing with."

"Of course." I was comforted by the lull of No-Mind and the easy rhythm of the Oneness Prayer deep in my inner sanctuary, and yet even those blessings couldn't stop the chill coursing through me.

"Good." There was kindness in Kendrick's face as he smiled at me.

I was about to ask how long we would be in Poseidia tomorrow when the ship's hull opened. I heard Ava and Hunter discussing something as they entered. Footsteps and soft laughter emanated from the hallway, announcing them before they again entered the control room.

"What did we miss?" Ava scanned our faces. "You all look like you've seen a ghost."

"We've been deliberating something equally elusive but not so transparent, I'm afraid," Kendrick replied. "The dubious Alaric, from our own Great Central Sun region. And whether or not he might be the lost king of Moldaaris."

"I knew we wouldn't return to find you chatting about the weather over tea and crumpets." Hunter took a seat next to Kendrick after Ava settled in beside Quenna. "Why the interest in Alaric?"

"Because we don't know his reason for being here," Kendrick grumbled. "His magnetism could make him the most dangerous embodiment of Lesser Light we're facing. And we don't want to be seduced." I could feel my face getting hot, as shameful thoughts of bare bronze skin forced me to admit I was aching for seduction. "I've asked Elysia to feel into him more deeply tomorrow. I'm hopeful she'll be able to provide a read on his true intentions by the day's end."

"I'll do my best." I could feel a momentary lapse in Hunter's Oneness Prayer at what Kendrick had asked of me. But those green eyes never sought mine. I had no idea what I would say to him, or how I would explain my actions—let alone my conflicted feelings. I could only pray I would find some way to make things right with Hunter. Because I couldn't let the Alaric experience come between us. If it hadn't already.

SEVEN

"Perhaps we could have that word now, Captain?" Hunter glanced at the others, but not at me, and my stomach plunged.

"Of course." Caution spilled like water over Kendrick's countenance.

"There's no easy way to put this," Hunter began. "But we've been betrayed."

"Betrayed?"

"Yes. By the Elders."

"What?!" Quenna's tone was shrill. And seething.

"Yes," Hunter replied. "Ahlaiele's been breached."

"In the name of Oneness!" Quenna slapped the chair's armrests. "How can you be sure?"

"El got a clear vision of it once she began feeling better," Hunter said. "Poseidia masterfully wields Dark Heart energy, which is what tainted our Elders. Addicting them so they must now gorge on her poison."

"I've long heard whispers of the Dark Heart's hallucinogenic powers," Kendrick murmured. "How they can hook even the purest heart frequencies."

"Yes," I whispered. "In my mind's eye, I saw the Elders first coming under the influence through long-distance communications. Messages extended in friendship and alliance, yet cloaked in evil intent. An unguarded moment, like an exposed vein, is all the opportunity the Dark Heart needs. Just the smallest prick, the tiniest taste of her frequencies, and the needing begins. Then nothing else matters to her junkies. Except feeding." Tears trickled along my cheeks. "Ahlaiele's once unrivaled rainbow of color is now swirling in shadow. Our fellow Light Rays have all become Dark Heart dependent. And our Elders are strung out on a drug so complex and powerful they no longer recognize themselves. Or their Highest Light purpose."

"How could we not know?" Kendrick shook his head. "Why was there no warning?"

"We had no expectations of such treachery so we weren't looking for it," I replied.

"So what about our mission?" Quenna asked.

"The mission was merely something the six of us could believe in," Hunter remarked. "It captured our attention so fully it never occurred to us it might only be a Lesser Light maneuvering." For several moments we sat in a bruised silence only death and betrayal can command.

"All right, crew," Kendrick said at last. "Quenna and I have been apprised of the situation. Now we must decide our actions from this point onward."

"Let me mind-message you two on that," Hunter suggested.

"Agreed," Kendrick answered. He glanced at Quenna, who nodded her readiness. They sank deeper into their seats.

Several minutes passed, as Hunter relayed our idea about the Oneness Prayer and the Circle of Emotion. Closing my eyes, I delved deep beneath my breath, resting in No-Mind as a way of holding space for Kendrick and Quenna. But also as a means of seeking respite from my own troubled thoughts. In No-Mind, I could escape the feel of Alaric, as his energy had not only uncovered but caressed every desire my body had secretly harbored all my long years. No-Mind also offered a break from my guilty heart, which scolded me for going against everything I'd ever learned about resisting Lesser Light urges. And in No-Mind, I could avoid the pit in my stomach, the one that deepened every time Hunter's eyes avoided mine. There was nothing but the void, until Kendrick's voice parted the silence.

"I see the congruency of this plan," he said at last, turning toward Quenna.

"Yes," she whispered. "It resonates truth. It's challenging yet to accept how we've been programmed to do exactly what feeds gui ..." Her voice trailed off. "But I believe the Oneness Prayer can work."

"As do I," Kendrick replied. "I believe Highest Light has guided and protected us thus far. And so even if there never was a pure intention on the part of the Elders to conduct our mission, nonetheless I think we should carry forth as best we can to see it through. To ground Highest Light into this bleeding ground. Because I for one still believe we may yet halt Gadeirus' plans for intergalactic control. Agreed?"

"Agreed," we answered as one.

"Of course, it appears we won't be returning to Ahlaiele in a few days, as we'd planned," he added. "We will need to consider alternatives. So moving forward, I want you all to keep your eyes and ears open for Highest Light promptings."

"There's also the matter of our essences, Kendrick." Ava looked uneasy as she searched our faces. "Any thoughts on how we might retrieve those?"

"I'm afraid that might become a diplomatic negotiation," Kendrick replied. "And yet honestly, I've had no time to give it any thought." He shook his head. "Highest Light willing, we should know more in a few days. It's imperative we keep our heads and stay calm." Kendrick stood, extending his hand to Quenna, who rose from her chair as if it were a throne. "Even as we prepare to retire for the evening, Quenna and I will be joining you in holding the Oneness Prayer. Realize tomorrow is a critical day for all of us, and these human bodies do require rest for maximum performance."

"I have a question before you go, Kendrick," Hunter said.

"Yes?"

"Will we have an opportunity to venture forth on our own after our obligations are met? I mean, it's not that hours of secret life-risking adventures and arrest-worthy activities won't be just all kinds of fun. But in case these are my last days, I intend to go out having explored all Poseidia can offer."

"Much of the day has been scheduled in order to assure our presence is seen and felt where most important," Kendrick replied, "but I see no reason why certain personal indulgences can't be accommodated."

"Poseidia, here we come!" Hunter grinned at Kendrick.

"Indeed." Kendrick smiled at all of us. "And on that note, we shall take our leave."

"Good night, y'all," Will said. His voice was even more gravelly than usual. "I figure we won't be far behind."

Kendrick nodded, and then he and Quenna strolled through the arched doorway leading to the lavatories. For a long while the rest of us sat in stillness.

"You look as tired as I feel," Ava said to Will at last. "Perhaps we should consider getting some rest."

"Come, my lady." Will sprouted from his chair, offering Ava his hand. "Let's find out what this thing humans call 'shut-eye' is all about."

"Of course." I noticed he kept hold of her hand as she turned toward me. "Elysia, if you need anything at all, don't hesitate to wake me."

"Thank you, Ava. I will."

"And Hunter, don't keep her up late," she warned, pointing her long index finger at him. "More than any of us, she needs time to recuperate."

"Thanks, Mom!" Hunter grinned as Ava and Will left the room. And then the one thing I'd been both craving and dreading finally happened. For once I wasn't sick or in need of saving. I was simply alone with Hunter.

EIGHT

To curb my angst, I tried concentrating on my breath, which was too shallow and rapid to be calming. My heart hammered away at its cage of ribs, trying to break free of all the emotions I desperately wished to restrain. When finally I looked up to see those green eyes watching me, I prayed for the strength to be as noble as he so obviously was.

"Hey, you," he murmured.

"Hey, yourself." All the feelings I was doing my best to suppress had lumped in my throat, strangling me to hoarseness.

"Come on. Let's go to the Tranquility Room so we won't disturb anyone."

"All right." I could barely breathe as I followed him to the ship's most peaceful space, my heart pounding hard as the door closed behind us. I thought for sure he heard it as I stared up into the hard lines of his face.

"You look like you're thinking too much." He slid onto the couch where he'd healed me earlier and motioned me over. I sank next to him, our legs nearly touching.

"Probably so." For some reason, I found it awkward to look at him. So I studied the floor, as he rested a hand on my knee.

"You're obviously hurting, El. Can't you tell me what it is?"

"I'll be all right," I shrugged. "Really I will. I'm feeling quite well, as a matter of fact."

"You know I'm not talking about your general state of health right now. Energetically I can see you are, in fact, doing much better in that department."

"Hunter, I don't know what you mean—"

"I think you do." He leaned closer, his posture still perfectly balanced. "And it has to do with Alaric."

There. I knew he'd seen it, and now he'd voiced it. I couldn't avoid the subject any longer.

"What about him?"

"Come on, El." Now it was Hunter's turn to examine the floor. I could feel his wave-like energy pulsing into my body where he touched me. "I know what he ... did to you."

"Really?" Out of nowhere, my anger flared. "Well, that makes one of us."

"You don't know? How could you not? " He clutched my knee. "For the sake of Oneness, El, he violated you!"

"Other than the obligatory hand kiss, he didn't touch me!"

"He didn't have to," Hunter whispered, raking thick fingers through his hair.

"Hunter, listen—"

"To what?" His eyes blazed with fury. "To you telling me he didn't lay a hand on you? And that you don't know what happened?"

"But that's the truth—"

"It's not the whole truth and you know it!" Hurling himself from the couch, he whirled to face me. "He was able to ... to reach inside you, to pleasure you somehow, without even the slightest physical contact. You tell me how I'm supposed to be okay with that!"

"Hunter, please." I scrambled to my feet, stunned by the hurt coming off him in waves.

"You tell me how I'm supposed to be okay with the Captain's directive! To you spending even more time tomorrow with that ... creature!" He squeezed his eyes shut, and I could sense the tears he was blocking. "Please tell me how I'm supposed to stand by and watch him disrespect that which I hold most sacred."

"Oh, my dear." I cradled his face in my hands. His cheeks felt like sun-baked stone, and for several moments we simply stood like that. Energetically, I kept insisting he let me in, to allow me to share in his pain. And yet I could feel his wall, the one he'd built by willing himself to bear this burden alone.

"You are my most special love, Elysia." He opened his eyes, and their misty vulnerability touched the very depths of my soul. "I want nothing more than to be able to express my feelings for you. In all ways."

"I know," I whispered. "With all that I am, I know that's true."

"But because you are so precious to me, I want any expression of love from me to honor you in the deepest of ways." Tenderly, he took my hands in his. "I told you before, I want to savor you. To cherish and adore you. I want to go slowly."

"Yes, I know."

"Then help me, El." He kissed each of my hands, his eyes pleading with mine. "Help me honor you. By honoring yourself."

"I'm not sure I understand—"

"Don't let him have you," he begged. "Don't let him devour what I long simply to taste."

"How could I possibly want that? To be ... consumed?"

Tears filled his eyes, and he buried his head in my shoulder. "It's going to be okay," he said quietly. "It's all part of the One. I know that to be true."

"I know," I agreed, but my voice lacked conviction.

I flashed back to how out of control I'd felt with Alaric. I would agree it was all part of the One, that it would somehow have to be all right. But I didn't know how I could possibly honor both Hunter and myself when it came to Alaric.

In the darkest recesses of my soul — those places I could never hide from a truth I didn't want to face — I knew it was inevitable that Alaric would try to have his way with me as he had before. And yet as depraved and disgraceful as my mind shouted he must be, my heart and soul simply refused to listen. In spite of everything, I honestly didn't know if I had the strength to resist him.

What did that say about me, I wondered. About my character, my integrity, my dignity? My sanity? I felt as if my whole world had been upended, and the longer I thought of it, the more I knew I simply didn't have the energy to keep this tumult inside. I stifled a shriek, but the effort drained me. I believe, had Hunter not been holding me, I would have collapsed to the floor.

"Shhhhh," he whispered, and his lips made their way along my collarbone. Slowly, carefully, he kissed my neck. I thought I might pass out, either from the guilty recollection of how Alaric had somehow evoked the same feeling in me, or from the nearly painful pleasure Hunter was sending throughout my body.

"You've made me feeble," I managed.

"Do you want me to stop?"

"Do you want me to remain capable of forming sentences?"

"Not really," he murmured in my ear, and we both laughed. I wriggled in his grasp, trying to subdue the heat rising within, the feeling that simultaneously was producing chills and gooseflesh all over me.

"Not fair." I was astounded at how ready my body was to explore his. With parted lips, I traced the hard line of his neck up to his jaw. As I did so, the muscular arms wrapped about me trembled.

"Not fair!" With ease, he lifted me from the ground, then allowed me to slide back into his embrace. He flushed, his eyes fiery and intense, his breath heavier than normal. The look suited him. He'd never been more handsome.

"Kiss me, Hunter."

"I believe I have been. Or were you not paying attention?"

"I meant on the lips."

For what seemed like an eternity, he caressed my hair, the curve of my chin. Then he cupped my jaw and lowered his head. I closed my eyes, eager with anticipation. I could think of nothing but what his mouth on mine would feel like.

Sweetly — with a tenderness my own fevered passions could never match — his lips brushed my own. Ever so briefly. It was like a drop of water after days in the desert. I opened my eyes, and saw he'd pulled away.

"Oh no. Please. You can't stop. Not now."

"El, I have to."

"Why?"

"Because we're taking things slowly, remember?"

"Says you."

"Yes. Says me."

"But —"

"El, we have the time to take our time," he whispered. "We're certainly in no rush to get back to Ahlaiele at this point. So we'll be here long enough to get to know these physical bodies. Every square inch, okay? I promise."

"Right now that's not helping."

"I know. But I do have a plan."

"Pray tell," I murmured, thinking to myself I should be content to stay here in his warm embrace.

"Tomorrow. When we're free from our obligations. We've been given time to explore on our own."

"And what exactly are you intending to explore? Poseidia offers many pleasures. Art? Music? Architecture? Culinary delights?"

"You." He held me away from him, his eyes soft and loving. "Just you."

"I think Kendrick was granting permission more for the art and music and such."

"Actually, Kendrick gave his blessing for personal indulgences. And you are the most personal thing I'm looking to indulge."

"Oh Hunter, I wish —" I began, but I stopped myself. Wishes seemed pointless.

"What is it, El? What do you wish?"

"That we could be here under different circumstances, without care for missions and duty," I sighed. "Perhaps as intergalactic tourists, coming to Poseidia simply for ocean breezes and renowned cuisine."

"Yes," he whispered. "I wish that, too."

"Maybe tomorrow we could pretend it's that way. Even if it's just for a little while."

"I don't see why not." He wiped a tear ready to drip from my chin. "But for now I think we both should get some sleep. We need to be on top of our game tomorrow."

"All right."

"Come with me." Hunter offered his arm and the dimpled grin that enamored my heart. Yet when I was finally nestled in the travel pod, I had to admit I wasn't thinking of Hunter. Forbidden gold-green eyes and pleasuring lips were what eventually lured me to sleep.

NINE

As we descended the ship's ramp, beauty in all its forms besieged my senses. I wondered if Hunter and the guys had been this giddy when they left after breakfast. The breeze wrapped me in a welcoming scent of gardenia, jasmine, and fresh sea spray. Drinking in my first view of Atlantis, I felt intoxicated.

The Seraphinite had touched down on a flat plain just south of the labyrinthian canals encircling Poseidia. Looking out across the stone landing strip where we stood, I saw multiple crafts spaced evenly apart. The diversity displayed among the ships spoke to Atlantis' position as an intergalactic gathering place. Many were similar in design to our own, but an equal number were unlike anything I'd ever seen.

A powerful rustling came from behind me. I turned to see a hawk land on the ramp's handrail. The raptor was female, her mottled brown plumage and brick-red tail feathers regally displayed. Sharp copper eyes pierced my depths, and I knew she would be watching over us. Yet before I could say anything to Ava and Quenna, she took flight.

Watching her soar carried my gaze to the horizon. In the distance, three concentric circles of turquoise sea surrounded Poseidia's shores. Buildings bearing clean, simple lines loomed above canals caressing thin strips of land. With crystalline walls and metal roofs, the whole of Poseidia glowed in the early morning light.

To the north, mountains of black, white, and crimson towered like sentinels over the capital below. The rock of the cliffs shimmered as if alive, red-faced and laughing, daylight tickling chiseled chins and noses.

"Gorgeous," I whispered.

"Unbelievably so," Ava murmured. She looked polished in our crew's black dress uniform, its pants and shirt pinstriped with the hue of our individual Color Rays. "No matter how many trips I've made here, I never tire of her beauty."

"She truly is majestic." Quenna smiled as she gazed upon the landscape, like a queen greeting another monarch. "I cannot imagine growing weary of this view, either."

We didn't wait long before a hovercraft approached. It lowered to within a foot of the ground. Then three tall men, dressed in white tunics with metal belts, stepped from its disk-like surface.

"Ava, my dear!" The shortest of the three marched up to Ava and hugged her heartily. "My goodness it's been a long time! You look positively gorgeous in this form!"

"Kenaseus, thank you for your kind words. How are you?" Ava seemed genuinely delighted by the red-haired man's embrace. "It's been longer than I care to admit."

"Welcome home, my friend." Kenaseus released her, turning merry blue eyes upon Quenna. "My lady, how pleased I am to see you again this morning."

"Thank you, Kenaseus." Quenna extended her hand for him to kiss. He obliged, then grinned at me.

"And you must be Elysia."

"Good morning, Kenaseus. It's an honor to meet you."

"The honor is mine." He motioned to his two companions. "Please let me introduce Jonastus and Perraseus. They serve on the city's diplomatic relations committee with me."

"My ladies." Jonastus had curly dark hair, a slender frame, and a gentle tone that immediately put me at ease. He was the tallest of the three, with a kind face and soft features. Rather angelic, I thought.

"Please let us know if we can do anything to make your stay more comfortable," Perraseus said. He was muscular with brown hair and large, gray eyes. His angular face exuded self-assurance.

"Gentlemen, thank you." Ava beamed at our hosts. "We so appreciate you attending to us. Will you be taking us into Poseidia then?"

"Yes, of course," Kenaseus laughed, his wide chin dimpling. "You wouldn't deny me the opportunity to catch up with you after all these years, would you?"

"Absolutely not!"

"Shall we then?" Kenaseus clasped Ava's hand and placed it at his elbow. "Gentlemen, if you will be so kind as to escort Quenna and Elysia onto the hoverdisk."

Perraseus offered his arm to Quenna, while Jonastus moved to my side.

"Thank you," I said as I gazed into beryl blue eyes.

"You're most welcome, my lady." His voice barely rose above a whisper, and yet it carried perfectly to my ears.

"Please. Call me Elysia. Or better yet, El."

"All right, El." That sweet smile suggested he was pleased I wished to be less formal. "And you may call me Jon."

"Okay. Jon it is, then."

I placed my hand just above his elbow, feeling the sinewy strength that belied his thin frame, and together we boarded the hoverdisk. There were no walls or rails. I wondered how we would stay on its shiny metal surface.

"The hoverdisk uses gravity to hold us aboard," Jon said in that same soft voice. "You can move about if you wish once the disk is in flight, but it may be more challenging to pick up your feet than what you're used to. It's just the way gravity locks you onto the craft. So you needn't worry about falling off."

"Good to know." I smiled at him, wondering if he had just read my mind or if all new visitors ponder the same thing when asked to board the flying disk.

"It's a short ride to Poseidia, and then Kenaseus is going to show you some of the sights and let you visit the markets before you're needed at the palace."

"Also good to know." Again I grinned. "It seems you're more aware of the day's itinerary than I am."

"It's my duty to know." Those eyes, so trusting they melted my heart, searched my face. "Just like it's my honor to inform and protect."

A whole-body chill trembled me. I could still feel the ease and rhythm of the Oneness Prayer, purring along just beneath the level of conscious thought. If I'd had any doubts, I was now certain his angelic resemblance was no coincidence.

"Thank you, Jon. That means more than you realize."

"No thanks are necessary. Believe me."

"I do believe you," I whispered. "And yet I enjoy offering gratitude when someone extends an honest heart to me."

"Consider mine extended." Again he looked at me with such openness it made me teary. "And think of me as forever grateful in return. For all you will be doing here."

Before I could respond, the hoverdisk eased from the ground. As the wind teased my ponytail, Ava beamed back at me.

"This is going to be such fun, El!"

"It already is!"

In silence, we soared toward Poseidia. As we neared the outer canal, Perraseus pointed out a school of dolphins. They were flanking many merfolk, who appeared to be taking turns diving. The ones emerging from the sea were handing baskets to those on black, rugged cliffs. As I watched, a sinking despair washed over me that made me feel like I was drowning.

"They are pearl divers," Jon explained. "In the king's service."

I nodded, too overcome to speak, and shut my eyes against the impressions flooding me. It was odd; the mermaids looked so peaceful and the dolphins seemed so joyful. And yet there was an undeniable feeling of hopelessness. I knew the divers were slaves. Unquestionably,

I'd just seen one area we would need to ground in Highest Light, and we weren't even two minutes into our flight.

"My ladies, we will be passing over the outdoor shopping district soon," Kenaseus boomed in his deep voice. "But before we land and explore the street vendors, I want to fly over the capital city and let you experience her beauty from above."

Below us, the markets by the sea begged for closer inspection. I could scarcely take in the diverse crowds or the dizzying selection of wares as we whirred along. I was grateful for the distraction from the depressing reality of the pearl divers, and yet I felt I must not forget what I'd seen. In my heart, I swore to Highest Light I would make a difference for the merfolk as the hoverdisk slowed and turned.

We were heading straight for Poseidia's epicenter. Pearly bridges telescoped out from the city, traversing the canals encircling her like spokes from a sacred wheel. Her skyline inspired a sense of perfection; each building stood in harmony, proportion, and balance with its neighbor. Many of the roofs were domes or pyramids—a gleaming array of gold, copper, and silver atop pastel-colored stone and precious ivory. She was lovely.

"Ahead is the Grand Temple," Kenaseus remarked. "And the building just to the right of the Grand Temple houses our most famous crystal, the Tuaoi Stone."

The Grand Temple stood in Poseidia's center, at the island's highest vantage point apart from the towering cliffs to the north. Its crystalline frame, carved with sacred geometry, formed an iridescent geodesic dome. Next to the temple stood an oval structure, made of polished white stone and topped in gold. On Ahlaiele, we'd been told the oval building housed the world's largest known crystal—what Kenaseus had just referred to as the Tuaoi Stone.

The building's roof was fully retractable, such that the cylindrical crystal held within could be raised, rotated 360 degrees, and aimed at any angle. Being able to maneuver the crystal so easily allowed the Atlanteans to beam information and energy around the earth, channeling from the crystal through the temple's pyramid crown. The structure's sacred symbols then intensified and transmitted the desired vibrations to a network of pyramids around the planet. These precisely placed structures served as receivers, dispersing the gathered energy as needed within a specific region. All in all, the system provided balance and harmony, since at any given time at least one of the pyramids was optimally positioned to capture solar, lunar, and star energy and then share it—powered by the extra frequencies the Tuaoi Stone supplied.

"Now on the left is Your Majesty's palace," Kenaseus bellowed. "All you see around and beyond the castle are the king's splendid grounds, which I hope we'll have time to tour with you later."

I'd been wondering why Kenaseus had said so little about the Grand Temple and the Tuaoi Stone, and now our attention was being drawn to Gadeirus' estate. The palace was a huge square at its base. Rounded columns rising five stories high bore a copper dome overlaid with gold and silver. I supposed it was considered too much to take in, let alone comment on, with so little time on our tour.

"There will be an opportunity to see these sacred sites," Jon whispered. "But not today."

"No?" I felt puzzled. "Kendrick had given us the impression we would have some time at the end of this day to explore at our leisure. I was especially hoping to see the Tuaoi Stone."

"Recreation time is indeed built into the schedule. And yet exploring the Tuaoi Stone is strictly forbidden."

"Forbidden? Since when? Before leaving Ahlaiele, we were told we'd be taking a tour."

"It's a recent development. The king believes enemies are lurking in Poseidia's shadows. Dangerous adversaries who are simply waiting for an opportunity. And he's determined not to give them one."

"An opportunity for what?"

"Seizing power. Because whoever controls the Tuaoi Stone can rule the world."

"I see." Kenaseus was pointing out secondary temples and educational establishments, but I wasn't listening. Back on Ahlaiele, we had discussed the importance of accessing the Tuaoi Stone to transmit Highest Light across the planet. I felt sure the Elders had warned Poseidia's king we would attempt to usurp the crystal's power if we survived our flight. I closed my eyes and reminded myself the development didn't matter. Highest Light would find a way—of that I was certain—in spite of appearances and circumstances.

I opened my eyes and glanced at Ava and Quenna, who were smiling and chatting with their companions while Jon and I stayed silent. I could feel him as readily as I'm sure he sensed me. I wondered yet again why it seemed the others on our mission had such an easier time than I did of connecting with their joy and simply letting themselves have a pleasant time. Intellectually, I knew it had to do with the deeper space I held, and the higher intensity with which I felt, but that didn't make me long for their carefree attitudes any less.

"My ladies, we will be arriving at the markets momentarily. I can hardly wait!" Kenaseus' childlike enthusiasm was infectious. "Prepare to be overwhelmed!"

As Ava and Quenna laughed, I glanced up at Jon. He looked at me with compassionate understanding, and I knew he realized Kenaseus had just uttered aloud my mantra for survival on this earthly plane.

TEN

The hoverdisk descended swiftly, halting in an open area seemingly reserved for such crafts. Glancing around, I saw row after row of similar vessels, all appearing to defy gravity by resting a foot or so from the ground. But there were also many other shapes and designs floating from mere inches to a few feet above the black stone. I wondered to myself how anyone would know which disk was whose since so many of them looked alike and — at least as far as I could tell — there were no identifying markings.

"Each disk has a crystalline chip imprinted with the owner's energy," Jon said as he helped me from the craft. "It guides the owner back to it through an automatic positioning system, which most people choose to feel as a vibration. Then once you reboard, the disk responds via voice or thought command." I nodded, unsure if I felt uneasy or relieved to realize either Jon was two for two in anticipating my unspoken questions regarding the hovercraft — or else he could actually read my thoughts.

"My ladies, welcome to the best place on earth to feast your eyes — and your taste buds!" Kenaseus roared good-naturedly. "You're about to experience the finest foods, wares, art, and music available anywhere. Poseidia's Artisan Market District is a collective made up of the most creative minds from around the universe. Just observe the crowds here, which are an everyday occurrence, and you'll begin to see how much we appreciate artists."

"Wonderful!" Ava clapped her hands in delight. She openly enjoyed all things Poseidia, particularly these markets by the sea. "Where should we begin, Kenaseus? Surely you've put together orientations for tourists on a tight time schedule before."

"Oh, indeed." For a moment he fell silent, rubbing his chin. "Given the short amount of time at our disposal, I believe we should head straight for the bread. Unless there are objections, of course."

"You're going to love the bread!" Ava gushed at Quenna and me. "I don't believe it's as much a food as an art form."

"Why bread, as opposed to cheese? Or spices? Or cacao, even?"

asked Quenna. Her inquiry was something I'd been wondering myself, yet my quiet nature generally kept me from asking such things.

"An excellent question, my lady," Kenaseus answered. "When you're in the bread section, all those other delights—cacao, cheeses, spices, and so forth—are available to be tasted on the bread itself. So it's like having multiple exquisite tastes and scents all combined and available in a single section of the market."

"Well then. I don't need further convincing," Quenna replied. "Elysia, how do you feel?"

"I'm good with the bread." Our party stared at me, and my face flamed. I did my best to ignore the heat—although I don't think I did a very good job. "Besides, Ava is so excited. I'd hate to see her disappointed."

"Thank you, dear." Ava squeezed my shoulders. "No one is going to be disappointed today if I can help it. Least of all with the bread. I guarantee it!"

"It's settled then," Kenaseus laughed, his eyes creasing to jovial slits as he motioned for us to follow. "Come this way. We'll cut through the silk rugs, and then we're practically there."

Kenaseus gestured for us to make a left on the next cross street, where throngs of shoppers seemed to triple out of nowhere. I could have easily gotten distracted observing the various forms of life milling about between the brick and stone buildings. Many were human, but an equal number were an eclectic assortment of hybrids. Several appeared to be tall, humanoid aliens in colors ranging from gold to green to blue. There were also shorter, dwarf-like beings with beards wearing what looked like some type of military uniform. I also saw any number of combinations of animals—crosses of birds and reptiles that resulted in fierce-looking creatures, hybrid goats and horses, and other species I couldn't readily identify. As we moved through the thick crowd, I felt endless attempts to plug into my energy field. I needed to be cautious, and so I amped up my focus on the Oneness Prayer, which helped me navigate the landscape of hungry gui density as if I were wearing an emotional suit of armor.

As we made our way along the cobblestone passage, I caught sight of the rugs hanging on display behind the vendors. I was struck by their loveliness. Even in the side street's early morning shadows, there was enough light to reflect the silk threads' luminescent quality. Each hanging rug, trembling in the breeze, resembled a living tapestry.

Vivid images of birds, animals, flowers, plants, and geometric shapes of all kinds nodded and waved as we passed. Kenaseus was chatting with Ava, and the others seemed to be trying to hear him above the buzzing masses as we marched toward the bread. But I was enamored with the elaborate beauty before me. The rugs seemed to carry deep emotion, which was something I hadn't expected from a material object. Only Jon seemed to notice how intensely I was experiencing their rich colors and designs.

"Each one is made by hand, so no two are alike," he said in that hushed voice, which always easily reached my ears, in spite of the fact we were navigating an area rumbling with sound.

"They are stunning. I'm drawn to them for reasons I don't fully understand."

"Many are made by the merbeings." He slowed to my halting gait. "Merfolk are the epitome of complexity, both in their emotional bodies and in their weavings. They are highly empathic."

"It makes sense now. I can tell how the merfolk are feeling through these rugs. I had no idea an object could convey that depth of resonance."

"Then prepare to be endlessly fascinated here, El," Jon said, smiling at me. "Because this artisan market mostly carries items that resonate deeply. Including the bread."

"So I keep hearing," I replied, and we both laughed.

As we neared the end of the rug vendors, I turned to ask Jon something and bumped into someone.

"My apologies." Green eyes widened in surprise — and recognition — when they met mine. "Do I know you?"

"Well, I — I mean, we've never met." The red-haired merbeing's words were carefully chosen, for all of her fluster. I could feel what she said was true, and yet it wasn't the whole truth. Nor was she whole herself, I observed, as she limped away from me on two leg-like stumps.

Her eyes were so like mine, they haunted me. And their sadness punctured my heart. As I stared after her, a sickening feeling began to rise, strangling my breath. It was a sure sign Lesser Light had found an opening, and for a moment I simply had to stop and stand still.

"It's all right, El." Jon's tone was calm, and yet even his soothing presence didn't help bring me back into focus on the Oneness Prayer. I squeezed my eyes shut — hard. As I did my best to get my breathing under control, I felt Jon's arms go around my shoulders and guide me somewhere — presumably out of the middle of the street. I dared not open my eyes. I was better able to drop down again into the Oneness Prayer with them closed.

"Breathe, El," he whispered, his lips right by my ear. "Just breathe. And remember Highest Light."

"Yes," I managed to say. Warmth pulsed from his palms, and immediately the Oneness Prayer began flowing through me again. I don't know how long I stood there before, all of a sudden, familiar waves of light opened my throat. Then just as quickly as I'd become ill, I felt like myself again.

Opening my eyes, I glanced around to see Jon had whisked me into a small area behind one of the rug vendors, where they'd neatly piled empty boxes and cartons. The large stacks provided some measure of protection from curious onlookers, and I was glad it seemed no one had taken notice of me. Looking up, I could see Jon's relieved face. And beyond that, a gaze of pure intensity, from green eyes so like my own.

"Hey, you," Hunter murmured.

"Hey, yourself." I shook my head in disbelief. "What are you doing here?"

"Oh, the usual," he teased, his eyes twinkling. "Typical damsel-in-distress stuff. Some life-or-death healing work. But you know, it's all in a day's work."

"How did you get here so quickly?" I could feel my face flushing at the thought I'd once again disrupted Hunter's plans and spoiled his off-duty leisure time.

"Did you think I wouldn't be watching out for you?" His loving voice brought tears to my eyes.

"No, I—oh, it's not that," I stammered. "I just—I mean—"

"El, I apologize for interrupting." Jon's near whisper nonetheless commanded attention. "But if it's okay with you, I will leave you in Hunter's most capable hands for the moment, and catch up with the rest of our party."

"Of course." Secretly I felt grateful he'd saved me from further awkwardness. "And Jon?"

"Yes?" His angelic face held a quizzical expression, making him even more cherub-like.

"Thank you. For taking such good care of me." Tears splashed from my lashes, but I wished to express my gratitude even more than I wanted to preserve my composure.

"The honor is mine." He bowed, one hand over his heart. "I will see you both shortly at the bread vendor area."

"Yes, you will," Hunter replied, locking forearms with Jon. With that, my Atlantean guardian angel turned and melted into the crowd. Which left me face-to-face with my Ahlaielian guardian angel.

"I'm sorry, Hunter. I—"

"It's okay, El." Stepping toward me, he caressed my cheek. "Everything's all right."

"But things got out of control again," I protested. "I just couldn't get myself back in sync with the Oneness Prayer."

"It felt to me like you were surprised by something, and then Lesser Light was able to infiltrate your defenses. Is that what happened?"

"Essentially, yes. It was strange. One of the merfolk seemed to recognize me."

"Merfolk? You mean the mermaids who dive for pearls?" He shook his head. "I don't understand. What was a mermaid doing in the market? And how in the name of Oneness could she possibly recognize you?"

"That's what I wondered, too. It was odd. She had eyes like mine," I said. "But it was her sadness that overwhelmed me. And once I saw she was hobbling on stumps instead of a tail, I became quite ill."

"Stumps?"

"Yes," I whispered. "There are some very unnatural things going on here."

"Indeed there are." He swept long bangs from his forehead. "I suppose we were warned as much. All we can do right now is breathe and show up, fully present, in this moment." Gently he grasped my shoulders. "Are you ready for that?"

"Yes."

"Then come on. We should get to the bread vendor area so our absence won't draw undue attention."

Before I could reply, he'd turned and was surveying our surroundings. Hunter was nothing if not watchful. Then without another word, he took my hand and we began walking through the market. I could feel his energy surging through my skin where our fingers touched. I felt altered, and I realized he'd surrounded me in a vibrational bubble to prevent any further incidents. I began to worry he was using too many of his own frequencies to shield me, when he eased his pace and leaned in close.

"I'm all right, El," he whispered in my ear. Briskly his lips grazed my cheek, and even that small gesture raised gooseflesh along my body. "Just go back to the Oneness Prayer. I'll take care of the rest."

"Okay." I knew I was in no position to argue. He squeezed my hand before once more lengthening his stride.

We reached a cross street, and Hunter confidently turned right. It appeared we'd entered the food area at last. Multiple spices scented the air. The tables brimmed with woven baskets bearing fruits and vegetables, in all shapes and sizes, among countless colored bottles of oil. As we passed vendors who specialized in mead and cheese, I began to smell what could only be the bread we'd been hearing so much about.

Toasted seeds dotted the first steaming loaves I saw. Behind the tables, bakers were busy popping fleshy dough into a wall of ovens. As Hunter slowed his steps, I tried to take in the magnitude of the selections. Large slabs and small rolls lined the tables, in colors ranging from milky white to mocha brown. Everywhere I looked, beings of all shapes and sizes stood sampling bites of bread from tiny gold napkins shaped like stars. And across every table, wrapped packages of these heavenly delights were being swapped for Atlantean currency.

The crowd was so dense I'd become pressed in behind Hunter. From this vantage point, I could see nothing but his broad shoulders towering above me. He held my hand against the small of his back as he inched forward. Abruptly he stopped, and I felt an uncharacteristic flinch in his energy, making my heart drop. With a sense of dread, I peeked out from behind him.

Just ahead was Kenaseus, guffawing and gesticulating with two other men I assumed must be Atlantean, as they were dressed in similar white tunics with metal accents. Ava stood further to the right, a joyous grin on her face as she spoke with a group of hybrid species. Her genuine happiness at once again being on the island's soil permeated her whole being, and for a moment I wondered if I could ever feel that level of contentment here. Or anywhere, for that matter.

Before I could get lost in my musings, though, a magnetic energy began to pull at me. Its field was so strong I nearly lost my balance and fell against Hunter. A wave of fear swept over my body, as I recognized who was drawing me. For several moments I managed to look at the ground, but the tugging only intensified. I felt powerless to resist. My head lifted as if by force, and my gaze locked with Alaric's. Another ripple surged through Hunter's energetic system, and yet I felt frozen in place, unable to move or act in a way that could diffuse the tension rising among the three of us. I'd known this moment would arrive at some point today. But it had come much sooner than I'd anticipated.

"Down we go, into the lair at last," Hunter muttered. "The sheep meet the wolf. The ones risking slaughter, eye to eye with the one who slaughters." Ever so slightly he shook his head. "And I know not who will blink."

ELEVEN

Before I could reply — if indeed I would have been able to speak — Hunter stepped to the side, exposing me. Once again we began advancing, and I could feel my heart hammering away as I realized we were mere steps from what I feared was Lesser Light's pure embodiment. I felt as if a sheath of protection had been removed, though Hunter yet gripped my left hand, and I could still feel his energy moving in comforting waves up my arm from where our palms touched. But that's not all I was feeling.

Alaric's frequencies were altogether different from Hunter's, but no less potent. The reptoid's laser-like vibrations were pointed and cold next to Hunter's, and yet they were equally as riveting. Alaric had somehow connected systemically to me; anywhere I focused in my body I could feel his energy's metallic quality. His gold-green eyes continued to bore into me as Hunter and I approached. It was only when we were less than 10 feet away that he removed his gaze from mine.

I was acutely aware he'd been watching Hunter hold my hand, and for the briefest possible millisecond I thought I felt a deep jealousy emanating from him. But it passed as quickly as it had appeared, whatever the true feeling may have been, and I realized I was in no position to be objective about what I thought I was perceiving anyway. By the time we were standing in front of Alaric, he emitted only cool nonchalance.

"Good morning, Alaric," Hunter said, his tone friendly.

"Good morning, Hunter." Alaric's smooth voice seemed oddly quiet.

The two locked forearms, and I sensed respect welling up in the reptoid. I don't know what I'd been expecting. Perhaps some kind of egoic male strutting over the complex triangle of emotion we all shared. And yet there we stood, the very picture of civility. It was another side of Alaric, one which epitomized genteel grace. As he conversed good-naturedly with Hunter, I found myself wondering if he could possibly be the same reptile who'd made such overt sexual advances toward me.

"Alaric, let me again present Elysia," Hunter said after many pleasantries had been exchanged. He rested his hand on the back of my waist and coaxed me forward. "It was challenging to pull her away from the silk rugs, but somehow that was accomplished."

"I see," Alaric replied, his sensuous lips curving into a smile. His eyes turned toward me, but this time there was no energetic locking. "My lady." He bowed and reached for my hand, which I extended reluctantly. I found myself holding my breath as he kissed the back of my fingers. Again he behaved like the perfect gentleman. I felt more uncomfortable than ever.

"Alaric."

"It's a pleasure to see you again, Elysia." Graciously he released my hand. "I trust you've been enjoying the market thus far."

"Yes, I—I have been," I sputtered. My face flushed, which made matters worse. Somehow being around the more arrogant Alaric was easier, as it seemed to engage more of my inner queen. But this mannerly reptoid made me feel like an anxious teenager. "There's just so much to see. I'm sure it would require several days in order to take it all in."

"Either that or going with an experienced guide." He looked at me without emotion. "Being with someone who knows the lay of the land can make all the difference."

"Elysia—there you are!" Kenaseus bellowed before I could consider what Alaric had said. The statesman's hair shimmered like fire in the sun, which finally had risen high enough to warm our area of the market. "Have you had a chance to sample any of the delightful breads yet?"

"Not yet."

"You must eat up, my dear, so we can explore at least some of the other vendors before we have to leave for the palace. Which is in less than an hour." Looking beyond me, he caught sight of Hunter. "And you must be Hunter, are you not? Ava's told me so much about you." Kenaseus locked forearms with Hunter, and the two of them began to talk, leaving me alone with Alaric once again. That is, if anyone could be alone with someone while in the midst of thousands.

I became self-consciously aware of how he towered above the other tall men. I started to feel intimidated, then exasperated at myself over why I should have such a reaction to him. And then I noticed a delicate grounding of my internal angst. It was as if a spider had spun fine silk around my anxiety and hidden it away in a web somewhere. Cautiously, I raised my eyes to his. That gold-green gaze was still. Tranquil even.

"Here, my lady." In his impossibly large hand, he held out to me one of the star-shaped napkins. On it was a sampling of golden-brown bread, with large pores and a thick, seed-studded crust. There appeared to be at least three different spices sprinkled over it, and a touch of greenish oil drizzled on top.

"For me?" I peered up into his face, realizing I was trying to feel into him, to see what this gesture really meant. But either he was devoid of feeling or else so expertly masked I could get no reading.

"For you." Gently, he reached with his other hand for mine. Once I'd extended it, he nestled the napkin in my palm. "Please."

"That's very thoughtful." I realized I truly didn't know what to say. "Thank you."

"You can thank me by trying it." The smile on his face actually touched his eyes, warming them. For some reason I couldn't explain, I felt tears surfacing. So I looked away, pretending to study the bread. It smelled divine as I lifted the sample from the napkin to my mouth.

I wasn't prepared for how utterly amazing the bread tasted. Its lighter body was soft and chewy, with a hearty crust. The herbs added a slight sweetness, a zest of citrus, and a pungent boldness simultaneously. And the drizzled oil must have contained basil and rosemary in its olive-green richness. The longer I chewed, the more flavor was released. I couldn't quite believe how such diverse tastes had come together so harmoniously, in such an exquisite treat.

"Alaric, this is beyond delicious!" I beamed at him, still chewing.

"Wait until you try this one." He handed me another napkin, and I got the sense he savored sharing these delicacies with me. While I finished swallowing the first sample, I examined the second. This one was a deep brown bread, with nuts as well as seeds embedded in its thick crust. It, too, was dusted in herbs and bathed in oil. Feeling emboldened, I popped the sample in my mouth without hesitation. Just like the first, its taste was multi-layered, complex, and yet exceedingly complementary. If anything, I thought this second sample was even more delectable than the first.

"Of all the hundreds of samples here, how did you know I would like these so much?" I really wanted to know the answer, and on some level didn't even care I was showing how eager I was to learn it.

"I just know certain things. And here, I do know the lay of the land."

"You most definitely do." My voice sounded distant even to my own ears. I felt dreamy, as if I were having a déjà vu experience of some kind. I noticed he was looking at me with an expression I could only describe as tender, and again those tears seemed to come out of nowhere, stinging my eyes. I couldn't explain why I was feeling so emotional, or why I felt compelled to engage him further. "Alaric—"

"There you are, El!" Ava's enthusiastic tone matched her embrace. She stumbled upon us out of the crowd. "And hello again, Alaric! I hope you've been well since I saw you last evening."

"Very well indeed, my lady." He kissed her hand, but before any more could be said, Kenaseus and Hunter strode over and stood beside me. And then Jon and Perraseus joined us as well.

"All right, everyone. I want to move our brief tour along so you get to see a little more of the market beyond the breads. We should have time to visit a few more vendors before I need to get you to the palace." Kenaseus surveyed our group. "Does anyone know where Quenna is?"

"She was with Kendrick and Will not long ago," Ava answered. "I thought they were right behind me."

"I will find them," Perraseus offered, his gray eyes confident. He turned and the crowd consumed his muscular frame. Out of the corner of my eye, I saw movement above and to the right of where we stood. The hawk landed on some stacked crates in an opening between two of the bread booths. I could feel her copper gaze boring into me as foreboding filled my body. Something had happened to one of the crew.

"While we wait, let's decide where we shall land at the palace once it's time for us to leave so it will be easy to reconvene," Kenaseus suggested. "There are multiple parking areas available for flying crafts. Hunter, did you hop a hoverdisk to the market?"

"Yes. Kendrick flew Will and me here this morning." I realized the pinched look on Hunter's face meant he'd also intuited something was wrong with one of our friends. Fear's keen blade stabbed me, slicing away whatever silky threads had earlier bound my angst within its web. My heart rammed my ribs as Kenaseus continued discussing parking possibilities.

No longer listening, I stared at the ground, focusing with all my might on the Oneness Prayer. It wasn't long before I felt more grounded and peaceful. And yet as I rested in the inner quietude, I became increasingly aware of something. The calm state wasn't of my own doing.

Hunter stood to my left and Alaric to my right, both channeling energy to support me. I was, it seemed, in the midst of the Lemurian symbol I'd described to Hunter only the day before. I was the middle dot on my very own open-ended Circle of Emotion. But the oddest thing was I could neither sense nor see the gap that should have existed between Alaric and me. And that frightened me most of all.

TWELVE

I closed my eyes, trying to focus harder on the Oneness Prayer. I realized both Hunter and Alaric were observing me, each in his own discreet way. Breathing deeply, I did my best to surrender to the energy both men were supplying, thus creating no resistance. Being receptive in this way helped me sink deeper into the Oneness Prayer, and from that void I finally felt more peaceful. In the immediate background, I could still hear Kenaseus and Ava and the others chattering, and beyond that was the market's general drone.

I opened my eyes and saw Perraseus dash behind me. A fresh wave of apprehension washed over my heart; he carried the emotional vibration of worry. Perraseus approached Kenaseus and whispered in his superior's ear. Kenaseus' somber expression told me something dreadful had indeed come to pass.

For a few moments, Kenaseus listened and nodded. Gently he touched Perraseus on the shoulder. Then he surveyed our faces, motioning us closer. Gone was the twinkle in his eye. Before us stood the statesman ready to do damage control, and I felt my heart in my throat as I wondered what in the name of Highest Light could have happened—and to whom.

"My friends, there's been an unfortunate development, and I wish to speak plainly to you about it," he began. "Perraseus has informed me Quenna has fallen gravely ill and is being transported to one of our care facilities, accompanied by Kendrick and Will."

"Oh no!" Ava exclaimed. "What happened?"

"My dear Ava, at this time I simply don't know," he replied. "However, Kendrick has sent word through Perraseus that it's more important than ever for you to represent Ahlaielian interests at today's diplomatic relations gathering. But first, you are to step in for Kendrick by honoring a private audience that's been arranged with the king. He's at a summit assembly in the nearby mountains, and Jonastus and Perraseus will be escorting you there to meet with him before returning you to the palace."

"Of course." Ava said. "Do you know if Will is going to stay with

Kendrick at the care facility?"

"I have my orders to bring him to your meeting with the king. Kendrick wants him to support you in this diplomatic mission." Kenaseus looked at Hunter. "And I've been instructed to fly you to the care facility. Kendrick believes you may be crucial to Quenna's recovery."

"Certainly." Hunter's jaw had hardened to stone. "Anything I can do to be of assistance."

"Good." Kenaseus nodded before turning to me. "And that leaves you, my lady. Kendrick thought it best for you not to come to the care facility, as he expressed concern you were still adjusting to our denser atmosphere. However, he didn't want to stress you by having you arrive unescorted to the gathering, either. So I've been ordered to bring you back to the ship."

"I'm a big girl, Kenaseus." My face reddened as I spoke, seemingly contradicting the point I was trying to make. "I'm quite capable of attending the gathering without an escort."

"I understand, my lady. And yet I have my orders."

"But—"

"My apologies, Elysia. However, there's really nothing I can do. Kendrick's directive was quite clear."

"But I—"

"I will escort Elysia to the capital." Alaric's velvety voice was quiet but commanding. It stopped me cold. I felt hushed surprise ripple out among the group, and an unguarded spark of jealousy from Hunter before his energy subsided back beneath the Oneness Prayer. Alaric turned to me and bowed. "It would be an honor, my lady."

"I'm confident the entire Ahlaielian assembly here appreciates your gesture, Alaric." Kenaseus still wore that well-mannered smile, although I could tell he was uneasy. "And yet her presence at the gathering isn't even required."

"Perhaps it's not required, but it most certainly is necessary," Alaric replied, his voice unhurried and as smooth as silk. "I'm sure I don't need to remind you how eager many of the intergalactic federation members are to meet with the Ahlaielian delegation. Much anticipation has been building around expanded trade and consciousness development through contact with those from the Great Central Sun region." He turned steady eyes on Hunter. "It may send a mixed message— perhaps even indicate a wavering of support—if there isn't at least one Ahlaielian representative at the gathering from its commencement. Given the current unrest among the federation as a whole, that is."

"Yes, well, Kendrick has issued his orders." Kenaseus' voice sharpened. "There's nothing to be done about it now."

"On the contrary." Alaric's buttery tone was hypnotically pleasing.

He made even a disagreement sound harmonious. "One of you needs to mind-message Kendrick about Elysia. Now." Again he looked at Hunter, and I caught my breath. "Or I will."

"I simply think disturbing Kendrick with this issue at the present time is overstepping boundaries," Kenaseus urged, practically begging Alaric to drop the issue. "It's highly inappropriate. It goes against all established protocol. And—"

"I'll do it." Hunter spoke firmly, decisively, his eyes never leaving the reptile's. "Alaric is right about the federation and the importance of us doing nothing to undermine their confidence in our mission."

"Hunter, listen to reason," Kenaseus pleaded. "You can't possibly mean—"

"I agree with Hunter and Alaric," Ava interrupted. "We must do what's best for the mission."

Even as Kenaseus reluctantly backed down, he and Ava continued discussing her upcoming meeting with the king. It appeared Kenaseus was now concerned she may be inappropriate in her dealings with His Majesty, given her demonstrated ability to disregard accepted custom and protocol. While they continued their banter, I stopped listening altogether. My gaze was on Hunter, and my feelers on Alaric. Both were patiently still. Hunter had already closed his eyes, and I could feel him broadcasting to Kendrick. I dared not look at Alaric. But I caught a glimpse of Jon. His face looked so gentle, so reassuring, and as our eyes met he gave me the slightest nod. I knew he was telling me all was well and not to worry. Which served as a reminder once again to breathe deeply—something I still kept forgetting to do.

A short time passed, and Hunter's eyes opened. Kenaseus was still debating Ava and didn't notice.

"It is decided," Hunter announced. "Kendrick sends word Elysia is to attend the gathering." Showing no emotion, he looked at Alaric. "And Alaric is to be her escort."

My face flamed again, and yet I knew I couldn't show any type of reaction, especially since all eyes were upon me. I clung to the deep breathing, like a drowning woman clutches a raft, and prayed the inner stillness that was once such a natural part of me on Ahlaiele would somehow grace me at least with its appearance, if not its essence.

"All right then," Kenaseus replied after a long pause. "Did Kendrick happen to relay a passcode with his message? All diplomatic missions are carefully monitored for security and safety reasons, and any change in orders must be documented with a passcode." His statesman's smile faltered as he took in Ava's disapproving look. "Strictly an adherence to protocol is all."

"Yes, Kenaseus. He gave me a passcode," Hunter muttered, and I could feel weariness welling up through his words. "Would you like me to write it down for you?"

"Please." Kenaseus produced a pocket-sized crystalline tablet and a writing instrument. Hunter scribbled something, and Kenaseus nodded. "Yes. That is the correct passcode." He looked around at our party before his eyes settled on Alaric's. "We should take our leave. Is your hovercraft near the west entrance?"

"No."

"All right. Then we shall part company with you here." Kenaseus locked forearms with Alaric before enveloping my hands in his. "My lady, I'm looking forward to seeing you later this afternoon."

"The pleasure will be mine, Kenaseus." I smiled with a spunk I didn't feel as Ava grabbed me, hugging me hard.

"It's going to be all right, El," she said through tears.

"I know." I released her and wiped at my own eyes. Then Perraseus brushed my cheek with his lips. Jon was close behind, and he gave me an encouraging smile before he, too, embraced me.

"I have a little something for you, El," he said in his comforting tone. He let go of me and placed a small wrapped item in my hand. "You'll want to put this in your pocket for later. It's a reminder Highest Light is and always will be here for you."

"All right," I replied, tucking the bundle deep inside my shirt pocket as more tears surfaced. "Jon, I don't know how to thank you enough."

"You already have." He kissed my cheek. "I will see you at the gathering, once we return from the mountains."

"Okay." I watched him whisper something to Alaric. Then Jon and Hunter spoke briefly, before Hunter locked forearms with Alaric. It appeared more pleasantries were exchanged among the three of them before my beloved finally approached.

"Hey, you."

"Hey, yourself." I stifled a sob as he enfolded me in his arms. My frustration with myself rose higher. It was no time to be weak, and yet there I was, ready to collapse in his embrace.

"Shhhhh. We can do this. I've got your back, my beloved."

"I know. For as long as we're here."

"And for as long as you need me," he replied, "which had better be forever and ever." He held me away from him. His handsome face looked all the more dashing, dimpled with his most hopeful grin.

"And then some." I put on the happiest smile I could muster.

"It's just for a couple of hours, El." I knew his words were as much for himself as they were for me. Then he bent and kissed my cheek. "I love you."

"I love you, too," I replied as he turned to follow the others, leaving me in an awkward, ironic place with Alaric—alone again in a crowd.

THIRTEEN

For a few moments, I simply stood there, watching after Hunter and the rest of our party. I had so many feelings surging beneath my skin, and yet no outlet for either expression or analysis. The only thing I had was my breath, so I inhaled deeply to help center myself before turning to face Alaric.

Looking so at ease it brought envy to my heart, he neither tried to seduce me with his eyes nor did he rush to speak. His calm countenance suggested he could wait there all day with me. I recalled his broad brow and sculpted cheekbones from the night before, and realized he was much more handsome than I was comfortable acknowledging. I started to say something, then thought better of it. I smiled as I blushed, raking quivering fingers through my ponytail.

"You have no need to fear me, Elysia," he said at long last, as he studied the hair I continued to sift. "I mean you no harm."

"I'm just—I mean, I think I'm still getting used to the dense vibrations here." The words fell from my lips, clumsy and unsure. "Quite honestly, I'm not used to physical form, or processing all this emotional data coming in from everywhere." I was mortified I'd said too much, and yet exasperated I seemed compelled to want to share things with him all at the same time. I reasoned it was because I had no other way to process or integrate all I'd been feeling since coming to Earth. And yet deep down, I knew somehow it was much more complicated than that. "I may be feeling nervous in general at the moment, but I don't fear you."

"Liar."

"I beg your pardon—"

"My lady, you may very well be used to telling others whatever you wish and having them believe you." His eyes glowed mostly gold in the late morning sun. "But I'm not the others. And you clearly are quite frightened of me."

"How can you say that?" I said, emboldened with new energy. "It's true I'm experiencing fear, on a scale I never expected. Just like all emotions seem to be amplified for me here. But I most definitely am not afraid of you."

"Prove it."

"How?"

"By not flinching every time you look at me."

"What?!"

"You heard me." Alaric smiled politely, his full lips parting to reveal straight white teeth. "Your vibration literally trembles each time you meet my gaze."

"I don't know what you're talking about." My face flushed as I struggled to probe my own depths. To see if what he said could possibly be true.

"You most certainly do, my lady." He sounded so self-assured, and it annoyed me he could remain poised in the midst of my turmoil. "Your frequency is fear, pure and simple, in my presence. And I'd very much like that to change."

"My frequency's doing just fine, thank you." I thought back to what Ava had told me "fine" meant to humans, and it made me grin. I hoped my smile made it seem like I was making light of the situation. Part of me did feel like teasing him, but most of me was disturbed he seemed to see something I hadn't. And I had to admit he was telling the truth.

In my flustered state, I thought it best to try and turn the attention away from me. If that was possible. "But why even concern yourself with how I perceive you?" I asked. "When we met last evening, you weren't exactly the perfect gentleman. And quite frankly, you didn't seem to care what I thought or felt."

"You're absolutely right, Elysia. I extend to you my deepest apologies." His gold-green eyes radiated remorse. I had no doubt he was being sincere as he bowed before me. "Unfortunately, I was caught in my own painful vibration, and as such I behaved in a way that was both cruel and disrespectful. I do hope you'll forgive me."

"I can forgive you, Alaric. If you can accept I'm not fearful of you."

"I'm only trying to help you become aware of all you need to know in order to chart your course around Atlantis. Remember, I know the lay of the land here. And you most definitely need to be aware of what vibration your energy field is holding. If you're to navigate wisely, that is." He eyed me, as if considering something. "I will show you what I mean. Come with me."

Without another word, he grabbed my hand and practically dragged me along behind him. Whether it was his size or his energy, everyone steered clear of us. The crowd kept parting to allow our passage. I struggled to keep up, wondering what the rapid movement was really about. I noticed how large his hand was as it cradled mine, and how smooth. The skin was neither warm nor cold, but somewhere near neutral—and unbelievably soft. I could have become quite fascinated by how unique his skin was, if he hadn't suddenly hauled me down a narrow alleyway.

The shadows stretched deep, as lofty buildings snubbed sunlight from spilling onto the dark stone pavers. There were no vendors. The alley was lined with empty boxes and crates, evidence of the commercial enterprise just half a block back the other way, and yet there was a ghastly feel to it. I knew Hunter would be upset if he knew where Alaric had just taken me, and I realized in that moment how thoughts of Hunter filled me with guilt. I couldn't shake the feeling that somehow, deep down, I secretly craved Alaric's advances—and I would have no way of ever explaining that to Hunter.

Before I could think or feel anything else, Alaric pulled me into an opening among the stacked crates. Deftly, he spun me around until my back hugged the wall. And then his hands pressed against my shoulders, pinning me to the masonry. My breath was ragged from running to keep up with him, but also because I was terrified—and exhilarated. Sensually, Alaric slid one large palm up my neck to my throat, lifting my chin so I stared into gold-green eyes that held no emotion.

"Are you afraid?" His voice was sultry, inviting. His eyes, though expressionless, dared me to feel. And yet he didn't give me an opportunity to respond before he turned my head to the side. I caught my breath just as his mouth met my flesh. His lips were even softer than his hands. And warmer. From somewhere above I heard the hawk's cry, and yet I could take no comfort in her witnessing my descent into depravity. I bit my lip as he traced the line of my neck to my jaw, with kisses that knew no insecurities or hesitation. "Tell me how much you've been fearing me," he murmured in my ear.

"I am scared now," I whispered, wondering if he was going to stop. And secretly, shamefully hoping in the deepest, blackest part of my soul he wouldn't.

"What about before?" he insisted as he kissed my jaw, my cheek. "Tell me you were frightened, from the first time you saw me last night."

"Why?" My voice slurred as he continued to arouse me with his lips. "I admitted I was nervous. Isn't that enough?"

"No." He pulled away just far enough so he could stare into my eyes. Ever so gently, he caressed my cheek. "I realize I got off on the wrong foot with you last night, and again, I humbly apologize for that. I want you to trust me. But as long as you continue to lie to me, I know you don't."

"But I—"

"Truly I understand, much more than you realize, that you say and do everything from the standpoint of what's best for the mission." His index finger traced the line of my mouth. "And yet the mission will not fail if you tell me the truth."

"I don't know what to say." Tears misted my eyes, seemingly for the hundredth time that day. "Honestly. Because I'm confused when it comes to you."

"Tell me more."

"You ... make me feel things," I replied, my heart throbbing. This was a man I would never have to beg to kiss me.

"Yes." His lips brushed mine, and I caught my breath, trying with all my might to keep my wild emotions in check. "I do make you feel things. Many things that perhaps are ... unfamiliar."

"That's an understatement." Looking up, I expected to see him gloating. I was surprised his countenance, if anything, had softened into sadness. "Although it's not exactly that these feelings are unfamiliar. It's strange, really."

"How so?" His mouth was again on mine, this time a little firmer, a little more lingering.

"It's as if something inside has stirred that has long slumbered." I shook my head. "Almost like a memory."

"Almost." He kissed me again, delicately parting my lips with his before once more ravaging my neck. In that moment, I met my own wickedness and realized it mattered not how he knew to pleasure me so. Even if the rumors were true and he was an escort for hire, it made no difference. Were he to ask it of me, I'd pay any price to be this expertly enticed. I cried out as his teeth skimmed my skin, beyond caring if any audience could hear me—or what they'd think if they did.

"Alaric, please ... You're making me weak."

"Then I'm not meeting my objective. That very singular purpose I mentioned last night," he whispered. "All I want is for you to feel your own power. To remember it."

"Remember what?"

"That you need not fear me nor simply submit to me out of some distorted sense of insecurity." Again he withdrew. Just far enough to look me in the eye with an intensity and a tenderness I found overwhelming. "I want you to be the queen that you are."

The very vibration of his words cut through my fog and confusion and all my layered defenses like a well-honed sword. In one fell swoop, his blade of illumination sliced a lighted pathway into my soul's blackest recesses. Laid bare before me was the realization—stark and shocking and yet undeniably true—that I had known him before. In a past and distant life. A shared life at that. On Moldaaris.

"I am your queen," I breathed.

"No, my lady." His voice surprised me with its gentleness—

something I was still trying to get used to, as it went against all my preconceived notions of his armored strength. Yet it was the tears glazing his gold-green eyes that floored me. "Indeed, you are a queen, a royal by birth and training. You have ruled by my side. And you have loved me as completely as a woman can love a man. But you are sovereign unto yourself and belong to no one."

"For the love of Oneness." A flood of sense memory washed over me. I couldn't believe so much emotion had been buried inside, and that for all of my feeling capacity I'd never known it existed. But now I'd caught a glimpse of our former life, of its beauty and majesty. And the chemistry, which explained why I was so drawn to him in Atlantis. In spite of all circumstances, all potential for risk and hurt and loss. In my mind's eye, I saw myself as a hybrid being, part human and part dolphin. And there was more. So much more. "We had a child," I whispered.

"Yes." A tear trickled along his cheek. "We did."

"A boy we named Gyan. With your eyes," I continued, my voice distant even to me, as I waded into the deep waters of our collective past. "Black tousled hair. The most beautiful ivory skin. And a will stronger than either of ours."

"Yes." Alaric laughed softly as he cradled my face in his hands. "Much stronger."

"And we were happy."

"Very much so, my lady."

"And then ... there was to be another child." A lump swelled my throat, strangling my words. "A girl. She would have looked like me."

"Yes." He leaned closer, resting his forehead against mine. "She would have been the very image of you."

"But we—her—that welcome addition to our family never came to pass."

"No." Sighing, he enfolded me in his arms. For many moments he held me without speaking. "There was an ... event ... that took you from me. Just before you were ready to give birth. And it was this wound's memory that made me vicious last night."

"I know about your mission. About King Helionel. And the destruction of Moldaaris."

"So you've heard the legend of the lost king of Moldaaris," he mused. "Some of it is true. Much of it is exaggerated. As mythic tales become through eons of retelling."

"What part of it is true?"

"The only part that matters." Again he sighed. "The part where I watched Moldaaris vanish before my eyes. And take you and the children with it."

"Oh, Alaric." I clung to him. "I don't know what to say."

"There really are no words for some things. Only feelings."

I retreated from his chest so I could examine his face. There was sadness but also resignation in his eyes, and I felt acceptance born of the passing of centuries. I reached up — way up — to touch his cheek. He appeared to study me, to weigh something. And then he seized me, kissing me with a vengeance. I couldn't believe how it felt to have a passion equal to mine rising to meet me. His lips and his hands were every bit as hungry as my own. And his feeling sense was so finely tuned. Clearly he could follow me to the depths or the heights, or anywhere in between. I felt like I might pass out from arousal. But before that could happen he slowed his kisses, quelling the frenzy, until at long last he held me away from him.

"Don't stop," I whispered.

"It's not my intention to stop." His fingers slipped along the length of my neck. "I'm so tempted, Elysia. I could easily be an absolute brute and take you right here. Although my refined sensibility would prefer a slower, sustained union. In one of the island's most sumptuous beds."

"And yet you are stopping."

"I'm merely postponing, my lady." His mouth again found mine, and I felt the complex layers of desire he was masterfully keeping in check. "We are due to arrive any minute at the gathering. And while I'm all for throwing duty as well as caution to the wind where I myself am concerned, I won't risk your mission — or your reputation — for an exquisite interlude."

"The gathering!" I sighed heavily. "I don't know how my diplomatic duties could have escaped my mind so completely!"

"Hmmmm," he murmured. "Ecstasy or diplomacy? Which is more utterly captivating?"

Laughing, I examined my uniform, looking to see if I was anywhere near as disheveled as I felt.

"You look beautiful." His eyes were warm, approving, and with a hint of lust, which made me blush again.

"Thank you." I smiled up at him. "But I feel like I'm in no shape to face the delegation. And yet I fear there's no time to do anything about that. Are we far from the hoverdisk?"

"We won't be needing a hoverdisk."

"Why not?"

"Because I can teleport us there."

I shook my head. "You are full of surprises."

"It's kind of a specialty."

"No doubt." I tried to absorb the reality of him as my mind's wheels began to turn. "So before we go to the palace, perhaps you could teleport us back to my ship? I'd like to freshen up before meeting all the influential people on this island."

"Of course. Are you ready?"

"Yes." He bent to kiss me, and just like that we disappeared, right as his lips touched mine.

FOURTEEN

We arrived on time for the gathering, thanks to Alaric's teleportation ability. I was grateful for the opportunity to pull myself together back at the Seraphinite. We materialized inside a greenhouse, which wasn't far from the capitol's west wing. Beyond the crystalline walls where we stood stretched endless rows of roses. As visitors roamed among the splendid silken blooms, I felt panicked we may have been observed.

"It's all right." He stood behind me, his hands still grasping my shoulders. "No one can see us. We're invisible, until I say otherwise."

"Just another of your surprises?"

"Of course." His lips caressed my neck, and I leaned against him. "You're safe with me."

"I'm not so sure about that," I replied, and he laughed softly before stepping away. Taking my hand, he led me deeper into the greenhouse. It appeared we were alone. We passed some of the most resplendent blooms I'd ever seen, caged beneath quartz pyramids. I found their collective fragrance inebriating. He took me behind a tropical plant grouping, its giant leaves offering a perfect screen. Again he embraced me. And when he let go, the light wavered.

"We're now exposed, my lady."

"I'm not sure I like how that sounds."

"I know. But just stay with me. You'll be fine." There was that word again, the fear-laden acronym that made my own stomach want to shudder. And yet I knew I couldn't think about it now. He extended his arm, and I gripped his bulging bicep. Neither of us had changed our clothes from before, and it secretly thrilled me to think I would be moving among Atlantean officials wearing garments his hands had touched and teased. That bore our mingled scents.

Together we strolled out into sunshine and a light breeze through the greenhouse's open doorway. Even though he was so much taller, Alaric's gait somehow matched mine step for step. As we ambled among roses in every imaginable hue, I kept having visions or remembrances. I saw and felt us walking arm and arm amidst other royal gardens, across a sweeping lawn. In my mind's eye, I glimpsed a stone castle.

Pools with cascading waterfalls. Then a child's giggle filled my head, and I caught my breath.

"All the quartz crystal on this island magnifies one's emotional body, so memories can become hauntingly alive here in the denser vibrations." He spoke as if he'd read my mind, and I wondered just how precisely he could tell what I was thinking.

"Terrific. That's just what I've been needing—a magnified emotional body."

"Indeed." He placed his hand on mine, where it rested on his arm. "But you can use that heightened sensitivity to your advantage with these diplomats, you know."

"How?"

"Remember, you have a greater capacity to feel than most do. By focusing on a feeling that brings you electrically alive, such as joy, you can allow the island's quartz grids to magnify that energy. It will be more powerful than anything anyone else is feeling in the capitol. And it will render you absolutely irresistible."

"You mean it will take me beyond the utterly charming I already am?" Again he laughed. In the sunlight, his bronze skin glistened where his simple black uniform opened to his chest. And it was all I could do to pull my thoughts from that supple softness exposing itself below his collar.

"Yes, my lady. Even beyond the mesmerizingly beautiful, which you most definitely are as well."

"And what about you? Care to join me in absolute irresistibility?

"I thought you'd never ask."

Briefly we walked in silence. There was so much beauty to take in, everywhere I turned. Trees and shrubs and fountains and flowers graced our surroundings in abundance. Everything looked, smelled, and felt lush.

The garden path soon gave way to a marble walkway, which led to the capitol's wide steps. Though it loomed large in the landscape, the stately building nonetheless harmonized well within its setting, as every building in Poseidia seemed to do by design. Its white walls served as a canvas for a colorful palette of plantings encircling its entrance. Above us towered a portico, which sheltered the deep entryway. At the base of the steps, Alaric stopped and faced me.

"Remember to hold the emotion of joy, Elysia. I'm embodying it now. Can you discern it?"

"Yes." There was a noticeable "up" quality to his vibration, and it made me feel giddy as I consciously matched his frequency.

"Very good," he replied. "Now we're going to walk into this place, and absolutely own it. Understand?"

"Yes."

"You and I. Queen and king. Having the most enjoyable afternoon."

"I'm ready to have a good time."

"And I'm ready to give it to you," he murmured in my ear. I could feel myself flush as he again offered his arm. "Shall we?"

Regally, we ascended the grand steps. As we reached the portico, I saw several men and women chatting in small groups. I felt their eyes upon us as we crossed the expansive porch. Curious and disapproving glances, coupled with a rustling of whispers, made me think for a moment of his doubtful reputation. If what I'd heard about him was true, I wondered how we must look to them — a missionary on the arm of a prostitute — and then I shoved those unsettling thoughts from my mind. Even though I didn't yet know the truth, I cared not. I was filled with an elation I couldn't recall feeling. Servants moved here and there, dressed all in white and bearing trays of drinks and hors d'oeuvres. Alaric took two burgundy-colored beverages from a passing platter.

"Just a little at a time," he warned, as he handed one to me.

"What is it?" I brought the drink to my lips, smelling its fruity bouquet.

"A wine made from a combination of Atlantean berries." He studied me as he sipped from his glass. "It's one of the least potent elixirs they're serving, but nonetheless it can overwhelm the uninitiated."

"So proceed with caution?"

"Extreme caution." He smiled, and again I felt my face redden. I worried alcohol would only make my blushing more intense, and yet there was nothing I could do about it. It was customary to be polite in accepting offered foods and beverages so I took the tiniest taste. I was unprepared for how the drink's energy rocketed to my head.

"And this is one of the least potent options available?"

"I'm afraid so, my lady." He took an hors d'oeuvre from another servant's tray and offered it to me. "May I suggest you eat while you're here? It will slow the alcohol's effects. And may I further suggest you use the wine glass simply as a staging device?"

"May I suggest you are brilliant?" I chewed the spicy morsel before risking another nip. His eyes burned into mine as he laughed.

"Come with me," he whispered. "Before you become drunk and I become any more tempted to have my way with you."

Together we walked to the closest group, a party of three men dressed in white tunics with metallic belts. It was clear these men knew Alaric, who immediately introduced me. Feeling emboldened by the wine and uplifted by the joy vibration, I could have been mistaken for a Gold Ray from my planet, as I talked and laughed easily with them. It wasn't long before I realized I was savoring this type of social exchange.

With an eagerness I'd not anticipated, I moved with him among the elite. We met each group gathered around the portico's perimeter before migrating inside to a grand hall. High ceilings, adorned in what looked like engraved copper, reflected light from the chamber's large windows. The floors were polished white stone, inlaid with intricate sacred geometry. It was an impressive setting. But nothing was more awe-inspiring than Alaric.

He was an absolute master with people. He knew what to say at the perfect time—whether to a single person or a group—as well as the ideal moment to move on to the next social interaction. I found it easy to follow his lead. I just had to keep matching his frequency, and it seemed I too was gifted with the appropriate words. His idea to hold the vibration of joy was brilliant, as it seemed to make us an unstoppable charismatic force.

Beyond the surface smiles and polite questions about furthering diplomatic relations with Ahlaiele, I felt their revulsion and envy toward us in equal measure—both their prudish judgment of something I myself did not yet fully understand, and their hunger for the unmistakable synergy swirling between Alaric and me. I knew there wasn't a woman present who wasn't at some point fantasizing about what it would be like to make love to him, in spite of any qualms his questionable character aroused. And, strange as it felt, many of the men seemed to be lusting over me in exactly the same manner. I reasoned it had as much to do with this irresistible frequency we were holding as anything else. Although I realized it was possible the wine was simply going to my head.

As we were busy meeting and greeting, I kept noticing a woman monitoring us, even as she worked the room in her own right. She wasn't being obvious, but that was in fact what first drew my eye. Her beauty was striking. She was tall, with olive skin, almond eyes, and a physique that begged to be admired. I noticed I had to be especially mindful of my frequency around her. As much as I hated to admit it, I felt a competitive undertone I couldn't explain. And I found if I pondered her too long, I wavered rapidly out of the joy wavelength. Our eyes met a few times, and I grinned. She smiled and then looked away. At some point, it was inevitable we would come face to face.

As Alaric spoke with a small group including Vicastus and Bellaeus, I got called over to meet another visiting dignitary from the Great Central Sun region. Tyrius was stocky with a thunderous voice and a love of laughter. We had a most enjoyable conversation, and as we parted— which he only allowed me to do after a crushing hug and a promise I'd dance with him at the evening's ball—I felt like I was on a natural high. Turning to look for Alaric, I instead banged into the watchful woman I'd been avoiding. My half-consumed glass of wine spilled onto the floor.

"I sincerely apologize, my lady," she said, as two servants hurried over with towels. One of them bowed as he plucked the empty glass from my hand. "I should have been better about watching where I was going."

"Not at all," I replied with a smile. I was thinking how ironic it was for us literally to collide, considering how carefully we'd been evading each other. "I should stick either to walking or turning, but definitely not both at the same time." She laughed easily at my words, which seemed to break the tension.

"I'm Charlaeus."

"And I'm Elysia." I owned the joy vibration again, so I gave her my most dazzling smile. "Forgive me, but haven't I heard your name somewhere before?"

"I've known Ava for eons."

"Yes! Of course." I felt a profound relief I couldn't comprehend, and I wondered if I would ever get used to how complex and intense feelings were at this lower vibration. "I believe yesterday you met Kendrick, our captain."

"I did, yes." As she smiled, dimples dotted her cheeks, and I thought again how pretty she was. "I'm under the impression I may be showing you and your party around some over the next few days. I've lived here my whole life and absolutely love sharing a native's view of this island with those who are new to Atlantis."

"That sounds amazing." I felt Alaric glance over as he continued a conversation with Vicastus. "Can you tell me why you love it here so much?"

"I could, although it might take me hours to do so." We both laughed, and I noticed she'd also registered Alaric's brief observance of us. For some reason my stomach dropped, and I was left with a queasy sensation. She continued to speak, telling me of many wonderful things about Atlantis and Poseidia, in particular. But I barely heard her.

I was using all my focus and attention to keep up the appearance I was completely focused and attentive. Actually I felt quite ill, and yet I was determined to figure out how to balance myself. I suspected gui was simply beginning to feed as the wine clouded my head. So I grounded my energy even more firmly in the Oneness Prayer, which helped. As I stood there looking like I was listening to her, I became aware Alaric was channeling the joy vibration to me. In an instant, I felt normal. Genuine spark and enthusiasm replaced the queasiness, and once again I began to take in what she was saying.

"Have you gotten to see much of the island since you arrived?" Her face was open and friendly, as if talking about her beloved motherland had helped her relax. Although I wondered if perhaps the joy frequency was lulling her into a happier state.

"Mainly glimpses from a hoverdisk so far. Although Kendrick has promised we'll have time to explore and take in the sights and culture while we're here."

"Yes, he seemed committed to having all of you experience the wonders of Atlantis." Again, her gaze flitted toward where Alaric stood across the room. "There are of course the standard cultural offerings, such as art galleries and museums. And architecture is highly prized here, so while you're in Poseidia you should make sure you take a tour explaining the sacred geometry governing our skyline."

"I'd learned about the symbols and crystal grids prior to our arrival. About how Atlantis is an intentionally created place." The same servant who'd taken my empty glass returned with a filled one. I thanked him, and he bowed before darting off. I then looked back at Charlaeus, who'd subtly been studying me as I interacted with the waiter. Feeling a little self-conscious, I took a sip of liquid courage. "And so are there some special places to visit here that aren't exactly on the visitors' tours?"

"Absolutely. To me, the most magical spots are the island's natural hot and cold springs. Have you heard of them?"

"Yes. Is it true Poseidon created them for his bride?"

"According to legend, yes. But what I can tell you for certain is they are unbelievably romantic."

"Really?" It was hard to retract my mind from images of steaming water, lush foliage, and bare bronze skin. "I can only imagine what it must be like to visit the springs with your beloved."

"There are some secluded spots where the cold water runs right next to the hot. It's an incredible experience even if you're there alone. But being with the one you love brings it to a whole other level." She glanced again in Alaric's direction. "Alaric and I go riding there all the time."

"You do?" She nodded, and I told myself I would rather die than react. So I channeled my shock and agony as consciously as I could into the joy frequency while grounding myself in the Oneness Prayer. Behind this focused vibration, I was able to shield my true self. "I can't tell you how long I've wished to ride."

"You should come with us!" I wondered what she knew about his rumored escapades. And yet it was obvious neither the whispers nor anything she'd learned of the truth had prevented her from falling in love with him. She squeezed my arm, oblivious to my devastation, and for that I was grateful. "Alaric is a master rider. He taught me a couple of years ago, and I'm sure it would come naturally to you, especially since you love horses so much!"

"I would really like that, Charlaeus." It was true I'd yearned to ride for all of my long years on Ahlaiele. It was one of those physical pleasures I'd always dreamed about. Although riding under these circumstances would, for me, be sheer abuse. I took a larger sip of the wine, enjoying in some strange way how it stung my throat as I swallowed. "So you don't think Alaric would mind if I joined you?"

"Not at all." She beamed at me, and I couldn't tell if it was because the intense joy vibration I held was affecting her, or if she felt like she'd found a long-lost sister who adored horses as much as she obviously did. Perhaps it was both, and the wine was keeping me from being clearer. "I'm not sure if I'll have the chance to ask him before I have to leave. I've been trying to catch him since the two of you arrived, and I still haven't had the opportunity even to say 'hello'. But that's the way it is with these diplomatic affairs. I'll definitely ask him once he gets home after the ball."

"That would be wonderful." I was channeling so much suffering into joy now people were even more subconsciously attracted to me. Out of nowhere, groups drifted closer, and I could feel a multitude of mostly male eyes upon me, as if wishing to catch my attention even for a moment. "I'm sorry you have to leave early. So I won't have the pleasure of speaking with you again at the ball?"

"Right now I have to bring the kids to an art class we take together," she replied. "And then tonight I'll be staying in with the children. A diplomat's life here is filled with parties, which may seem exciting. But honestly, I prefer staying at home, reading and drawing and naming the stars from our balcony whenever possible."

"It sounds like a nice life," I observed. "How old are your children?"

"Six and four." Her eyes filled with love as she spoke of her children, and it touched me deeply, in spite of my sorrow. But before I could say anything more, Ava threw her arms around my shoulders.

"I'm so glad to see two of my dearest friends getting to know one another!" She hugged Charlaeus. "How's it going ladies?"

"I've been having a wonderful time with Elysia." Charlaeus looked ecstatic, as she relayed some of what we'd been discussing. Ava listened as I kept myself riveted on my vibration. For some time, I'd been aware Alaric was watching, and yet I simply couldn't think of him now. I glanced around at all the eager faces surrounding me, who seemed so hungry to talk with me. I said my goodbyes to Charlaeus and Ava, embracing them both before forging my way into another nearby conversation.

At one point, Will's eyes caught mine from across the room. He raised a wine glass to acknowledge me, and I toasted him in reply. With both Ava and Will now on the scene, I felt like I could perhaps relax a little more since the burden was no longer solely on me to represent our mission's interests. And yet I was so anguished I didn't know exactly how I was ever going to be able to look in the mirror once I allowed myself to come down from this channeled high. Or how — and when — I was even going to be in any shape to leave the building.

Unquestionably, I'd had more wine than I should have. But the thought of having to endure waiting around for Will and Ava made me want to scream. I dared not even imagine the torture of continuing to pretend I was okay once I was alone with them. Although I couldn't admit what was wrong, either.

The whole situation was overwhelming. It unnerved and electrified me how much I'd already learned about longing and lust and love — and betrayal — in one day. But I couldn't allow myself to focus on me or my issues. I just kept fueling the joy vibration, as more and more men found excuses to engage me in conversation.

When yet another dashing male handed me more wine from one of the servers, I began to think I really should take Alaric's advice and use the glass as simply a prop. I didn't quite know how I'd allowed myself to imbibe the fiery liquid so freely. If it was indeed supposed to be a numbing agent, then it wasn't a very strong one. But its seductive power I couldn't deny. As I raised the elixir to my lips, my fingers were intercepted by an impossibly large, soft hand I'd all too quickly allowed my heart to need.

FIFTEEN

"Don't mind if I do," Alaric said with a grin, confiscating my wine as he eyed my latest companion. With one swallow, he emptied half the glass. "How are you, Alanicus?"

"Really well, my friend. Really well." Alanicus smiled, but I could feel it was more like a snarl. Glancing at me with ice-blue eyes reminiscent of Kendrick's, Alanicus gulped from his glass and then turned to Alaric. "I talked to Charlaeus earlier. She seems elated these days."

"Well, her children are her life, you know," Alaric replied smoothly. "And her new position on the diplomatic relations committee allows her more time with them. So yes, I do believe she's quite happy."

"Not to mention that gives her more time with you as well." Even in my inebriated state, I could see much of Alanicus' boldness came from the wine. And yet I was secretly enjoying his blatant attempts to make Alaric squirm.

"I do my best to look out for her while I'm here." Alaric's voice was as silky and calm as ever. "Since Robaeus died, it hasn't been easy."

"But you're easy. Aren't you capala?" Wickedly, Alanicus laughed. "I'll bet your well-practiced pleasuring makes her forget all about Robaeus when you're in town."

"No drug or distraction—or deity—could ever do such a thing. Let alone me." Alaric's tone was hypnotic, and I could feel his vibration deflating Alanicus' drunken bravado. With another swallow, Alaric finished the wine and placed the glass on a waiting servant's tray. "Now, if you'll excuse us, my friend."

"Of course, capala." There was that word again. The way he wielded it there was no mistaking its meaning, though I didn't speak the Old Tongue. Alanicus seemed at a loss as to what else to say, so he reached for my hand, and when I offered it, his lips lingered too long to be appropriate. "I do hope to dance with you at the ball."

"My lord." I chose to ignore his comment. In his altered state, it was likely he'd forget most of what was being said to him anyway. I simply nodded and turned away. It was a relief to leave him. Yet Alaric was at my side, which felt like the most uncomfortable thing of all—and, beyond all reason, still the most desired.

As we walked, he gripped my elbow. His touch made me simultaneously want to run screaming in the other direction and throw myself into his arms. I shook my head, trying to clear it, and the room began to reel.

"Lean on me," he urged. "I'm taking you out of here."

"But Ava—"

"I've already spoken to Ava. She's aware you're not quite yourself, and she gave me her blessing to escort you from the gathering."

"But—"

"Object all you like, my lady." His voice was smooth and firm. "But we're leaving. Right now."

I couldn't argue. In fact I couldn't say anything more, as tears threatened my beautiful façade. Amazingly, I was able to smile and politely kiss several diplomats on our way to the door. More miraculous still was that none of them had any idea of what was truly going on inside of me. That thought made me return my awareness to spinning my misery into joy. Which I continued to do even as we descended the capitol steps, where I relied more and more on Alaric's muscular arm to steady me.

Outside, the sun was still strong. It felt good to walk in its warmth and allow the rose gardens' heavenly perfume to fill my head with something other than despair. No one was around, and as we passed the greenhouse we'd used before as a teleporting station, I began to wonder what Alaric's plan was. He'd said nothing at all to me since we left the gathering. And in my present condition, I couldn't trust myself to feel into him.

In quiet desperation, I staggered along at his side past large oak trees, their low-hanging branches draped in silvery moss. I'd been trying hard to inhale deeply when a dark shape moved up in the trees, startling me. As I lifted my head, I saw my hawk friend, settling on a lofty perch. In silence, she stared down at me, those coppery eyes conveying a stern reminder to reclaim my power.

Although I had no idea how I was ever going to be able to do that, I telepathically thanked her anyway. Reaching again for a calming breath I couldn't quite grasp, I continued on as Alaric led—beyond several stone seating areas, reflecting pools, and a number of trellises, around which were entwined spicy-scented vines. When we reached the last trellis, he guided me through its arched canopy.

It felt like a sheltered circle. There was a marble bench in the middle, and on all sides we were shielded by greenery.

"Please. Sit with me," he whispered.

I looked up into his face, and somehow all the claws I'd wanted to use to gouge his eyes lost their sharpness. Wearily, I sank onto the cool stone. He eased down beside me. Sitting so close to him, I was again aware of that swirling between us. For a moment, I shut my eyes, and the dizziness returned full force. Before it registered that I was close to passing out, his arms enfolded me.

Effortlessly he scooped me up. Even before I opened my eyes, I could feel the quality of the light had changed. When I looked around, I noticed we were in another outdoor sanctuary, surrounded by black steaming pools. Poking through the mist were tall ferns and fallen logs cushioned with moss.

"Where are we?"

"The most secluded of the island's hot springs," he replied. Still holding me, he ever so gracefully lowered himself onto one of the long-uprooted tree trunks. "I thought this would perhaps be the best place to help you ... recover."

"Recover?" I laughed weakly. "I'm afraid I'm beyond all hope of recovery."

"Elysia—"

"Put me down. Please." As if I were petals trembled from a wind-blown flower, he gentled me onto the log beside him.

"Take off your shoes and place your feet squarely on the ground."

"What?"

"You heard me," he said. "The electrons being given off in this rich soil will help ground and center you." There was no arguing with him once he said something so persuasively. Sighing, I slipped off my shoes and positioned my feet on the moss-covered ground as he'd told me to do. Then I looked up into those waiting gold-green eyes.

"Why didn't you tell me?" I felt my heart crowding my throat, rendering my voice raspy and weak.

"What could I have possibly told you, in these last few hours we've spent together, that's more important than what I have already shared?"

"Oh, I don't know," I began sarcastically. "Maybe, just maybe, letting me know Charlaeus is your long-time love should have been at the top of the list."

"You are my long-time love."

"Please, Alaric. You know what I mean."

"I do, my lady." His voice was mesmerizing. "Charlaeus is an old friend. Everything I said to Alanicus about her in your presence is true. I helped her through the loss of her husband three years ago. And I continue to offer support as much as I can, whenever I'm here. Which isn't that often."

"But you stay with her when you're in Poseidia."

"Yes. I do." He said it so calmly, so matter-of-factly, that I didn't know whether to commend his honesty. Or be enraged by it.

"And you can see she is utterly in love with you."

"Yes. And yet she's well aware of my feelings."

"Which are?" I didn't know if it was because I had my feet firmly planted in the moss or not, but it felt like some of the alcohol's haze was starting to lift. I leaned toward him a little.

"I care for her a lot. I empathize deeply with her loss, and her children's loss. But I'm not in love with her."

"And yet you choose to sleep with her."

"Yes."

Again I couldn't decide if I was more crushed or consoled by his candor. I had to admit I admired him for not trying to make excuses, or otherwise explain away his behavior. Although my heart was still not prepared for his direct manner, which felt so unsettling. I rushed to stand, and another wave of dizziness swept over me. With shocking speed, he caught me before I fell, gingerly laying me on the ground. He removed the clasp holding my hair, and a hefty ponytail no longer burdened me.

When I again opened my eyes, he was lying beside me, his head propped on one hand, while the other caressed my face. I could feel that swirling between us and realized I could change neither my passions nor his. I wanted to sob, to scream, to throw things. And I also wanted to be held and kissed and pleasured, in all the ways I knew this man was capable of. But then there was the crushing weight of guilt. Over Hunter. And Charlaeus. And her children. I simply didn't know how to reconcile all the complex and intense feelings yanking me in all directions. Not for the first time, I wondered how humans could live out their lives in such a dense, third-dimensional reality that allowed so much agony.

"Alaric, I need your assistance," I whispered. "I don't know what else to do, other than to ask for support."

"I'm here. And I will help you in any way I can."

"I feel like my passions are ripping me apart, from the inside out." I became aware of my heart slamming against my ribs, as if in response to my words. "I have this insane jealousy over Charlaeus, and yet I know that's not fair because of my own connection with Hunter. If I'm honest, their part in this drama makes me feel crippled with shame. And it doesn't make it any better to know it's never been my intention to hurt anybody. Nor does it help to feel like I'm drowning in my feelings for you. So I'm not exactly sure what I'm asking of you, other than to listen."

"I am listening." He continued to stroke my hair and my face. "Tell me, what feelings are drowning you?"

"Do I have to come right out and say it?"

"Yes. You need to say it." His voice was so velvety. So self assured.

"First, you need to be clear about what's causing so much anguish so you can make a different choice. One leading to a more peaceful vibration."

"All right." I met his steady gaze. "I realize I'm making my own misery. A suffering that springs from knowing you've finally surfaced, after all these centuries, returning to my awareness. And I've allowed the very remembrance of you — of us — to shake me to my core. I've allowed you to take me outside of everything I've known, and everything I've known to be true. Everything that's been so comfortable." For several moments, I paused. "My firmly held beliefs as to what constitutes Highest Light — and what is Lesser — have all crumbled beneath the weight of a heavy heart. A heart that now sees, for all these millennia, I've been condemning its yearnings as gui."

"So you believed your desires to be Lesser Light."

"Yes."

"Because ..."

"Because it's how I was raised," I retorted. "It's what we've always taught on other worlds, to any number of cultures looking to us for guidance. And it became my firmest conviction. That any vibration associated with the lower chakras had to be gui."

"Even if that vibration was unconditional love?"

"No one on Ahlaiele has ever experienced unconditional love in the lower chakras since our frequencies are too high to vibrate below the heart. So from an Ahlaielian perspective, any lower-chakra wavelength must be Lesser Light."

"I see."

"I can't say it ever made sense to me," I continued. "But I've never known how to reconcile what I feel with what I've been conditioned to believe. It was easier cursing myself in secret, and just living a hypocritical Highest Light illusion. No one around me could feel anything other than happiness and hope, as only the highest vibrations dwell on Ahlaiele. And no one sensed anything amiss in my depths because no one else had such depths. So because I had neither the courage nor the strength to admit my true feelings, for all these centuries I've hidden my longings behind a conscious intention to embrace Highest Light."

"And so you've been living a lie no one else could see."

"Yes," I sighed. "But these hidden aspects of me have somehow always suspected the truth. That something was incomplete. And now, at long last, I know why. It was like being half alive really, with no contrast, no opposite energy. Up without down. In and not out. Ice without fire." I swallowed hard, as more tears choked me. "All these parts of a spirit I've long disavowed. I now see they're sacred components needing to be reintegrated so I can experience wholeness.

And as tortured as I feel right now, I'm still beyond grateful to you." I shook my head. "You've unearthed these pieces of me long buried which, now exposed, can never be pushed back into the crypt, covered over, and forgotten."

"No. I'm afraid they cannot."

"And so it seems you've pulled me from the grave, only to hold warmth and light and a mirror to a phantom's face who long ago forgot her own countenance. Which has allowed me finally to see into my shadows. Into the whole of myself."

"Yes." He eased gentle fingers through my hair. "I do hold a mirror for the whole of who you are. Because you and I, our souls are in sync. I match you, vibration for vibration, through all of your layers and to all of your depths. There's no part of you I cannot show you, because there's no part of you I do not know."

"I thought I had that with Hunter. Until now."

"It may sound strange to your ears to hear me say this, but Hunter is exceptional." Leisurely, Alaric moved his hand across mine, where it lay on my abdomen. "I picked him myself. For you."

"What?" I bolted upright, and he caught me in his arms before nestling me back onto the ground.

"You're not yet ready to rise, so please lie still. And I will explain."

"Please." As much as I hated to admit it, I was begging now. "Although I'm not sure I'm ready for an explanation. How much more shock must I endure? My mind is spinning! It's being pulled down by this new current, this ... latest undertow." For the longest moment I paused, making every effort to regroup. To be brave. "But before I go under—before I lose my faculties completely—I'd like at least a glimpse of what drove me mad."

"You fully have your wits about you, my lady. In spite of the alcohol. Which is why you are able to feel and articulate so clearly." Slowly, rhythmically, he clasped and unclasped my fingers. The motion was sensual, and I caught my breath as gooseflesh erupted over my body. I looked at him with all the hunger I was feeling, and he gave a short laugh. "But I, on the other hand, must be mindful here. Because those eyes say a man could indeed drown his sanity, if he's not careful, in their desirous depths."

"A funny thing it is for a man speaking of desire to be worried about his wits, and not his heart."

"Not when his heart's fate has been sealed for centuries." Sweetly, with a tenderness that nonetheless tore at my already bleeding soul, he kissed me. Ever so deliberately, and with every ounce of his attention, he allowed his lips to convey eons of what felt like unwavering love. Faced with such steadfast emotion, I had no strength for anything but surrender. I gave in to his kiss.

There was ecstasy in the yielding. He pulled me to him, his hands in my hair, running over my body. For several magical moments, we rolled and writhed on a smooth, mossy bed. And then, all too quickly, he slowed his kisses, eased his touch, pulled away.

"I'd better tell you what you've asked of me." He brushed tangled hair from my face. "Or else soon I will be beyond words."

"All right."

"It was a soul-searing event, watching Moldaaris explode from our ship." He leaned his head on one hand, while the other cradled mine. "To this day, I can see it clearly. We all were numb with shock and grief. Later, our allies told us Helionel intended a second blast to take out our craft, but he'd generated so much force in order to annihilate Moldaaris he overloaded the crystals. Their lasers malfunctioned, at least long enough for us to escape. But we had no home left. No family to which we could return. Fortunately, we still had diplomatic ties all across the universe. We broadcast our situation and received many welcoming invitations. To start over. Make a new life. Have a different identity, if we so desired. We were nobles and knights, after all. Thirteen of us, with leadership and diplomatic skills that could translate into any number of paths of service."

"What did you choose?"

"At the time, I cared not what I chose, as I felt all choices that mattered had been taken from me." He ran his fingers along the length of mine and back, his eyes distant. I did my best to ignore how arousing it felt and simply listen. "All these centuries I've served as king, on the most remote planet imaginable. And though there was no need for it, I raised and trained an army. It gave me an outlet for my rage, and little else. But that was only after I made sure your spirit and our children's were safe."

"How exactly did you do that?"

"You really don't remember, do you?" I shook my head, and he continued. "On Moldaaris, I had been born into a royal lineage of shape-shifters. I possess abilities many cultures would attribute to shamans, such as teleporting, telepathy, and telekinesis. I can alter my physicality at will, taking any desired appearance. And I can track souls or retrieve them, if need be. Typically, I'd help other planets with this type of service as a diplomatic offering, in the wake of natural disasters or whenever there were massive casualties. How sadly, painfully ironic that my skills were to be required for my own family. As well as all of Moldaaris."

"How come our souls didn't just ascend into Highest Light?" I was spellbound not only by his story, but by how his words came to life for me through my own feelings and visions. And memories, which seemed to stir as I connected with his vibration.

"Normally that would happen automatically," he explained. "But when there's trauma or an abrupt, unexpected death, there's often bewilderment—and fear. And when someone dies in a fearful frequency, his or her vibration is too dense to be drawn to Highest Light." With the barest touch imaginable, he stroked my hair. "On that day, millions of souls were suddenly disincarnate. A situation made all the more complicated because Moldaarins are inherently immortal."

"Immortal?" I shook my head. "Then how—"

"Because crystal weaponry can be programmed to bypass and destroy genetic coding—even normally invincible immortality codes." His fingers traced the line of my face, down the length of my arm. "Our people had always lived in harmony, according to the rules of nature. But everything that transpired on that day was unnatural."

"How did you deal with millions of souls needing help?" I sensed the ghosts from that day billowing about us. I could feel the magnitude of this ancient trauma rising up. Such chaos and confusion from that lifetime's ending flustered my heart. I did my best to return to my breath. And listen.

"I was the only shape-shifter aboard the ship, but the others were all masters of holding space. So I channeled an energy vortex—a giant tunnel, if you will—that drew in all the disembodied souls. They were floating like falling leaves in the space where Moldaaris had just been." Briefly he paused, as if to recenter himself. "This vortex served as a doorway to other realms within Highest Light. And the others held space, guiding and assisting all of our people along this portal of light, as I then went in search of you and the children."

"And the children—I—"

"You weren't hard to find," he whispered. "I told you; there's no part of you I don't know. Your very essence has always vibrated to the same frequency as mine, so I felt where you were immediately." He caressed my face. "You'd been separated from our unborn daughter's spirit. But she wasn't far from you. And neither was Gyan. None of you recognized me, which is to be expected in the wake of so much pain. So I spun a web of light around each of you. And then entered the vortex with your energetic bodies in my arms."

"Oh, Alaric," I breathed. Reaching up, I touched his brow, his cheek, his lips. "For the love of Oneness. Are you—"

"I'm all right. Truly." He bent and kissed me firmly. It was as if he wanted to assure me he was grounded in the present moment, instead of lost in wounding of the past. "I want you to know why things unfolded as they did. And why I brought you to Ahlaiele."

"Okay."

"Each soul that moved through the vortex was drawn to a particular realm, based on the energetic frequency it was holding and Highest

Light's assignment of where its next life was to take place," he continued. "Our children went immediately to the Realm of Immaculate Innocence, a sacred Highest Light plane where loving ancestors would welcome and nurture them until they were ready for their next level of existence."

"As special as that realm sounds, I still know it was heart-wrenching for you to let them go." My voice was thick with tears. "I can feel how you were overcome with grief."

"Yes."

"And what became of me?

"You, my lady, were another story altogether," he whispered. "You'd foreseen some sort of cataclysmic event, and in fact begged me not to go to Atlantis." Tears moistened his eyes. "Worry is not your nature. You have the heart of a lion and more courage than any warrior I've commanded. Yet I believe your visions truly made you afraid of losing me, as you'd never before asked such a thing." Ever so gently he cupped my cheek. "Your concerns affected me so much I actually came close to bowing out of the mission. I felt torn between reassuring you and fulfilling my sworn duty as king to lead, serve, and protect. A responsibility I believed required my presence on this assignment." He paused, squeezing his eyes shut, before again meeting my gaze. "Ultimately, I persuaded you I should go, and in all the centuries since that choice has continued to haunt me. And at times riddle me with guilt."

"Highest Light, no," I sobbed. He fell silent, and I know not how many moments we stayed like that. But it was long enough for my crying — and his self-reproach — to subside.

"All the while I was away from your arms, you never again spoke to me telepathically of your concerns," he continued, his fingers dabbing my tears. "So I never even thought to ask or feel into you, with so much commanding my attention in Poseidia. But in hindsight, it seems fear consumed your thoughts and shaped your vibration for all the weeks I was gone. It must have, for your soul to have been bound so when you died." He shook his head. "Seeing you in bondage like that, well ... that's why I cannot bear the look of fear in your eyes. Least of all when it pertains to me."

"I have no words — I — "

"You need no words with me, Elysia. Only feelings." His fingers twisted my tresses as he kissed me hard. I could feel his urgency, born of centuries of separation. I moved my hands across his body. Everywhere was carved muscle. I slowed my touch, and I thought I felt him tremble. Then with the speed and grace of a panther, he moved so he lay beside me. Again, he kissed me, his lips unsatiated like mine, but there was a sense he'd regained his armored control. "You've nearly made me forget myself."

"I want you to forget yourself."

"Not yet," he whispered. "Not until I can have you to myself. For hours." He pulled back just far enough so he could look in my eyes. "I mean to make you remember what it's like to be uninterrupted. Unhurried. Untamed."

"Unchained."

"Yes," he sighed. A single tear escaped along his cheek. "And with all that I am, I mean for you never to be bound again."

SIXTEEN

I wanted nothing more than to stay in this magical place, in Alaric's muscular arms. Thoughts of his skin against mine in the steamy water made me blush. Softly, he laughed, as he turned my body, cradling me from behind.

"Soon, my lady. Very soon, you'll no longer wonder what lies beyond the water's edge." He rested his head on mine. "I will take you there."

"Am I that transparent?" I snuggled against him, watching fingers of sunlight caress the nearby ferns. Just below us, the vaporous pools bubbled and beckoned.

"You're that vibrantly alive." He pulled me closer. "Now there's one more engagement this evening for which you must be in attendance. And so I'll need to return you to your ship soon."

"I know. And yet my heart longs to stall you a little longer," I whispered. "I'm sure you realize you still haven't told me how you brought me to Ahlaiele. Or why."

"Yes. I realize that."

"If you'd prefer to tell me another time, I understand." I studied the swirling water, waiting for his reply. He didn't speak, and the silence grew uneasy. "If that would please you, of course."

"Many things would please me, my lady. If you were at my side," he murmured at last. "Midnight rides, the horses snort and blow, as wild and breathless as we, chasing the moon. Stolen glances, delighting in what's been taken, never to be returned. Jokes for two, as no one else could fit between such small and secret smiles. Deep, dark chocolate temptations, sweet sin shared from a spoon. Courting at court. Slow dances. Slower kisses. Where every heart watching weeps for its turn. Sunset swims, wet lashes, skin on skin. Whispers breaking as a boat gently rocks. You in nothing but my impossibly big shirt." His lips lingered on my neck, and I caught my breath. "Making love as a jealous sun rises, his glaring envy forgotten as we abandon ourselves to the morning."

"Such beauty in your words."

"I've spent endless nights being mindful of the meter and rhyme we shared. Which stretched into centuries of compunction, as my conscience cried out over every couplet lost."

"Oh, Alaric." Tears rippled down my cheeks, onto his sheltering arm. "Please tell me why you brought me to Ahlaiele."

"Even in death, you were so beautiful." His velvety voice was distant. "Just as you are now. Were you aware you look exactly the same as you did then?"

"No. Was my name—"

"Yes. It was Elysia."

"Some part of me remembered, as the name came quite clearly to me in meditation. And so I chose it for the mission. Yet it's curious why the surgeons made me in the same image as before."

"Your beauty was still in your vibrational coding, so they simply called upon the frequencies already within you in order to recreate your physical body. Besides, there's never a need to improve upon perfection." He paused again before continuing. "In spirit, you were still just as pretty, but pale. And your vibration was burdened with fear. Your eyes were wide with it, though unseeing, unfeeling. Unknowing. After I released the children, I was in a daze myself. I held you in my arms for the longest time, gazing upon your face, not knowing how I would ever find the courage to let you go as well. Even though I knew you would never know me again until I was able to release you to the appropriate spirit plane."

Again, he fell silent. I was listening so intently I barely breathed.

"Finally, I flew with you to the Highest Light realms, searching for a frequency that would let me know where your soul belonged. But there was no match. And yet there was a strong pulling from somewhere. I then felt my way along the tunnel, looking for the vibratory level clearly reaching for you. Although when I found it, I couldn't accept my discovery."

"What did you find?"

"That your soul was being called to Atlantis."

"What?"

"Yes."

"For the love of Oneness! Why?"

"Because fear had made your vibration dense and coarse. So much so, in fact, your spirit was too heavy to stay in the Highest Light realms. But you were a perfect vibratory match for Poseidia's chaotic energy. For all the experiments just in their infancy."

"What exactly are you saying?" I twisted in his arms so I could face him.

"That your soul was being drawn to Earth, to be born into cruelty and torture on Atlantis. And that through dying in fear, you'd changed the evolutionary path of your spirit." His eyes radiated a pain I felt in my heart. "You've always been a feeler, my lady. Any frequency you've vibrated you have done so with exquisite intensity. And so the fear you were holding was immense. Powerful enough to enslave you in Earth's third-dimensional density. Into a cycle of lifetimes destined to be ... heart-wrenching."

"And you could see all of this?"

"See and feel it. But I simply couldn't allow it."

"I'm almost afraid to ask. What did you do?"

"What any other shape-shifter would do in my position. I struck a deal."

"I'm not following."

"Walking between worlds is what a shape-shifter essentially does." I felt how much he wanted me to understand what he was saying, so I did my best to stay focused and listen. "I can move easily among the different realms. I know their many guides. And gatekeepers. And while some laws governing soul assignment are absolute — for example, a soul vibrating at a lower frequency is so heavy it will simply fall out of the Highest Light realms, no matter how many times it's brought there — others are more malleable. Often there's room for negotiation. For bartering and deal-making. And much of the final say depends on a realm's gatekeeper."

"So you bargained with a gatekeeper."

"Yes."

"On my behalf."

"Yes."

"To keep me from being born into a series of wretched lifetimes on Atlantis."

"Yes, my lady."

"I'm trembling," I whispered. "I don't know what you did to save me from that fate, but I'm feeling horrified. And sickened."

"Elysia —"

"What did you do, Alaric?"

"Shhhhh." His hands caressed my hair, my face. "I did what I had to do."

"And what was that?" I leaned away from him, searching his veiled eyes for a truth I knew I wasn't prepared to see. "What of your own soul did you sacrifice for mine?"

"I was out of options," he said at last. "I'd mind-messaged all my contacts. Guides, gatekeepers, guardians. None of the Highest Light realms could take you, even though many wanted to help me. But your vibration was so heavy it would have just kept dropping to the lower planes. And as soon as that happened, you would have been drawn to Earth, to be reborn in Atlantis."

"Who was she?" I felt my stomach heave, as a dawning horridness strangled my breath. "Oh, for the love of Oneness, Alaric! Please ... I can't be right."

"The gatekeeper to the Great Central Sun region has long been a powerful presence," he continued, his voice calm and comforting. "Her name is Linasia. She was the only one who offered to assist me. In fact, I think she's the only one who had the ability to help. She mind-messaged me, telling me to bring you to her, and we would come to some sort of an arrangement."

"More like a sentencing."

"It was a bargaining, pure and simple." He kept smoothing my hair in that relaxing way. "Linasia had worked with me before, helping me place other souls over eons of time. She had long taken notice of me. And yet she'd always respected my love for you as pure. It still was, even as I cradled your unresponsive energetic body to me. But I was desperate. And she was ... desiring."

"So she wanted you. In exchange for helping me."

"It was a little more complicated than that." He trailed a finger along my cheek, his eyes on another time and place. "Yes, she wanted me for herself. And yet she had a child, from a secret liaison with an Atlantean politician. Linasia had negotiated her daughter Carinnia onto the throne in Zachtronymus. It's the smallest, most remote planet in the Great Central Sun's furthest district. But Carinnia was no queen. She had no concept of fairness and holding space for the good of all. She simply liked wearing a crown. And she wanted a king."

"But how could this be? How could Linasia remain a gatekeeper while holding such a vibration?"

"Influence," he replied. "Political power born through long years of playing the game. Gatekeepers essentially are politicians, and they exist in the in-between realms. As such, their vibrations are allowed a good deal of fluctuation."

"What were her terms?"

"She would assign you to Ahlaiele, which had the strongest ancestry of healers in the Great Central Sun's realm. They would help transform your vibration, then birth you within that lineage. And there you would remain, as Ahlaielians are immortals with no real impetus to move beyond their task of preaching hope and love around the universe. And so I could be assured you would forever be living as a pure Color Ray, on a Highest Light planet."

"But what did you have to offer? In exchange?"

"I had to agree to let the Ahlaielians keep your memory erased of the children and me, as their Elders emphasized it would always create stress for you and threaten your ability to remain in their high frequency. They did extend to me the opportunity to select the soul who would become your companion, since all Color Rays are paired. That's how I came to choose Hunter. But I could never contact you. Although I would be allowed to observe you from afar when I visited the realm, as a way of making sure Linasia kept her end of the bargain." He gave a short laugh, devoid of all humor. "As if I needed to observe you, to understand everything there is to know about you. But at least I would be able to look upon your energy every now and again. It was the smallest comfort I could take, in a pact that otherwise left me raw."

"What are you not telling me? What else did you have to do?"

"Become Linasia's lover." He looked at me without emotion. "And marry her daughter."

For several anguished moments, I was stunned beyond words. I simply stared at him. This man who had bartered away any chance at future happiness for himself, in order to save me from a tortured existence. Thoughts of Charlaeus and even Hunter seemed distant, as my own woes paled in comparison to what Alaric must have endured — and for so long. Somewhere overhead I heard the hawk screeching, and something in her sorrowed cries shook me from my stupor. My hands flew to my face, and I sobbed. All the shock and sadness and sweet devotion were too much. Gently he wrapped me in his arms. I felt him channeling calming frequencies to me, and I allowed their healing vibrations to soothe my frayed spirit.

"You're right. There really are no words for this. For us," I said at last, rubbing my eyes. "Only feelings."

"Yes."

"And yet I realize there's much more for you to share." Even in my torment, I could feel more layers, other unpleasantness of which he had yet to speak. And which I sensed would be difficult to divulge. Like the rumors. "There's so much more I want to know."

"Yes, my lady. I promise I will tell you everything. But it may take some time. And right now I must get you back to your ship."

"I know. So you're coming to the ball?"

"Yes."

"And will you dance with me?" I looked at him flirtatiously. It was good to hear him laugh from his heart again.

"I will. If you haven't overpromised yourself to all the men from the gathering." He grinned at me. "There was quite a long list of them, you know."

"I know." My smug smile made him chuckle once more. "That was just my way of making sure you noticed me."

"Darling, you have my rapt attention." I felt a thrill move through me at the term of endearment. It was sultry coming from his lips. I looked at him, my soul bared, and then his mouth was on mine. Slow, sure and deep, as if he could kiss me for three days. I opened my heart as fully as I knew how, and I could feel the swirling intensify.

"Make love to me. Here. Now."

"Elysia—"

"Right now."

"I don't think—"

"I don't care about the ball," I murmured between kisses. "I don't care about the mission. I can't seem to concern myself with anything except trying, in some small way even, to begin making up for lost time. For all of this long, lost time."

"It's all right," he whispered, his lips deliberately slowing mine, quelling my frenzy. "You know, in all our centuries together, I never once denied you anything. My time. My attention. My support. My loyalty. My love. And never, ever my body." He laughed softly against my mouth, and the vibration filled me with pleasure. "I will not deny you beyond this evening's commitments. You have my word."

He kept kissing me, lighter and lighter, as he spoke. "Now I've promised Ava to deliver you back to the ship, and I intend on doing so. I further intend on meeting up with you at the ball so we may continue our flirtation. I mean to make you remember when we have courted at court. Dancing as foreplay, where everyone in attendance longs for such a union. For even a pirouette from that depth of passion." Chills coursed through my body as he nuzzled my neck. "You can leave with me afterward, or I can meet you in secret. Your choice. But the next choice is mine."

"Which is?"

"Where to take you."

"I honestly don't care where."

"You will," he whispered, bringing my hand to his lips. His eyes never left mine. "You'll see."

SEVENTEEN

Standing before the lavatory's mirrored wall, I examined the heavily made-up face staring back at me. Crimson lips matched my hair, which Ava had helped me wrestle into curly submission. Shadow and liner and mascara shrouded my eyes. Ava was chatting amiably to my left, as she labored over the makeup she'd been working on for what seemed like hours.

We both were being extra careful. Without Quenna's confident eye, Ava and I weren't sure what to do with all the brushes and cases and tubes. Unfortunately, Quenna's condition had deteriorated, and her medical team still didn't know why. While they ran more tests, she would be staying overnight in the care center. And so there we were, sorely missing her and her artistry and feeling sad and more than a little awkward. But it wasn't just Quenna's condition or the powdered mask making me feel not quite myself. Nor was it the slight hangover from my earlier overindulgence. It was looking into these green eyes, the windows of my soul, and having them reflect the depths of my being that had for so long been hidden from me. And the memories.

From time to time, since Alaric had returned me to the ship, flashes and edges and daggers of emotion alternately dazzled and stabbed me. I found I kept staring into the mirror, reminding myself of my name and that I was here on a mission, just to feel less like I was losing my grip on reality.

"How does this look?" Ava's direct question roused me from my reverie. I studied her handiwork.

"I think the right side needs to be blended more," I suggested at last. "Here, let me try."

"Thanks." She handed me the eyeliner and a smudging implement. I did my best to relax and come from that centered place inside, which made every task—even eyeliner—easier. I worked for a bit and then had her open her eyes. After going through the process a couple of times, I stood back and used my best critical eye to evaluate her.

"What do you think?"

"It looks great!" She blinked at her reflection in the mirror. "You must have been channeling Quenna!"

"I'm certainly no Quenna. But I redid mine enough, trying to get it right, that I think I picked up a few pointers."

"Elysia, you look lovely." She placed warm hands on my shoulders. "You're going to be quite popular this evening. I think every man there is going to want a turn courting at court."

"What?" Her words brought back something Alaric had said, in his whispers by the springs. Something about courting and the public and slow kisses. And me remembering.

"Courting at court." She turned back to the mirror, busying herself with mascara. "It's actually based on an ancient mating ritual still observed by some primitive Earth cultures. A would-be suitor pays an offering to the tribe, for the privilege of asking his intended to dance. She can refuse, at which point he can offer a higher bounty or lose what he paid. Either way it's a risk. She can say 'no' either because she's not interested or because she's enticing him into a flirtation to demonstrate her worth. Often a couple with clear chemistry will go back and forth at this stage, showing the tribe just how well matched they are. But a male not only has to win his beloved's heart—he has to compete against other males bidding for her, as a popular female will draw many suitors. And that's what I believe will happen with you this evening."

"You're serious."

"Quite," she replied, laughing. "Once—or if—she accepts, he then has the opportunity to dance alone with her. Those watching determine how fertile the match is likely to be by throwing currency into a basket beside the dance space. The idea is at the end of the evening, each woman is wed based on who the tribe felt was most appropriate for her. Although basically, she is betrothed to the suitor who raises the biggest dowry." She smiled at me from her mirrored reflection. "Courting at court has evolved largely into a flirting game among the nobility. No one is wed at the end of the night, obviously, and giant screens keep track of the pledges instead of having the royals toss money into a basket. It's all done in a playful and respectable manner, of course. Often it becomes high drama, as many who excel at courting at court bring a good deal of acting and dancing skill with them. In fact, nobles often come to the balls just to be entertained, to see who is best or new on the scene. The game itself usually is used as a fundraiser, making it popular at balls. Which is how it will be done tonight."

"You sound as if you're looking forward to it," I observed, wondering to myself just how terrified I'd be if I was chosen to participate.

"Oh, I've been to lots of balls, El. I think most of their games and pageantry are fun." She put down her mascara tube. "Here in this female body, I guess it feels like it will be some kind of reward for having to endure the hair and the makeup and the gown." Glancing at my robe, she motioned me toward the dressing area. "And speaking of gowns, we'd better get dressed."

Compared to the hair and makeup, donning a ball gown was easy. Mine was silk, strapless, and a shimmering dark green that reached within a whisper of the floor. The finishing touch was the present Jon had bestowed upon me earlier—an ornately engraved gold and diamond necklace, bearing two large emeralds and a ruby of equal size spaced evenly along its front. An open space floated between the emeralds, and I was elated every time I looked upon this physical creation of the Circle of Emotion. I knew it was no accident he'd gifted me with such an exquisite reminder of Highest Light's support. I also knew its story yet waited to be revealed. Perhaps this evening would present an opportunity for me to learn more. When I came out into the lavatory, Ava stood waiting for me, a vision of loveliness in a dove gray gown.

"Oh, Elysia. You're gorgeous!"

"Am I?"

"You are indeed. Like I said, I predict you'll be the belle of the ball."

"Well, I can honestly tell you I have much more modest goals than that," I replied, smiling at her. "Like not tripping on my dress or spilling wine on anyone. Or otherwise causing myself to blush."

"You're going to be fine," she said. When I looked at her, we both laughed. "I suppose I should rephrase that."

"No, really, it's good you made me giggle." As we entered the control deck, still chuckling, I saw Hunter and Will had been waiting. Their backs faced us, and they seemed deep in conversation. They sported Atlantean formalwear—black suits made of silk, with long jackets and elegant lines. As they turned, I felt self-conscious. It was the first time I'd seen Hunter since spending so much time with Alaric. I flushed when his eyes—so like mine—looked at me approvingly. My blush only deepened when Will let out a low whistle.

"You ladies are prettier than speckled pups," he said, staring as if he'd never before laid eyes upon us.

"You could say that again," Hunter murmured. His face was hard and gray, like chiseled stone. I hadn't been in touch with him since he returned from the care center, but I could feel how taxing his day had been. And yet I knew it wasn't healing work that had proven the most challenging.

"Thank you, gentlemen. You're both looking quite dapper yourselves." Ava's smile was big and warm as she kissed them. I followed, hoping somehow the gesture would help me feel less awkward. As my lips brushed Hunter's cheek, I saw his eyes close. And in that moment, I knew he was aware of much more of my heart than I'd hoped he would be—at least until I'd had an opportunity to explain. But I knew I couldn't focus on that at the moment, so I allowed myself instead to be grateful for Ava's gift of gab.

Effortlessly, she carried the conversation as we boarded the waiting hoverdisk — this one enclosed with a rounded, see-through top. I assumed its covering was to protect all the hours devoted to hair and makeup, as well as ensure our clothing was impeccable when we arrived. I recognized the king's royal crest engraved on the floor. It appeared the craft had been the mode of transport for Ava and Will since their meeting with Gadeirus.

Soon we were flying through the night, and I felt bewitched by the beauty below that was Poseidia. The markets were still going strong, illuminated by golden lamplights and vendor signs in a kaleidoscope of color. Poseidia's three concentric metallic walls were alight, their lustrous sheen brightened by sconces evenly spaced along the perimeters. Her ivory bridges and stone buildings were aglow as well, and an endless sea of copper and gold and silver roofs reflected a sophisticated luminescence.

Hunter maneuvered the hoverdisk as Ava and Will stood beside him, exclaiming about one particular building or view after another. I'd positioned myself at the back of the craft, where I could be alone and simply take in the magnificent sights. It was strange to see Hunter so silent. Even more odd was choosing to be physically apart from him, when just this morning I had craved his touch. It was awkward, and I knew I would need to make time and space to speak with him.

I couldn't allow our painful situation to become even more inflamed. I wondered at how the whole course and trajectory of my life had so radically changed in a few precious hours, and yet I knew what had been done could never be undone. The quicker I could make peace with Hunter, the easier it would be for us both.

Ahead, the royal grounds came into view. A virtual sea of light bathed the palace, illuminating its five stories along with its multiple gardens and orchards and the massive stable complex. Everywhere I looked, servants in white scurried to and fro, while thousands of elegantly dressed people milled about. The sight filled me with butterflies. I finally began to realize just how big of an event the ball really was.

Ava directed Hunter to the left of the main entrance, opposite the carriages lining up to deliver their guests. Once we came to a halt, three attendants approached. Two of them helped Ava and me to the cobblestone drive. The last spoke briefly with Hunter before flying off, making room for the crafts behind us.

Hunter turned to where Ava, Will, and I waited. I watched him take note of Ava's hand on Will's sleeve. Without slowing or hesitating, he came to my side and bowed, offering me his arm.

"My lady." He eyed me with what felt like distant appreciation, the way one would admire an acquaintance's painting or prized horse. "May I have the honor?"

"The honor is indeed mine," I whispered, placing my palm on his bicep. I sensed his guarded nature, which mirrored my own. Just like me, he was putting forth his most appropriate behavior. I did my best to breathe and let go of what fate had placed between us. I prayed I could stay in the moment, and for now simply enjoy that I was entering a grand hall, on the arm of a handsome and noble spirit I'd loved for centuries.

Slowly we walked, listening as Ava pointed out details or interesting facts. From the ground, the palace towered so tall I had to strain my neck to take in its roofline. I noticed candles flickered from each of its cathedral-like windows, and all of its pillars were wrapped in garlands of red roses, chamomile, rosemary, and bridal wreath.

"The carriages are the king's own, sent out to bring his closest friends and advisors to the ball," Ava commented as we passed the gleaming gold vessels hitched to magnificent teams of white horses. "And the flowers gracing the entrance are all highly symbolic," she continued. "These are plants of romance and remembrance, traditionally found at weddings, which set the stage for a night of enchantment. Historically, that's what a ball is all about."

As we approached the grand entrance facade, its marble stairs leading to a gilded doorway, I saw more and more guests preparing to enter. The tuning orchestra's pleasing promises beckoned from within. A salty breeze stirred, kissing my cheek, and I was reminded of how tranquil the ocean felt. In many ways, I wished I was preparing to walk barefoot upon her shores, instead of readying myself to face so many aristocrats. My pulse began to pound at the thought, and I caught my breath. Hunter placed his hand on mine and channeled a calming vibration to me. The gracious gesture was needed. In spite of any personal hurt he was experiencing, he still extended himself to me, in the most selfless way. I looked up at him, tears misting my eyes.

"Thank you."

"You can thank me by not crying, El." He looked at me with kindness, and I felt a part of him emerge from his hiding place. "I'd never want to be the cause of waterworks that streaked your painted perfection."

"I'll do my best. Although you're too late to keep me from blushing."

"It only adds to your allure," he remarked, squeezing my hand. "You look stunning."

"Hunter! So glad to see you, my friend!" Kenaseus was slapping Hunter on the shoulder before I could reply. His broad face was all smile, and his reddish hair glowed gold under the palace lights. His grin widened even more as he turned his eyes to me. "My dear Elysia! Your beauty is enough to take one's breath away."

"Thank you, Kenaseus."

"Best be prepared, my boy," Kenaseus said to Hunter as he winked at me. "She's going to be much sought after this evening."

"I'm aware," Hunter replied, the slightest smile curving his lips. Kenaseus chuckled.

"Very well then! I must say hello to the ever-popular Ava before I lose her in this sea of humanity." He bowed to me and then pivoted, throwing an arm around Ava's shoulders just as she and Will crossed the threshold. They paused inside the doorway, but Hunter guided me past them and into the grand foyer.

"I was hoping to speak to you before the ball gets underway." He paused, glancing about then glowering down at me. "Alone."

"All right." My heart was in my throat. I wished more than anything I'd had the courage to say something first. But I'd missed that opportunity, and now I needed more than ever to be brave. "Where should we go?"

"Out on the veranda." He steered me past a veritable wall of windows and onto an expansive patio. More rounded columns, rising into white arches, formed an elegant border. Fountains and flowering shrubs gifted sound and color to several stone seating areas. The retractable roof was open, and we found ourselves exposed to the stars. In spite of how crowded the palace seemed near the entrance, there were very few people here.

Side by side, we strolled, my hand still on his sleeve. He led me to one of the far marble benches before motioning me to sit. As he sank next to me, I looked into eyes that were weary but determined.

"So." He dropped his gaze, and I could feel him gathering his thoughts. I held my breath. "I can feel the change in your heart, Elysia."

"Let me explain —"

"There is no need." He folded his hands in his lap and proceeded to study them. "Even now — even here, where he is nowhere near us — I can feel your ... intensity for him. And his for you."

"You need to know why, Hunter." My fingers clasped his. "Why everything is unfolding the way it is. So quickly. He —"

"I don't believe I can bear to hear about it right now." He looked down at my hand on his, and thick bangs fell across his forehead. "I'm not sure I want to know."

"In the name of Oneness, I never, ever meant to cause you pain," I breathed, withdrawing my hand as tears threatened their mascara banks. "Please let me explain."

"Pain I can live with." He grew quiet as a couple walked past us, arm in arm. "Betrayal is another matter."

"I can understand why you would feel that way. But I think if you can just hear me out, I —"

"Please try to see my point of view." He closed his eyes, as if the sight of me had become too much to endure. "This morning when I left you, I thought—I knew—we were in love. And by the time I saw you this evening, your heart had completely turned away from me."

"Not turned away," I insisted. "Opened to a deeper understanding."

"Opened to what? Are you hearing yourself?" He scowled at me, his anger finally surfacing. "Alaric has gotten so far inside your head you aren't even making sense!"

"The whole story makes perfect sense. If you'll only—"

"No. Not now. Not ... here."

"But you brought me out here to talk about it. Didn't you?" I felt some of my inner queen emboldening me. "If you didn't want to hear about it, then why ask?"

"Because it's not just my personal feelings at stake here." His eyes blazed into mine. "I'm concerned for the mission."

"The mission. Really!" I glared at him, not bothering to hide my indignation. "What does this have to do with the mission? Especially since we've gone rogue anyway and are completing our assigned tasks only because of our commitment to Right Action!"

"Everything," he said. "Alaric has so influenced your energetic field I believe it's fair to say you've been compromised by Lesser Light influences. And in this state, I'm not confident you'll be able to carry out your duty of grounding in Highest Light frequencies, in the required under-the-radar manner." He shook his head. "Rogue or not, the rest of us are unquestioningly loyal to Right Action. And we simply can't sustain any more deception from within our own ranks."

"What are you saying? That I'm unfit to serve? To carry out my duties?"

"Just saying it's a concern."

"Let's get something straight. Right now," I hissed at him. "From the moment we landed, I've been inundated and overwhelmed and overcome with any number of discordant frequencies. I've nearly died twice in less than 24 hours. And you know what? I'm still showing up. Still serving Highest Light—not Lesser—and obeying Right Action. I'm still here, doing my utmost to fulfill my duties. To the best of my ability. Every. Single. Moment." I shook my head at him. "So spare me the 'it's not personal' speech. Remember who you're talking to. I can feel just how personal this is to you, Hunter. And I would appreciate you sitting with that, letting the truth of it filter down past your rage. So we can come to a peaceful understanding between us. Which is truly what I'm concerned about."

For several minutes, we sat in silence. I couldn't believe how, after all these centuries together, this was the only real disharmony I'd experienced with him. And yet I realized this was also the first conversation I'd had with him since rediscovering such a huge part of who I was. Finally, he looked at me, his eyes softer.

"Forgive me, Elysia. I didn't mean to be so rude," he whispered. "I do need some time to think. To process and to feel." He placed his hand on mine. "I will prepare myself to be able to hear you."

"Thank you."

He stared at me, as if perhaps seeing me for the first time. The "me" I was just uncovering myself. "You'd better go back inside," he said at last. "I'm sure the ball is underway by now."

"Are you not coming?" I could feel how keeping his rage contained had exhausted him.

"Not now. I'm going to stay out with the stars for a while." He managed a smile. "But you should go ahead. They tell me you're going to be in demand this evening."

"Hunter —"

"No, it's okay, El. Go on. I'm doing what I need to do to take care of myself."

"All right." As much as I wanted to comfort him by touching his cheek, I knew I needed to refrain. I rose from the bench. "Until later then."

He nodded. Without another word, I turned to go. Quickly, I crossed the patio, as if speed would somehow hasten the healing of our hearts. In spite of the fact things were nowhere near resolved, I felt grateful we'd begun a dialogue.

As I returned to the grand foyer, I saw hundreds of people arriving. I felt intimidated, and then I remembered Alaric's description of me, of how I'd always been. Before. A balanced queen, someone courageous and confident. With the heart of a lion. I knew she was there still inside. I'd glimpsed her, had touched her even. Alaric had a way of drawing her out, and yet the part of me I was rediscovering knew my own happiness and sense of power depended upon me being able to channel her myself. And learning how to do so in such dense energies seemed crucial. If I could just find a way to stay in her vibration, perhaps I would no longer be sending out the damsel-in-distress frequency the men in my life seemed compelled to answer.

I retreated behind one of the plants lining the foyer's perimeter and closed my eyes. I knew maintaining balance here, with only half my essence, was my particular challenge. I'd have to rely on my intention to meet me where my natural resources had been siphoned off. I prayed to Highest Light for guidance as I opened to Source. I did my best to tune out my surroundings and simply breathe beneath my anxiety. Beneath the Oneness Prayer we all hummed, and into the deepest void I could reach.

While the whole of the palace was poised to celebrate and make merry, I'd plunged into the darkness within. Into a beautiful and mysterious world I'd either never known existed, or more likely, hadn't remembered. In my mind's eye, I'd fallen into a cave, an abyss alight only with candles illuminating ruby walls. There I could see the most magnificent throne.

Her seat of honor, shaped from the blood-red stones of her chamber. On the floor, encircling the throne, was a gold inlaid image. The same design of the necklace I was wearing. In that moment, I was gifted with knowledge. I understood the missing piece of myself — the essence that had been split off — made me no less potent. No less whole. All I had to do was draw from the circle, and I would be drawing from my power. All of it.

In my mind's eye, I ascended the throne. I'd never dreamed how warm and yielding stone could feel. I placed my feet on the ground, connecting with the circle. The floor began to glow a warm gold as the circle pulsed. A blast of what I could only describe as pure male power shot into my body, such that my eyes jolted open.

For a moment, I breathed hard, as if I'd just emerged from a deep dive. As my breath slowed, I became aware of how different I felt. It went beyond the Oneness Prayer, beyond any sensations I'd experienced on Earth so far. It felt like an integration of male and female, a deep acceptance that finally had led me to embrace and allow all I was to begin to step forward. I searched for words and kept returning to something Alaric had said — there are no words, only feelings, for some experiences. And I was way beyond words right then.

Looking out at the crowded room, I no longer cringed. I inhaled deeply, trying on my newfound confidence, and stepped forward from where I'd hidden. For the first time since arriving on Earth, I was aware of energy flowing up from the ground, through my legs, and into the center of my heart. It felt grounding and comforting — encouraging even — and so I allowed myself to be filled. As I moved into the room, I recognized the energy as life force itself, emanating from the whole of who I was. My posture straightened. My head lifted.

Then I sensed a tugging, a familiar energetic caress. Pausing, I turned in the direction of the entryway. Through the open doors, I watched Alaric emerge from one of the king's carriages, his eyes smoldering into mine. He was in the company of a woman, and I found even that awareness neither bothered nor intimidated me in my present state. If anything, I held my head higher before nodding slightly, flirtatiously, allowing my full power to reflect from my eyes. And then I turned and walked toward the ballroom. Something was definitely stirring within — whether a memory or a refreshed sense of being, I knew not. What I did know was the hunt was on. I'd just laid the burning scent. Now it remained to be seen how he gave chase.

EIGHTEEN

Before entering the ballroom, I thought it best to check my makeup — as well as the eyes that all of a sudden felt radically different. I followed a stream of women along a hallway, which led to a lavatory. Once inside, I crossed its alabaster expanse to a back wall of well-lit mirrors and sinks where several ladies preened.

As I approached, the first thing I noticed was my improved posture. I looked as straight and proud as Hunter. My neck seemed so much longer with my head carried high. A woman with shoulder-length brown hair in an ivory gown was washing her hands at the sink nearest me. I recognized her as the lady who'd emerged from the king's carriage with Alaric. She noticed me and moved over.

"Please. There's plenty of room," she called over her shoulder, her raspy voice friendly. "My name is Arianna."

"Thank you, Arianna. I'm Elysia." I couldn't help wondering about her connection to Alaric. In this more balanced state, I didn't feel jealous — only curious. And for that I was grateful.

As I approached the sink, her dark eyes met mine in the mirror's reflection. She smiled as she dried her hands. Then she noticed my necklace, and her smile faltered. Flushing, she looked away. I could feel her hoping I hadn't noticed.

"Arianna, are you all right? Are you unwell?"

"My apologies, Elysia." She continued toweling her already-dry hands. "I am well, thank you. I believe I was simply struck by the beauty of your necklace. I have a friend who wears that very design in a ring but has never been able to explain to my satisfaction the meaning behind it. I'm very drawn to it, and I'd like to learn more. And yet I've never seen anything like it anywhere else." Her composure regained, she studied my face. "I'm native to Atlantis, and all Atlanteans are wired to be curious about shapes and symbolism. Do you know what this design means?"

"I've read it was a symbol sacred to Lemuria," I replied. "And it's meant to represent the choice of love over illusions of separation, such as fear or pain. But beyond that, I do not know."

"I see." She studied the gemstones a moment more and then shrugged. "Somehow it speaks more emotionally to my heart, though. On some deeper level."

"Yes. I feel the same way."

"Ah well. Perhaps there's no reason for what a woman's heart simply knows," she said at last. Eyeing me, she smiled again. "I so hope to see you at the ball. Where we may continue our conversation."

"I'd like that very much."

"Very well, then." She touched me lightly on the arm, before turning and walking from the lavatory.

Somehow, as we'd been conversing, the bathroom had emptied. I found myself alone in front of a mirrored wall. Smiling at my own reflection, I was again fascinated by how different I looked. I reasoned it was merely because I felt so different.

The sight of my smile made me look twice. I couldn't believe how much brighter it seemed, how much happier. But my eyes were what really drew me as I gazed in the glass. For one thing, they were calm. And from that serene place radiated a sense of self I couldn't recall feeling. Not once, in all my long years on Ahlaiele. I'm sure I must have felt it when I lived on Moldaaris. Although that particular sense memory had not yet surfaced.

I pulled out a brush and powder and eyeliner, even though I could see nothing in the mirror that needed retouching. Still, it felt good to hold the tools of adornment in a new light. I swept powder across my lips, then retraced the line of my eyes. Instead of focusing on makeup as a burden, I chose to think of it as a means of perfecting my actor's mask—the disguise that would not only allow me to have fun with the evening's coming drama but also would help shield me as I looked for opportunities to begin grounding in the Highest Light energies of hope and love. Which is what we'd come to do.

Perhaps Hunter questioning my ability to perform my duties had helped light a fire beneath me, sparking me to seek action as soon as I could find an opportunity. As I stood there before my reflection, I prayed in earnest to Highest Light to use me as quickly as a way could be found, as a vessel for the upliftment of the planet. I figured there would be no better place to begin than the palace, which seemed to be the epicenter of Lesser Light on Earth. And there'd be no better time to start than that very moment.

Returning the makeup to my purse, I left the lavatory. My steps echoed on the stone, in the currently deserted hallway. As I made my way toward the ballroom, I noticed an entourage emerging from a corridor across the foyer. Dozens of couples were still chatting or strolling about in the entrance hall, and yet they gave a wide berth to this distinctive group, which was made up of perhaps twenty people in all. About half looked like uniformed guards, with neatly sheathed sabres at their sides. Another three or four were servants, dressed in white and carrying trays of wine bottles, crystal decanters, and stemware. The others were tall men, some swarthy and the rest fair-skinned, who appeared also to be wearing uniforms. But these were no foot soldiers. Their pastel suits were finely cut, with pearl and gold buttons and detailed brocade. It wasn't until I caught sight of the tallest one, however, with his gold and jeweled crown, that I realized I was about to bump into Poseidia's new king.

I wanted to laugh. I couldn't believe the opportunity before me. As I gave thanks to Highest Light for such a rapid response to my prayer, I neither slowed nor hurried my pace. Instead, I continued walking, my head high, as one by one the men noticed me. I was curious that, for once, I didn't blush. The guards and servants, trained to avert their eyes, nonetheless kept finding ways to glance at me, bringing a secret smile to my heart. The men in the king's inner circle, however, were not so subtle. I could feel bold, open lust in more than one of them. Then the king's raven eyes found mine.

He had wavy black hair and what looked like a day's beard growth. An opulent gold-belted surcoat covered his muscular frame in a deep ivory silk. He also wore matching pants and a nearly floor-length cloak. He stopped and whispered something to the sandy-haired man on his left. Removing his cloak, the king handed it to one of the servants. When he sauntered toward me, he was alone. The entourage simply stood waiting. And watching.

Our steps met in the middle of the foyer. On Ahlaiele, I'd been well-versed in how to greet royals. I was prepared to be gracefully formal with this king. And yet the fact he was approaching me — alone — made it clear he was throwing all formality to the wind. Instead of offering me his ring to kiss, he extended his hand for mine, the same way any other Atlantean male would do as a sign of respect.

"My lady," he said in a deep and melodious voice. He bowed, kissing my hand. "Welcome to Poseidia. I am Gadeirus."

"Your Highness. My name is Elysia." I curtsied as I met his gaze.

"Are you waiting for your party?" He glanced around, smiling politely, his cupid-bow lips revealing pearly teeth.

"I am part of the Ahlaielian delegation. They are expecting me in the ballroom."

"I see." He tilted his head, studying my face. "I am delighted to make your acquaintance, Elysia. Would it please you if I escort you inside?"

"It would please me very much." I grinned at him, aware of the unexpected turn of events. A hunt was on, and with none other than the king himself.

"What would please me is if you'd agree to join me. At my table."

His dark eyes took in every nuance. I could feel his curiosity and his desire beneath a carefully cultivated masquerade. In that moment, I realized what all the blossoms beckoning romance to the palace façade revealed.

"It would be my honor, Your Highness."

"Very well then. But please, you must call me Gadeirus."

"All right, Gadeirus." He offered his arm, signaling the entourage to move on ahead of us. Then he strolled with me toward the ballroom. Just like Ava, Gadeirus was gifted in making small talk. He commented on various paintings and pointed out architectural details we passed. And yet all the while I could feel him registering my responses. Absorbing them, as if he wished to commit every subtlety to memory.

"Tell me, Elysia." His beautiful deep voice sounded casual, as if he were preparing to board a hoverdisk instead of enter a grand hall where everyone had gathered to honor him. "What is your favorite flower?"

"The lotus."

"Why the lotus, my lady? And not, say, a rose?"

"Because a rose is usually sheltered, as most gardeners grace it with an attentive eye." I knew his seal featured a rose—and that was why roses in a rainbow of colors had carpeted and draped what I'd seen so far of the palace—so this was no random question. "It is pruned and protected, watered and fed. All in the hope it will one day burst forth from a tightly held bud, raising perfect petals to a welcoming sun. It would be highly unusual, for a flower so loved, not to deliver its promised beauty." Momentarily I paused, registering his rapt attention. "But a lotus, well, its path is not so privileged. It is buried in mud. Deep beneath still and murky waters. There is no guiding hand, no warmth and nurturing in the depths. Only its own essence, seeking fulfillment. And through its striving, its loveliness lifts—unstained—to the surface."

He stopped just shy of the ballroom. His entourage marched through the arching doorway, where they were greeted by thunderous accolades. I could hear someone addressing the crowd inside, amid loud whistles and clapping. He turned me to face him, his fleshy palms consuming my hands.

"Well, my lady. Whether you are the unspoiled progeny of silt and clay or a dedicated gardener's handiwork, I know not. But you are the most beautiful of blossoms."

"Thank you, Gadeirus. You are most gracious."

"Shall we?" Again he offered his arm, and together we entered the ballroom. The floor trembled beneath boisterous applause. It was so deafening that had the king said something to me, I would never have heard him.

The oval room was cavernous, open five stories high, with balconies overlooking a black and white dance floor. The walls and ceiling were intricately carved white marble. Cascading chandeliers, which gave the convincing appearance of waterfalls, somehow defied gravity. They floated mid-air, streaming from near the ceiling to within a dozen feet of the stone tiles below. Faceted quartz prisms shimmered along their lengths, casting ripples of shadow and illumination. I looked out at the crowd, and felt the sweet anticipation of knowing that sooner or later I would feel Alaric's gaze from somewhere among the thousands of faces.

Gadeirus paused once we reached the center of the ballroom, marked by an inlaid marble replica of his coat of arms. The crowd quieted as the lights dimmed, and the orchestra eased into a waltz. Gadeirus again turned me toward him, clasping my hands.

"Perhaps I should have mentioned there is a first dance, which traditionally is mine to perform." His eyes twinkled wickedly. "It is customary for me to choose one of the High Council members as a partner. But I would be greatly honored if you would dance with me instead."

"The honor is mine."

"Very well, then. If it pleases you, I will have your stole and purse waiting for us at the table."

"Of course."

He signaled a servant, who rushed over. Gadeirus placed his hands on my shoulders, allowing my stole to slip into his long and delicate-looking fingers. It was a sensuous movement, as if he were undressing me, and the crowd cheered. His eyes never left mine as he lifted my hand, the one holding the purse. Then he gave my things to the servant, who fled from the floor. But his hand lingered with mine there in the air, and he slid his fingers along my palm.

Again the crowd went wild. I could see this was some sort of prelude to courting at court. I turned the back of my hand toward him so I could motion with my index finger for him to follow me as I retreated three steps. The crowd laughed and cheered, and whistles pierced the room.

Eyes smoldering, he strode toward me. I drew deeply from my cave's golden circle, channeling hope up through my feet until my body brimmed with it. With consummate ease, he took me in his arms, and we waltzed as if we'd done so for years. He led with the lightest touch, making him effortless to follow. Around and around the room, we hovered and spun, his eyes searching for mine as I smiled and looked away.

From the ronde to the slip pivot and every crisp step thereafter, I allowed my balanced queen to flirt with his kingly persona. This dynamic enhanced a palpable chemistry between us, one the crowd clearly felt. Quickly the balconies filled, with onlookers on every level, as we seemed to float along the polished marble. They clapped as we whirled. And as I spun, I created an invisible web of hope, a matrix that would later help ground in love.

As applause swallowed the last chord amid a standing ovation, Gadeirus brought my hand to his lips. It was as I'd hoped. Neither the king nor anyone in attendance had sensed my intention, or seemed aware at all of the energetic structure now pulsing throughout the grand hall. The crowd cheered and whistled, screaming my name in approval. Still holding my hand, he led me from the floor as another waltz commenced. This time numerous couples took up the dance. Soon the chamber was alive with beautiful movement.

Four of the king's bodyguards joined us as we made our way toward the back wall. Briefly, he whispered to one of them, who hurried off in the opposite direction. Gadeirus never returned my hand to his sleeve, which would have been the mannerly thing to do. Instead, he interlaced his fingers with mine as we walked, a very intimate gesture for a king to extend to someone he'd just met. Clearly, though, he had no interest in strict protocol. And my only focus was to see how the drama, laid before me by Highest Light, played out.

It seemed hundreds were waiting to extend a greeting or give their regards as we passed. Efficiently, the king nodded and smiled, steadily moving among the crowd. I suddenly became aware of Alaric's eyes upon me. I felt the more discreet side of his energy, with its fine, spider-silk threads. From somewhere.

I could barely see two feet in front of me, with so many people crowded around. Ahead, I finally glimpsed a round table on a raised platform. Several servants were attending. Perhaps 30 people had already been seated. As we approached, they stood.

"My friends," Gadeirus called out. "May I present to you Elysia of Ahlaiele."

He brought me around to each of them. I felt like the king's shiny new toy and did my best to be attentive and polite. Most of the women were friendly and perhaps a little envious. The men were courteous, and yet the ones who'd lusted after me in the hallway felt particularly distant—out of respect for Gadeirus, I'm sure—as the king was not bothering to hide his own interest in me. But there was a complicating factor, a rather large one, that quickened my pulse. Alaric was a guest at the king's table.

He'd been placed almost directly opposite from where I would be seated. I called upon all of my focused attention to stay grounded and draw from my deep cave's golden circle as we inched closer to him. When we came to Arianna—whom I'd met in the lavatory and was presently standing beside Alaric—she embraced me warmly.

"My dear Elysia. I'm so pleased you'll be at our table."

"You know my sister?" Gadeirus asked, a quizzical smile curving his lips. He had no idea what a large piece of the puzzle he'd just put together for me.

"We met earlier," I replied. "I'm very much looking forward to continuing our conversation."

"And I as well. Elysia, you're a splendid dancer."

"Thank you." I grinned at her. "Your brother is an excellent lead. He makes it easy."

"Dancing is a passion I readily indulge," Gadeirus replied, pleased by my compliment. "But you're about to meet the one who has most helped me hone my skill. He's the most gifted dancer ever to visit Atlantis, at least of whom I'm aware." I noticed as Gadeirus brought me to stand in front of Alaric, he gripped my hand more tightly. "Alaric, this is Elysia."

"Yes. I've had the pleasure." It took all my concentration to gaze upon him casually. He looked dashing. Beneath the crystal lights, his sable and gold hair glistened. He was dressed in black silk, expertly tailored to accentuate his physique, with a daring unbuttoned collar.

"And so we meet again, my lady." His eyes were carefully controlled, but I could feel a whisper of that swirling sensation as I stood close to him. He reached for my free hand, and when I placed it in his, he brought it to his lips. That's when I saw the ring flash on his fourth finger. The very sight of it nearly stopped my heart. Two emeralds and a ruby of equal size, set in engraved gold, with an open space between the emeralds.

"The pleasure is mine, my lord." I allowed a taste of my balanced queen to tease his lips. He smiled as he released my hand, but not before sending a subtle sensation throughout every erogenous zone in my body. Politely I nodded, and then Gadeirus steered me toward where we would be seated.

"Would you care for champagne?" Gadeirus asked as we all took our seats.

"Please." I knew I shouldn't refuse. He motioned for a waiting servant to pour. Around the table, champagne flutes were filled. Then he stood, a smile spreading his pillowy lips.

"My dear friends, I would like to propose a toast," he said in a tone accustomed to speeches. He held his glass high, and around the table fluted stemware rose in response. "Thank you for your support. For your kindness and camaraderie throughout this transitional period. I am deeply honored by your presence here this evening." He looked around at each face as he spoke, every bit the polished politician. "We have come here together for the purpose of celebrating. Of lauding old connections and cherishing new beginnings." For the briefest moment, he glanced at me before grinning around the circle. "May you find this to be the most enchanting of evenings."

He raised his glass to his lips, and the rest of us followed suit. I could feel the champagne's powerful energy just by holding the crystal vessel, so I took the smallest sip possible. The evening was far too important— on a number of levels—for me to risk becoming inebriated again. I was keenly aware my self-restraint was being monitored on two levels: by the sharp raven eyes of the king, and by Alaric's seductive energy field, which wrapped around me like a lover's warm skin.

"Are you not pleased with the champagne?" Gadeirus asked once he'd taken his seat. "I would be happy to replace it with another, if you'll tell me what taste would appeal."

"The champagne is wonderful, Gadeirus." For the barest moment, I allowed my eyes to hold Alaric's. "I'm simply pacing myself is all."

"Very well, then." He drank freely from his glass, obviously accustomed to its effect or uncaring about it. "I have a surprise for you."

"For me?" I stared at him, question marks in my eyes. His black gaze glowed with mischief. And desire. Before I could say anything else, two servants brought a massive floral arrangement to our table, exchanging it for the existing red-rose centerpiece. A striking crystal vase, round and deep, was placed on a crystal candelabra. The vase was filled to overflowing with red lotus flowers.

As I looked around, I saw an identical display being swapped for the roses adorning each table. Similar bouquets began to line the dance floor, set upon candelabras at least seven feet in height. Lotuses laced with candles were also being secured along each balcony's perimeter. Then one by one all of the candles were lit. Five stories of balconies alight. Five stories of lotus blossoms. Incredulous, I gaped at Gadeirus. He laughed as he handed me my champagne.

"To essence seeking fulfillment," he whispered, clinking his glass to mine. Ever so carefully, I took another sip as he drained his champagne flute. I wondered just how much he might be able to consume without showing impairment. My feeling was quite a lot.

He looked ready to ask a question of me, when I saw Ava and Will approaching. The king must have noticed the delight on my face for he stood and warmly greeted them.

"It is most wonderful to see you again, Your Highness," Ava said, curtsying before him.

"The pleasure is mine, my lady." I realized he didn't tell her to call him by his name, and it made me wonder just how many liberties he'd already extended to me. "I hope you will be joining us on the dance floor."

"Yes, Your Highness," Will answered. "Dancing's a particular passion of Ava's."

"Really?" Gadeirus raised his eyebrows as he looked at her. "That is something we share. I hope you will do me the honor of dancing with me this evening. If Will doesn't mind, of course."

"Not at all," Will replied, a smile gracing his lips.

"Your Majesty, I would love to dance with you!" Ava gushed.

"Then perhaps you will join me for this waltz?"

"Oh yes, Your Majesty!" She giggled and kissed Will on the cheek. Gadeirus leaned toward me, and for a moment I thought he was going to kiss me as well.

"I will return shortly," he whispered in my ear. "At the conclusion of this dance, I will make an announcement about courting at court, to get the pledging underway. But after that, it's my hope to dance with you again."

"Of course."

"Good." He looked at me with a mixture of wistfulness and lust, before offering Ava his arm. Once they were swallowed by the crowd, Will lounged into the seat beside me.

"Hey, kiddo."

"Hey, Will."

"I sure was surprised about you and Hunter," he observed. "And you and Alaric."

"No one's more surprised than I am."

"Look," he murmured, "either you feel a damn thing, or you don't. And nobody I know feels more than you do on depths and levels I'm sure I can't even begin to comprehend." He placed his hand over mine, where it lay against the armrest. "No worries now. He'll be all right. Hunter is adjusting."

"Is he here in the ballroom?"

"He was. Until you danced with the king." Will eased back in his chair, lifting a glass of champagne offered by a passing servant. "That may have dilled his pickle a bit."

"Yes, of course. But the opportunity—"

"Brilliantly played, El!" Will laughed. "The hope energy in this room skyrocketed when you were on that floor. Even now it seems to be holding."

"Let's see how it unfolds throughout the evening." I glanced at him as tears filled my eyes. "I can't tell you how much it means to me, Will. For you to be supportive of my feelings."

"Hey, you know what, kiddo?" He looked at me, his face suddenly serious. "We're all in this together. And if we survive this mission, I know I just want each of us to be happy. However the hell that looks, or whatever it takes. Or wherever it leads. Period."

"You're going to make me cry."

"Well, we can't have that now," he said and then kissed my hand. "Seeing as how I feel like your big brother and all, and I've got just a little bit of a protective streak in me, I'd like to ask you a couple of things. That is, if you don't mind."

"Ask me anything."

"What all did you find out about Alaric?" He sipped the champagne, his eyes never leaving mine. "Does he really sell pleasure for profit, like Quenna had heard? And if he does, are you sure you can live with that?"

"It's a long story. One I tried to tell Hunter before the ball, but he's not yet ready to hear me." For a moment I was quiet. "Alaric is a shape-shifter, the lost king of Moldaaris Kendrick spoke of. And I was once his queen."

"Lords with swords, El!" He leaned closer, his eyes fiery. "Are you sure?"

"Positive," I sighed. "He was the father to my children, and he watched from his ship as Moldaaris exploded, killing me and our son, as well as our unborn daughter. Because I died in fear, my soul was destined for Atlantis, where I would have been subjected to all her laboratories' unspoken cruelties. Alaric saved me from that fate by bartering away his own. He struck a deal with a gatekeeper, which is how my soul was born on Ahlaiele, and ultimately healed from its debilitating fear. In return, he had to enter a loveless marriage, and be subject to any number of unpleasantries over the last thousand years. Just to keep me safe."

"Well, I'll be."

"So I honestly don't know yet if he's been selling pleasure for profit. There have been many things for me to discover. And remember, since much of my memory was wiped out as a condition of me becoming Ahlaielian." Tears again stung my eyes. "But I can tell you this. If he did become a paid escort, then in all likelihood it was part of the deal to save me."

"Oh El, honey." In an instant Will was on his feet. He pulled me from my chair into a hug. "It's all right now."

"I know."

"Please forgive me all my probing. It takes a real man, who's really in love, to endure all of that. And for so long."

"Yes," I whispered. "Yes, it really does."

"And what matters now is you're in love with him."

"I am, Will. With all that I am."

"Well then. I'm happy for you, kiddo." I watched as his dark eyes recovered their mischievous sparkle.

"Thanks, Will. Perhaps you and I could dance later this evening."

"I'm mighty flattered, El, but from the looks of things, your dance card is full."

"What?"

"Bidding's already begun for courting at court. From what I've heard it always does, way before the king ever gets around to making an announcement." He smiled at me. "Take a look at this tabulator everyone was issued at check-in. Now maybe it's because you walked in on the king's arm. Or maybe it's because you look finer than frog's hair in that dress. But according to the numbers so far, you're the most sought-after partner this evening. Bidding wars seem to be underway for every scheduled dance when it comes to you. Of course, all the proceeds go to charity. So see how you're supporting Highest Light just by being popular?"

"I don't know what to say."

"These are only opening bids, mind you." He pushed unruly black locks behind his ears. "It doesn't mean, really, that these are the men who will ultimately win the right to dance with you. Other bids are still pouring in."

"So basically, strangers who want to dance with me are paying a lot simply for the right to ask."

"Not only that," he replied. "There's also the option to vote on a couple you'd most like to see dance together. So throughout the evening, there are dances showcasing the most requested couples. And right now you're at the top of that list, too."

"What?" I simply couldn't imagine how the evening appeared to be unfolding. Of course, I knew it was being orchestrated by Highest Light. It would have to be, in order for all of these things to be lining up the way they were. "So who is it the masses most want to see me with?"

"Well, not surprisingly, many of them want to watch you dance with the king again." He looked at me and grinned. "But that's not their top choice for you."

"Pray tell, then. Who is?"

"Alaric."

I grabbed Will's sleeve. "How? How in Highest Light could that be possible? We've barely spoken to one another since entering this ballroom."

"Well, it's like we preach till we're blue in the face," Will answered. "The principles of energy are happening all the time, whether we see or feel or believe in them or not. And so I think the crowd is picking up on the energy that's between you and Alaric. Your unbreakable connection. Something so powerful it's pulled you from Hunter, which is no small feat."

"The king won't approve."

"Prob'ly not," he chuckled. "But I'll be damned if that's gonna stop you."

NINETEEN

Once Will left, I noticed the king's table had emptied. Taking a centering breath, I made sure of my connection to the cave's golden circle and felt gratitude for the window of opportunity alone. Highest Light had cracked open a doorway, allowing me to sneak through in order to continue my mission of grounding beneficial frequencies within the palace. I welcomed the breathing space, the chance to go about unnoticed, before the time when I would again be thrust into the spotlight.

Walking the floor's perimeter, I kept my eyes averted, my focus inward, and I intended with all my being to move unseen among the masses. Even within this privileged crowd, I felt so much unworthiness. Such lack of self-love. I realized I shouldn't be surprised, because how else could misery thrive unless the influential had been gazing too long across the Circle of Emotion's gap? I caressed the necklace, running a finger along its emeralds, feeling the space between. And set my firm intention to draw Poseidia's eye from the void.

With each step, I brought forth as much love as I could channel, wrapped within the grounding arms of hope, and offered the message to the room. Tremendous energy flooded me. The stone surfaces hungered for the healing vibrations and gulped all I fed them. I realized how long Lesser Light's separation frequencies had permeated their porosity. But love was stronger than separation. Once love was grounded in hope, all else flourished.

Beneath my energy field, I felt the Oneness Prayer humming. I also sensed Hunter shaping the energy I planted, strengthening and supporting it. I felt relieved he was now working as my partner in that way we'd always collaborated best. Everything seemed right as I continued my secret dance, my solo of purpose around the ballroom.

Even in the midst of performing my work, I had one selfish desire—to see Alaric among the twirling bodies. He was not hard to find. Between his height and relaxed grace, he commanded attention. He was dancing with Arianna, who laughed as he guided her across the floor. Watching him, I felt hypnotized. He was equal parts artist, seducer, and feline. And when his gaze penetrated me as he whirled past, I felt — with every fiber of my being — his intention for the evening to be ours, in every possible way. I closed my eyes for a moment in order to quell the ecstasy wanting to take me right there and then.

Not wanting anyone in the sea of people to notice — and wishing to bring myself back to my Highest Light assignment — I forced myself to step away. Although it made my breath catch to think of what it would be like to dance with him. If Will was right, it looked like I may get that opportunity. At last. A taste of courting at court. With my Moldaarin king.

My body vibrated with excitement just thinking of it. There would be no way of hiding or diminishing the energy between us in front of these thousands of spectators, I realized. I had to trust Highest Light would help me channel that exquisite frequency for the good of all.

In my heightened sensual state, I knew I would be that much more magnetic, and I sensed that was also something Alaric wanted me to realize. To feel and own my power on this planet meant to do so completely, and that involved embracing my sexuality. Not the flawed idea of submitting in order to please another, which was so rampant on Earth. But to enjoy and share from the richness and depth of my inner beauty, my own strength and self-worth. I finally truly understood it would take me being at my most complete, my most empowered, to succeed in my mission. And reclaiming all of myself involved shifting my beliefs regarding Highest and Lesser Light.

I could no longer blindly believe the lower chakras emanated only Lesser Light. Alaric had mentioned unconditional love and the lower chakras. For all my centuries on Ahlaiele, it's what I'd long hoped and secretly believed — that sensuality could be sacred instead of shameful. There was such a sense of Right Action, of personal empowerment about redeeming the whole of who I was, instead of dividing parts into Highest and Lesser and judging them accordingly. And it was only by the grace of Oneness I'd managed to tap into that power for myself, within those very walls that evening.

I still couldn't believe how balanced I felt. Later, when the work was done and it would somehow, somewhere just be me gazing into Alaric's eyes, I thought there could be no more sublime sensation than to be able to share of myself, to express my love for him from this centered space. But that would have to come after the task at hand.

Onward I moved, channeling and grounding, until I'd circled the room. At the completion of my sacred duty, I was standing far enough from the king's table so as not to attract attention. And my timing could not have been better. The orchestra was slowing into its finale.

I watched as the sandy-haired man from the king's entourage appeared on a dais. The orchestra fell silent, and the crowd applauded.

He raised his hands and waved, eliciting cheers and whistles.

"Honored guests, for those of you who do not know me, I am Desineus," he said in a deep voice. "It is my privilege this evening to introduce to you a man who represents the ideals we hold dear in Poseidia. A man whose commitment to our people has been demonstrated over the years as a ranking member of Poseidia's governing council. His hard work and dedication to bettering the lives of every Poseidian have earned him the highest title in the land. But tonight, in celebration of just how successful he's been at ensuring the good life here for us all, we have orchestrated this enchanted evening. This magical night, in the hopes of bettering the lives of the many underprivileged that still live on the outskirts of Atlantis — and beyond." Desineus paused, his blue eyes scanning the crowd as he allowed for polite applause. "Tonight, it is my deepest honor to introduce to you His Royal Highness of Poseidia, King Gadeirus."

Desineus bowed as Gadeirus strode to the podium. The two spoke briefly before Desineus left the stage. Gadeirus grinned, looking out at the wildly cheering masses. The uproar continued for nearly a minute and then Gadeirus held up his hands, gesturing for silence.

"My friends. I'm both humbled and honored by your enthusiastic turnout this evening." Again the audience erupted, leaving Gadeirus snickering. As the crowd quieted, he continued. "Tonight is indeed an enchanted evening. A most special time for us to come together, in support of those less fortunate, so we may all in turn be uplifted." He paused, allowing those assembled to applaud, which they did so more respectfully. "I'm pleased we will be honoring an age-old custom here at the palace, one dating back to the beginning of recorded history. Many of you may indeed be aware of this tradition, which began as a form of early courtship, and which now serves as a modern-day opportunity for high-stakes intrigue and mystery, romance, and yes, even rebellion."

More whistling applause ensued.

"Tonight, you will have the opportunity to participate in the most innovative dance being done in the world, which for centuries has been called 'courting at court'. Where, if you're willing to take the risk, you may dance with the partner of your dreams. That is, if the object of your desire says 'yes'. And of course, if nobody outbids you."

Explosive laughter echoed throughout the hall.

"Ladies and gentlemen, may I draw your attention to the screen behind me?" As he motioned toward the display, it lit up. "You see before you a listing of the dances marked specifically for courting at court. There will be seven of them, in addition to three dances where you have the opportunity to bid on the couple you'd most like to see dance together. For a grand total of ten. Courting at court will be interspersed with other dances, where anyone is free to step out on the floor. But for the courting at court numbers, we ask you to stand or sit back and watch unless you are one of the lucky two who will be in the spotlight."

Once more the crowd cheered.

"Now for more details regarding courting at court, I'd like to turn the podium over to a beloved member of our diplomatic relations committee. Ladies and gentlemen, please welcome Kenaseus."

Gadeirus applauded along with the audience as Kenaseus hurried across the dais. His red hair gleamed under the chandeliers, and his grin was as huge as I'd ever seen it. There was no mistaking how much he enjoyed his duties. He waved to those gathered, and they whistled even louder. He bowed to Gadeirus, who then left the stage only to be intercepted by four of his waiting bodyguards. As well as several supporters who were ready to engage him.

"Ladies and gentlemen, I am most honored to be here. And it is my supreme pleasure to be able to introduce those who may be new to the concept of how courting at court works." He paused as the crowd grew silent. "May I turn your attention back to the crystal display behind me? As King Gadeirus noted, there is a listing of the dances earmarked for courting at court bidding. Beside each dance, you will see a box showing the current bid. Next to that are names and pictures — secured at registration — of the party who's placed the highest bid so far, as well as the intended partner. Bidding may continue via the crystal tabulators issued at registration until five minutes before the scheduled dance is to begin, which allows the winning party and the intended partner time to approach the stage. So what you see on the screen could change at any moment, as someone bids a higher amount to get a desired partner to the top of the list for one of the dances."

Briefly he waited, looking out at the hushed assemblage before continuing. "You will also see a countdown beside the dance that's up next. The countdown will show you how much time is left to bid and hopefully become the winning bidder of that dance. If you're the winning couple, please proceed to the stage immediately. The winning bidder will inform the orchestra what type of dance will be performed, while the intended partner will wait in the center of the floor as the music begins. The winning bidder will then signal the start of the dance by tapping the crystal chime you see here." He pointed to several tube-like crystals of varying lengths, hung from an arching metal stand perhaps eight feet in height, that had been placed in front of the dais. "Are there any questions?" Voices like fallen leaves rustled across the ballroom, but no questions arose. Kenaseus glanced up at the crystal screen. "Very well, then. The first courting at court number begins in 15 minutes, after this orchestral interlude. Thank you for your kind attention. May you all enjoy the magic to come!"

The crowd clapped as Kenaseus melted into the masses. Murmurs swept the ballroom's five levels. Excitement and anticipation were palpable, and everywhere I looked I could see people tapping on their crystal tabulators, engrossed in those tiny displays. I peered up at the giant screen, which showed I was to be dancing the first dance with none other than Tyrius, my newfound friend from the Great Central Sun region. I remembered how I'd enjoyed our conversation earlier in the day, and I thought it would be fun to dance with him. Unless someone else outbid him in the next few minutes, that is.

"Hello, El." That quiet voice was most welcome to my ears. I glanced to my left and into Jon's reassuring eyes. He looked especially angelic in an ivory suit.

"I'm beyond happy to see you, Jon," I said as I hugged him. "There's so much I want to say to you. So much to thank you for. And so much I'd like to ask."

"I understand. And all of your questions will be answered, I assure you."

"I know there isn't time for a conversation now, as it looks like I'm going to be dancing in a few minutes."

"So I see." Jon laughed as he eyed the crystal screen. "In fact, it appears you will be kept quite busy dancing this evening."

"But can I at least ask you about your gift?" My fingers fiddled with the emeralds at my neck. And the gap between them. "Where did you get it? Why did you give it to me? And why does it match the ring Alaric wears?"

"What you've asked could take a while to answer," he replied in his calm tone. "But I will tell you anything I can, once you've first had the opportunity to speak with Alaric."

"I understand," I whispered. "So much is happening, Jon. And so fast. To say it's been a full day would be the understatement of the century."

"I know." Tenderly he touched my shoulders. "But it's all Highest-Light inspired. And at all times you are being loved and supported and guided."

"Forgive me for interrupting, my lady. And hello, Jonastus." Gadeirus had approached out of nowhere. His raven eyes flashed disapproval at Jon's hands on me.

"Your Highness," Jon replied, bowing. "I will take my leave now." Turning to me, he kissed my hand. "You're going to have the most splendid evening." He grinned his seraphim-like smile before disappearing into the crowd.

"Truly I did not mean to interrupt your conversation, Elysia." The king's dark eyes told another story. "I simply wanted to wish you well with courting at court. And tell you it is my hope to win your hand for more dances this evening. Would that please you?"

"Yes, of course." I gazed at him from the space of my balanced queen. He dropped his eyes, and ever so slightly bowed his head. "Right now, though, I believe I should begin making my way to the dance floor."

"Very well, then." His lips lingered on my hand. "I'll be watching."

Flirtatiously I smiled, which seemed to please him a great deal. As I walked away, I could feel his strong need to control, his quick temper, and his jealousy. I felt it was the alcohol beginning to crack open his well-cultivated mask, and I realized I'd have to tread cautiously. But I knew I shouldn't think on it now. Already I could feel thousands of eyes upon me, as I made my way along the side of the dance floor. I was just tuning in to make sure the connection to my inner cave was strong when Alaric appeared.

"Hello, love," he said, taking my hand. As he raised my fingers to his lips, his ring flashed in the chandeliers' softly moving lights.

"I so want to kiss you right now," I whispered, my heart racing at the sensuous way he'd said 'love'. "Among other things."

"Soon. Much sooner than you think." His fingers brushed my chin. "I will come for you."

"You'd better." He laughed, decidedly delighted as he slipped into a sea of faces. I caught sight of the crystal screen, whose countdown indicated there were six minutes before the dance. I was thankful no one had yet outbid Tyrius. I noticed something else as well. Bidding on one of the dances was skyrocketing. The figures began escalating so rapidly the running tally blurred. Fascinated, I looked to see which dance had suddenly sparked so much interest. I couldn't help but grin when I saw it was one of the dances for most requested couple—starring none other than Alaric and myself.

TWENTY

"Elysia!" I turned toward the voice booming my name. Striding up to me, arms nearly as wide as his grin, was Tyrius. He was dressed in a taupe suit with detailed embroidery. The color complimented his dark skin and curly brown hair. Beneath the chandeliers, light reflected off a scalp exposed by his deeply receding hairline. I glanced at the crystal screen to see we had three minutes before we danced. "How are you, my dear?" He clutched me to his barrel chest. "I'm delighted to be courting at court with you. And I'm positively thrilled to be going first!" Releasing me, he clasped my hands and rolled his eyes. "All right, so technically the king was first. But I shall be first this time!" We both laughed, and it warmed my soul to be able to feel so light-hearted.

"I'm happy we will be dancing together, Tyrius," I said, still amazed I could be looking forward to something that mere hours ago had terrified me. "So tell me. How did you want our scenario to unfold?"

"Hmmmm." He rubbed his chin, his brown eyes brimming with mirth. "I think you should play hard to get. But not too hard." He chuckled again. "I've been courting at court for years, and I've always wanted a partner who could play into the drama of it. Who could really help put on a show."

"I can do that." It was like those words simply popped out of my mouth. I wasn't sure why I'd said them, but somehow they felt like the truth. "Just tell me what you envision."

"Really, my lady?"

"Really."

"Well, I'd like to tell a story. Of a passionate couple who love each other, and yet are often at odds." His eyes became serious. "It's actually the story of my wife and myself. I say white and she says black. Or I insist it's down and she swears it's up." He shook his head. "Marceilia had to remain at home to care for her ailing mother, and I miss her dearly. But I would be thrilled to be able to tell her how I danced for her. For us!"

"Then we shall dance for Marceilia. It will be my honor."

"Oh, Elysia. I don't know how to thank you."

"Just tell me what dance we're going to base our story on."

"The tango!" Once again his face lit up. "It's our favorite."

"The tango it is. I will follow your lead. But be prepared for a few surprises!" My words again shocked me. Why was I saying such things?

Tyrius laughed heartily as Kenaseus reappeared on the dais. Thousands clapped and whistled. Then the orchestra stilled, and it seemed every eye in the room was either on Kenaseus — or upon Tyrius and me.

"Good evening and welcome, ladies and gentlemen!" Kenaseus bellowed. "It's time to begin courting at court. First bidder up is Tyrius of the Great Central Sun region. And his intended, Elysia of Ahlaiele." The crowd shrieked when I took my position on the coat of arms. While I watched Tyrius trot over and whisper something to the band leader, I prayed for Highest Light to move through me as we danced, so I would be able to ground in loving frequencies for the benefit of all.

The violins began, sweet and soaring, as Tyrius hurried to the crystal chime. He struck a longer tube, and a deep tone permeated the ballroom. The full orchestra responded. As its rhythmic melody lulled the chamber, Tyrius implored me with his hands. He dropped to one knee and I turned a quarter step, crossing my arms and raising my chin high. Undaunted, he grasped a handful of lotus stems from a nearby arrangement. He pivoted, displaying them beneath my nose. I eyed him with a 'maybe' smile, and the crowd applauded as I again turned my back.

Scurrying around me, he pushed the flowers into my hands, and I shoved them back at him, such that they fell to the floor — except for one. I seized that stem and shook it at him, as if we were arguing. Tyrius then snatched the flower and tried to take me in his arms, but again I resisted — to the delight of the crowd. He persisted and I backed up, hurling one shoe at him. Before I could toss the other one, he'd grabbed that hand. Wrestling the shoe from my grip, he threw it to the floor, as thousands cheered and clapped. I tilted my head to one side, and he cocked his to the other. He offered me the lone flower, and this time I accepted — to booming applause. I inhaled its essence as he offered his hand. Grasping the stem between my teeth, I placed my hand in his. Then his other arm enveloped me. And we began to move.

Crisply we danced, in perfect time with the orchestra's staccato stops and starts. Tyrius was graceful for such a stout man, and he channeled pure passion while we circled the floor. At one point, I passed the lotus stem from my lips to his — a sensual move that garnered enthusiastic applause. Our steps alternately pivoted and stalked one another, neither he nor I relinquishing control. Dramatically, he released me to a swing-out position, then whirled me in. More stalking, more pivoting. As soon as I stopped spinning, he tossed the lotus and took me in his arms. Then he dipped me just as the orchestra exhaled its final note.

For a moment there was silence, and then the crowd roared. Tyrius lifted me to my feet, and we bowed several times to a standing ovation. We hugged, and I found myself giggling, which brought even more whistles from the audience. I glanced up at the crystal screen, where bids were still racking up for us. Tyrius bowed to me, and I curtsied. I gathered and slipped on my shoes before he led me to the side.

"Elysia, I don't know how to thank you! That was spectacular!"

"We had fun, didn't we?"

"Yes, my lady! I cannot believe how you captured the essence of my wife. It's as if you were somehow able to feel her—even become her—and then express her so well through the dance." Tyrius shook his head. "I've courted at court for more years than I can count, and I've never had an experience like this."

"Your clear passion for Marceilia made it easy for me to understand and then help convey your feelings," I explained. "That to me is the most beautiful thing about dance. It's not so much the steps, but the feelings being communicated."

"You are a rare woman indeed." Tyrius kissed my hand. "May I escort you to your table? I believe you'll be dancing again before long, if the screen is correct."

"Thank you. But I believe I will get some air first."

"I understand." He bowed once more. "I do hope to see you again before the night's end, my dear."

"Of course." I smiled before turning away. Couples flooded the floor as the orchestra slowed into a waltz. I checked the crystal screen, and it appeared the next courting at court number would commence in 15 minutes. It was one of the most-requested-couple dances, and thankfully I was not part of that pairing. My next scheduled dance was the one after that, so I figured I had perhaps half an hour before needing to be back in the ballroom. As I walked toward the doorway, many people paid me compliments or thanked me for putting on such an entertaining performance. I smiled and expressed gratitude for their kind words, but I kept moving purposefully toward the exit.

Feeling the need to regroup, I set my intention to continue on unseen until I'd escaped the ballroom. It was amazing how reining in my energy made me quite invisible. In no time, I was making my way through the foyer. I thought revisiting the veranda might be a way to give myself some quick meditation time. I hoped against hope its expansive space would be quiet, like it had been when I was there earlier with Hunter. As I entered its broad patio I felt fortunate, because it appeared deserted.

I passed several fountains before pausing in front of a sculpted image of dolphins and mermaids. Staring at it left me wistful. It was like gazing upon family that once was, long ago, to which I could never return. Mesmerized by the falling water, I sensed the sea yet churning in my blood. I had a striking sense memory of breathing underwater. Then I felt a familiar tugging behind me, stirring me from my reverie. Turning, I looked into Alaric's loving face.

"I told you I would come for you."

"Yes, you did. And amazingly we are alone."

"Earlier I set up a deflection shield, just outside the doorway. It allows you but no other to enter." He looked attractive and relaxed, with his hands in his pockets. Shirt open to mid-chest. Bronze skin begging to be touched. "We won't be disturbed."

"You are indeed a man of many mysteries."

"It's a Moldaarin thing."

"Of course it is."

"You were amazing before." Like a panther, he eased toward me. "I could feel you remembering so much."

"It was like a dream and a memory all in one," I mused. "One thing is clear. Dancing has been a fever of mine."

"Yes, darling. You loved it as much as the ocean. And that is saying a lot."

"Alaric, I know there may not be time now, but if you could I'd like you to tell me something."

"What is it?" He brought my hands to his lips, causing my body to tingle. The moon had just risen, round and pregnant with glory. His emerald and ruby ring shimmered in her fertile glow.

"What is that ring you wear? And how is it connected to this matching necklace Jon gave me this morning?"

"This necklace was my engagement gift to you. I had it made to match your eyes." He traced his fingers along my neck, across the gemstones' outline. "You insisted I bring it with me on that last mission, as a kind of good-luck charm."

"Oh my," I sighed. "When I was studying earthly lore before coming here, a book of Lemurian teachings literally fell off a shelf and opened to that symbol."

"I'm not surprised." A tender smile curved his lips. "You've been guided and supported all along, in your journey to come to Earth. To complete your mission and return to me."

"Yes." I closed my eyes while he caressed my shoulders. "And the ring?"

"It's my wedding ring."

"Of course." Chills coursed my spine, as a very clear image of my own matching band appeared in my mind's eye. I knew there had been a diamond, emerald, and ruby engagement ring as well, designed to fit seamlessly above the three central stones. All of which I knew had been lost in the destruction of Moldaaris. "I'd read the symbol served as a reminder of how emotions work here on Earth. Of how we need to focus our feelings intentionally. A metaphor for giving our attention to the things we love within its unbroken line, as opposed to what we've not healed across its gap." I shook my head. "But in my heart, I feel it's much deeper than that."

"Yes," he whispered. "Symbols representing deep concepts can carry multiple meanings. What the Lemurians said about the image representing the conscious choice of emotion is a valid interpretation. But it's only one translation, and not the original one." He looked away, as if hearing something in the distance. "Like the story of the lost king of Moldaaris, the emblem's original legend has been mostly forgotten over the centuries."

For several moments, he stared at the necklace, deep in thought. "This is a Moldaarin representation of the ultimate love story. Of the constancy of the heart. It's a snake, who according to our lore is the archetype of the loyal lover. Stones are placed at the head and tail, with a ruby in between, at the heart. The head and tail are alpha and omega, lover and beloved. They represent you and me, our joined ruby heart forever connecting us along the unbroken perimeter. The gap between the two emeralds indicates that, no matter the circumstances or hardships or separations, you are never any further from me, as I will always love you just the same. From alpha to omega and back, through our coupled heart. Unconditionally. And irrevocably," he murmured. "I knew my work would often take me from you, and I wanted you always to have with you a symbol of my eternal fealty. At the time, I had no idea just how vast alpha to omega is, through our coupled heart's passageway. I knew not how far I'd have to go, or how long I'd have to wait, in order to be with you again."

"In the name of Oneness." Tears flooded my painted features, and there was nothing I could do to stop them.

"It's all right." His voice was hushed as he took me in his arms. He spun his spider-silk energy around me, cocooning my heart. From that soothed place, I reached down, deep down within myself, and reconnected to my cave. I sensed the golden circle pulsing around me, and once again I began to draw from it. Slowly I pulled away, so I could look into his eyes.

"Alaric, I—"

"Shhhhh." He pressed a finger to my lips. "We will breathe as one this very night. You have my word." Pulling a handkerchief from his pocket, he dabbed my tears. "But first, I have to return you momentarily to the world of men."

"I'm sure all this crying has washed away hours of effort," I laughed. "And I care not. Besides," I added, "my magical tools are in my purse.

Wherever it is the king took that."

"You mean this?" Alaric's eyes glowed as he presented me with my small green bag.

"Where? How?"

"I have my ways. And I felt you would want it."

"I should go, so I can be ready for courting at court."

"Here. The lighting is perfect. Allow me." He took the bag and led me to the bench beside the dolphin and mermaid fountain. "I have a practiced hand. And a trained eye."

I sank onto the stone bench, looking up as he slid down beside me. "Why?"

"Elysia, you have never, in all your long years, liked makeup." He opened the bag and, withdrawing a small tube, began touching up my foundation. "Not that your natural beauty ever called for it. But there are those occasions when a costume or mask is an asset. Such as for courting at court. Many nights I have sat with you so, highlighting and adorning an already perfect masterpiece, before we would dance."

"Where do your surprises ever end?"

"Why should they?" We both laughed, and then his face grew serious. "Now hold still and let me revel in you."

TWENTY-ONE

As I entered the ballroom, I felt refreshed and ready to face the evening. I'd checked Alaric's work while in the lavatory, and I couldn't believe what a lovely job he'd done. My face looked flawless. It made me smile to think a manly man had such a gift with women's powders and potions.

It seemed I'd chosen a good time to return. A couple was in the middle of courting at court, and all eyes were on them. I was able to move unnoticed through the clapping and cheering. As I approached the king's table, I saw the guest chairs were empty. Only Gadeirus and Desineus had claimed their appointed seats. Drawing nearer, I watched Desineus whisper something to the king before taking his leave. Gadeirus then turned to me, his black eyes sharp as he stood and kissed my hand.

"My dear Elysia." His voice held a softness that couldn't quite blunt the edge I felt beneath his polished exterior. "I've been missing your company."

"They say absence makes the heart grow fonder."

"Yes, they do, don't they?" There was a wariness in his eyes I hadn't seen before. "Please. Sit with me."

"All right."

He held my chair before taking his own. The crowd began applauding and whistling, as the couple finished their routine. I glanced up at the crystal screen, where bids were still registering for them. I wanted to be aware of the schedule, since I thought I'd need to head toward the center of the floor any minute. Although I saw another couple was about to perform, which I found curious. Of course, I realized anyone was free to bid, and at any point there could be someone else garnering the most money. Yet my curiosity turned to a bone-deep chill when I saw my name had dropped off the screen entirely except for one dance. I was now only listed as a participant in one of the most-requested-couple dances. And it was not the one with Alaric that my heart— and even the crowd—so desired. But with the king.

I grounded and centered myself, drawing from my cave and

reinforcing my power from its golden circle. Looking around as casually as possible, I saw all of the men from Gadeirus' entourage. They were stationed discreetly in a rough semi-circle, from a few feet to several yards out from us. I realized the king must have had his henchmen keeping the guests away from the table, presumably so he could pull some sort of power play with me.

Regardless, I knew above everything else I needed to remain calm. If I allowed myself to react in any way, I would pull myself out of alignment with my own authority. Clearly, I needed to tread carefully. Before coming to Earth, I had studied plenty of human nature. I knew the kind of controlling ego it would take to fix the bidding and remove me from being chosen at all for courting at court would never be able to rest without rubbing it in my face. Without trying to engage me. So I decided to let him reveal himself. As I expected, it didn't take long.

"You are quiet, Elysia." He turned in his chair so he could rest his hand on mine, where it lay on the armrest. "Is something wrong?"

"It's an odd thing," I answered, my voice steady. "Just a short time ago, my name was scheduled for the next dance. And the next three also."

"Was it really?" If he was trying to feign surprise, he didn't do it well. "I hadn't noticed."

"Indeed." His tone inspired me to an even deeper place of power. And in that space, another interesting fact jumped out at me. "Well, according to the screen's current data, I'm still the most requested partner of the evening. And yet I'm only slotted for one more dance. I do find that unusual, don't you?"

"Courting at court is always unpredictable," he replied. I could feel the oversight escalating his anger, as he hadn't thought of having my 'most requested' status altered along with everything else. "But you will dance. With me. Which is how it is meant to be."

"How it is meant to be is up to the audience to decide," I said without emotion. "But if I'm not going to be stepping out for charity, I most certainly wish to dance for myself." I made a move to stand, and he grabbed my arm, jerking me back into the chair. Instantly, I felt Alaric's energy surge from within me. I knew he was watching and on his way. I also felt Hunter's livid response to my field being violated. I sent them both an 'I'm okay' message, and then I allowed my balanced queen to permeate my being. Gadeirus' movement was so forceful I could feel how it had caught the attention of some in the crowd. I glanced at the fingers digging into my bicep, before staring into bloodshot eyes. "Let me go."

"Why?" He pulled me toward him, squeezing harder. I smelled alcohol and rage coming off him in waves. I could feel him searching for fear, for a disempowered place from which he could feed. "You seem to like men touching you."

"I'm afraid there's been a misunderstanding here," I said, ignoring the pain in my arm. "You see, a big part of my job as a missionary is cultivating respectful, mutually beneficial relationships. Now I'm sure I don't have to tell you the importance of wit and charm in developing loyalty and good will. Am I witty and charming? You bet." I smiled at him. "But if anything, being personally charismatic gives me the power to be picky about who touches me. And who doesn't." Leaning closer to him, so our lips nearly touched, I glanced between his mouth and his eyes with the full force of my being. "Unhand me. Right now."

"I will release you when I'm ready," he fumed. "And not a moment before."

Calling on Highest Light, and channeling as much power as I could, I stood and wrenched my arm back. Perhaps because he was inebriated, or perhaps because Highest Light had gifted me with strength, he slipped in the chair from where he'd had so much weight leaning against my arm. Several guests turned to look in our direction. I felt his entourage splitting their attention between monitoring the crowd and watching me, and wondering what action they should take.

He moved to grab me again but I stepped away, off of the raised platform. As I did so, I saw not only Alaric, but Hunter, Will, and Jon encircle the king's table. I could feel their composed alertness. Gadeirus got to his feet and once more lurched toward me, just as Tyrius pushed past the closest of the king's men to stand by my side.

"Elysia, my dear!" I noticed he reached for the hand that hadn't been in the scuffle with the king, bringing it to his lips. "I'm so pleased to find you between dances."

"And I'm delighted to see you, Tyrius."

"I thought I'd come persuade you to dance with me again." His eyes appeared jovial, but I knew he was showing up for me as part diplomat and part bouncer, and it was clear he cared not which role he'd need to play.

"I would be honored. I was just waiting to learn the king's intention." I stared at Gadeirus. "I know he may need to leave the ball earlier than expected, due to unforeseen circumstances. And I was waiting to see if he wanted to dance our most-requested-couple dance before he goes. That is, if it would please him to do so. And if he wanted to arrange it."

Gadeirus glared at me, and yet I could also see respect for my cunning. He knew I had the upper hand, as I'd just about made it impossible for him to stay at the ball. Because to do so, he would have to face me on the dance floor. That would mean being present to the injury he'd caused me. As well as staying in my empowered energy field — something I knew made me intolerable to him now that he had succumbed to the raging bully within. Bullies always feel impotent in the presence of true personal power. And a bully—when confronted from a place of balanced empowerment—always backs down. Gadeirus was no exception.

"You are ever thoughtful, Elysia," Gadeirus muttered. "I'm afraid I will not be able to honor our performance after all. The hour is arriving when I must deal with these ... unforeseen circumstances."

"I understand, Your Highness." I curtsied, as his cupid-bow lips skimmed the hand of my unharmed limb.

"Now if you will please excuse me." He nodded to Tyrius before striding from the raised platform. I noticed four of his bodyguards had been waiting on the periphery, and they fell in line around him as the king marched toward the ballroom's entranceway.

"Come and sit, my dear," Tyrius whispered. He wrapped an arm around my waist and guided me back to where I'd been seated. Pulling a handkerchief from his pocket, he covered the flesh where Gadeirus had gripped me. Looking around, I saw Ava hurrying through the crowd. She bounded up the platform as Alaric, Hunter, Will, and Jon stood like an impenetrable force in front.

"You are hurt." Gently she hugged me, tears welling in her eyes. For the first time, I turned my attention to my arm where droplets of blood were staining Tyrius' handkerchief.

"Yeah, well, you should see the other guy." I smiled, and both she and Tyrius laughed as Hunter came over to us.

"Let me help, El." Hunter's eyes were solemn, and I felt his concern. He'd gotten towels from somewhere. Ava stepped aside to let him next to me, and he removed the now-bloody handkerchief. Gadeirus' nails had gouged deep ravines. I'd tuned the wound out so completely I hadn't realized how much he'd been hurting me.

Just then a servant arrived at the table with cotton, bandages, and what I assumed were healing liniments. I knew one of my own entourage must have requested the soothing agents, and I felt gratitude embrace me. As the servant set down the tray, his eyes took in my injury. I felt sympathy for me mixed with disgust over the king's actions.

"Thank you so much." I smiled, extending energetic gratitude to him. "I appreciate your help." For a moment, his eyes widened. Then he returned my smile and bowed, before hurrying away.

"I told you earlier you're a rare woman," Tyrius said, as he watched Hunter clean my lesions. "You handled the king masterfully. And still, in the midst of your suffering, you thank his servant. I'm humbled by your example."

"Your words are very kind," I replied. "Actually, I'm quite surprised by the king's actions. Perhaps our dance was too much for his refined taste?" I looked to catch Alaric's eye, as I was beginning to suspect the real issue was that someone had told the king we'd been spotted together on the veranda. But he was gone.

"Refined? Ha!" Tyrius shook his head. "Our dance was a work of art, a pure expression of the heart. And if it upset him, then he is as unbalanced as the rumors suggest."

"What rumors?" Ava asked.

"Gadeirus was a very controversial choice to be crowned king of Poseidia," Tyrius sighed. "His twin brother Atlas has for years been the Atlantean overlord, the most powerful elected position on Earth. Atlas was appointed by his father Poseidon, and he was also given dominion over the surrounding ocean. Meanwhile, Gadeirus and three other nobles were made kings of Atlantis' vast continent. Gadeirus has long ruled the extremities, toward the more remote Pillars of Hercules."

"Bet that really stuck in his craw," Will muttered.

"Indeed it did!" Tyrius' dark eyes looked troubled. "Both brothers have a reputation for a rough and brutal nature. But Gadeirus has twice the ego and perhaps three times the ambition. Poseidon knew this, which is why he gave Atlas the most control."

"Then how did Gadeirus come to power in Poseidia?" Ava asked.

"Mysteriously," Tyrius replied. "The last Poseidian king drowned, under suspicious circumstances. At least that's what I've heard. Gadeirus petitioned his brother for the throne. Being overlord, Atlas has the authority to appoint a king. He selected Gadeirus, in spite of the governing council's strong caution to choose otherwise."

"At one time Ahlaiele was closely allied with Atlantis." Ava's face reflected the gloom in her voice. "Serving as an ambassador here is how I came to love this island so deeply. But starting with the last king invitations to come and share ideas arrived less frequently. I only knew that ruler through intermittent communications and never once visited under his reign."

"And this king is much more unstable than the prior one." Pausing, Tyrius watched as Hunter began the healing work on my arm. "The situation is complicated even further, I'm afraid, because of Gadeirus' addictions."

"He sure was belting back the bubbly," Will observed, his black eyes narrowing.

"Alcohol's not even his drug of choice," Tyrius said. "Through his considerable influence, he has long traded on the black market for the finest mind-altering drugs in the universe. He's also begun cultivating hallucinogenic plants on the palace grounds, from what I'm told. And he imbibes freely, seemingly uncaring of his duties and responsibilities. In fact, during his inauguration, the palace was filled with daze-inducing smoke." He shook his head. "I'm not meaning to sound judgmental here. Normally, I'm okay with people making their own choices regarding what they put in their bodies. But I do believe a king should be held to a higher standard. Especially when he's shown himself to be dangerous."

"I have to agree with you, Tyrius," Ava muttered.

For several minutes, there was silence as everyone sensed the intensity of the energy Hunter was channeling. In my mind's eye, I could see red waves of inflammation moving out of me. Before long, the red dissipated, and then I saw blue and green waves funneling in. I looked up and found myself peering into Hunter's focused stare.

"Hey, you," he said.

"Hey, yourself."

"How do you feel?"

"Good. Really good."

"You should rest for a bit." He studied me carefully. "Your energy field is still restructuring."

"How'd she do, doc?" Will asked.

"Very well," Hunter replied. He brushed back bangs that had flopped across his forehead. And then he removed the towel he'd draped over my arm. I heard Tyrius gasp. Looking down, I saw my skin was completely unmarked.

"Like it never happened," Tyrius marveled, as Ava hugged Hunter. "You should come and visit my home, Hunter. It's one of the Great Central Sun's remote outposts. It is beautiful and quiet. And we have many stones our own healers use in their work." Tyrius smiled. "Tell me, Hunter. Do you ever use gemstones in your healings?"

Ava, Will, and I all laughed.

"They are laughing, Tyrius, because I've always loved working with stone medicine, on planets where it's available," Hunter replied. "And I would be most honored to visit you and your people."

"Then consider yourself formally invited!" Tyrius slapped him on the shoulder, then turned his attention to me. "So, my dear Elysia, how can I help you? Do you need to eat something? Rest?"

"Actually I'm quite well now." At that moment, I saw Alaric slip from the crowd. Something in his eyes beckoned. "Well enough to dance the king's dance after all."

"What?" Ava's head whipped toward the screen. "But that dance has been erased. I'm sure it was only a matter of minutes before they changed it, once Gadeirus left."

"Perhaps," I said, rising from the chair. I walked over and stood beside Alaric. "All the more reason to put in an appearance."

"You can't be serious—" Ava began.

"Oh, she's serious," Tyrius bellowed. "Most serious!"

"Yes." Hunter's voice was slow and firm, and I felt the conviction beneath his words. "An exclamation point to the evening. An energetic example of hope and inspiration for all." Hunter looked from me to

Alaric and back to me. "And love."

"But how in tarnation could this be done?" Will asked. "Never in a million years would they bend the rules now."

"Leave that to me," Alaric murmured.

TWENTY-TWO

As Alaric spoke with Hunter, I was showered with good-luck hugs from Ava, Will, and Tyrius. Then my eyes turned to Jon, who'd stood like a sentinel at my side. He'd remained quiet throughout the incident with the king, and yet I had felt his unwavering support. I hugged him fiercely.

"Thank you, Jon. For your silent strength. You're such a blessing."

"And you are an inspiration." His angelic face beamed serenity. "I told you earlier you were going to have the most splendid evening. And I believe that's going to start right about now."

"I believe so, too." I smiled at him as Alaric approached. He and Jon locked forearms, exchanging hushed words, before Jon faded into the crowd. I looked up into gold-green eyes that watched me carefully. He laid his hand where the king had clawed me.

"Hunter assures me your tissues have healed. I just want to know how you're feeling."

"I am well, Alaric. Really." I stepped closer to him. "In fact, I seem to have an opening in my dance schedule. Do you know of someone who might be interested?"

"Any man in this room would be interested." He traced my neck with fingers that shivered me. "Come with me, love."

He offered his arm, and together we navigated the crowd. It was very much like moving through the market earlier. People sensed us nearing, and a path simply parted. I glanced at the crystal screen, which showed the next courting at court dance was to begin in five minutes. Ahead, I could see a couple clearly waiting their turn.

"Please stay here," he said. Before I could reply, Alaric approached the couple. The woman embraced him, and I watched as the man clapped his shoulder. For several moments they spoke, and the couple nodded. Both of them peeked at me at one point, as Alaric continued to talk. The woman hugged him again, although this time she looked close to tears. Yet all I could feel was joy emanating from her. I was trying to imagine what he could possibly have said to them when Alaric returned to my side.

"We're on. We'll just be starting a little early, so it's obvious no one will be bidding on us."

"Let's do this." It was now two minutes until the scheduled dance. I wondered what the audience would think since there would be no way to lay money on our performance. But I realized I couldn't worry about that. Again, Alaric eased his way through the crowd, this time seeking the orchestra conductor. It was apparent the two were friends. Briefly, Alaric spoke to him, and a huge grin creased the conductor's face. Just like with the couple moments before, I couldn't help wondering what he'd said to spark such a smile.

As Alaric closed in on the chime, the conductor motioned with his hands. The music quieted and the crowd stilled. Removing his suit jacket, Alaric tossed it onto the dais as thousands of females whistled. He grinned as I, and every woman present, applauded his physique.

The orchestra birthed a slow and sensual melody—only strings—while he unbuttoned and rolled his white sleeves to the elbow. Enthusiastic catcalls and clapping ensued. From what Gadeirus had said, Alaric was a legendary dancer in Atlantis. I was sure he'd long been a favorite at courting at court. And judging by the squealing females, the pleasure-for-hire rumors only enhanced his allure. All around me, I could feel aroused curiosity, as thousands questioned what was going on—and why this pleasant impromptu intervention wasn't on the schedule.

I strolled toward the coat of arms. Once I stood on its center, surrounded by its ring of red roses, the crowd sensed our intention to dance and took to its feet. Five stories of murmuring echoed around me, followed by five stories of jubilant cheers, which drowned out the music. Glancing at the musicians, I could see they cared not. All of them were chuckling. It felt like they didn't often get to see authority challenged or rules broken, but enjoyed it immensely when such disobedience ensued.

The king's men, however, apparently did care. Six of Gadeirus' henchmen swarmed the dais, only to be intercepted by Hunter, Will, Jon, and Tyrius. Seconds later, Kenaseus and Ava joined them as well.

There was much talking and careful attention to appearing civil, although I could feel surprised anger in the king's confidants. The audience, relishing the danger of defying Gadeirus' rules in his own house, grew rowdier. Soon calls rang out.

"Alaric!" the crowd cheered.

"Elysia!" they responded.

Finally, the king's representatives and my friends left the stage. An ear-splitting standing ovation followed.

I prayed to Highest Light with every ounce of my intention, offering thanks for letting our performance proceed. I asked for aid in anchoring joy through the dance. For the ability to weave love into the hope gridwork I'd already grounded within the space, as well as the chance to awaken the memory of Oneness inside every heart gathered. I felt the power of the opportunity, the sacredness of the moment at hand.

Our composition opened with a rest in the measure, the masses' hushed silence a prelude to Alaric striking three chimes. The minor chord carried through the chamber, blending in harmony with the orchestral strings. I watched over my shoulder as he inched closer. Never could he have looked more like one of Earth's big cats. I could feel every muscle twitch, every feline motion, even before it occurred. He stalked me, coming ever closer. Without touching, we began to circle one another to the sound of wild applause.

"Every man in the room desires this dance with you," he murmured, moving in perfect rhythm with me. "But on this steamy night, would it please your body to rise and drop as the lion leads?"

"That depends." I channeled my balanced queen. "Does he offer me his courage?"

"Yes." Reaching behind my head, he pulled pins from my hair. The crowd went crazy, as red curls cascaded down my back.

"And his loyalty?" I tilted my head, as his fingers kept releasing my tresses.

"Oh yes." The last of the pins clinked to the floor. He ran his hands through my hair, his face hovering this close to mine as we spiraled and the audience shrieked.

"Will I feel his passion?" Trailing my fingers along his face and chest, I pushed him away, though I let my eyes singe his.

"Most certainly." Smiling, he brushed his index finger along my cheek, lifted a lock of fallen hair behind one of my ears. Then his hand cupped the back of my neck, drawing me to him. I spun away from his grasp, even as my gaze continued to flutter between his lips and eyes.

Again he approached. This time he offered his hand. I extended my palm and retracted it, as if I'd changed my mind. With easy grace he grabbed my fingers, gathering me to him, before releasing me. We turned from one another then pivoted back, until we were face to face. It felt even to me like he would kiss me at that point. Instead, he raised his hands to mine, and we began to move in flirtation position, as the crowd exploded in whistling applause.

"And does he love me?"

"Yes." Once more he came close enough to kiss me, but didn't. The audience, stirred to a frenzy and yet unable to bid on our dance, tossed paper currency to the floor. "On this steamy night, would it please your body to rise and drop as the lion leads?"

"Yes."

"And would you marry him?" Removing a ring from his pocket, he knelt and reached for my hand. The audience screeched and stomped, and my heart nearly hammered its way out of my chest to the beat of their rhythmic stamping. I couldn't hear the orchestra as I placed my left hand in his. Tears again threatened the perfect eyeliner Alaric's own hand had so masterfully drawn. For several moments I simply gazed at him. As the crowd began to quiet, he smiled. "Elysia, will you marry me? Again?"

"Yes." I nodded emphatically, ensuring everyone could see. Such a boisterous roar rocked the ballroom. Although courting at court had been derived from a mating ritual, I was certain none of those gathered had ever seen an actual engagement unfold quite like this on a dance floor. Five levels of paper money fluttered down, covering the floor like so much confetti. He placed the ring on my fourth finger. It was a perfect fit. Looking down, I could see it was a diamond, emerald and ruby design—exactly as I'd envisioned in my mind's eye. In one smooth movement, he arose and enveloped me in his embrace.

"I had it remade. For you," he whispered as he whirled me across the floor.

"It's beautiful. I'm beyond words."

"You are beautiful. And as I've told you before, you never need words with me. Only feelings."

Together we twirled, each pirouette expressing elegant precision. Alaric made courting at court effortless. I clearly felt the next desired step through his unwavering intention. Each moment in his arms brought back strong sense memories of how seamlessly we'd danced during all those centuries before.

After a series of staccato steps, he slid with me to the floor. My head tilted back, and he nuzzled my neck with lips that barely brushed my skin. Knowing fingertips slipped over my gown's silky length, while the crowd clapped and cheered and whistled. More money rained upon us.

For the briefest moment, he pressed deliciously against me. Then he pulled me up into a rapid rotation, lifting me higher and higher so my legs extended out before draping me backward over one shoulder. Still spinning, he slid me ever so sensuously down the front of his body. When my feet touched the tile we began moving our arms and hips to the rumba, delighting the spectators. Again and again, he turned me, stirring the money mounding around us like so many fallen leaves. Our movements were brisk and then leisurely, as the audience continued its enthusiastic applause.

While we each slid a leg low and away—hands clasped and foreheads touching—the music changed. We rose into a sultry tango. His head and mine were one as we moved. He kept looking from my lips to my eyes. It was easy to see my Moldaarin king was in no hurry.

As the music reached its crescendo, the crowd seemed to be holding its collective breath, waiting for him to kiss me.

They started chanting, "Kiss! Kiss! Kiss!"

It was what Alaric had been waiting for. Ever so sensually, his lips found mine. While the audience tromped about and cheered, our bodies continued the most intimate tango that could be danced.

When the orchestra slowed to its finale, he tipped me back, my throat exposed. His lips grazed me, neck to ear, as the music ceased. For a moment, there was stillness. He raised his head until his eyes scorched my own. And then he devoured my mouth, his tongue possessing mine, to the roar and tremble of thunderous applause. People on all five stories whistled and cheered as he finally broke our kiss to lift me beside him. He held my hand in the air as more money streamed down. Lotus blossoms were being hurled as well. Laughing, he took me in his arms and kissed me again. Thousands erupted with shouts of "Encore!" I glanced at the musicians. All of them were standing and clapping.

We bowed once more before ascending the dais, where he threw on his jacket. Then he dashed with me through the drifting cash, along the dance floor's edge and toward the door. Everyone in the room seemed to be screaming "Encore!" as we darted from the ballroom. Past paintings, plants, and deserted hallways in the empty foyer, he hurried me toward the veranda.

Once there, he scooped me in his arms and hastened to the bench near the dolphin and mermaid fountain. Sinking onto its stone surface, he ravaged me with eyes no longer veiled by duty or obligation. I could feel the unbridled fire he was finally allowing to burn, after all these centuries. It quivered me. His hands twisted in my hair, his lips seizing mine.

"I love you, Elysia," he panted at last. Tears splashed from his lashes. "I've never stopped. Not in all these centuries we've been apart."

"I love you, too."

"Now you have to decide, darling," he whispered, his lips against my ear. "Are you going to leave with me? Or would you prefer I meet you later, in secret?"

"I'm done with waiting," I replied. "And since thousands of people just watched us practically make love on that dance floor, I don't see any reason for secrecy." He laughed against my skin. "I'm going to leave with you."

"All right." Gently, he set me on my feet as he rose to stand beside me. He took both my hands in his. "You should know Gadeirus' seers already have been observing us. And they will be monitoring our every movement, from here on out."

"I suspected as much. But it matters not."

"You are sure?"

"Yes. They will be watching whether we're together or apart. And I desire to be with you." Wickedly I grinned at him. "Let them watch."

"Indeed. Then there's just one more matter I'd like to settle before we go."

"And that is?"

"I want things to be right between us. Clean and pure, as they always have been," he said. "I realized today how hurtful my relationship with Charlaeus was to you. And so I returned to her place after leaving you at your ship, and I told her what had happened. I believe in my heart she understood, even if it was difficult for her to hear—as it was for Hunter." He brought my hands to his lips, kissing them both, and then for a long moment he stared at my engagement ring. Finally, his eyes met mine. "I want you to be comfortable and confident in my commitment to you. I want you to know there is no other woman in my life, nor shall there be. And to that end, I want to marry you. Tonight. If it would please you."

"Tonight? But how—"

"The 'how' has already been arranged." He smiled at me. "Ava and Jon and the others will soon be waiting for us by the ocean. I have a good friend who's a minister. He has agreed to meet us there. Of course, I made it clear we would commence only if it's what you also wanted."

"What about what you want?"

"I simply wish to be with you for the rest of time," he murmured, stroking my hair. "I would love to marry you, right now, so there's no more lingering." Softly he laughed. "I've already waited a thousand years, you know. But I will happily pause longer for what feels right to you. If you would desire a large ceremony, for example, or something particular—"

"No." I looked up at him, at this man who had already loved me through death and beyond. At this man who had been the father of our children. Who had suffered and bled for centuries so I would be spared. "I already told you. I'm done with waiting. I am ready, right this minute, to marry you. And I can think of no greater cathedral than the ocean's shore."

"It's settled then." He kissed me again. "Shall we?"

"There's just one thing."

"Your purse?"

"How did you—"

"My dear, when it comes to you, I know these things," he whispered. "Come with me. I had Jon leave it on the next bench over. And yes, because it will make you feel better, I will retouch your magnificent canvas." He caressed my cheek. "Although, as I've told you, there is never a need to improve upon perfection."

TWENTY-THREE

It wasn't long before we were sauntering hand-in-hand along the shore. Alaric had teleported our shoes somewhere before leaving the palace with me, so we were in our bare feet. Sinking step after step into sugary sand felt blissful after an evening in dressy shoes. The breeze gentled our hair, and under the expectant moon the waves crested white against the sky's dark edge. Everywhere above us, twinkling stars winked encouragement. We would have to walk a bit in order to reach our wedding party, but I was glad of it. Dolphins played in the surf, their clicks and whistles a friendly escort.

"They've come to welcome you, Elysia," Alaric observed. "And show their loving support."

"I can feel that." My voice sounded far away and dreamy. Being this close to my ancestral family flooded me with memories. I recalled swimming among them—not only on Moldaaris, but right here in Poseidia—and I realized in that moment Earth was more of a home planet to me than Ahlaiele could ever be. I remembered being happy just playing games. Riding their backs beneath the waves. Exploring the ocean's deep magic they so enjoyed sharing. I felt how it had been to breathe beneath the surf—as easy as it was right then inhaling air. And how seamless the transition had once been between worlds. For a moment I paused, watching them. "I so wish to be among them again."

"You will. And soon." Alaric slipped behind me and wrapped me in his arms. We stared out at the water, her rhythmic lapping at the sand a comforting sound. "We could go for a swim after the ceremony, if you'd like."

"As much as I yearn for those waters, there is another thirst I'd first like to quench." I turned in his embrace. Eagerly, his lips parted mine. And a vivid memory washed over me, causing me to catch my breath. "You've made love to me on this very beach."

"Yes."

"More than once," I murmured while erotic images filled my mindscreen.

"Yes. Part of our honeymoon was spent right here."

"Part of it?" I shook my head. "There's so much to recall. And I want to remember everything."

"I know." Slowly, ever so sweetly, he kissed me again. "Do you feel this sand beneath your feet?"

"Yes."

"Earlier today, I told you the quartz on this island may make you more emotional, as it reflects emotion like a mirror. Look around you, Elysia. Every grain of sand here is made of quartz. And quartz stores memory, which is essentially vibration. The stronger the vibration, the more readily its imprint is held." He ran his hands through my hair, down my back, and then clasped my hands. "In all my long years, I've never felt a stronger vibration than the one we share. And when essence meets essence, when our flesh fuses, and I am breathing your breath and you mine ..." His stare practically seared me. "There is nothing more passionate. Or powerful. And this silica has borne witness to our love. The full intensity of it. Multiple times. Over many centuries." He brought my hand to his lips. "So you needn't worry so much about remembering. This sand has seen it all, and kept a blush-worthy record which — if you ask it through your intention — will reveal anything you wish to know."

"Alaric," I whispered as my eyes misted. "You amaze me."

"What would amaze me is if I could marry you without tending to any more of your tears." We both laughed, and he took me by the hand. Again we walked, on the wide expanse of shoreline, with the dolphins at our side. Beautiful buildings and lights loomed in the distance. We seemed to be heading toward restaurants and hotels. And humanity. But for a few minutes more at least, we would be delightfully secluded.

"Would you tell me about Jon?" I asked. "I knew from the moment I met him he could be trusted. I feel like he's family somehow."

"That's because he is." He smiled at my wide eyes. "Jonastus was born in Poseidia, the son of a prominent restaurateur and his artist wife, who emigrated here from Alpha Centauri. We were good friends, and every time we came to Atlantis we visited them. Many sunsets we spent together, sharing stories until the wee hours at their restaurant, which was by the water's edge. Both of Jon's parents were storytellers so it's interesting he's naturally quiet."

"I can't get over this image I have of him in my mind's eye. He looks like an angel," I mused.

"That's what you would say to his mother." For a moment, he paused. "You always called him your precious angel. From the time he was born. For hours sometimes, you would sit with him and his mother in her studio. Erinasia taught both you and Jon to paint. And next to Jon, you were her favorite model."

"Really?"

"Indeed," he replied. "She always remarked on your exquisite natural beauty. The symmetry of your face. The curves of your body. And those green eyes." Again, he fell silent. I felt emptiness and resignation beneath acceptance—hallmarks of the ancient wound he carried for me. He was about to tell me of another tragic loss.

"One day, when I'd just returned from an overnight mission, you greeted me with haunted eyes. You said we needed to go at once to Atlantis, that something wasn't right with Jon. I never questioned it. We left immediately. When we arrived, we came by the restaurant and found it had closed. Upon inquiring at the neighboring shops, we learned Erinasia and Kennastus had gone sailing one afternoon and become lost. Their vessel was found with no one aboard. Their drowned bodies were discovered days later. It was odd because they both were accomplished sailors."

"It feels like foul play."

"It was," he sighed. "When I later searched for them in the Highest Light realms, they told me they had been murdered through dark magic. Along with other prominent citizens who had donated money to political factions looking to end the experiments. Which at the time were in their infancy."

"What about Jon?"

"He'd been at school the day his parents went sailing. Because neither of them had family ties here, and since no one listened when Jon asked to send word to Alpha Centauri and Moldaaris, he was shipped off to an orphanage on one of the continent's poorest and most remote outposts. An orphanage we later discovered was surrounded by a crystalline force field, designed to block any type of telepathy. Which allowed its caretakers to use the children as laborers, until they could be sold into the underground slave trade—with no means for their mind-messaged cries to be heard."

Alaric put his arm around me as we continued to walk. "I will never forget the look on your face when we found him. He'd been in the orphanage for a month. He was 11 at the time. Jon had kept a couple of charcoal pencils and a small sketchbook with him—the only things he'd been able to bring from home. You knelt beside him, and he looked at you with that peaceful expression he always has. He said to you, 'I knew you'd come. I've been drawing you here.' And then he showed us his sketches. Each one was a perfect rendering of you with those haunted eyes. Every evening, after brutal hours toiling in unthinkable conditions, he'd been drawing your likeness, hoping you would feel him. Knowing if anyone could, it would be you." Again, Alaric paused, squeezing my shoulders. "You hugged him so hard. He was calm, but there was such pain in your face. All I could do was keep reassuring you all would be well from that day forward."

"For Highest Light's sake," I breathed. I could feel my body trembling.

"Hey," he whispered, stopping to cradle my face in his hands. "Things really were quite well from then on. Jon came to live with us, and we adopted him as our eldest son. Later he grew into the perfect older brother, once Gyan was born. And in the thousand years since you and the other children were taken from me, I've been so grateful for his gentle, loving soul. It's been an endless blessing he chose to settle in Atlantis, and not Moldaaris, once he reached the age to make such a choice."

"Yes. I know that's all true." I had allowed something about the emotional intensity of Jon's story to unground me. I found I needed to draw more deeply from my inner cave's golden circle, and once I was again able to feel its strengthening waves channeling up through my feet, I felt much better. "I think it's just the impact of that memory. It's still very emotional, even after all these years." I shook my head, laughing. "Tell me, Alaric. Do we have any memories that aren't intensely emotional?"

"You realize intensely emotional experiences make the best remembrances, don't you?" Ever so tenderly he kissed me. "And we are about to make another such memory. We've reached our cathedral."

The shoreline curved like a horseshoe. In the moonlight, tall grasses waved to us along the dunes. From a gnarled cypress nearby, I heard the hawk's cries, and my heart soared knowing she'd be watching. Across from the cypress, rising from the white powder, stood a crystalline formation. It was round, with a natural arched doorway, yet I could see it was actually a collection of thin crystal points, emanating out in all directions from what appeared to be a massive shell and silica matrix. A structure that must have stretched at least 30 feet in height and diameter.

The gorgeous cluster had the look of an ice fortress, which felt even more special in such a tropical paradise, but the vibrations coming from the formation were anything but icy. Energy pulsed and surged, in and out, like a benevolent giant breathing warmth and light.

"What is this place?" I asked, looking around in wonder.

"We are standing in one of the most sheltering beachscapes this island offers. That crystalline configuration is selenite, which typically rests and grows underground, in hot caves. But its loveliness rises here on Poseidia's shore as well. A testament to the magic that is so much a part of Atlantis."

The closer we moved to the selenite, the more light I could feel humming through me in waves. And the more sense memory. It was as if the crystal blades were cutting through eons of cobwebs, and at the same time its fiber-optic fingers were reweaving lost or tattered ties. I knew when I touched it there would be a sensation not unlike a rocket blasting through my body. Alaric led me to the doorway and paused, his fingers laced in mine. Drawing as deeply from my inner cave's golden circle as I knew how, I placed my free hand on the spiky surface.

I cried out just as Alaric steadied my shoulders. I felt his spider-silk energy soothing me, opening me. Easing the light transmission's passage. Clean and clear and white-hot it throbbed, until I began to wonder if my physical body was breaking into pure light. Closing my eyes, I focused on my breath and my cave with its golden circle. In some manner of time—I knew not how long—it was as if my inner world had synchronized with the stone.

Removing my hand, which was blazing hot, I stepped back. Alaric released me. I opened my eyes and saw a tall man, in an ivory robe, lighting the room's myriad of candles. His white hair reached his waist. He moved slowly, with a mindfulness suggesting he'd long embraced this rite as a meditation. When the last votive flamed to life, he turned toward us.

"Hello, Elysia." His voice was deep, his sable eyes sharp and clear. He took my hand such that I felt cradled in comfort and love.

"Hello, Andolphicus," I replied. "Thank you for coming. I'm so very honored you will be marrying us. Again."

"My dear, you've been missed."

Ava, Will, and Jon entered the structure. Releasing Andolphicus' hand, I walked with Alaric toward my friends. I laughed to myself when Tyrius' broad form marched through next, as it seemed I'd made a steadfast comrade for life. Then I saw something else, something that completed my hopes for the day. Hunter stepped into the room, right behind Tyrius.

In an instant, I flew across the space, throwing myself into arms that finally felt ready to embrace me. Here was my Ahlaielian soul mate, the frequency Ray I'd thought was my eternal love. Until that morning, when my eyes began to open to all the rest that I was. He hugged me hard, and I couldn't help but sob against his broad shoulder. Silently he held me, his familiar healing energy surrounding my heart, and as I quieted he pulled away so he could look at me.

"Hey, you."

"Hey, yourself," I whispered. "You have no idea how much it means to me that you're here."

"I have a vague notion," he replied, and we both laughed. "Just as I'm beginning to realize the depth and scope of your connection with Alaric." He looked at me through damp eyes as he took my hands in his. "I simply wasn't ready to listen before the ball, El. And I apologize for that. But after I spent some time alone, I got to talk with him. And I found I couldn't help liking him." For a moment he paused. "Then Will told me what you'd shared with him. What you'd tried to tell me that I wasn't able to hear. About Alaric being the lost king of Moldaaris. And you being his queen." More tears dripped down his face. "It definitely put things in a different perspective for me. And then when things went down the way they did with the king, Alaric is the one who shadowed the nobles and made sure Gadeirus was not going to cause any further problems. He really took charge and made sure you were safe. Which impressed me."

"You could not make me any happier than by getting to know him."

"Actually, I felt like I was getting to know you both when I watched you dance." He took out a handkerchief and dabbed my face. "That performance was more than a work of art. It was a work of love. I still can't quite believe how many intricate layers of love you were able to weave and ground when you were interacting with him. Seeing that ... well, I could deny neither the energy nor the emotion. Alaric seems to be able truly to meet you and match you in your depths. It's what I think you've always longed for, during all our long years on Ahlaiele. And as much as I love you, I believe he is right for you."

"Oh, Hunter —"

"I love you, El," he murmured. "Of course, Ava has been trying to grab you practically since you came over to me. So you'd better say a few words to her and the guys, and then I believe there's a wedding to attend."

"I love you so much, Hunter." I squeezed his hands before embracing Ava.

"My darling, sweet sister. I'm here for you, as always." She released me, cupping a hand to my face.

"My dear Elysia!" Tyrius interrupted before I could say anything else to Ava. "It brightens my heart to see you so happy." He hugged me with gusto. "Your dance with Alaric made me cry. In all my years of courting at court, I've never witnessed such a thing. It's only fitting you should marry him after that!"

"Thank you, Tyrius. I truly am honored you are here." I smiled at him, as Will eased his arm around me.

"Hey, kiddo." He kissed my cheek. "You're just radiating love. And beauty. And he is so damn lucky."

"I really appreciate that, Will." I grinned at him before moving to stand in front of Jon.

"Didn't I tell you it was going to be a wonderful evening?" Jon asked as he took me in his arms.

"You did indeed," I whispered. "I love you, Jon. So very much."

"And I love you." Gently he released me, his calm blue eyes filling with tears. "It is a blessing beyond words to have my mother back in my life."

"My precious angel." I smiled at him through fresh tears, before turning to look into the wise and serene face of Andolphicus.

"Here, my dear." He had me digitally sign a crystal tabulator before instructing Jon to add his signature to the marriage certificate. Then slowly he made his way over to where Alaric was talking with Hunter. Once they'd signed as well, I watched Hunter and Alaric embrace. My heart soared as Alaric and Andolphicus then walked with me to the chamber's center.

"Please, my friends. Come closer," Andolphicus said in his welcoming tone. Feet shuffled sand as everyone moved behind where I stood with Alaric. "We are gathered here today, in the presence of Highest Light, to celebrate the sacred blessing of holy matrimony between Elysia Catrice Odai and Alaric Grayson Ardere. Within the sanctity of marriage, nothing is of more importance than love. It is love that brings you here before us this day. It is love that unites your hearts and spirits. And as your lives continue to interweave as one pattern, may you remain as a steadfast example of love's constancy. Of how love believes, abides, endures, and triumphs. Would you please face each other and hold hands?"

I turned toward Alaric. For a moment I simply drank in his beauty. He clasped my hands in his and smiled, his teeth flashing white against smooth, bronze skin.

"Alaric Grayson Ardere, do you take Elysia Catrice Odai to be your lawfully wedded wife? Do you promise to love, honor, cherish, and protect her, forsaking all others and cleaving only unto her forevermore?"

"I do."

"Elysia Catrice Odai, do you take Alaric Grayson Ardere to be your lawfully wedded husband? Do you promise to love, honor, cherish, and protect him, forsaking all others and cleaving only unto him forevermore?

"I do."

"Very well then. May I have the rings, please?" Jon stepped forward and handed two rings to Andolphicus. The minister then closed his eyes and held the rings toward the heavens. "May Highest Light duly bless these rings, as eternal symbols of your love for one another." Andolphicus then presented Alaric with my ring. "Alaric, please place this ring on Elysia's finger as you repeat after me."

Looking deeply into my eyes, Alaric repeated line for line the vows Andolphicus uttered. "I, Alaric Grayson Ardere, take thee Elysia Catrice Odai, to be my wife. To have and to hold, in sickness and in health, for richer or for poorer. Please accept this ring as a token of my undying devotion, of my promise to love you forevermore. And with this ring, I thee wed."

Once Alaric had finished, Andolphicus handed me Alaric's wedding band, and it was my turn to say my vows to him. After we'd exchanged rings, Andolphicus smiled at each of us.

"Alaric Grayson Ardere and Elysia Catrice Odai, as the two of you come together, united before us in the sacrament of marriage, and as you this day affirm your faith and love for one another, from this day forward shall you be one another's home, comfort, and refuge. In as much as the two of you have agreed to live together in holy matrimony and have affirmed your love for each other by the uttering of these vows, the giving of these rings, and the joining of your hands, I now pronounce you husband and wife. Ladies and gentlemen, may I present to you Mr. and Mrs. Ardere. Congratulations! Alaric, you may kiss your bride."

Slowly and deliberately Alaric kissed me, enfolding me in his arms as everyone clapped. Then Will stage whispered, "Dang! Y'all take a breath," which yielded laughter and a few cat calls. Alaric released me, took my hand, and kissed my fingers. Then we turned toward our small wedding party. There were many hugs and well wishes, and a good number of happy tears as well. It wasn't long before everyone but Ava had drifted outside. She gave me one last squeeze.

"Don't worry about showing up tomorrow, Elysia. We've got it covered."

"Are you sure? But I—"

"I am most sure, my dear," she insisted. "I'll handle things with Kendrick. And I think it's a good idea Gadeirus doesn't see you right away."

"I would have to agree."

"I will be in touch with you about the following day. There is a black-tie dinner in the evening you might enjoy. You've already laid the groundwork for our mission here, and the rest of us will see what we can do in the next two days with that foundation. But for now, I just want you to enjoy yourself."

"I love you, Ava." I clutched her tightly. "And thank you."

"I love you, too." She released me and kissed Alaric. The two of them spoke briefly, and then she was gone. I watched Alaric move toward me with cat-like grace.

"Let's say goodnight to Andolphicus." I nodded, and he took me by the hand to where the minister was gathering his things.

"Shall we help with the candles?" Alaric asked, hugging our friend.

"Oh no. You two should go and begin your life together. Again!" Andolphicus laughed as he embraced me.

The beach was empty when Alaric escorted me from the selenite structure. We walked a bit before he picked me up and spun me around. I giggled, and as he set me back on my feet, his hands curled in my hair. Hungrily, his lips gorged on mine, and I felt the promise of sweet surrender. I couldn't believe we had actually come to this place in time, where we could be alone and without thoughts of the mission for a while.

"Come with me, Mrs. Ardere," he whispered at last. "Our pleasure awaits."

TWENTY-FOUR

As if by magic, the double doorway parted. Alaric whisked me over the threshold while the chandelier eased into brightness. Then he lowered me so my bare feet kissed the travertine. With a wave of his hand, the doors drifted shut. He turned to me, an act of pure serpentine grace, and I caught my breath when he touched my cheek.

"Before I forget myself, I'd like to show you around." Clasping my hand, he ambled with me through the foyer. The high ceiling was fashioned of engraved gold. Silk the color of sand shimmered on walls hugged by gilded moldings. "The hallway on the left leads to the lavatory. The one on the right to the dressing rooms. You will find there's a complete wardrobe, filled with the latest Atlantean styles, all in your size. Although you're not going to be needing any of that for a while. A very long while."

"How did you—"

"Lay of the land, love." He laughed as we entered a suite bathed in seascape colors. Above us arched a domed ceiling, even higher than the foyer's. Etched gold trim teased the edges of three turquoise walls. The fourth was all glass. Its sliding doors stood open, and I heard the surf as if I were standing with my toes touching her. There was a large sitting area, with blue and beige and aqua couches and chairs. Red lotus bouquets lined the room, and in the dining area a regal buffet had been spread across a linen-clad table.

"Are we expecting anyone?"

"No. That's to ensure you get some nourishment. You've barely eaten all day, and I will not have you passing out on me."

"I'm not hungry."

"You will be." He cradled my face in his hands. "You should accept one insatiable appetite begets another. And you'll see it requires sustenance to pace yourself." He laughed again as his lips skimmed mine. "After all, I need you to be able to keep up with me."

"I think I'll have no trouble."

"Please, Elysia. Humor me, darling." There was a mixture of love and outright concern in his gold-green eyes. Taking a cup from the table, he held it to a covered vessel's spigot. A steaming brown broth filled the mug, which he then handed to me. "Start with this."

"What is it?" I could feel the liquid's dense and complex layering of nutrients through the porcelain. Its salty taste was savory. He poured some for himself as well, drinking deeply before he answered.

"Bone broth." He eyed me carefully. "Made from seaweed, vegetables, and a whole fish that's simmered for days. It's like a fine wine, really, made richer and more beneficial over the course of time. It's a deeply nourishing food. And you need to be deeply nourished." Worry knotted his brow before he smiled. "It pleases you?"

"Very much."

"Let me show you the rest of our accommodations," he suggested. "You're standing in the most exclusive hotel room in Poseidia. I had to pull some strings in order to procure a reservation on such short notice." Alaric grinned, and I couldn't imagine anyone refusing that seductive smile anything.

"We've been here before," I murmured, glancing around. "Our first wedding night."

"Yes! You really are remembering more and more." His arm cradled my shoulders, and I felt his disquietude rising again. "You're chilled."

"It's nothing." I'd felt cold since we left the palace, but there'd been so much to occupy my attention I barely noticed. "The broth is helping."

"There's something else that will help even more." He removed his suit jacket and had me slip my arms through its impossibly large sleeves. "Do you remember?" He led me past a palatial bed, adorned in aqua silk. As we neared the windows, a second suite appeared to the right. We walked through its rounded doorway and soft lights winked on, illuminating an all-white room.

Like the adjacent chamber, this sumptuous space seemed all the more expansive because of its seamless window wall. Beside the glass rested another opulent bed, its spread already turned down, revealing silky sheets. In the center of the room were two large in-ground pools. Together they formed the shape of an infinity symbol. Just beyond the pools were towel-stacked shelves and hooks bearing thirsty robes. Opposite the shelves was an alabaster fireplace, its massive firebox flickering orange and gold. I found my eyes being drawn back to the water, as another powerful sense memory filled my mindscreen.

"The first time you ever made love to me was here," I whispered. "Right here, in these vapors. The island's hot springs are funneled into this pool, and the cool springs into that one." I knelt by the mist, dipping my fingers into its penetrating heat. "Gyan was conceived here as well, although that was centuries later."

"Yes. The first time our hearts beat as one was here. And yes, Gyan's conception came from these waters." He crouched beside me, touching my cheek. "Go on and finish your broth, love. I'll bring a tray from the other room." Rising in one elegant movement, he seemed to glide into the adjoining suite.

I teetered to my feet, but that process felt anything but elegant. Downing the last of the broth, I hoped it would help rejuvenate me. Honestly, I didn't want to admit it but—even in such magnificent surroundings with the sexiest of men—I felt drained. I remembered there was a lavatory in this room, toward the back. Trudging the chamber's vast length, past more pretty plants, I entered the bathroom.

Automatic lights blossomed to a soft glow as I set my cup on the marble vanity. Scrutinizing myself in the mirror, I thought I appeared a paler shade of porcelain than before. But I was surprised to see my makeup didn't look like the melted mask I'd envisioned. In fact, it had held up well, considering how much crying I'd done. I wondered if that didn't have something to do with Alaric's expert hand.

Thinking perhaps I needed to be paying more attention to human self-care, I used the facilities and brushed my teeth to see if it would help. Washing my hands in the hottest water imaginable, I practiced channeling my balanced queen up from my inner cave's golden circle. I could feel massive amounts of energy coming into me, and after a minute or so I looked in the mirror. My color had improved, and I was once again aware of a pulsing up from the floor through my legs—a sign I was more balanced and grounded.

Feeling more like myself, I made my way back to the in-ground springs. While I'd been gone, Alaric had dimmed the lights and lit candles around the room's perimeter. Using a touchscreen, he adjusted the surround sound system as I approached. From every direction, classical music quelled and calmed me, though its comforting cadence seemed unable to still my heart. Pausing by the fireplace, I basked in its warmth while I gaped at his unbelievable physique, at the lustrous locks of sable-gold hair grazing his collar. He turned to me, his eyes sultry and smoldering. He moved toward me, grasping a cup from a tray settled on a bedside table. I caught my breath as he held the vessel to my lips.

"This is raw cacao," he murmured. "You'll love it." It tasted heavenly. As we shared the rich elixir, his bedroom eyes never once left mine. By the time we finished, I felt as aroused as if he'd been kissing me the whole time. He peeled his jacket from my arms and let it fall as he embraced me, his lips finding mine. I felt frenzied, nearly panicked with desire. But his hands only moved slower, his mouth more deliberately. I felt his intention to set an unhurried pace, and so I decided I would allow my body to rise and drop as the lion led.

He faced me away from him, smoothing my hair aside so he could kiss my neck. With adept fingers, he unfastened my gown. It tumbled to my ankles, and then he turned me toward him. Lifting me easily, he freed me from the dress and slid me down his body. I unbuttoned his shirt, forcing myself to adopt the same leisurely manner he was using to undress me. Once the white silk slipped from his fingers, his hands found my hair, his lips parted mine, and then he began to undo my bustier.

Piece by piece, our clothing piled around us as the fire crackled and sighed. At long last, there was nothing between us, nothing separating us but skin. For a few precious minutes, we simply stood in the lightest embrace, staring at one another. His body was beautiful. It put any picture or painting I'd ever seen to shame. He looked at me, looking at him, and smiled. Sweeping me up in his arms, he carried me into the steamy spring.

"So gorgeous," he whispered.

"You're the one taking my breath away."

"Oh, I haven't done that. Not yet." He kissed me deeply, so fully present and tuned in to my every response, it was bringing me to a rapid crescendo. I wanted to stay slow, to lock into a largo rhythm with him in this most sensual of dances, but the feel of him, all rippling muscle and pleasuring lips, kept quickening my pulse. I found it harder and harder to cool my desire as he masterfully stoked the flames. He began touching me more intimately, and I dug my nails into his shoulders.

"You're making me lose myself," I breathed. "I don't have the strength or the will to hold out much longer."

"Then don't," he urged. "My love, I want you to lose yourself." His mouth lingered on mine, driving deeper, then slowly surfacing until our lips barely brushed. Again and again he kissed me so, as he continued his feather strokes. "I want you simply to let go. To surrender."

"Alaric, I think I—"

"Yield to me."

"I feel like I might—"

"Yield to me," he repeated, his lips and fingers and then his eyes gently insisting. "Elysia, yield to me."

Staring into his fiery gaze, I felt a release I'd forgotten could be so powerful. Arching my back, I screamed. He continued his kisses along my neck, holding me as I spasmed against him.

I wasn't sure how long I cried out. Or how much I clawed him. Eventually I collapsed against his shoulder, sobbing.

Without a word he nestled me to him. I felt his spider-silk energy supporting me. Scooping me into his arms, he took me from the spring, clasping towels from the nearby shelf as we passed. Carefully, as if I were made of eggshell, he set me on my feet and dried me. Then he wrapped me in one of the robes before donning one himself.

He carried me to the bed, where he slid me under the sheets. I closed my eyes as he retreated to the other room. Within minutes he returned with a tray that he rested on the nightstand. Tossing his robe onto a nearby chair, he crawled in beside me.

"Here," he whispered, taking a bowl from the tray.

"What?"

"Try this." He placed a dark colored berry between my lips. "Do you like it?"

"Yes." I opened my mouth as he popped two more berries inside. Nibbling at the fruit himself, he regarded me with a satisfied smile.

"What?" I grinned at him, feeling a touch self-conscious.

"Nothing," he murmured, continuing to feed us both berries. "And everything." He chewed thoughtfully, his eyes soft in the candlelit shadows. "It's been a thousand years since I've pleasured you. And it's been that long since I last truly allowed myself to experience joy."

"But ... I mean, you ... well — "

"I'm not concerned about my own release, love, since that's what seems to be worrying you so." He caressed my cheek. "We will get to that. In due time. I've made it clear I'm in no hurry, haven't I?"

"Yes." Tears leaked from my lashes.

"Oh, darling." He wiped my misty eyes. "For a thousand years, it was the memory of your face, your breath, the scent of your skin, the feel of your hair — and the sound of you crying out in reckless abandonment — that sustained me. I never stopped thinking of you, through all the dark days of my contractual marriage, and all the lonely hours I've spent throughout the centuries. Can you possibly fathom what it means to me to share of myself again with you? To be able once more to look upon those eyes? To feel your body against mine?"

"Your words touch my heart in its deepest place," I whispered. "Truly, I don't know what I can say. But I know what I desire to do." Leaning across him, I took the bowl from his hands and placed it back on the bedside table. Opening my robe, I let it fall from my shoulders. I saw the longing in his eyes, reflected in the quivering candlelight. He pulled me to him, kissing me hard as my hands explored his body. Laughing quietly, he rolled with me, laying me back against the softness of the sheets.

"Have you recovered then?" He smiled at me, his fingers tracing my mouth.

"Miraculously."

"You are sure?"

"Positive." I began touching him, in seductive ways I was only beginning to remember, as if to convince him of my certainty. At first, he looked at me with surprise. Then he kissed me, consumed me. I could feel his arms begin to quake as he held me. His lips trembled against mine, and that tremor passed through my body as shivery delight.

"Can you feel what you're doing to me?"

"Yes." I continued my light caresses. "Melting the serpent's icy defenses."

"Yes," he sighed, closing his eyes. "I've been cold inside for such a long time."

"I know." I kissed his jaw, his neck. "And you were brooding about me catching a chill."

He laughed again and — opening his eyes — held my head so he could stare into the very depths behind my gaze. Intensely. Hypnotically. So erotically. I could feel how he was completely present with me. How he was exposing his soul to me, and I bared my spirit in return. Slowly, ever so slowly, he pressed himself against me. I could feel myself opening. Expanding. Welcoming.

"Breathe with me," he whispered. Together we inhaled, and exhaled. Over and over, his eyes never leaving mine. He wrapped me in his embrace. I felt a deepening connection, a merging that led me to breathe in as he breathed out. And then he inhaled as I exhaled. I lost track of time and space. Everything but his gold-green eyes, the rhythm of his breath. And the feel of him as he moved inside of me.

Another dance had begun. He held me with his eyes and his breath, at first clearly leading, giving everything of himself to me. All I had to do was receive. Then there was a natural shifting, a long exhale for the deep inhale, and at those times I led, and gave, while he received. Back and forth we went, giving and receiving, building and plateauing — until we reached the peak of pleasured arousal. But this time I found no release.

This time we held each other in a suspended state of ecstasy. The feeling was exquisite. I knew not how long we stayed like that. But at some point, the sun began to rise. And Alaric smiled.

"Would it please you to surrender with me?"

"Yes," I sighed. "Oh, yes."

Breaking eye contact, he began to kiss me again. Deeply. And fervently. Clasping my hands, he held me to the bed, as his lips and his body continued to urge. To demand. I could feel him right there with me, as an inward spiraling surge of energy began to build. Again he looked at me, moved with me, deeper and higher at the same time. I heard myself gasp right at the moment he caught his breath. And then we were writhing, and crying out, and holding each other as wave after wave passed through our bodies.

After, there was only bliss. And love. For a long moment, Alaric rested his forehead against mine. Then he turned me on my side, curling up to me from behind. His warmth lulled me, and I felt I was about to lose consciousness.

"Beyond words," I whispered.

"Only feelings," he murmured in my ear. Then in his arms, I fell fast asleep.

TWENTY-FIVE

Panting, I bolted upright. Sunlight streamed through the glass wall by the bed, and for a moment I didn't recognize my surroundings. Then Alaric's hands were on my shoulders.

"Shhhhh," he whispered, his velvety voice so soothing. Like the sound of the surf slowly returning to my awareness. He'd been propped up on pillows against the headboard, but as I looked at him he slid with me under the sheets. "Just a dream."

"You're the dream." I reached for him, caressing his face. "Are you even real? Or simply some figment of my insatiable imagination?"

"I may be immortal, but I assure you I am blood and bone. And desire." He pulled me to him, and I raked my fingers through his thick hair as those knowing hands and lips began exploring my body. Perhaps I was still in a heightened state of arousal from our hours of love-making. But I could feel myself building all too quickly to pleasure's pinnacle. "Alaric, please slow me," I sighed. "I can't seem to find a way within myself to bear such bliss for long."

"Oh, but you can," he murmured. Slithering up my flesh, he rested his weight on his elbows as he cradled my head in his hands. Once more his gaze lulled me, braking me to his sensual rhythm. In he breathed, and I breathed out, and before long I was again transported to that euphoric holding place with him. Then he rolled with me, raising me so I was sitting on top of him. I looked down into his unwavering stare.

"You can bear anything when you are rooted in your power. And I mean for you to remember how, as I want you to own fully who you are. To know your sovereignty. To sense it as thoroughly as you feel me now against you." Ever so gently he moved beneath me, easing and encouraging and readying. "Last night you and I merged within my power. And it was exquisite. Yet there is another dimension of intimacy waiting. Becoming one within your power will take us deeper. Much deeper. And then when we can flow between your essence and mine, well ..." Wickedly he grinned at me. "You'll see."

"Deeper than last night? How is that possible?" I shook my head as he laughed. "For me, the earth trembled as the heavens danced. I was lifted beyond all time and space as you made love to me. In the name of Oneness, what could possibly lie beyond ecstasy?"

"Trust me," he urged. "A woman's power reaches where a man's cannot. It's why balancing the masculine and the feminine within— which we all have—is the path to wholeness. But even the most balanced whole feels pleasure sharing of itself through sacred union."

"For as long as I can remember, I've wanted to believe in sacred union," I whispered. "What I've experienced with you feels nothing less than holy. And yet— "

"Your Ahlaielian training has taught you otherwise."

"Yes."

"You feel on some level it must be wrong to feel such passion. And power."

"Yes." Out of nowhere shame flared, moistening my eyes.

"Experiencing a woman's power is what a man craves of her most, whether he is aware of it or not."

"Why?" I ran my hands along his muscled torso, my body shivering in response.

"Because physically, he's not equipped with her gift of a sacred inner vessel," he replied. "Which is a direct conduit to the Divine. If he's blessed with wisdom, he may meld with her and worship in her vessel's chapel. More often than not, his lack of understanding makes him angry. He senses what he doesn't have, and his frustration goes on to reject the feminine within himself which, if he'd only embrace it, would be his path of redemption. But instead he endlessly pursues a female to possess, on some level hoping to capture connectedness through her."

For a moment he paused, studying me thoughtfully. "Try as he might, though, what she has he can neither possess nor command. It's an ironic state of affairs, as the very thing he most wants to have and control, he never will. Such is the plight of men, in their ignorance. Although he may indeed hold sway over the realm of doing, from there he'll never reach her. Or himself in his entirety, for that matter. Doing has no path to being, and it's her dominion over being that is the seat of all creation. Of being able to receive and be one with all that is." He caressed my cheek. "It's why many men fear and try to diminish women. Because a woman in her power can rule the world."

"Teach me."

"You already know," he said, a smile parting his lips. "You have reigned before like no other I've known. And you will remember. You've already begun, by rediscovering your inner cave."

"How did you know?"

"It's the chamber where a woman's beingness dwells." Lightly his fingers caressed my abdomen. "I could see it in your eyes once you'd opened her passageway again."

"So you're talking about drawing energy from that space." I moved my hips, opening and descending to receive him.

"You've been doing that." His hands whispered along my thighs. "I'm talking about being that space."

"How?"

"Just feel," he replied. "I will take you to the doorway, on the crest of a white wave, which you will come to recognize as male power. But you must enter alone, into the Divine Feminine. You must feel your way. And then, once you settle, it's my desire you will invite me inside to pray with you."

"You make me sound like a church."

"You are my church." Tears glistened in his gold-green eyes. "Your body is my temple. And I come to you to worship. To be with you, bearing witness to the Divine for all that is. To express my faith and my undying love."

"I so want to believe," I whispered. "I feel like the sinner who's lost her way. For centuries I've been raging against my temple, fighting to keep my desires and my guilt from consuming me. When all along it sounds like what I've really needed to do is simply be engulfed. And in surrendering to the flames, have my faith validated. My guilt assuaged. My power resurrected from the ashes."

"Precisely," he smiled. "Now look at me, love." His gaze intensified. "Simply feel. Then take me inside your cathedral. And offer me communion." I steadied my breath, falling deeper into his eyes. He inhaled and exhaled with me, over and over. We breathed as one. I continued to move with him as his flesh fused with mine, and in my mind's eye I saw a white wave forming. I pictured him there, breathing me into the silence beneath the wave. I felt myself sinking. Under the whitecaps, I caught sight of my inner cave, and her ruby-walled chamber beckoned me.

Just when I thought I'd reached her sanctuary, I felt another deepening. As soon as I slipped inside her walls, I began to fall through a black mist. Deeper and deeper, descending into stillness. Into beingness. On some level, I was aware my body was tensing, and some distant part of myself heard Alaric catch his breath as I contracted around him. Then the mist took me, becoming a void, the unformed form of all that is. I began breathing in the essence of all that is, and I felt a tremendous expanding within my heart. It was as if I'd merged with universal flow, and I could feel its sacred waters in my veins. Within this indescribable place, I opened myself to him. Softly, slowly I continued to unfold, as he entered the space I was holding. Until I was he, and he I, and then we were lost in Oneness, floating in the blissful sea of all that is.

I know not how long we drifted, before wave after wave came over me, and through him, and our cries echoed on and on in the void, carrying us back from her black waters. Breathless, I embraced him, resting my head against his chest. For several moments I lay there, listening to him pant as he clutched me. At long last he shifted, propping himself up on one elbow, loving me with those eyes.

"You heard my prayers," he whispered.

"Yes." I placed my hand over his, where it lay against my cheek. "How you exalt me."

"And how you hold me within this sweet rapture." Sweetly he kissed me. "I love you with all that I am, Elysia."

"And I love you." The serenity in his eyes stirred memories of how carefree he'd once been. Before so much heartbreak. So many centuries of longing.

"I want to make sure you keep your strength up, love." His lips grazed my neck. "We should eat something."

"Okay." I knew better than to argue, even though I couldn't imagine being more satiated than I was at the moment. But I could feel he knew what I was thinking anyway.

"Your appetite will come," he said as he slid from the bed. "Your other appetite, I should say." We both laughed as he slipped on his robe. "Would you like to go out for breakfast? Then maybe a late-morning swim?"

"Sure. I'll just shower first." As I rose, I glanced around for my robe, running quick fingers through wildly tangled hair. Then I saw him leaning against the door frame, arms folded, watching me. Just standing there, so unbelievably sexy.

His stare aroused me and made me feel a little self-conscious, too. "What?" For the first time in a long while, I blushed.

He sauntered to the clothing piled by the fireplace. Clasping his shirt from the night before, he crossed the distance between us and enveloped me in a silky softness that smelled like him. That sweet scent of sandalwood and musk. I tunneled my arms through its seemingly endless sleeves. And then he grasped its billowing front, pulling me to him. He kissed me hard, his hands running over the shirt as my fingers opened his robe.

"I don't know if I can ever look at you long enough," he whispered. "Or touch you often enough."

"Why don't you shower with me?" I smiled at him invitingly. "Maybe we both can look and touch a little longer."

"You realize we may never again leave this hotel room, don't you?"

"You realize I don't care, don't you?"

"All right, but on one condition." He continued to kiss me, moving down my neck with his mouth as his shirt slipped from my shoulders.

"You're so demanding now that we're married!" I teased, and he laughed. "What is it, dearest?"

"You need to eat something. Please." Squeezing my arms, he released me and walked over to the bowl of berries from the night before. Popping a couple in his mouth, he returned to me, bowl in hand. "I promise to get you a proper meal very soon. But for now ... please, Elysia."

I nodded, and for a few minutes he fed me berries. Then he placed the empty bowl back on the table. Dropping his robe on the nearby chair, he eased toward me, and the sight of him made me tremble.

"What?" His eyes were playful.

"I was just thinking how we may really not be leaving this hotel room. At least not for a long time." I lowered my arms, allowing his shirt to fall free of my fingertips. "A very long time."

"Come with me, Mrs. Ardere," he whispered, sweeping me into his arms. "A very long time is about to start right now."

TWENTY-SIX

For breakfast, Alaric brought me to a café by the water. We'd walked barefoot, holding hands, he in lightweight pants and a sleeveless tunic, and I in a shoulder-baring dress. We lounged at an outdoor table, sharing from multiple dishes, each one rich and satisfying. As his inner ice melted, he became more talkative. The sound of his speaking cradled me. It was the sound of home, of love and protection and strength and surrender, and I knew I would never tire of it.

When we finished, he pulled our shoes from a lightweight pack. Then he took me on a walking tour of the island's historic district, with its shops and restaurants fashioned in an earthy architectural style — one that predated the city's crystalline downtown skyline. There stood stone and stucco structures, with cobblestone streets and window boxes dressed in poppies and posies.

As we explored, I learned he loved showering me with gifts. He had an exceptional eye for what pleased me, and a talent for observing an item of clothing and knowing if it would fit me or not. He paid for what we bought from a thick stack of currency, and every time he reached for the bills my heart ached, as I suspected what he'd exchanged of himself for the money. At some point, I knew I'd uncover the truth behind the whispers. But I simply couldn't dwell on that right now.

By the time we returned to the sand, where we once again slipped off our shoes, he was carrying a large bag of silk outfits, perfumed oils, and some special dark cacao beans. And the warmest, softest robe I could ever have imagined. Here and there along the beach, people ambled along, or stretched out on blankets, or splashed in the sea. But for the most part, we had plenty of space to ourselves.

We'd only walked a short distance before Alaric spread a coverlet and set down the bag and his pack. He had me sit as he retrieved a hairbrush. With a serpent's grace, he slid behind me. I turned to look at him, question marks in my eyes, and he smiled.

"You've always loved having your hair brushed, darling." He ran light fingers down the sides of my head, gathering any strands that had fallen in front of my shoulders, and swept them onto my back. "I thought it might please you before we take our swim."

"Thank you, Alaric. You dote on me so."

"Cherishing you brings me great joy." Slowly, he brushed my locks, sending tingles up my spine. "I've had centuries to think about all the ways I've missed treasuring and pleasuring you. The end result is a very long list. Basically, you should know I intend to adore you exhaustively. And I'm just getting started."

"You should know I adore being adored exhaustively." I tilted my head back, basking in the unbelievable sensation the bristles teased from my skin. Reaching behind me, I ran my hands along his outer thighs. The brush stilled as he nuzzled my neck. Then he reclined on the blanket, pulling me on top of him, my hair tumbling onto his shoulders.

"I can't seem to quench this thirst for you," I murmured against his mouth.

"You can drink all you want."

"But the more I drink, the more I want."

"Then the more I will pour."

"I'm nearly overflowing now."

"I want you wet." His voice was silk seduction as he eased his kisses. And then for a long moment he paused, combing his fingers through my hair, his eyes soft and gentle on mine. "Come. Let me love you in the sea." Playfully he grinned at me. "Let's make the dolphins jealous."

Then he was on his feet, offering his hands to pull me up. He looked at me, eyes ablaze, as he unbuttoned my dress. He stripped it from my body, revealing the strapless suit I wore underneath. He lifted the tunic over his head, letting it fall as he stepped from his pants. Muscles bulging, he stood before me, his beautiful body barely covered in swim trunks.

I gawked, until he grabbed my hand and started running with me. Into the waves we crashed, and then he cupped water and threw it at me. It was cold on my body, and I screamed before lapsing into giggles. I tossed water toward him, which he dodged with feline agility. Quickly, I moved closer, slapping both hands into the waves and spraying him thoroughly. He laughed and grabbed me around the waist, carrying me as he waded deeper.

When the water was lapping at his shoulders, he turned me so I faced him. His lips found my neck, his hands molding to my body. The sun glinted off his sable and gold hair. The water's temperature had become warm and inviting. I wrapped my legs around his waist, drawing him nearer. And then a gentle bump nudged my back. Surprised, I glanced around and saw a dorsal fin swimming away. It joined a group of eight gray fins encircling us.

"Look, Alaric!"

"They've come for you, love," he replied, grinning as the dolphins clicked and whistled. "I told you we'd make them jealous."

As we acknowledged them, the dolphins swam closer. One in particular approached me, and I knew it was the one who'd tapped my back. I also knew it was a male, and as I peered into the gentle eye he turned toward me, I felt his loving presence. The dolphin moved his head into my hand, just below his eye, as if he wanted me to caress his cheek.

"He's telling me he's missed me," I said, tears dripping down my face as I touched him.

"No one in the universe, beyond myself and Jon and your dolphin extended family, knows the excruciating pain of being separated from you for so long." Alaric's own eyes dampened. "You're in their blood, and they yours, and so any descendants from your lineage will feel that ancient connection. And love."

I continued to pet the dolphin, and he glided around me so I could have access to the rest of his body. Always he came back to stare at me, and I got the overwhelming message he wanted me to swim with him.

"His name is Kavi, and he wants to take me somewhere." My voice was dreamy. I could feel the dolphin holding a vibration that was opening me, altering me. Awakening me. "Something he wants me to see. From before."

"In the Old Tongue, 'kavi' is a seer of the sun, direct perceiver of Truth, who reflects to the rishi's mirrored moon, such that Truth may shine forth day and night," Alaric whispered. "His kavi to your rishi is the most powerful visionary coupling. He most certainly can help you access and expand your ability to see, on every level."

"He says he will help me see the unseen again."

"Go with him," Alaric urged. "Remember, you can breathe underwater. You just need to surrender to the fear blocking the memory."

Once more I peered at Alaric, who nodded encouragement, before turning to Kavi. The dolphin waited patiently, his dorsal fin in my hand. He sensed my trepidation, and I understood he wanted me to feel safe. I heard his clicking rhythm change, and I realized he was telling me he would go slowly. That he would help me uncover and embrace a deeper layer of myself, where so many of my memories had been hidden away. Taking a deep breath, I mind-messaged Kavi I was ready, then grasped his fin. He swam off, circling around Alaric and keeping me above the water's surface as I gained my balance and bearings upon his back.

The sense memory was amazing. Before long, I had a visceral knowing of how natural it had once felt to swim as one with a dolphin. I relaxed my grasp on Kavi's fin, and as soon as that happened, his clicking changed again. I realized he was asking if I felt ready for the plunge. I told him I was, but even though I knew I should be able to breathe underwater conditioned response had my heart hammering.

Gradually, he swam deeper. Once the water swallowed my neck, I gulped a final breath, and then together we dove to the ocean's bottom. It was still shallow, yet I understood he was moving out to sea.

I opened my eyes wide and found I could see quite well in the aqua underworld. But my big challenge was upon me—I needed to breathe. Doing my best to relax, I released my lungs and prayed to Highest Light for the strength to trust. Pausing at the end of the exhale for as long as I could, I inhaled.

It was like another dimension opened in my body. I felt the water inside me, much heavier than air, but I also sensed a rapid-fire transformation taking place on the cellular level. It was like my hybrid system had flicked a switch, and I was suddenly fueled by water instead of air.

I had not anticipated such exhilaration. Riding along on Kavi's back created an unbelievable high, and as I again reached a deeper level of acceptance and comfort, he began to pick up speed. The sea floor blurred as we whizzed along past a dizzying array of unusual and brightly colored creatures and fish. Through grasses and above crevices and caves, we raced.

Before long I spotted an eye-shaped opening in a scarlet rock formation. Kavi swam inside and paused. Blue-green crystals cast a soft translucence from where they were embedded in the walls. I noticed a tunnel at the rear, and Kavi clicked at me, communicating he would be waiting when I emerged. But it was clear I must enter alone.

Releasing his fin, I slid from his back. He gave me a supportive look before darting from the cave. I turned and looked about me, feeling into the space. The aqua lighting was stunning. And eerie. It was quiet energetically, like a tomb, yet I knew every thought and movement was being observed.

I swam to the tunnel's round entrance. The alcove's luminescence lit perhaps the first three feet of the passageway, and then it became black as a moonless night. In those few feet, I could see the walls were made of rubies, in glittering druzy formations. I realized I would have to feel my way.

Moving into the opening, I sensed expansiveness, like being inside a giant womb. In the void, I became aware I possessed a type of sonar echolocation ability, which afforded me a detailed map of my surroundings. I felt such appreciation for the gift's discovery and wondered how a talent so profound could still be working when most of my other natural abilities had been muted—or thwarted. I reasoned it must have to do with my hybrid lineage. Something as ancient and as deeply a part of me as being able to breathe underwater. Something no passage of time — or crystal scalpel — could diminish or alter.

Feeling elated and grateful, I continued swimming for some distance before reaching a back wall with three openings. I sensed I was to enter the one on the left. Inside was an even more spacious chamber. I continued on, moving through the blackness. Then the chamber curved, and as I hugged its rounded wall, I began to see a faint yellowish glow. Within the deep red rocks, crystals emitted a golden light. The further I inched along, the more sunny the crystals appeared, until at last it seemed as if I'd emerged in broad daylight.

Ahead were four throne-like chairs encircling a luminous sphere. The chairs were fashioned from the same druzy rubies as the walls, and they were surrounded by a glowing ring set within the chamber floor. I knew this was the location Highest Light had shown me, from which I funneled energy to my own inner sanctuary, the seat of my personal power. A gilded stand cradled the crystal. On the chair facing me perched a woman with long auburn hair, not unlike my own. She was a mermaid, with golden scales and a fiery ruby in her third eye. Keenly, she watched my approach.

"Welcome, Elysia." Here in the depths the mermaid spoke to me telepathically, but in my mind's ear her voice held a fine chime's resonant tone. "You do not remember me. Not yet. But we are old friends. My name is Khrestes."

"It is an honor, my lady."

"Please. Sit with me." She extended a porcelain hand toward the chair opposite hers.

"Thank you." I sank into the enormous stone seat. It felt surprisingly comfortable, its rounded shape embracing and supportive.

"I'm sure you're wondering why you are here." Her eyes, so like fine lapis, were somber.

"Yes," I whispered. "Something troubles you, Khrestes."

"These are troubling times, Elysia." She sat with perfect posture, much like Hunter, and I noticed how her hands gripped the armrests. I braced myself for what she was about to say. "As you are aware, Earth's balance of power has been tipped. Dangerously so. It's the real reason for your Ahlaielian mission — the Highest Light purpose — and it reaches well beyond the betrayal. But you don't yet realize the full magnitude of what we are all facing."

"How did you know —"

"I'm the merbeings' prophet. The ocean's oracle." Again she looked at me, and I realized her pupils were mirrors. "I know you understand some of the levels of deception that have been proliferating. That from Atlantis there are those who have infiltrated places as distant and pristine as Ahlaiele. And that it's only by the grace of Oneness you and your crewmates survived the trip to Poseidia at all."

"Yes."

"You are aware of how your essence was split, under the guise of being able to complete your undercover assignment." I nodded as she leaned forward. "But as in the cosmic wheel of life, the interdynamic and interdependent nature of yin and yang, half the essence can't long survive on its own."

"What are you saying?" A dawning truth was rising within. But I wanted to hear her say it.

"You are dying." She surveyed my energetic nature. "You have the blueprint of an immortal. But that coding was switched off when the male half of your essence was removed. And to ensure your destruction, in case by some miracle you survived the trip here, your female essence was reprogrammed to begin a rapid disintegration."

"How rapid?"

"A couple of weeks, at the most." Again she studied my energy. "Although your heart is surprisingly strong, beyond what I would have expected. That's why Alaric has been mystified. And worried. He senses the crumbling beneath, but when he looks at you, he can't bring himself to see beyond your beautiful and vigorous heart."

"And my crewmates? Are they dying as well?"

"Yes." Her eyes were grave. "Although none of them have your depth and breadth of heart, a gift you inherited from your sea family. They are pure Color Rays, and as such they're already weakening. That's why Quenna became ill almost immediately, as her primary strength has always come from her now-severed male essence. Her Color Ray is also a predominantly masculine one so she is the frailest. But the others' demise will become evident in only a few days."

"I see." I closed my eyes, taking in her words, digesting them. I breathed of my power, and when I again looked at her, I felt only stillness inside. "We require more time, Khrestes. Our mission needs to be carried out. Or an alternate plan devised, as I understand you're about to tell me the rest of the story, and how we're heading toward some danger we'd not anticipated." She began laughing as I looked at her, puzzled.

"Only you would be able to speak of the mission and alternate plans when I've just told you your death is imminent." She shook her head, and I could feel her admiration. "That courage is just one aspect that made you the most powerful reigning queen, the ultimate maharani, a thousand years ago. And why you are so desperately needed here now."

"I'm here in service of Highest Light, and I mean to uphold and inspire Right Action with every fiber of my being until the mission is completed. Or I draw my last breath." I smiled at her. "Seeing as we may not have a lot of time, you'd best tell me what it is we're up against."

"All right." Again she looked at me with a mixture of affection and awe. "Let me begin with a sound healing, which will help unlock the memories subdued by the Ahlaielian frequencies since your birth there. Once your memory has been reclaimed, it will be easier for you to understand all I'm about to share."

"Thank you, Khrestes. I'm very grateful."

"The gratitude will be mine, maharani, if I can bring you back to me." She took a deep breath, and then the most astonishing song poured forth from her depths. I closed my eyes, allowing the vibrations to open and align me. Images and feelings hurtled past my awareness, and I felt release after release tremble forth from my diaphragm and spine.

As I sat back in the chair, my hands and feet quaked, loosening the restraints my soul had accepted in order to be a vibratory match for an Ahlaielian life. Khrestes' voice was so pure, so lovely, it was easy to lose myself in its freeing frequency. When her song finally stilled, it took all my will simply to open my eyes. My body felt paralyzed.

"Rest, Elysia. Your energetic body has not yet fully reintegrated into the physical. Once it has, you will be able to move."

I couldn't even nod my head, so I simply closed my eyes. It was as if a whole new inner world had been gifted to me. I felt such clarity, such congruency, as I could finally access thousands of years of experiences. Soon I became aware of energy surging through my legs from the stones beneath my feet. As the frequency flew up my body, I felt an unfreezing, a reanimating. When the vibrations reached my head, I opened my eyes. Khrestes was observing me from her mirrored gaze.

"That was incredible."

"You're looking much more like yourself, Elysia." A huge grin lifted her lovely heart-shaped face. I stared at her, and for the first time I really recognized who she was. Who she'd been to me. How the merbeings and dolphins were so intimately connected, like cousins within a family. And how she'd been one of my closest companions and allies, in all the long years of my life before Ahlaiele.

"Oh, Khrestes." Even in my mind's ear, my voice trembled with tears. "To gaze again upon your face and fully see it—after all these eons—is truly a gift."

"Welcome back, dear friend!" She clapped her hands in delight. "We have all missed you so."

"To be back, to be clear and present to what was, and what is—it's indescribable." I smiled at her. "I feel amazing for someone at death's door."

"I have endured many things in this mostly timeless existence. But after a thousand years of darkness to have my sister returned to me only to be taken away again in a few short days ..." She shook her head. "I'm not sure I can bear it."

"Highest Light will guide us. And a way will appear. Of that I'm absolutely certain." I felt the truth of my words, manifesting as a wave-like opening at my crown. "Perhaps if you tell me what I don't yet know about the power play at hand, it will be a first step toward a solution."

"Yes. Of course." I could feel her gathering her thoughts. And preparing to relive unpleasant past moments. "There's no easy way to say this, so I will simply begin speaking. I suppose I should start with King Helionel. And his obsession with you."

"Obsession?" I felt into my newly reactivated memory banks, but this was not a remembrance of mine.

"Yes," she murmured. "From the moment he laid eyes on you, if I'm honest. And the parallels with Gadeirus are chilling, as you will see." She paused, her voice the barest whisper in my head. "I remember it well. Helionel had recently been crowned king. You were here on holiday with Alaric, and the two of you were invited as visiting dignitaries to the palace. There was a ball and an evening of courting at court. The king did win a dance with you, but when you later took to the floor with Alaric, the entire palace was mesmerized, completely erupting in applause. And amazement. It created a fierce jealousy, you see, because first of all he couldn't have you; you were already married. And to another powerful king, one of Poseidia's staunchest allies. Secondly, even if he could find a way to have you, he knew there was no way to duplicate the intensity of the relationship you shared with Alaric. Believe me, he explored that option, bringing the best witches and spell-casters from across the universe to the palace. But they all told him the same thing. No spell or potion could divide two immortals united in vibratory harmony. And no magic charm could be conjured to make you love him instead of Alaric. So finally, he decided the only way to end his own suffering was to destroy the two of you."

"I remember Helionel," I mused. "He was short for an Atlantean and exceedingly polite. Friendly, even. But obsessed?" I shook my head. "If he was obsessed with me — or out to decimate us, for that matter — I knew it not."

"Neither you nor Alaric realized," she replied. "Which is to be expected, actually. I've never seen two people more wrapped up in each other. When you were together, you couldn't fathom the existence of another's longing." She sighed, swallowing hard. "In hindsight, that made you vulnerable."

"But ... to destroy an entire planet? Annihilate her people? Over me?"

"Ego spun off from balanced mind and divorced from the heart is a ruthless and sinister thing," she answered. "It cares not whom it hurts. Or what it obliterates, in the name of getting its way."

"Yes. And once the hellhounds are unleashed there's no calling them back is there?" For several moments I simply breathed, rooting myself more deeply within my power. "Help me face this unpleasantness, now that it's rushing right at me. Helionel had something to do with Alaric's fate after my death, is that right?"

"Yes."

"Tell me. How was Helionel involved in Linasia's pact with Alaric?"

"Linasia is a consummate deal-maker," she began. "She's always played both ends against the middle. She mind-messaged Helionel as soon as she learned Alaric was seeking a gatekeeper to help with you. Helionel, of course, thought it was a golden opportunity to enslave Alaric under someone he could control. But Linasia made it clear she wouldn't do it unless the king agreed she could use Alaric for her own pleasure. And she also wanted an exorbitant amount of money."

Khrestes squeezed her eyes shut, before once again gazing at me. "Helionel agreed to her wishes, but on two conditions. That Linasia also make Alaric marry her daughter, chaining him in a loveless marriage, as part of the deal. And then besides bedding him herself — something the King knew would be an endless torture for Alaric — Linasia was to prostitute him at every opportunity." Slowly, Khrestes shook her head. "It was Helionel's idea to sell Alaric's body to the highest bidder at the end of every courting at court ball being held in her domain, or in Atlantis. Or anywhere under Poseidia's influence, for that matter. Such that all these places where Alaric had been loved and respected as a king, he was stripped of his dignity, and seen through new eyes. The eyes of desire, yes, but also disdain. For the wealthy both admire and abhor their sexual servants. And so his new line of work was run like a private auction, overseen by Linasia, who wooed only the wealthiest women to compete for his ... services."

Khrestes gaped at me, and I could feel the torment behind her mirrored eyes. "The king wanted to take something Alaric had loved and fashion it into a prison, forcing him to be with women over and over again who could never be you. And in the meantime earn a tidy sum, since Alaric was always highly prized."

"For the love of Oneness." My voice cracked in my mind's ear. "I knew about Linasia. And Carinnia. And Quenna told me of whispers in Poseidia, about Alaric selling pleasure for profit. But I didn't realize —"

"There's never been any pleasure in it for him, Elysia. Or much profit, as the bulk of the proceeds have always returned to the reigning Poseidian king," Khrestes muttered. "Only self-reproach, as the most noble of kings became a whore to keep his end of the bargain with Linasia. To keep you safe."

"Highest Light help me!"

"Alaric himself doesn't know Helionel was behind the deal's details," Khrestes continued. "To be honest, he was so devastated after losing you I think he chose not to feel any more into the situation. In fact, it's how he survived over the next several centuries. Just performed without feeling. He cared not about anything after you were gone."

"I am beyond words," I whispered. "What endless horrors he has endured on my account."

"Elysia, I apologize," she began. "We don't have to—"

"Yes," I interrupted. "Yes, we do. I need to know, Khrestes. All of it. No matter how brutal."

"If you insist."

"So Helionel died a long time ago?"

"Yes." She sighed. "Centuries have passed since he transitioned after a state dinner. Many say he was poisoned, as he was most despised. And that's what I see as well. Atlanteans are long-lived, but not immortal. There have been three other kings between Helionel and Gadeirus. It's why the experiments have dragged out so long. The rulers since Helionel had no real heart for them. They were mostly content to bask in Poseidia's bounty and pay lip service to the factions pushing to expand such brutal measures. But that was before Gadeirus. None of Helionel's successors have been able to capture his cruelty quite like Gadeirus."

"And Carinnia?"

"She wasn't immortal, like her mother," Khrestes answered. "In many ways, she was similar to the shut-down Alaric. Very cold. Icy, even. Her smile never touched her eyes. But unlike him, she was shallow at her core. Elegant possessions and traveling in style were all that interested her. They spent a great deal of time apart, as he would often be away on a courting at court date. Carinnia took to traveling on her own, staying in posh hotels and catering to selfish whims, which included trying every known hallucinogenic. By the time she married Alaric, she had already suffered a raging addiction problem for years. And that dependency led to her untimely death."

"What happened to her spirit?"

"She was reincarnated. If it wasn't for her mother, she would have been born into the hellish experiments taking place in the tunnels beneath Poseidia," she said. "But once more Linasia worked her magic. Carinnia was reborn as the daughter of a wealthy nobleman on the outskirts of Atlantis, where she could again have beautiful possessions and travel as she wished."

For a short time Khrestes was silent, as she tuned in to Carinnia. "She has cycled through the circle of birth and death a couple of times since then. But she's still in Atlantis, living as a lord's wife currently, due to her mother's influence. And as such many things are exactly the same, on the soul level, with her."

"And Linasia?" I could feel my throat constrict as I uttered her name. "Is Alaric free of her now?"

"Still a gatekeeper. Still pretty much unchanged, in these thousand years." Khrestes eyed me carefully, and I knew I was not going to like what she was about to say. "You freed him, Elysia. As soon as you took physical form, he felt it. The moment you departed Ahlaiele, he left the Great Central Sun region. For good. Although I must warn you of some things."

"What things?"

"Linasia retains deep ties with Atlantean royalty and the High Council. And she is insanely jealous of you. She may as yet play a part with Gadeirus, depending on how things unfold." Her voice was hushed in my mind's ear. "Tell me. Have you considered why they chose you for the Ahlaielian mission in the first place?"

"We were told it was our centuries of devotion to Highest Light principles," I replied. "Which is probably the only true thing they said. And yet we were never supposed to uplift Atlantis with our convictions. We were meant to die for them."

"Yes," she whispered. "But Gadeirus specifically requested you. Partly for his own pleasure, and partly to draw Alaric back to Atlantis. I will tell you more about what he wants with Alaric in a moment. But first I'd like to make you understand Gadeirus has been obsessed with you since he moved into the palace and saw your painting."

"What painting?"

"The one Helionel commissioned, after the first time he watched you dance with Alaric." Her eyes took on a faraway look. "That night everyone longed either to be you, or to be Alaric holding you. There was an artist to the court in attendance, and he captured in pencil a magical moment between you and Alaric, which he subsequently began shaping into a painting. That is, until word reached Helionel about what the artist was working on."

"I'm sure it enraged him."

"Indeed it did. Helionel himself went with his guards to arrest the young man, who'd set up his easel in the public rose gardens, next to the capitol. But when Helionel saw the half-finished work, he couldn't help but be taken by such an exceptional rendering. So instead of arresting the artist, Helionel paid him a large sum to finish the piece — except with his own likeness in place of Alaric's."

"And this painting still hangs in the palace?"

"Yes," Khrestes sighed. "In the king's bedroom."

"Of course it does." I laughed, shaking my head.

"You should also know Gadeirus had an artist rework the painting once again," she added. "Now it bears an image of Gadeirus dancing with you."

"Of course it does."

"Gadeirus is just as brutally off-balance as Helionel was. If not more so, because of his addictions. And he has amassed even larger and more powerful crystalline weaponry than what was used to destroy Moldaaris." She looked at me sadly. "He has also reinvigorated the labs, beginning extensive experimentation into hybrid beings. He has imprisoned or maimed many of the mermaids, choosing the ones with hair and features similar to yours, and then surgically having them altered or bred with other hybrids in order to create a harem that suits him. And that's not all."

"What else?" My mind flashed to the hobbled merbeing from the market. She must have been one of the harem experiments, as her features were indeed similar to mine. "How deep is this blood bath?"

"Gadeirus is looking to create a race of dumbed-down shape-shifters. He thinks they would make superb soldiers and easy-to-control sorcerers," she answered. "Alaric is in grave danger, not only because of his connection to you—but because there's never been a better shape-shifter than your Moldaarin snake king. That's the main reason Gadeirus wanted to draw him back to Atlantis. He would love nothing better than to capture Alaric and have his mad scientists dissect him. Find out how he does what he does. While imprisoning you as his own."

"Seems Gadeirus has gone to a lot of trouble for someone who has at best weeks to live."

"He's known all along his psychic surgeons can repair your essence. They're the same ones who split your soul."

"I see." Closing my eyes, I prayed to Highest Light for inspiration and guidance. Moments later, ideas began to flash before me. "Tell me, is the grounding in of hope and love I did at the palace holding?"

"Yes. And so far it has gone undetected."

"Good. I know Hunter and the others had been planning to strengthen and reinforce it."

"Yes. And that seems to have all gone well, in spite of their waning energies."

"All right. So what I'm getting is the dolphins and the mermaids can work together, using sound frequencies to keep my friends alive, while we work toward a more permanent solution. Do you see this as a viable option? At least in the short term?"

"I do." Her eyes had that faraway look again. "The combination is stronger than either on its own. And more likely to counterbalance the unnatural alterations. Especially if the Ahlaielians are immersed in the healing vibrations during sleep."

"Good. That can be arranged. Just tell me where they need to be."

"The beach is best," she replied. "Within the selenite structure, where you were married. It will magnify the healing energies."

"Perfect." I paused again, collecting my thoughts. "Now as for the more permanent solution. What if we reclaim the surgically removed essences?"

"It would be a great idea." She shook her head. "Although the ones in charge of them have cloaked them well. They're somewhere beyond my sight."

"A shape-shifter could track them, no?" There was a long silence before she spoke, and in that space I could hardly contain hope's buoyancy bubbling within.

"Yes," she said at last. "A shape-shifter could track them."

"Alaric could find them." I squirmed in my seat. "I know he could!"

"If anyone could do such a thing, it would be Alaric." She studied me with her mirrored eyes. "Yet the way is fraught with danger, Elysia. The whereabouts of your essences is behind a veil, but I do see multiple Lesser Light guardians keeping watch. They are mighty. And they will see him coming."

"Not if they see me first."

"What are you —"

"I'm no shape-shifter, Khrestes. But there is something deep within me, something ancient and beyond words, that can bring the most powerful kings to their knees." I looked at her intently. "Energetically, I seem to be the latest plaything to the unhinged ego. And the bigger, the better. Surely, as an instrument of Highest Light, I can mesmerize Gadeirus. Then through that act, create a diversion to distract the guardians. Long enough, anyway."

"Never in a million years would I think you could do such a thing," she whispered. "Not even if you were in a healthy state." She gazed at me, through me, with her mirrored lenses. "But your heart ..." She trailed off, lost in a vision. "Your heart is all hope and fire. And love. It speaks to me only of possibilities. It sees none of the risks. Or why things could never be so."

"All around us is death and danger. But there is also the promise of hope. And healing. And happily ever after," I murmured. "Ultimately we experience what we choose. Emphatically and decisively. And I choose happily ever after. For us all."

"Come here, my sister." Khrestes stood with open arms, and I hurried into her embrace, crying in witness to all that was behind and between us. And before us. Then she stood back from me, clasping my hands. "I love you so much, Elysia. I am here to guide and support in any way I can. And I will be at the beach at sundown, with our extended family, to receive you and your friends."

"I love you, too, my dear Khrestes." I squeezed her hands. "And I thank you, for all you have done—and continue to do. Highest Light willing, we'll be laughing about this one of these days."

"I so hope you are right, maharani," she replied. "With all my heart, I hope that."

TWENTY-SEVEN

Kavi surfaced where he'd first encountered Alaric and me. I slid from his back, and he again turned his cheek toward me. I petted him, thanking him for helping me reclaim what had been lost to me for so long and for being my underwater wings. Playfully, he nudged me with his nose, then he glided back out to sea.

Diving beneath the water, I swam until it was shallow. When I emerged onto golden sand, I saw Alaric approaching. He moved so beautifully in his body, the very picture of grace. I came closer, and he stopped. I stilled myself as I watched him watching me. Tilting his head, he smiled and then covered his mouth with his hands. I heard him catch his breath. He ran both hands over his forehead and through his hair. I could see his lower lip begin to quake as I closed the gap between us. Without a word I embraced him, and his arms came fast and hard around me.

Sobbing, he buried his face in my shoulder. He clung to me, and I felt his emotional floodgates open, releasing centuries of heartache and strict self-control. I cradled his head and the small of his back as the weeping subsided. Still he gripped me. For the longest time we simply stood there, clutched in each other's arms.

"Never did I dare to hope," he murmured against my skin. "Not in all these centuries did I think you would ever fully know me again." He held me away from him, his eyes vulnerable as he studied my face. "I was so happy just to have you back. I could have spent eternity being grateful for your partial remembrances of all we are. Of all we have done, and all we have felt." He caressed my cheek, my lips. "And yet I am gazing into eyes that can look upon every shared experience. Touching lips that can taste every sweetness, from all our long years together." Smiling, he shook his head. "To have you resurrected from my soul's most devout prayer seemed an unbestowable blessing. Yet here you are."

"Indeed I am," I whispered. Reaching up, I held his face in my hands. "I can see, and taste, and feel. All of it. Every precious moment."

"Khrestes brought you into alignment." He was looking at me, through me, assessing the oracle's attunement.

"Yes."

"And yet ..." His voice trailed off, as he felt into me. "Something has been worrying me. Your heart is beyond radiant. But I think it's distracting me from something in the depths. Something—"

"Yes, Alaric," I interrupted. "Something is before us that we need to address." I took his hand in mine. "Let's chat for a while. And I will tell you everything."

"All right, love." His feeling sense was back on high alert as he walked with me to the blanket. Pulling a towel from his pack, he dried me. Noticing the gooseflesh pimpling my body, he grimaced, and I felt his concern escalate as both the sun and gentle breeze were exceedingly warm. He wrapped me in the robe he'd bought, and once again had me sit down. Quietly he slid behind me, the brush resuming its delightful trek through my wet locks. "Something ... unnatural is causing you to chill so easily."

"Yes. There was a ... separating that occurred on Ahlaiele, prior to us coming here."

"Separating?" The brush continued its steady strokes, but I could feel his misgivings growing.

"It was a condition we had to accept, in order to go on the mission." I paused, carefully choosing my words. I wanted him to understand, but at the same time I didn't want to feed his uneasiness. "Psychic surgeons split our essences, taking half from each of us. The male part was extracted from Quenna, Ava, and myself. While Hunter, Will, and Kendrick had the female part removed."

"Go on."

"We were told it would help us blend in better here. That it would make us seem more like the Atlanteans, and raise fewer suspicions, if it appeared our culture was also choosing ego-based identities over light-derived completeness." My voice was hushed. "We were told it was an easy procedure to restore ourselves to wholeness, once we returned to Ahlaiele." I shook my head. "We were told many things. All of which are untrue."

"Poseidia's taint has indeed spread to the far corners of the universe." He kept smoothing my hair, as he processed what I was sharing. "So there is a weakness now in each of you, as a result of this severing."

"Yes."

"And this weakness is what has made Quenna so ill."

"Yes," I sighed. "Khrestes told me Quenna succumbed so quickly because she moves through the world in a more masculine way, being born of a more manly Color Ray. Not to mention it's male energy that grounds the soul in these physical bodies. So her loss of the male aspect of herself was felt most acutely."

"I see." He fell silent, and I allowed myself to be lulled by the brush's rhythmic caress. "Since it's male essence that brings energy and warmth and vitality, I can understand how the severing has left you tired and cold and without appetite," he continued. "Just as Quenna has become incapacitated, I'm sure different imbalances are manifesting in the others. Although there's something else I can't quite sense, something you're not yet telling me."

"There is." I pulled away from the brush, and turned to face him. "Alaric, the others and I, we were betrayed. Abandoned by Ahlaiele. Because we'd always held fast to Highest Light and Right Action. Our Elders realized our devotion. Just as they knew we had enough power among the six of us to counteract their corruption. The defilement brought about by the addictive Dark Heart energies, which Atlantis so skillfully dispenses." For several moments I paused, stunned by how raw this realization still made me feel. "The Dark Heart poisoned them all. Until they were no longer Highest Light, but Lesser. And so they kept their new allegiance concealed, bringing in seers and scientists to perform the surgeries and place us in our new physical bodies. I'm now certain the tech support team came from Atlantis."

"Yes," Alaric whispered. "Poseidia specializes in such alterations."

"Indeed," I murmured. "And then computerized frequencies were planted in our ship's mainframe, which were supposed to cut off oxygen and life support. We were meant to die long before arriving here." Again I shook my head. "The Elders knew killing us would effectively remove all resistance to the Dark Heart overtaking Ahlaiele. And yet, by the grace of Oneness, there was a problem with the frequencies. Some sort of glitch. We were spared, but—"

"More like postponed." His face was expressionless. "What you're trying to tell me is you're dying."

"Yes."

"In the name of Oneness." Ever so softly, he touched my hair, my cheeks, my arms, and I could feel him looking through me. Beyond me, to some other realm. "Your heart is so strong and fine. It simply has not accepted a death sentence. It keeps channeling more energy from the earth, through your inner cave, to compensate for the lost essence." For a time he fell silent, his gold-green eyes studying something. "The others don't have your heart, and so they weaken by the hour."

"Khrestes told me the same thing," I replied. "She will be meeting us at dusk, with the mermaids and dolphins, and they will be doing sound healings. On the beach. In the selenite formation, where we were married."

"That will buy some time. And yet it won't fix the problem."

"I know."

"But I can." He clasped my hands, drawing them to his lips. "I can track your essence. Bring it back. Along with those of your friends."

"I knew you were going to say that. And so I discussed the possibility with Khrestes." I looked at him, at the light glinting off his sable and gold hair. At his sun-bronzed skin. At the devotion staring down at me, from gold-green eyes that nearly stole my breath. "Alaric, there's such danger awaiting you. I—"

"Really?" His smooth voice dripped sarcasm as he laid me on the blanket. There was a light in his eyes I couldn't interpret. And a deep, cold stillness that made me realize how formidable he could be. "I don't fear this blackness. I have long walked among risk and shadow. I am prepared. There's nothing more deadly than a snake before the strike. So consider me coiled." He smiled as he kissed me again. "Now tell me of these perils."

"Our essences are somewhere beyond Khrestes' vision," I murmured against his lips. He began kissing my neck, and I sighed, trying to keep my focus. "But she could see they were being protected. By multiple Lesser Light guardians. Who would be waiting for you."

"Yes." He caressed me beneath the robe, and I pulled him closer. "They're watching because they know I will come. It's all part of a scheme Gadeirus devised in his insatiable quest for power."

"There's more you should learn."

"About Gadeirus?" His lips and hands continued to explore. "And his obsession with you?"

"How did you know—"

"Is it not obvious?" He kissed me again, more deeply this time.

"But his interest in me is only part of the issue." I sifted his hair with my fingers. "Khrestes told me he wishes to capture you, to have his puppet scientists dissect you in order to figure out how to make a race of shape-shifters. Because once they learn how to duplicate shape-shifting abilities, they will further engineer their creations to be good soldiers and sorcerers. Slaves, essentially, who will obey blindly, never questioning their motives. And who knows what Gadeirus would do with such an army. With that kind of power." I shook my head. "He's already been experimenting on the merfolk. And I can't bear the thought of that happening to you."

"Darling, I've long known what Gadeirus wants of me." He traced my jaw and my lip with his thumb. "I told you I know the lay of the land here. I'm aware of the need to be mindful. I realize he had you embodied to fulfill his lustful longings. But he also understood you were the one thing that would not only draw me here, but perhaps make me—shall we say—less cautious."

"So Gadeirus probably knows what has become of our essences."

"Indeed he does," he murmured. "He had them put in the one place I would know best where to find them. And least wish to go."

"Are you saying you know where they are?!"

"Yes, I'm saying that."

"Where?" I could feel the heaviness of resignation in his body, and it filled me with dread. "Oh no. Alaric, please. What has Gadeirus done with our essences? And why is it where you'd least want to go?"

"They are with Linasia." He combed his fingers through my tresses, his eyes distant. "Under her watch. In the very castle where I lived with her daughter."

"For the love of Oneness." My eyes brimmed with tears. "Perhaps they meant us to survive the initial trip here after all. So you'd attempt to retrieve the essences, only to be returned to the hellish prison from whence you'd escaped."

"The others were not meant to live," he replied, his eyes still focused on a distant horizon. "But you were. Gadeirus' advisors knew enough about hybrids to realize you possessed sufficient strength to endure the lack of life support. You would simply have slipped into a hibernation-like state, where your body would reset itself and begin functioning on its own again once oxygen was provided." Briefly he quieted, deep in thought. "As long as you survived, Gadeirus knew I would come for you. And return to Zacktronymus without question."

"But you cannot." I slipped my hands along his bare chest, his skin smooth and warm in the sun. "There must be another way. I just can't allow—"

"I'm going, love." He kissed me firmly. "It's the only way. Because we don't have much time. And because I know what must be done. As well as how."

"Alaric, no—"

"It's all right, Elysia." He eased himself on top of me. Supporting his weight on his elbows, he held my head in his hands. "I do not fear Gadeirus. Or Linasia. If this were a battlefield or a game of chess, I would say they've made a clever move. Those with wisdom would not react in fear or with a sense of defeatism. But instead honor the shrewdness. Say 'well played'. Take the lesson offered by acknowledging a worthy opponent—and know the adversary better as a result. Then act from what has been learned, from a centered place of strength. Only from that balanced state can Highest Light flow unimpeded. And that flow is what will take us where we need to be."

"I know you speak the truth," I whispered. "But to have you go alone, with no one watching your back. It doesn't feel right."

"To be a shape-shifter is to be alone, in terms of the work I do." Again he kissed me. "No one can see or follow me, not if I'm aligned with Spirit. Not unless I'm distracted." He smiled knowingly at me. "And the one thing that drives me to distraction is you. Don't you see that's why I couldn't possibly take you with me?"

"Yes." I stared at him, my heart in my eyes. "But I desire very much to go with you."

For several moments he peered at me. Then he looked away, laughing.

"What bewitchery is this?" His lips grazed my neck. "How is it my iron will and steadfast resolve are crumbling before you?"

"It's a gift," I whispered. I twisted my hands in his hair, bringing his lips to mine. "One of my strengths. It's how I can help you. And why you should take me with you."

"You would be the death of us both, love." He took my hands and held them against the blanket.

"What if I were our salvation?" Again I looked at him, as I drew from my inner cave. "To be someone's obsession is to have a powerful hold over what they perceive. It's not just Gadeirus who is infatuated with me, you know. Linasia is as well. I can feel it."

"I don't think—"

"I know it's not what you had in mind." I shivered beneath him, feeling a wave of cold overcome me as he bit my neck. "I also know you're just trying to protect me. So tell me I'm wrong. Tell me a man ever notices a beautiful woman before another woman does. Tell me Linasia hasn't been enamored of me since the days of Helionel." My voice quivered as my teeth began to chatter. "Tell me she isn't crazy jealous of me. And that she hasn't begged you to make love to her as if she were me."

"Darling, please." He kissed me hard, as if to drive out my insistence on wading into these unpleasant waters. He pressed against me, and I could feel the quality of the light change. I opened my eyes and noticed we were on the floor of our hotel room, by the hot spring—blanket, bags, and all. In one quick movement, he was on his feet.

Before I could say anything, he'd scooped me into his arms. The room was cool, and gooseflesh crawled over my skin. He'd noticed it even before I did, as he carried me to the side of the pool, where he stripped me of the robe.

"Come with me. Into the warmth," he whispered as he removed first his own and then my swimsuit. "I don't want you using your strength to maintain your temperature." Gently he took me in his arms again, and then waded into the spring. Once he'd reached the level that was neck-deep for me, he eased me down so I could lean against the side of the pool. "While you were meeting with Khrestes, I arranged to have some food waiting for us. Rest here for a few minutes, and I will bring something to you."

"Alaric, thank you—it's just—"

"No arguments, love." He cradled my face, so he could look into my eyes. "I know you're not hungry. But your body needs fuel to keep producing energy to compensate for your missing essence. And for my thoughtless vibrations."

"I don't know what you mean—"

"I will explain once I've brought you something to eat." He placed a finger against my still shivering lips. "I'll be right back." Lifting himself from the water, he grabbed a towel from the glass shelf and dried his body as he slipped into the other room.

For several moments, I closed my eyes and rested my head against the marble. The heat felt like a hug as it enveloped my freezing flesh. I noticed the fatigue was back, though, which seemed to go hand-in-hand with the wintry bitterness inside. Yet I had to admit I was starting to wonder why I was insisting on going to Zacktronymus. Some help I would be if I couldn't even keep myself warm and upright for a few hours in a row.

Minutes later, Alaric returned with a tray. Placing it by the pool's edge, he lowered himself into the water beside me. Then he handed me a bowl and spoon. Steam rose from the fragrant liquid. Taking a bowl for himself, he eyed me carefully, as if he thought I wouldn't eat unless he watched.

"Thank you." I sipped the soup. It was hot and pungent, deliciously spiced, with multiple vegetables floating in its reddish broth. "What is it?"

"Deluxe bone broth, you might say." He smiled as he swallowed the hot liquid. "Do you like it?"

"Very much." I started to say more, then thought better of it.

"I know what you're thinking." His velvety voice was hushed. "You're wondering what I meant about my thoughtless vibrations. But even more than that, you want me to answer you about Linasia."

"Yes. Tell me I'm wrong, and I'll accept you at your word."

"You're not wrong." Momentarily, he studied the soup before once again meeting my gaze. "Everything you said is true."

"Everything?"

"Yes."

"And so you don't think I could be helpful with her?" He placed his bowl on the edge of the pool. Then he poured hot tea into a cup on the tray. His eyes stayed on the tea as he began to sip. I put my mostly finished bowl down and took a step toward him. "Hey," I whispered, placing my hand on his cheek.

"Let me pour you some tea." He set his cup down and reached for the teapot, turning so my hand slipped from his face.

"I'll have tea in a bit." Moving closer, I grasped his shoulders. And I turned his big body so he faced me. I could feel his complex layered web of protection, as if a spider had spun it from steel. Finally, he looked at me, his eyes veiled. And somber. "Whatever it is, Alaric, it's all right. Please. Just don't armor yourself against me."

"I have no defenses for you." His voice was a bare whisper. His fingers traced my cheek, the curve of my neck, down the front of my body. "What you're sensing is the coping mechanism I long ago created. For dealing with Linasia. And everything in her world. It's conditioned response, nothing more. But it is a thoughtless vibration to be holding in your presence—one born of a frozen heart—and for that I most humbly apologize. As I resolve to hold a higher frequency."

"It's all right," I murmured, touching his chest. "There is such harshness in that remembered space. Such brutality. And rage."

"Indeed." His eyes had that faraway look again, and I knew he was gazing upon the past. "For a long time I channeled my pain into those frequencies. I was often beyond rage, which took me to a silent, icy space. Now, all of these centuries later, speaking of Linasia is something I can do and remain detached. But the idea of you going into her den, where she would like nothing better than to claw out your heart, brought up that well-rehearsed reaction. Which is what you'd begun to feel from me when we were on the beach. And what prompted your chill."

"Yes."

"I spent eons in that deathly cold," he continued. "I was numb emotionally, but I could still think and speak. And perform. It mattered not that I was in a cage. Fate had already placed me in prison. And I gladly remained behind bars, in order to keep you safe and peaceful."

"You should have let me go, Alaric." Tears escaped my eyes, as I looked upon the man who had sacrificed all of himself for me. "Just let me reincarnate in Atlantis."

"No, love." He took me in his arms. "Watching you begin a cycle of lifetimes worse than death would have been much, much more terrible. I realize now how long I kept myself in such a low vibrational state, devoid of hope or joy, which simply perpetuated my prison term." Slowly he ran his hands along the length of my body. "I never stopped loving you. But I came to believe in my despair. I felt only the distance between what once was—and what I feared could never be." He shook his head. "It was only when I began to allow myself to think of you—of the real, actual, physical possibility of you—after so many centuries, that things began to change. Not my external circumstances—that would come later. But first it was my attitude that had to shift."

"You began to hope." I grinned at him, as I had felt hope's distinctive upward energy surge as he'd been speaking.

"Yes." He smiled at me. "A series of what one might call 'coincidences' occurred, which were so dramatic I thought one of two things was happening. Either I was losing my mind altogether. Or Highest Light wanted me to liberate myself from my self-imposed sentence and would somehow provide a way back to you. If I could just become impeccable with my frequency."

"Tell me. How was Highest Light getting through your arctic layering?"

"By sending me flowers." He touched my cheek. "Red lotuses, to be exact."

"That's our flower."

"Yes. The blossom on our coat of arms. The bud on my lapel when we would court at court. The petals covering this very floor the first time I ever made love to you." Slowly, and with such feeling, he kissed me. "For me, the red lotus had always been such a pure symbol of our love. Of our open hearts, and our passion."

He stroked my hair, his eyes once again focused on things past. "I first felt Helionel's hand in the bargain I'd struck with Linasia when I realized not just some, but all the things I'd ever really loved sharing with you were being cast in a distasteful light. Traveling. Horseback riding. Sailing. Swimming. Courting at court. Being king and queen. Flirting. Sex. I found myself in a position where I was expected to experience all of these things—only not with you. The wicked irony fueled my rage, and iced over my heart, for centuries."

"Khrestes said you didn't know about Helionel."

"Even a seer cannot peer fully into my depths, love. All snakes abhor outright exposure, so the ability to sink unobserved into obscurity is a gift. It's a blessing feelers like you and I share." He continued to caress my hair. "On her own, Linasia would not have thought to go for my jugular. She was mostly interested in getting her needs met. But she was easily swayed by Helionel. And he wanted to drive home every nail in my crucifixion. Yet in spite of their efforts to keep me in a place of suffering, neither Helionel nor Linasia ever taunted me with a red lotus. Looking back now, it seems the lotus could have been an obvious means of torture. However, its significance was the one thing I'd shared with you that they somehow overlooked. Or Highest Light all along had a plan for this sacred plant. I would say centuries passed without me ever laying eyes on its ruby loveliness."

"Oh, Alaric," I sighed. "I'm glad something stayed precious to you in all those difficult years."

"I sense Krestes told you of Linasia's backroom bargaining. How I was routinely sold to the highest bidder she could orchestrate while courting at court." He was watching me closely, and I held his gaze with all the love I felt for him.

"Yes."

"The deal I struck with her was unclean on so many levels," he whispered. "Bartering away my body and soliciting my soul were dirty lines in the contract. My every cell felt the stain. Only the remembrance of you—and the lotus as a symbol of you—remained pristine within me."

"Heart of my heart." Fresh tears fell from my face. "You kept your honor, rising as unsullied as the lotus, over and over—through all these dark, muddy waters." Lovingly, he wiped at my cheeks, even as his own eyes moistened. "All I see is your untouched magnificence."

"Elysia." His voice was so soft. Fragile, even. He looked at me, in that way he had of looking through me. "Let me get you dried and settled. And then I will tell you about the red lotuses."

"All right." Before I could move, he'd gathered me in his arms and was carrying me from the spring. Once he'd dried my hair and body, he slipped me into the absorbent softness of one of the robes. As he fastened a towel around his waist and dried off his hair, I sat on the bed's edge. Then he was beside me, sliding my legs between the sheets.

"Are you comfortable, darling?" Removing his towel, he nestled beside me.

"Very."

"Then I shall tell you about the flowers."

"Please. There's nothing better than a great love story, you know." He laughed, kissing my forehead.

"Indeed." For several moments he lay still. I could feel him unlocking a vault long sealed. "Even though I could teleport among the various planets for my courting at court dates, I usually traveled by starship. I found it oddly comforting to be sitting among strangers who knew nothing of me. Or the nature of my journey."

Softly he sighed. "Five years ago, on a return trip from one of the bigger planets in the Great Central Sun region, I was waiting at a transfer station for a craft to take me to Zacktronymus. Near the boarding platform, I was approached by a woman and her daughter, who was perhaps six years old. The woman smiled awkwardly at me, saying she didn't know why, but her daughter had seen me standing there, and then insisted her mother get me a gift from the station's florist. And it had to be this particular gift.

"The next thing I know, a beautiful green-eyed child is staring at me. With your eyes. I was completely taken aback. And then the girl handed me a bowl with a blooming red lotus. She said, 'This is for you, to let you know you don't have to be sad anymore'. I was beyond words. With tears in my eyes, I hugged them both. I could feel the first cracks in my frozen heart begin to spider outward." His voice wavered with emotion. "For the rest of the trip, I held the bowl so tightly it's a miracle it didn't break. And I thought of nothing but you.

"From then on, the red lotus just kept showing up. In unexpected places. And incredible ways. I found, after seeing not a single blossom for centuries, all of a sudden I rarely entered a castle where I wasn't greeted by some sort of red lotus arrangement right near the door. Out of nowhere, I was being adorned with red lotus boutonnieres again, as if they'd mysteriously come back into fashion. I found more and more of the women who'd paid so much money for me were less interested in my body. Instead, they longed to hear about the woman I so clearly and completely loved. And though I never once mentioned a red lotus, these women would often send me home with a bowl of them. It happened so frequently I'm sure Carinnia, if she'd still been alive, would have wondered about it. Even in her mostly drunken stupor, she would have questioned why the castle was filling up with red lotus flowers."

"How amazing," I mused.

"It was." He hugged me to his chest. "For five years, I was being prepared. The seed had been planted, and my only duty that mattered was tending it. Feeding it, watering it, nurturing it. And in order to do that, I knew enough about energy seeking its likeness that I realized I would have to heal my rage. As well as release any emotional charge with Gadeirus and Linasia. Because only pure love would draw your virtuous heart to me."

Another pause ensued, and I could feel him moving through that other space and time. "It was during this period I felt particularly vulnerable, and during my visits to Poseidia, I developed a friendship with Charlaeus. Her husband had just died, and she'd loved him dearly. I felt we could relate to each other's passion for another. But our relationship became something deeper for her. For me, she was some sort of remedy for my loneliness, a byproduct of too often being in the forced company of others."

He took a deep breath, and I could feel my heart in my throat. "At the time I didn't realize it, but she was helping me heal. She served as the bridge that was leading me back to myself, where I could rise from the murky depths and be ready to open up to you again. Now I can see the whole of my path was being guided by the metaphor of the lotus. But also the symbolism of the bamboo tree. Do you know of it?"

"Doesn't it have to be tended for four years on sheer faith alone? Because nothing springs forth from the ground?"

"Yes," he replied. "And then in the fifth year, in a flash of forceful growth, it shoots 80 feet in the air, in a matter of weeks."

"And so in your fifth year —"

"During one of my courting at court dates, I learned Ahlaiele would soon be sending a delegation to Atlantis. Energy poured from my crown down through my body, and I knew Highest Light was letting me know you would somehow be a part of it."

"What did you do?"

"I offered up a prayer of thankfulness," he murmured. "And vowed to perfect my thoughts in the little time left. Because I was determined this opportunity, when it finally came, would be mine for the asking." Again he stilled himself before continuing. "I gave myself permission to feel my love for you, and I did my best to allow you to flow freely through my veins once more. At every opportunity I spent time thinking of you, and expanding my heart. I practiced gentleness and patience and kindness. And I cultivated my Atlantean connections, because I realized knowing intimately the lay of the land here would only be helpful in reconnecting me with you. Through the workings of Highest Light, I befriended Gadeirus' sister Arianna. And she introduced me to the rest of the family. Including Gadeirus, who was not surprisingly most interested in me."

"I'll bet he was."

"On multiple occasions, he invited me to the palace. For dinner and dancing. I instructed him in the subtle art of courting at court, of which he seemed most eager to learn. I realized he was desperately lonely, and he pined for you in a way that began to feed my compassion, facilitating my own healing."

For another long moment he was quiet. "Once, I arrived early for a dance lesson with him. I was shown into a parlor, which overlooked one of the rose gardens. As I waited, I peered out the window and saw an artist working feverishly on a painting. I was struck by how much the man was feeling from his canvas, and I was curious what subject would arouse such passion. He appeared to study the light and several sketches, and then moved his easel in such a way so I could gaze upon his subject. Which was you, dancing in the arms of an as-yet unfinished Gadeirus. Surrounded, of course, by red lotus blossoms." He shook his head. "But just like the painter, I could sense the original energy embedded in the work. The postures and expressions were ours, and still quite powerfully held the energy of you and me."

"Khrestes mentioned this painting," I replied. "It was inspired by us courting at court the first time we met Helionel. Who had himself painted over you long before Gadeirus ordered the image reworked to include his own likeness."

"Staring out that window, I could appreciate how any man would want to be the one holding you," he whispered against my forehead. "I just kept looking at your face, remembering the feel of your body beneath that silk gown. How it had felt courting at court with you that evening, all those centuries ago. Among a red lotus garden they'd prepared for the express purpose of honoring our coat of arms." Quietly he laughed. "I thought of that painting before we danced last night. I felt so exhilarated, so alive, when suddenly there were five stories of red lotuses surrounding the dance floor. It was as if the whole Universe inspired me to propose."

"My love." I kissed him, and he took me in his arms. He unwrapped my hair, his mouth on mine as he laid me back against the sheets. I felt him tremble. Deeper layers of his ice had surfaced. Determined not to feel the cold, I channeled love up through my inner cave as powerfully as I could, from my heart to his. Sighing, he held me closer, and soon the tremor subsided. I tried to free myself from the robe, and for a moment he pulled away.

"Are you sure?" That smooth voice was so tender. So caring. And careful. "Perhaps I should dry your hair, so you won't chill. Or maybe you will want to eat a little more first. There's also the tea, which you haven't touched —"

"It's you I desire," I said. "I want to make love to you with all that I am, now that you're more than a beautiful, blessed shadow of a memory to me. I want to experience fully all of who you are, as I once did." I could feel a wave of desire rise up through my body, and I kissed him deeply. Nimbly his fingers opened my robe, lifting me to release it from my shoulders.

"I am beyond words, love," he whispered in my ear.

"And I'm nearly beyond feelings." I moved beneath him, opening and inviting, as he pressed against me. "There's only here and now, between pleasure and surrender. Where I intend to linger."

"And where I will hold you." Sweetly and sensually he kissed me, and in that timeless moment, there was simply a free fall into ecstasy.

TWENTY-EIGHT

Afternoon sunshine sparkled on the stemware, creating lemon-water rainbows. We had the spacious deck to ourselves, as other patrons had chosen to stay indoors, where the temperature was artificially cooled. I was grateful to be soaking up the heat of the day, comfortable in a belted gold tunic with matching jacket. More activity stirred than when we'd ventured out earlier. Seemingly everywhere small children darted about, digging moats and building castles and making mermaid shapes in the sand. Their occasional squeals of delight filled me with joy. Throngs of couples strolled the beach, and in the mellow waves all manner of beings were splashing and swimming. Alaric sat across from me, his bronze hand covering mine, as he placed our order. Inhaling the salty air, I offered up my thankfulness to Highest Light that I could be feeling such happiness.

"You look radiant, love," he said when the server left. Alaric was wearing light pants and a collared shirt open to the chest. The sleeves were rolled to the elbow, revealing his muscular forearms.

"I feel euphoric. You have that effect on me."

"Do I now?"

"Absolutely intoxicating."

"Then I don't know which of us is more inebriated. You are a potent potion. And I have happily indulged." The server returned with hot tea, which she poured into a cup for me before setting the teapot on the table. Alaric thanked her as she left, and then for several moments he simply held me with his eyes. "Being with you brings me such pleasure," he said at last.

"Keeping your company is a wish fulfilled. Truly I want for nothing."

"There's something I'd like."

"Anything."

"Ride with me." Fire flickered in his eyes, and my own passion stirred when he mentioned horses. "We still have plenty of daylight before we need to be back for Khrestes and your friends."

"Let's go!" I practically leaped from the table. He laughed as he caught my arms.

"Not so fast. You've got to eat something first." Solemnity straightened his smile. "You need to keep up your strength, Elysia. Until your essence is reintegrated, you have to be very deliberate about food and rest."

"I know," I sighed, dropping down again at the table. "You're right, of course. I suppose the idea of riding with you, after all these centuries, simply made me forget about lunch."

"I realize you're not hungry, darling." He topped off the tea before placing the cup in my hands. "And I understand other things are more appealing to you now than food. But you need to promise me you will eat regularly, in the short time I must be away from you. I've already made arrangements with the hotel to bring nourishing meals in my absence. Whatever you would like, from any restaurant or from room service."

"Absence? But we haven't—"

"There's really nothing to decide, love." He sipped lemon water in the sunlight, his wedding ring flashing against the glass. "As I've said to you, I know what must be done. And I have the skill to do it. But I need to go alone."

"Alaric." I barely had breath to whisper his name as the server returned with our food. While he chatted with her, I set down my tea and hobbled to the railing. I visualized air filling my lungs, and I gripped the weathered wood as I felt for my inner cave. Being upset made it more challenging to ground and center myself within my power. I asked Highest Light for help. Then Alaric was loosening my hands, interlacing his fingers with my own as he rested his head against mine.

"It's all right. Shhhhh." I leaned against him, my body cold and trembling. He let go of my hands and engulfed me in his arms. I could feel his spider-silk energy settling me. His breath found mine, and he helped breathe me into a peaceful state. "Sit with me and eat."

"But I—"

"Please. I will discuss anything you'd like, and I promise I will hear what you have to say. Just first come and have lunch with me." His words were mesmerizing. After all these centuries, I of course knew he could hypnotize simply by speaking. Yet considering how raw I felt, I welcomed his spell.

"Okay." Wearily I sank into my seat. He eased beside me and began filling bowls and plates for us from the different dishes covering the table. The food was delicious. Multiple steamed vegetables in pungent sauces. Grilled fish and sweet potato soup, and salad with soft cheese and walnuts. Had I been hungry, it would have been a heavenly culinary experience. As it was, I so appreciated the pleasing taste and warmth, and yet in spite of all the savories before me, I found I had to make myself eat. But Alaric was right—the meal produced the desired effect. It wasn't long before the tea and the food warmed me, and I began to feel more like myself.

"That's more like it," he said, caressing my chin. "Your color has returned."

"I'm so grateful for your care." I smiled at him. "I do feel better. Much better, in fact. And I do promise to be more mindful of eating. I cannot allow myself to weaken. Or you to worry."

"It does my heart good to hear you say that, love." He clasped my hand. "Worrying about you is the biggest interference I could have. And it serves none of our purposes."

"I know." I could feel the balanced queen once again ascending her throne, channeled through my inner cave. "I believe I can finally hear you, Alaric. With me being in a more delicate state, I accept I must find another way to help you, to assist us all, besides accompanying you to Zacktronymus." I peered at him, my heart in my eyes. "But I intend to be of service. I sense there's an important duty yet I must perform. Even if it's in your absence."

"Nothing is more important to me than securing your essence and making you safe and strong again. Nothing," he whispered. "And to that end I will abide, knowing it means I must leave you for a while. That parting in and of itself is enough to give me pause, if I allow it. Which I cannot, and still keep my absolute focus on what needs to be done. So when I sense you are speaking of putting yourself consciously in harm's way—especially now, when you're needing support yourself—my heart is not only cautious. But worried." Leaning over, he kissed my cheek. For a moment his lips lingered on my skin as he sighed. "How can I convince you the most powerful action you could take right now is no action at all?"

"You speak of wu wei," I murmured. "The act of non-acting. A means of leading by flowing with what is. By moving through life naturally."

"Yes." He squeezed my hand as the waitress cleared the table. While he spoke with her, I again felt such gratitude for him. And when he looked back at me, his gold-green eyes nearly made me catch my breath. "You've always been a master at embracing wu wei, darling."

"Expertise easily flows from what feels right and true," I replied. "And just as Mother Earth continues to spin around the sun shining on us now, with no notice being taken of her revolution, and just as the trees and flowers simply grow without striving, I promise you not necessarily inaction but Right Action. To holding fast to my deepest sense of flowing unseen with what is. And from that level of wu wei, surely I will evoke no angst within you."

"You are a seductress of semantics if I've ever met one." He laughed as he kissed me. "Why don't you tell me where your sense of Right

Action is leading you? And I will let you know if it worries me or not."

"Left to your own devices, you would have me bolted and barred behind our hotel room's imposing doors."

"I won't deny that would bring me some measure of comfort." He smoothed my hair with his fingers. "Although lock and key would not long hold you. Not with you remembering your power. And looking for a way to wield it, however silent and unseen the intention."

"Would you have me do nothing then? While you bare your throat in the she-wolf's lair?"

"I would have you stay still and self-caring until your essence is restored. Before you give in to the urge to bare your throat in the king's lair."

"What makes you think—"

"Because you are so much like me, love." The waitress returned with a single dish and two spoons. Alaric thanked her before turning his gaze back to me. "Because we are in parallel situations here. You with Gadeirus, and I with Linasia. Because I can feel you feeling into my task at hand. So you can see how to distract and deflect within your sphere of influence in order to help shield me." He lifted breeze-blown hair behind my ear. "Because you would do anything to save me. Except save yourself first."

"I would do anything to save you," I whispered. "Every time I feel into this situation, I am guided to a singular thought. That distracting Gadeirus—and keeping him off-balance—would prevent the puppet-master from pulling his marionette strings. And as a result, Linasia should be easier to mesmerize."

"You know so many of my ways." He smiled at me, although his eyes seemed focused on some distant horizon. "You could easily be a shape-shifter in your own right. Yet Gadeirus is a bigger challenge than Linasia."

"Because of his ego?"

"Because he's violent." Alaric traced a finger over my arm, where Gadeirus had cut me with his nails. "His addictions make his rage— and his cruelty—even more unpredictable. You called out the abuser in him, which means he'll be looking to draw blood the next opportunity he gets. Or worse. So if distracting Gadeirus is your perceived sense of Right Action, then I'm afraid it worries me very much indeed."

"I would never seek purposely to worry you. But Gadeirus needs to be addressed. And powerfully so, I might add. How else do you see being able to retrieve our essences?"

"By going tomorrow. When he will least expect it. He will already have his focus diverted in a number of ways. It's my understanding there will be diplomatic meetings all morning and afternoon. And he will be highly anticipating seeing us both at the palace dinner."

"But your absence tomorrow evening will raise eyebrows."

"By that time, his suspicions will no longer have a direct bearing on me obtaining the essences, as I should have them in my possession. And be en route to friends I've already mind-messaged, who have the skill set to be able to restore them." He paused, studying my reaction. "Once the restoration has taken place, however long that takes, then I will come for you and the others."

"Exactly when did you plan all of this?" I gave him my best bedroom smile. "I thought for sure I'd had your undivided attention." He laughed as he hugged me to him, the muscles of his arms rippling against my back.

"If we weren't in a public place, I would show you just how rapt my attention has been," he whispered in my ear. "As it is, I could recount for you every sigh, every shiver. I could recite every time you were beyond words. And when you took me even beyond feelings."

"I'm headed somewhere beyond feelings right now. But it's somewhere between blunted and numb." I pulled away just far enough so I could see his eyes. "My body's trying to deaden the feeling place in me, Alaric. So I can be brave. All these parts of me are wild with fear at the idea of being away from you. Because of the very real danger of losing you. All over again."

"You are brave, love. It doesn't mean there's an absence of fear. Just a determination to go on in spite of it." He cradled my face in his hands. "This is just a brief but necessary detour on our journey together. I want you to keep thinking of the 'happily ever after' part. Because we are going to have that. And soon. With everything I am, I promise it won't be another thousand years."

"I'm going to hold you to 'happily ever after'. And 'soon'." Briefly, longingly I kissed him.

"Before the sun rises, I mean to explore with you even more ways of how 'happily ever after' is going to look and feel. And taste." He reached for the spoon and dish the waitress had left. "Try this with me."

"What is it?"

"A local specialty. Made from raw cacao, honey, and rum, along with rich spices."

"It's really good," I mumbled, my tongue thick with the sweet delicacy he offered. Bite by bite, he fed us the cacao dessert from a shared spoon.

"There's a place I'd like to take you. On horseback. Where we could be alone for a while." His gold-green eyes held the same longing I felt. That there wasn't enough time between now and when he was leaving for us even to begin feeling satiated, before once again facing a period of separation.

"Take me," I whispered. He smiled wickedly, his eyes burning into mine as he lifted my hand to his lips.

"As soon as I settle our tab." In one supple movement, he rose from his chair. Before I could reply, he was halfway across the wooden deck. I watched him disappear inside the restaurant's glass doors, and then I walked to the railing to wait.

Looking out at the turquoise water, I selfishly wanted as many as possible of the last hours before Alaric left to be ours. Every time I thought of his absence, my heart stumbled, and I felt the sting of tears. I knew he was right, though. I couldn't focus on my fear or else I would feed it, allowing it to grow. I had to find a way to keep my attention tuned to a higher vibration, one that nourished my hope instead. So I closed my eyes, steadied my breath, and prayed to Highest Light to guide and protect him. In my mind's eye, I saw him returning to me, and lingered in the excitement of what it would be like for him to touch me again after time apart. Then, as if on cue, I felt his lips on my neck.

"Let's get you into something more appropriate for riding." Taking my hand, he led me down the deck stairs. I felt him tuning in to see if any passersby were observing us. At the bottom of the steps, he took me in his arms and kissed me. I melted against him as the light shifted, and then we were standing in the midst of our hotel room.

Gently, he guided me to the dressing area. We entered the first of two well-lit oval chambers, with ivory walls and multiple mirrors. I examined the rows of hanging clothing as he slipped into the room beyond. Changing in front of the mirrors, I noticed my color was still pink, and so far I'd kept warm. I was just fastening my belt when I felt him watching. I turned to see him dressed in similar earth tones, sleeves rolled to the elbow, with boots raising him at least another towering inch.

"You look beautiful," he murmured.

"You're quite dashing yourself."

"Are you ready?"

"So ready." A silken finger slipped along my lip, and once more the light changed. I looked around and saw we were shielded behind some tall grasses, outside a large barn complex. The structures were a silvery metal, with copper roofs and trim that gleamed in the midday sun.

"Come with me." Hand in hand, we approached the idyllic setting. Beyond the stables stretched open pasture, with select shade trees and ponds teeming with herons. To the right curved a path leading into the forest. Before I could absorb any more of this loveliness, we reached the barn, which smelled of hay and feed and leather. A short, stout man with brownish-gray curls lugged buckets along the stable's center aisle. I heard him whistling as he hastened toward where we stood, in the barn's wide double-door entry. Looking up, he chuckled as his dark eyes crinkled.

"Hello, Alaric!" He thumped the buckets down and hurried over. "I'd heard you were visiting. How are you, lad?" Vigorously he and Alaric locked forearms.

"Very well, Dehk." Alaric placed his hand on Dehk's shoulder. "I'm most happy to see you."

"Aye." He slapped Alaric good-naturedly on the back. "And who is this stunning woman?" Dehk asked, turning friendly eyes to me.

"This is Elysia, my wife," Alaric replied. "Elysia, this is Dehkonius, a very old friend of mine."

"Not that old, I hope!" Dehk laughed. I felt questions turning in his mind, as I'm sure he'd often seen Alaric in the company of Charlaeus. He reached for my hand, softly kissing it. "Lassie, it's an absolute pleasure to meet you. Please call me Dehk."

"Thank you, Dehk." I smiled at him, appreciating how he made me feel immediately comfortable. "I look forward to getting to know you."

"Likewise, dear." He grinned at me before turning brooding eyes on Alaric. "So where've you been hiding her, lad? And why wasn't I invited to the wedding?"

"Elysia and I have been in love forever, Dehk, but circumstances had us living separate lives. Until quite recently," Alaric explained. I could feel Dehk reading between the lines as Alaric spoke, but he said nothing. "We were married last night, on the beach."

"Well, congratulations then!" He hugged us both. "I feel honored to be seeing you on your first day as husband and wife."

"Thank you. I really wanted Elysia to meet you." Alaric smiled at the older man. "You're one of my most trusted friends here on this island, and I have some business that will take me away for a short while. I'm hoping if she needs anything—"

"Say no more, lad. I'm here for you both. And Elysia, you might as well consider yourself adopted. Because this boy's always been like a son to me. So anything you need—anything at all—you come to me."

"Thank you," I replied, touched to the point of tears.

"It's all right, lass." His own brown eyes moistened, and I realized he was much more of a feeler than he'd probably acknowledge. "So," he said, looking from Alaric to me and then back to Alaric. "Are you looking to ride today?"

"Indeed we are."

"Come on, then!" We followed him along the stall-lined aisle to the open door at the back. Off in the distance, I could see several horses grazing. "Elysia, can you keep up with this lad on horseback?"

"I'm going to do my best."

"Will you be needing a saddle?" His eyebrows arched as he studied me, and I knew he was curious about my skill level.

"No saddle, Dehk. And no bridle."

"Ha! So she is gonna give you a run for your money, my boy!"

"So it appears," Alaric murmured, his eyes loving me.

"Would you like me to bring some of them over, lassie?" Dehk asked. "Or do you want to see who shows up?"

"Definitely who shows up."

"She's a woman after your own heart, lad," Dehk said as he winked at Alaric.

"She is indeed."

I closed my eyes, and in my mind I summoned a steed that would wish to merge with me, much as my dolphin friend Kavi had done earlier. I felt energy bolt through my heart, and I looked up to see an all-black horse galloping toward us. Both Alaric and Dehk began laughing. When the mare stopped in front of me, blowing on my outstretched hands, I turned and looked quizzically at the two men.

"Not only a run for his money, but on his favorite horse!" Dehk was clearly amused. "None other than the lovely Sanadara herself has graced you with her presence, lass."

"She's magnificent," I whispered, petting the mare's mane that hung well below her neck and admiring her sleek conformation.

"Aye. That's what 'Sanadara' means in the Old Tongue. And she most surely is magnificent. As well as picky about who rides her." He scratched his chin. "I've been here for a good number of years, and Alaric is the only one Dara willingly has come to. Until now."

"I'm honored," I told Dara, who nickered while Alaric admired me with his eyes.

"Who will come in her stead?" Dehk asked, turning to Alaric.

"He's on his way," Alaric replied. Just then I heard the distant rumble of hooves. From across the field, a horse seemed to float toward us. He was the color of gray marble, and looked as if he'd been chiseled by an artist's hand. The horse was tall and showy. He shook his head as he ran, and I could feel his keen fire. As he neared, I noticed his mane and tail had practically every possible color — white, gray, blond, red, brown, and black. Abruptly he slid to a stop in front of Alaric.

"Not in a thousand years would I have ever thought," Dehk mused.

"It's time for many things that haven't been considered in a thousand years," Alaric said, glancing at me as he petted the gelding. "Hello, Avalon."

"So Avalon is particular about his riders also?" I glanced between Alaric and Dehk, who were both laughing quietly.

"Avalon's so fussy he's never had a rider before, lass," Dehk explained. "Strictly a pasture ornament. He's had plenty of trainers. Learns easily enough. The boy knows what to do. He simply never wants to do it. But any number of horse people have kept trying to get him to cooperate, because he has the smoothest, most graceful gaits I've seen." He shook his head. "Maybe you had to show up before he felt he was ready."

"Maybe so." Eyeing the horse, I could sense his clever willfulness was matched only by his courageous heart. "He fears nothing. But he wants clarity and confidence in a partner, or else he will walk all over someone. Most riders possess one or the other, not both. So he brings out where someone is insecure. And most trainers can't face a horse showing them that shadow of themselves." As I spoke, Avalon yawned and then began licking and chewing, which was the sign of a horse relaxing in the presence of truth. I looked at Alaric. "If you can get the mare out of your heart for a while, you have exactly what he needs. And he can reflect much to you, about daring to hope for that one special connection. Even if it's against all odds, and a thousand years in the making."

"Such wisdom has never been laid bare before me like that, child," Dehk whispered. "That horse has never really been seen—not by any of the trainers certainly. Not like that. But you are more than a seer, aren't you lass? More like a direct channel of Highest Light." His dark eyes regarded me. "You are what we'd call a rishi, in the Old Tongue. One who speaks truth from Highest Light."

"She is all of that. And then some." Alaric's tone was hushed. "Which is another reason we may need your help in the coming days, Dehk. She's caught the fancy of none other than Gadeirus himself. And his shadow has not particularly cared for the truth she has spoken."

"Understood, lad." I felt him reading between the lines again, and I knew he was a man who would act in the face of a crisis. "Anything you need, Elysia. Anything. Just mind-message me. Or one of the horses if for some reason you can't get through to me. All they need is the barest image. And we will come to your aid."

"Oh, Dehk. Thank you." I was so moved I could hardly speak.

"It'll be all right, lass." Affectionately he cupped my chin. "Now are you ready for Dara?"

"I am." Taking a deep breath, I eased into Dara's space. Her ebony coat shone like obsidian in the sun. Telepathically, I asked her to back up, and she retreated three steps. In my mind's eye, I held a picture of us riding as one. Slowly she knelt beside me, making it easy for me to climb on her back. I twisted my fingers in her mane. And then I asked her with my feeling sense to circle: first at the walk, then the trot, and finally the canter.

She performed flawlessly. It was exhilarating once again to be in such harmony with a horse. One last time we looped the paddock's perimeter before stopping in front of the men.

"Well done, lassie!" Dehk grinned up at me, approval all over his face. "Well done!" He turned to Alaric. "You'd best get a move on, or else she's going to leave you here in the dust."

"Indeed." Alaric approached Avalon. The horse blew on his hands. Alaric backed him up just by asking clairvoyantly. Once Avalon stood still, Alaric gripped his mane in his left hand near the withers. With easy grace, he swung himself onto the gelding's straight back. They circled around and came to a halt next to Dara and me. "Are you ready, love?"

"Yes."

"We may be out late," Alaric warned his friend.

"No worries," Dehk chuckled. "The main thing is for you kids to have fun. If I'm asleep when you return, you know what to do."

"I do at that." Alaric turned Avalon and headed at a leisurely pace for the woodland trail. I guided Dara alongside him, and it brought back many happy times from centuries ago. Not only did we have horses on Moldaaris. But we rode any chance we got when we came here as well.

"I remember this trail," I said.

"I'd hoped you would. Are you up for an adventure?"

"I might be persuaded." Before he could respond, I signaled Dara and she galloped away. I heard Alaric's laughter and Avalon's rapid hoofbeats behind us. But I was thrilled to be in the lead. I had an idea where Alaric wanted to take me, so I sent Dara the mental image. I sensed she knew her way around these woods, and I simply allowed my body to mold to hers as we flew along the tree-lined path.

Just ahead the trail split, and Dara bolted to the left. We raced through thickets and brush. She had to jump two downed logs soon after we made the turn. I could no longer hear Alaric and Avalon behind us; there was just the rustling of branches and greenery. The path narrowed, and she slowed as the terrain became more rugged.

Up and up we climbed, until we reached a knoll at the top. In the distance I heard rushing water, so I knew we weren't far. We continued along the mist-covered path. After rounding another curve, I caught my breath at the spouting splendor of a waterfall. Then, I turned and grinned in spite of myself. Avalon stood in a grassy clearing, Alaric sitting tall on his back.

"What a surprise," I called out, riding up to meet them. "However pleasing it is to see you, I thought for sure we'd be here first."

"Dara took you the familiar way," he replied with a grin. "Avalon happened to know a shortcut."

"Well done. I know when I've been bested." I teased him with my eyes. "So I will humble myself before you. If the offer still stands, I believe I'm ready for that adventure now."

"You mean I don't have to persuade you?"

"I think I might like being persuaded." I reached over to him, tracing my fingers along his thigh. "Just because I said I'm ready doesn't mean I wouldn't like a little coaxing."

"I must warn you." He slid from Avalon's back. "I can be very enticing."

"Then tempt me." He pulled me from the mare into his embrace. The horses grazed as he kissed me, his hands in my hair, running along my body. Sweeping me into his arms, he carried me behind the waterfall and inside a cave with a stunning view of the cascades crashing outside. Steam spewed from cracks in the red and black stone, filling misty lagoons all around us. He removed his boots, and then ran his hands down my legs.

"You won't be needing these," he whispered, freeing my feet of footwear. Slowly he rose, his fingers undoing my shirt, as I loosened his belt. Once we'd shed every stitch and stood skin to skin, he ushered me into one of the vaporous pools. "People tend to flock here in the evenings, after the sun has set," he told me. "Although on this day, I set up a deflection shield. Because I wanted you all to myself."

"I love it when you're selfish."

"And I love it when I can love you selfishly."

In the cave's deep womb, I felt neither cold nor fatigue as we embraced. There was nothing but our rhythmic sighs, as endless as the effervescent water, until we lost ourselves in our breath.

TWENTY-NINE

The horses halted in a meadow overlooking the waterfall. On the edge of the daisy-strewn field, jasmine wrapped its tendrils around the trees in a sweet lover's embrace. From atop a towering oak, the hawk swooped in front of us, flashing her mottled body and red tail feathers. She screeched across the clearing, landing in an aging elm, its branches buckling beneath her.

"So you've a messenger, love," Alaric observed.

"She showed up the first time I left the ship. And she's been making her presence known ever since."

"Hawks are one of the most powerful guides in this realm." For a long moment he studied her. "She has much to teach. And she will shelter you, should the need arise."

"Yes. I feel that, too." He reached for my hand, lifting my fingers to his lips.

"Happy?"

"In every sense of the word." The late afternoon sun glinted off his still-moist sable and gold hair. He grinned, his teeth starkly white against bronze skin.

"Are you warm, love?"

"I am."

"We should head back soon. I want to get you out of those wet clothes before dinner."

"You're always thinking about getting me undressed."

"Only for the last few thousand years or so." He kissed me deeply, his lips lingering on mine with such tenderness it left me tearful. Suddenly Avalon snorted, stamping his hind leg, and we both laughed.

"I suppose he has only so much patience for pursuits of the heart," I said, patting the gelding's gray coat.

"He'd rather be wooing a trail he's never before blazed." Alaric rubbed Avalon's neck, before turning soft eyes to me. "Let's ride back along the beach."

I nodded, and we mind-messaged the horses to walk on. Side by side we crossed the meadow, before Alaric led us down the winding trail at the waterfall's edge. The path was well-packed earth, punctuated by rocks and flanked by stands of oak and elm. A warm mist rose off the water, and on the exposed slope hibiscus, gardenia, and plumeria blossoms greeted us with their vibrancy. All along the trail, hummingbirds and butterflies flirted with the flowers.

Everywhere I looked was beauty. In spite of all we yet had to face, I couldn't believe how fortunate I was. To be able to remember fully who I was and to reconnect with my heart's one love were such precious gifts. When we finally trotted onto the shore's golden sand, I felt wrapped in gratitude.

Riding bareback was the closest thing I'd experienced on land to swimming atop my dolphin friends. It was like flying, and I felt my heart trying to soar right out of my chest as we galloped through the foamy water. We rode past restaurants and retail establishments until Alaric slowed Avalon's pace and turned him from the ocean. Dara and I followed, and it wasn't long before I saw our destination—a beautiful wood and copper stable, nestled between two hotels, with hitching posts and hay off to one side.

Alaric stopped and slid from Avalon's back. As the gelding sifted through dried bermuda, Alaric walked over to where Dara and I waited. "I thought we could leave the horses here, where they will be cared for as we have dinner and prepare to meet the others," he suggested. "And then we could return them to Dehk's later tonight, if that pleases you."

"Of course. I've always loved late-night rides with you."

"My sentiments exactly, love."

"Alaric! How've you been?" A thin man approached us from the barn. He and Alaric locked forearms. I dismounted while they talked, thanking Dara for melding with me.

"How are you today, Mrs. Ardere?" The man had a gruff voice, with shoulder-length brown hair and blue eyes. He extended his hand as he came to meet me. "My name is Kevonious, though most folks call me Kev. I'll be caring for your horses this evening."

"Thank you, Kev," I replied. "Please. Call me Elysia. It's nice to meet you. And I appreciate you looking after Dara and Avalon here."

"My pleasure, Elysia." He took a lead rope and eased it over Dara's neck. "Dara's been here on many occasions with Alaric. But I must say I'm surprised to see Avalon. I'll bet Dehk just about flipped."

"For sure, no one was more surprised than Dehk." I patted Dara's neck. "You know about Avalon then?"

"All the horse people on the island know Dehk and his horses. And Avalon's kind of a legend. Perhaps more so in his own mind, though." We both laughed as Alaric returned. It appeared he'd already settled the gelding inside.

"No hurry in getting back here tonight," Kev said.

"Thanks, my friend." Alaric again locked forearms with him. "It will be late. I'm just not sure how late."

"That's fine." Kev bowed his head toward me. "Nice meeting you, Elysia. I'll be seeing you."

"Nice meeting you, too." I smiled at him as Alaric took my hand.

"Would you like to get changed and go to dinner?"

"Sure." He hugged me before leading me behind a tall border of decorative grass. In an instant, he brought us back to the hotel, where we exchanged damp riding clothes for dinner attire. As usual, he was ready first. I'd just slipped on a long copper dress when I felt his presence. Looking up, I smiled at just how resplendent he could be in a collared shirt and black pants.

"Need any help with that?" In the room's floor-to-ceiling mirror, I watched as he approached from behind.

"Putting it on? Or taking it off?"

"On for now," he whispered. "But only for now. I have other plans for you later."

"What plans?"

"You'll see." He kissed my neck as I fastened the gown's gold belt. "But I'll give you a hint. You'll not be needing this lovely frock. Or any manner of dress, for that matter."

"I'm intrigued, Mr. Ardere."

"That's just how I want you, Mrs. Ardere. Now let me take you where the locals eat."

In a heartbeat, the light altered, and we were in another part of the island, near the shipping docks. He eased his arm around me as we stepped out from behind some stacked crates. We ambled along a pier that led to a wooden shack, with a copper roof long weathered to green.

The establishment was low-key and crowded. We sat outside, on casual tables with benches, overlooking the busy dock with cargo ships coming and going, loading and unloading. When the food came, it was steaming hot and plentiful. And unbelievably delicious.

I did my best to eat as much as possible, in spite of my lack of appetite, as I knew we faced a busy and important evening. At the very least, my efforts pleased Alaric. Afterward we strolled along the pier, watching as the sun slipped close to the sea before he teleported us to the selenite formation.

Inside the crystalline structure, I felt its welcoming energy pulse through me. We were the first to arrive, and yet there was already a table set with serving trays, heated carafes, and vessels dispensing fruit-infused water. Beside the buffet were neatly stacked dishes and cloth napkins. And adjacent to the refreshments was a row of blankets and pillows. I looked at Alaric quizzically.

"I created a deflection shield so we wouldn't be disturbed, and then

I made some arrangements with the hotel," he explained, tracing a finger along my cheek. "The others are going to need nourishment and warmth even more than you do."

"Thank you," I whispered, and he smiled.

"They are here, love. And we need to tend to them." I nodded, and together we walked through the arched doorway opening to the ocean. The sun's brilliance had faded to frailty, but she had strength yet, just enough to bleed the last of her life force along the horizon. Just enough to see four silhouettes trudging toward us.

I felt their labored steps, and a rising sadness. Will and Kendrick managed smiles as Alaric locked forearms with them. Ava burst into a grin when she saw me, but it seemed to exhaust her. And Hunter's eyes, normally so like my own, appeared sunken in his chiseled face.

"Hey, you." Hunter sighed as my arms wrapped around him.

"Hey, yourself."

"Elysia." Ava's quiet voice still bubbled enthusiasm. "I'm so glad to see you!"

"And I'm so glad you're here. Let's get you inside." I could feel her gratitude as Hunter and I half-stumbled with her into the selenite structure. Once we lowered her onto the waiting pillows, Hunter eased himself beside her. On Ava's other side, Will and Kendrick gingerly reclined, as Alaric assisted. Just then a wave of grief swept over me, and I looked into Hunter's waiting eyes.

"Something has happened to Quenna," I murmured.

"Yes." He sighed, clasping my hand. "I'm afraid she made her transition earlier this afternoon."

"Oh, Hunter."

"There was nothing more I could do, El," he said wearily. "She was in the depths of a coma, with no male essence to spin energy into sustenance, no matter how much I channeled in."

"It's all right. You did all you could, and she's in Highest Light now." I kissed his cheek. "It's time to focus on you and the others." He nodded as I moved to check on Ava. Tears trickled from her eyes, their steady stream slicking her hair.

"I can't believe Quenna's gone, El."

"Shhhhh." I held her face in my hands. "I'm sure she's looking down on us as we speak, itching to organize our efforts here. I know she would already be redoing the way the food and beverages are set up."

"Of course she would," Ava laughed weakly.

"Have you eaten anything?" I think I finally realized how Alaric had been feeling with my lack of appetite, as I watched her slowly shake her head. "You need nourishment, Ava. Even though I know you're not hungry. Alaric has been after me to eat since the wedding, and I must say it has made a big difference for me." I held her hand in mine, and it felt as if her fingers had been dipped in ice water. "Would you eat if I bring some food over? Please?"

"I'll try."

"Good girl." I brought a blanket back for her before joining Alaric, who was preparing a tray. I could feel his spider-silk energy embrace me as I took two cups from the waiting stack.

"Make sure you have some bone broth yourself, love." He turned a spigot, releasing rich and salty goodness into a cup. "I need to make sure you keep your own energy strong. You will want to join Khrestes soon, as she has arrived."

"I promise you I will." I filled a cup I was holding half full of broth, and downed it in two large swallows. Laughing softly, he kissed my cheek.

"Would you like to take this platter over to Kendrick and Will?" he asked. "I believe Kendrick especially would like to see you before you go. And I will bring a tray to Ava and Hunter. As well as more blankets."

"Of course." I met his gaze, my heart in my eyes, before taking the serving vessel from his hands. He was emanating such a strong field of gentleness and confidence, which the selenite structure was magnifying, and it seemed the perfect frequency to foster relaxation and healing. I did my best to adjust my vibration accordingly, as I carried the tray to where Will and Kendrick were lying. Kneeling beside Kendrick, I touched his hand, which felt warm and withered.

"My dear Elysia." Feebly he squeezed my fingers. "Thank you for initiating a plan to aid us. Much of this journey so far has been ... unexpected."

"Of course." Tears leaked from my lashes. "Kendrick, I'm so sorry about Quenna."

"I know, dear." There was a break in his whisper. "She's in Highest Light now, though. So we all have much to be grateful for."

"We do indeed." I picked up the vessel of bone broth. "Please drink this. It's deeply nourishing and should assist in the healing process."

Slowly he propped himself up on one elbow. He took the broth and gulped it. I then placed a plate full of meat and vegetables in front of him, and I could see he needed no encouragement as he began wolfing the food. Patting his shoulder, I moved beside Will, who was also leaning on his elbow. Deep dark rings encircled his eyes, although he looked as relaxed as ever.

"Hey, kiddo."

"Hey, Will." I hugged him, feeling how his lean frame had thinned to bones and skin in just two days. "How are you feeling?"

"Like I was rode hard and put up wet," he muttered, and yet he winked at me. "I sure as hell have taken being an immortal for granted all these years."

"I think we all have." I smiled back at him. "I have some broth and other food for you to eat."

"Sure thing." He took the cup from my hand and, like Kendrick, inhaled it. I then gave him the plate.

"I've got to meet with Khrestes, but Alaric is here if you need anything." I kissed him on the forehead as I arose.

"El, you should know how grateful we all are." He looked up at me, his ebony eyes serious.

"You're family to me, Will. So I'm going to do anything within my power to help."

"I know it," he replied. "By the way, you're lookin' like married life is agreeing with you."

"Being married makes me so happy!"

"It sure as hell shows." He reached for my fingers, kissing them gently. "You go on now. We're in mighty fine hands."

"You are indeed." I smiled again before turning to find Alaric's eyes on me. I walked over to where he stood, filling another platter.

"Hunter at least has an exceptional appetite," he remarked.

"So do Kendrick and Will."

"Must be the male essence trying to compensate." I could sense him feeling into me. "Are you still warm enough?"

"I am. Thank you for asking."

"Your well-being is so important to me," he whispered. "Are you ready to meet Khrestes?"

"Yes." I kissed him before grabbing some towels and hastening through the doorway. Outside it was dark, but I could feel the dolphins as they circled beneath the waves. It was a night pregnant with hope, as round and full as the sky's swollen lunar orb.

A warm breeze teased my hair as I dropped the towels and slipped from my dress. Wearing nothing but skin I crossed the beach, feet sinking into cool sugar until my toes touched the tide. The water wasn't cold, but it shivered me nonetheless. Goosebumps erupted across my body and so I paused, feeling for my inner cave.

As I waded deeper, my dolphin friends began clicking and whistling. Kavi nudged me and then surfaced. I patted the cheek he turned to me. In the calm black waves, I grabbed hold of his dorsal fin. Easing myself onto his back, I felt expectant as he swam toward the lava formations nearby.

Approaching the cliffs, I heard a humming. I became aware Kavi was leading me between two submerged rows of mermaids, who I sensed were preparing for the sound healings. Around and across our path, multiple dolphins dove and jumped, playfully escorting us to where I knew Khrestes awaited me. Reaching the bubbled walls, I could see they formed a horseshoe shape.

I asked Kavi to dive with me, to take me into the heart of the horseshoe. Gracefully, he glided with me beneath the water's surface. From there, I felt the sea dwellers' loving support even more clearly. Looking around, I saw more merbeings bowing their heads as we passed. Deeper and faster we swam, until we reached the ocean floor. And there, on a circular crystalline formation with twelve mermaids, sat Khrestes.

"Elysia! Welcome, maharani!" Her lapis eyes emanated love from their mirrored depths as she communicated to me telepathically. "Please. Come sit with us."

"Thank you, my friend." I hugged her before taking a seat to her right. As I studied the fresh-faced mermaids, I bowed my head to acknowledge each one. Their waist-length hair floated around and above them, mingling many hues. Some were redheads, but there were also blondes and brunettes, and even one with silver locks. Brown, blue, green, and gray eyes gazed back at me as they returned my gesture. I could feel each one feeling into me, with a sense of wonder. And respect.

"You are looking exceedingly well." Khrestes' keen eyes absorbed my energetics, as a knowing smile brightened her heart-shaped face. "Matrimonial bliss is agreeing with you. Not to mention having such a strong shape-shifter funneling energy to you is having a most desired effect. More than I realized it could."

"Funneling energy?"

"You didn't know?" Softly she laughed, shaking her head. "Of course you didn't. Because he would never tell you. And he knew you'd never feel it."

"I don't understand —"

"Alaric has been channeling universal life force to you. Culled directly from the Great Central Sun, which once provided warmth and nourishment to your home planet of Moldaaris. It's what your body's very particles are made of, so it's an ingenious way of giving you the energy you need. And in such a way that, unless you were feeling for it, you'd never know. Very, very clever is your Alaric. He is now grounding that energy in for the others, too." Tilting her head, she eyed me carefully. "Haven't you noticed you've been feeling stronger? Warmer?"

"Yes, but I thought other factors were at play." I shook my head. "I've been better with eating and self-care and being in my inner cave's energetic space. So I didn't realize he was supporting me in that way."

"He can't help himself, really." She smiled at me. "He loves you so. And he's so strong he's not harmed by harnessing light for you." For a moment she fell silent. I could feel her studying me more deeply. "Of course, your own efforts have been helping a great deal as well. You've finally applied enough pressure yourself to slow your mortal wound's bleeding. Which in turn better allows your energetic system to hold and assimilate the life force he channels." Again she was quiet, as if considering something.

"What is it, Khrestes?"

"Gadeirus' seers and scientists have been watching Alaric." In my mind, her voice had quieted. "They've never before been able to observe him at work long enough to understand his energy makeup. To learn how he does what he does." She looked at me soberly. "He's coding the channeled energy effectively enough to hide it. It's just that Gadeirus has the best seers tracking him. And so even a blank trail is still a pathway, one that is bound to expose him eventually. Alaric realizes the risk. But he's putting himself in even greater danger than before, Elysia. Especially if they can determine, and then use against him, whatever his weakness may be."

"I have to stop him." Alarmed, I sprang from where I was sitting, just as she grabbed my arm.

"Your interference will only give them more of what they want." Her mirrored eyes shimmered. "They're watching you, too. Your gifts and strengths are also things they yearn to understand — and eventually duplicate. If Gadeirus weren't so enamored of you, I'm sure they would have captured you long before now and dragged you to the labs beneath the city."

"I can't just sit here—"

"Nor should you, dear. We will begin the sound healings momentarily, and I'd like you to participate at least for a little bit, because your energy system will benefit both from the giving and the receiving." She smiled at me, her red curls floating out behind her in the tame ocean currents. "As for Alaric, I've just asked the dolphins to use their sonar to scramble his already-shielded transmissions. That should further slow the seers' efforts."

"Thank you, Khrestes." I sighed, sinking back onto the quartz ring.

The formation was a smooth circle, approximately three feet high and 20 feet in diameter. Around its perimeter, the mermaids began to hum in multiple keys. I felt how their voices joined and strengthened those of their companions I'd passed on my way here. The quartz amplified their vocal frequencies, and I sensed the merfolk's unified intention to transmit the healing sounds to the selenite formation via the crystal's laser-like focusing ability.

Just then several dolphins appeared. They encircled the ring, their clicks and calls and squeaks blending and harmonizing with the mermaids. Khrestes nodded to me, and I added my voice to their vibration. Then Khrestes began to sing, a haunting and hypnotic melody that spiraled wave after wave of energy through my body.

Closing my eyes, I focused on my breath—on giving and receiving through vocalizing. I felt altered, transported into an angelic realm of sound. I surrendered to its beauty and power, until I felt Kavi's gentle bump against my back. I opened my eyes and saw Khrestes staring at me. She continued to sing, even as she mind-messaged me I should return to the others. I nodded before grasping Kavi's fin. And then he carried me swiftly to shore, through a complex tunnel of sound co-created by dolphins and merfolk.

In the shallow waters I slipped from his back, patting his cheek before he again raced out to sea. As I stepped onto the sand, I could feel intense energy vibrating up my legs and pulsating from my palms. Glancing around, I noticed the beach was deserted. And I wondered how much of the solitude was due to Alaric's deflection shield and how much was simply the focused intention of the sound healing, allowing only our party within its reach. Before I could think on it further, I felt my beloved's spider-silk energy engulfing me.

I looked up to see Alaric approaching. I hurried my pace, so eager to feel his body against mine. It was mere moments before I heard the thud of linens and a sack hitting the sand, joining towels and the dress I'd dropped earlier. Then his arms were around me, holding me to him, his lips on mine.

"Such beauty emerging from these waters," he whispered. His fingers combed my hair. "And such energy coursing through you."

"Yes." Looking at him, I felt the wave-like throbbing magnify, merging and building with the swirling always between us. "Such intensity it nearly takes my breath away." I touched his cheek. "How are the others?"

"They are well." He continued to stroke my hair, and I could barely believe how luxurious it felt. "They're sleeping. Nestled for the night, wrapped in Khrestes' restorative song of the sea."

"Which leaves us."

"Yes." In the dark he dropped before me, onto his knees. He lingered there, his tongue tracing my navel, exploring my hips as I trembled beneath his touch. "I told you earlier I had plans for you."

"You did." I bit my lip as his mouth continued its descent along my body.

"Somewhere special I want to take you," he said between kisses.

"You could take me right here."

"If you wish it." He gazed up at me, his eyes hungry but deliberate. And not for the first time, I realized how he so elegantly embodied urgency without ever being rushed.

"What I wish is to explore all I can with you this night," I replied, tracing my finger along his full lips. "Whatever you ask of me, my heart will answer 'yes and more yes'."

"Elysia." His velvety voice was hushed as he rose to his feet. He took me in his arms, pulling me close. "Ride with me once more. And then after, let me surprise you with an exhilaration you've not had in more than a thousand years."

"Oh yes. And more yes." I took a towel for my hair, while he groped in the bag for fresh garments. Once I dressed, he teleported us to the hotel, where we left the wet things. Then he returned us to the stable.

It seemed late. Kev had left the lights on outside for us. I sat on a bench near the hitching posts as Alaric went in to settle up with him. Looking around at the gardenias and jasmine blooming by the barn, I felt overwhelmed with gratitude to be experiencing such joy in this tropical paradise. For a moment I simply closed my eyes and gave thanks to Highest Light. And then Kev appeared with Dara.

"Hello, Elysia," he said in his gravelly voice. "I've got Dara here for you."

"Thanks, Kev." I smiled as I rose to greet him. "I hope you've had a good evening."

"Any evening with the horses is an enjoyable one." He grinned back at me, his blue eyes twinkling. "Can I give you a leg up?"

"I think I'll be okay." In my mind I asked Dara to kneel. She lowered herself to the ground and I climbed on. As she got to her feet, Kev let out a low whistle.

"I've not seen her do that before."

"Perhaps no one's asked her," I replied, and he laughed as Alaric rode out on Avalon.

"Thanks again for everything," Alaric said.

"Don't mention it," Kev called up to us as we headed toward the ocean. "Enjoy the ride you two. It's a perfect night for it."

"Indeed." Alaric smiled as I moved Dara to Avalon's side. "Ready?"

"Just tell me where."

"Another route to Dehk's," he murmured, although there was fire in his eyes. Avalon sensed it too as he fidgeted, looking ready to bolt at any moment. "Dara knows the way." And with that he galloped off, quickly leaving us behind. But not for long. I found I barely needed to urge the mare on, as she relished the chase.

Down the deserted beach we blazed, where low tide had left a wide berth of wet sand. There was only the sound of surf and hooves and us laughing beneath a jovial moon and a million amused stars. I leaned forward, asking Dara to catch the gray gelding. She moved to the outside, toward the water, and closed the gap. Once she was beside him, the two horses merged into a matched rhythm, snorting and blowing and showing they loved to fly every bit as much as we did. I felt so alive, her back beneath me, moving with me as the fervent wind kissed my hair and caressed my soul.

Before long, lights and sleeping establishments gave way to silent, sandy stretches. Once we left the beach a fern-lined path appeared, and as the dew fell we slowed, entering a misty forest maze. All around us seeped the scent of cedar and fir and earthy dampness. And then we came upon a meadow where horses grazed, their heads lifting as we passed. In the distance I saw the well-lit back of Dehk's barn. Alaric smiled at me, one eyebrow raised, and I knew that was my invitation.

Dara and Avalon sped off together. It was a dead heat all the way to the gate, where they slid to a dusty halt. We slipped from their backs, and Alaric opened the latch. Then we watched as they thundered across the paddock, into a far pasture. Swinging the gate closed, Alaric took my hand. He pulled me to him among the knee-high timothy and clover.

"I've so missed times like these, love."

"As have I."

"There's a place I promised to take you," he whispered between kisses. "Would it please you to go?"

"Yes."

No sooner could I blink then the light had adjusted, and I saw we were standing in shadows by the water's edge. Stretching out from shore was a well-lit pier, the tide licking its pillars. Row after row of magnificent vessels were docked on either side of the wooden walkway. There was a quiet creaking as boats bumped their mooring buoys.

Lacing his fingers with mine, Alaric led me along the weathered platform, past yachts and crafts for fishing and sailing as seagulls scolded from above. Near the end of the pier he stopped, turning me to face one of the largest boats in the marina. She looked to be all glass and steel, with wide expanses of floor-to-ceiling windows. Glancing at her bow, I saw the name Red Lotus as he nuzzled my neck.

"Surprise."

"Is she yours?"

"Ours, love." He wrapped his arms around me, and his warmth comforted me in the cool night air.

"She's gorgeous."

"Like you. And she has the best bed in all of Poseidia."

"Why is that?"

"Just the right firmness," he replied, his teeth grazing my throat. "Combined with the sea's easy rocking. A glass ceiling that opens to the moon and stars. And a view in all directions."

"It sounds perfect. As long as I'm the one sharing that bed with you." No sooner had I uttered those words than I regretted them. I was stunned by my lack of sensitivity to all he'd been through, with so many women, in order to spare me so much. "Alaric, I apologize. I don't know why I said that."

"I do." His voice was hushed. "And it's all right. I know what you're thinking, beneath your desire."

"But I really wasn't thinking. Which is why I made such a heartless comment."

"Yet in the back of your mind, you're wondering if a woman gifted her to me. For my services. And you assume I've been bedding Charlaeus here."

"I really don't—"

"I know you think you don't care." He turned me to face him, his hands on my shoulders. "I also know you love me. But still ..." His voice trailed off. He looked at me, his eyes damp. And vulnerable. "In all these centuries without you, I've mostly kept myself numb to my circumstances. Yet the depraved distance from blissfully wed and wealthy king to kept man has been a long-suffering journey."

"What you've endured on my account—"

"I would eagerly bear again, to keep you safe," he murmured. "When our considerable fortune was lost with Moldaaris, I found myself in a position where the favor of others is what provided for me. Though my stature among them had changed, I still moved among the elite, and so I've been afforded many luxuries over the years. Hovercrafts and hotel privileges and fine dining and custom tailoring." He touched trembling fingers to my lips. "Yes, this vessel was a gratuity, right down to her fine silk sheets. But I've not slept in them. And the only woman I've brought here is you."

"I'm so sorry!" I threw myself against his chest, sobbing. "I don't know what catty jealousy possessed me. Please forgive me."

"There's nothing to forgive, love." He rested his chin on my head as he held me close. "I understand. These are our insecurities surfacing— something I've told you all the quartz here encourages. Your fears regarding other women. And mine of feeling defiled." His voice enveloped me, soothing my soul. "The boat was gifted to me not long after I found out the Ahlaielian delegation was coming. I was allowed to choose from among the finest yachts. I cared little for engine size or cargo room. It was all about making sure the bed was nurturing, the ambiance inviting. That it would be the very best for you, the most romantic, as it once was, when we had such a vessel in these very waters. A craft I sold soon after you died, as I couldn't bear its reminder of all we could no longer share."

He paused, closing his eyes. "But when I learned you would soon arrive in Atlantis, I was determined somehow I would draw your pure heart to me. Even if you never again fully remembered who I was. Yet to do that, to attract your vibration to mine, I needed something to help me focus on all those centuries I felt untainted. So I could remember—

and begin to hold the frequency of—feeling worthy of you and the sanctity of our love. Red Lotus helped me do just that."

"Alaric, please." Tears thickened my words. "Feel into me, my love. And know that none of it matters. Absolutely none of it. The truth is it's your very essence—your heart and soul—that honors me. Your exquisite body is my temple. And it's sacred." I kissed him with everything I felt inside. "It rips at my heart to think on any level you still feel unworthy. You have to let me help you change that. Because I cannot let you return to Linasia as long as there is a shred of that feeling in your frequency. It could prove to be your weakness with her, and it would only serve to complicate your task. You can feel the truth in my words, can you not?"

"Yes." He sighed, leaning his forehead against mine. "And so we'll not dwell on my practiced vibration. That only feeds it. I would prefer a pleasurable diversion."

"Anything."

"Let's take her out this night, with only the stars as lookouts." He smiled at me through moonlit tears. "Where we will once again feel a boat cradled by the sea, and lose ourselves in the rocking."

"Yes and more yes." Gathering me in his arms, he carried me up the boarding ramp and onto the waiting vessel.

THIRTY

Alaric led me through the boat's lavish interior before taking us out on the open water. Near some of the island's outcroppings, he dropped anchor while I busied myself lighting candles. In the third-story bedroom, I breathed in the votives' honeyed fragrance as well as my surroundings.

Floor-to-ceiling windows, with open privacy shades and glass doors leading to a deck, set the stage for the view we'd have come morning. The room itself was a blend of sleek and sumptuous. Rounded chairs in gold and red silk shimmered on a matching area rug. Teak flooring embraced the platform bed, its edges swimming with carved dolphins. The bureau's crystal vase cradled a red lotus. I smiled to myself, and then I could feel him watching me. Turning toward the bedroom door, I saw Alaric leaning against its wooden frame, hands in his pockets. And hunger in his eyes.

Maybe it was because this night would be our last together for I knew not how long, but I ached for him with an intensity bordering anxiety. As the sound of surf on rock crashed through the open windows, he crossed the room, graceful and slow. He slid the gold spread from the bed before drawing me to him. While his lips urged and invited mine, his fingers unraveled me from my clothing. I stripped him of his attire, and then his hands were in my hair, running down my body.

Pulling me onto the bed, he nestled me in red silk sheets. Then twice he pleasured me to release, before ever so tenderly pressing himself against me. I fell into the depths of his gaze as our flesh fused in the candlelight. And in the softness of breath and caresses, and the gently rocking arms of the waves, essence met essence. Time had no meaning in his embrace. Hours must have passed in the stillness and the ecstasy. And there we'd remained, in sacred union, as the sun's voyeuristic rays dared peek through the windows.

"You're so beautiful. Inside and out. From those eyes to the very depths of your heart," he murmured against my lips, his hands on my back, clasping me to him beneath the sheet.

"And I'm so blessed." I touched his hair, his jaw, his shoulders. "This face. This physique. This sweet and seductive spirit. I can't believe these things you do to me. The way you make me feel."

"I've told you before: I come to pray. Your body is hallowed ground."

"Then let me offer you sanctuary. Please, Alaric. Don't leave today."

"Elysia, I—"

"Please. Somehow I made myself believe this dawn would never break. Yet now it's here."

"It's all right, love. Surrender with me."

"But I—"

"Surrender with me," he urged, moving beneath me, his eyes never wavering from mine. I could feel a wave building and caught my breath, trying to stall the moment even as the sheet fell from where it had draped my body. But the feel of him inside was so sensual, his gaze so hypnotic, that the wave crashed through in spite of all my dams and defenses. I clung to him, crying out as we spasmed together, with the sun's strengthening rays bursting forth across our bodies.

Collapsing against him, I melted as his warmth surrounded me. For several minutes we neither moved nor spoke. Then I sighed as he pulled the covers over us, his muscular arms encircling me from behind.

"Only feelings," I whispered as my tears stained the silk pillowcase.

"Yes." He rested his head against mine. "And our feelings will carry us through this time apart, love."

"It's just—" I began, stifling a sob. "I don't know how to let you go."

"You're not letting me go," he insisted, his soothing voice in my ear. "You're allowing me to take care of the one thing remaining between us and our happily ever after."

"Isn't there another way?" I shifted in his embrace, rolling so I could look at him. "The ancient texts all talk about there never being just one way up the mountain. Can't we find another route? One that doesn't take you from me?"

"No other path is both swift and unseen. And lined with the element of surprise—all of which are to our advantage—if I go now."

"Maybe I'm just too emotional to be clear. But I'm uneasy. As if a feeling of déjà vu were upon me." I felt my lip quivering. "It's how I felt once before. The only other time I've begged you not to leave."

"Elysia," he sighed. "I must go. Your very life depends on it, as well as the lives of your friends. Besides, it's in my blood to do such work. I love it. You know I do."

"I know. You always have." A sad smile tugged at my lips. "But what if you simply continued to funnel universal life force to me? Especially if I used my intention to support the regeneration. Perhaps that would be enough to help my body recreate its missing essence. And that could lead to a way of helping my friends."

"So Khrestes told you about that." He laughed quietly. "It would be a helpful measure. But it's no solution. It won't restore your immortality. Or work quickly enough to help your friends much at all." Sweetly, he kissed my forehead. "I want you to know once I leave for Zacktronymus, I won't be able to channel that kind of energy for you any longer. Too easy to track."

"Nor would I want you to." For a moment I was quiet, my heart in my throat. "Then there's nothing I can do to change your mind?"

"There's nothing you can do to keep me from saving your immortal soul, love. Because I intend to have you to myself for eternity." He smiled as he caressed my cheek. "I'm kind of selfish like that."

"Alaric—"

"Shhhhh. It's all right."

"I wish to believe it really is all right. Because I know it's the only vibration that will lead us to happily ever after. So I'm doing my best to believe, in spite of how things look right now," I whispered against his chest. "Maybe discussing some of the more practical matters will help me feel more centered and grounded. Tell me when you're planning to leave. And when you promise to contact me. So the sea of silence I fear won't stretch as endlessly between us."

"Remember the balanced queen you are." He kissed me lovingly, lingeringly, as he smoothed my hair. "I've never known someone so powerful. Or brave." Holding me away from him, his eyes were soft. "Your heart will always be your guide when it comes to me. I will speak to you through your heart, in a voice that is unmistakably mine. It's a form of mind-messaging, but harder to trace. And I will do so at six o'clock, well before the start of this evening's dinner."

"All right. And when will you be leaving?"

"As close to now as possible."

"What?! But you haven't had breakfast. And the boat—"

"There are provisions in the kitchen. And you may return the boat to its slip, if you wish." He smiled as he slid from the bed. "You've always loved captaining a ship."

"Indeed," I replied, pulling my suddenly heavy limbs from the sheets as if I were treading quicksand.

"There are clothes for you as well, darling. Next door over." In seconds he'd donned pants and a shirt and shoes. Then I heard his swift steps on the stairs, just as I was opening the adjoining closet's polished wood door. But I simply stood there, sliding hangers back and forth. Taking a deep breath, I shook my head, trying to clear my daze. I decided I needed to become decisive, whether I felt that way or not. Calling forth my best balanced queen, I grabbed the very next outfit I touched. Soon I found myself wearing beige slacks and a sage-green shirt.

Making the bed, I picked up the piled clothing we'd worn the night before and tossed it all in the closet's hamper. As I closed the door, I caught sight of my reflection in its mirrored inside panel. My face was pale but determined. So determined, I thought, and that realization gave me hope. I took one last look out the room's expanse of windows, at the breathtaking seascape. Then launched myself down two spiraling flights of stairs.

Rapidly I made my way across the open living quarters to the kitchen. Waiting on the counter were two steaming mugs of cacao. Before I could say a word, he was scraping some sort of vegetable dish from a pan onto two plates.

"I hope you're hungry." He grinned at me, and I could feel his commitment to keeping things as upbeat as possible. I smiled back, as best as I could from the space of my balanced queen, and realized it would serve Highest Light for me to match his attitude.

"Actually, I am." Even though I wasn't, I'd made up my mind I would eat whatever he placed in front of me. "You're very good for whetting the appetite, Mr. Ardere."

"I was referring to food, Mrs. Ardere." He and I both laughed as he strode through the living area with the plates. "Come sit with me on the deck," he called back and I followed, carrying the mugs.

Outside, it was gorgeous. Turquoise water sparkled around us, translucent and calm. Seagulls and pelicans passed overhead, on a mission to reach the black rocks nearby. I joined Alaric at the deck's oval table. For the next several minutes, we ate and talked and laughed and sipped the cacao, as the sun continued its rapid rise. When the plates were empty, he reached across the table and clasped my hands.

"It's time for me to go, love."

"I know."

"I will message you at six."

"I feel I need a 'Plan B'. If for some reason you're delayed—for any reason—what next?"

"Then I will message you at midnight. But I won't be delayed."

"Is it safe for me to message you?"

"Not at first. I would need to be long gone from Zacktronymus. Or else they will hear you." He smiled, and I could feel him willing me not to worry. "Best to wait until you hear from me. And you will be hearing from me."

"All right."

"I'm not going to say goodbye, you know. You are never, for the rest of eternity, going to hear me utter that word to you."

"I can live with that," I whispered, as he came around the table and helped me to my feet. "Promise me something."

"If I can at all."

"That you will only think of your magnificence once you leave my arms." I gazed at him, my heart filling my eyes. "That you will remember how you've demonstrated your worthiness and purity over and over. And that I love you, in your entirety, with all that I am."

"I promise," he murmured, his eyes soft and warm. "Remember I love you, darling. From alpha to omega and back, through our coupled heart." Once more he kissed me. "I will return as soon as I can." And with those words, he disappeared.

THIRTY-ONE

Staring out over the open water, I felt a bleak and utter loneliness void my heart. My legs drained, and I sank back into my seat. Yet I knew I couldn't give in to weakness now. Then, as if in answer to my unspoken fears, I heard the hawk.

Glancing at the jagged cliffs, I met her scrutiny. I felt her urging me to be brave, to stand in my strength, to honor myself, which was the only way I could honor him. And us. Sighing, I sent her my gratitude as I called on my balanced queen. I did my best to be the energy in my inner cave.

It took a while, but my heart stopped trying to beat its way out of my chest. It took longer still to quell the nothingness inside, but I just kept refocusing my attention, as she'd reminded me of what I knew. That I could help myself and Alaric only by remaining positive and hopeful. When I regained my feet, I felt energy once more coursing up my legs, which made me thankful.

As I prepped to return the boat, I realized having these duties was helpful not only for passing the time, but for keeping an appropriate mindset. I wondered if that's another reason Alaric had brought me out on the water the night before he left, in order to give me small tasks — a focus — to help keep me out of my head for a while. And thus outside the frequencies of fear and worry.

It would be just like him to do something like that, I reasoned. My "very, very clever Alaric", as Khrestes called him. The one who would think of everything. Who was now doing everything possible to save me, much as he did a thousand years ago. Although this time around, I was very much conscious and present and aware, and I could choose to think and act in beneficial ways.

I vowed to myself as I cleared and washed the breakfast dishes that this time I would be doing everything within my own power to help us reach happily ever after. How that would look, or what I would need to do, I knew not. But I trusted Highest Light would reveal Right Action, allowing me to travel the path of flowing unseen with what is, the sacred route of wu wei.

After I put away the dishes, I returned to the bedroom to collect the previous day's clothes. Reaching into the hamper, I piled our things into a laundry bag I'd found hanging inside the closet. But as I grasped Alaric's shirt, I caught his sweet scent, and sadness overcame me. I dropped to my knees, breathing heavily of his body's pleasing perfume.

As I drank it in I began to weep. Rib-heaving sobs gave way to guttural cries, and there on the floor I curled myself around his shirt. Before long, I'd spent all my emotional currency. Finally, I stood, promising myself that would be the last self-indulgent neediness I'd allow.

Perhaps it was because crying allows a cathartic release, but I felt better. I washed my hands and face in the lavatory, then smoothed my hair before grabbing the laundry bag and heading for the stairs. Once I reached the living room, I realized I hadn't made any arrangements for getting back to the selenite structure — or for how I would be navigating Poseidia at all, now that Alaric would no longer be teleporting me everywhere.

I took a deep breath, determined to think only pleasant thoughts. About how things always worked out for me. Or Alaric's exquisiteness. I knew it was the right mindset for making positive things happen, and I was sure there'd be places to procure hoverdisks near the marina. So I put worries of transportation out of my mind as I weighed anchor. Lowering into the captain's chair, I willed myself to think of Alaric's kisses, and then I piloted the boat back toward land.

From out on the sea, Poseidia dazzled me. Her modern lines, her crystalline structures, the whole of her white and pastel loveliness lured my gaze and captured my soul. Not for the first time, I wondered how such beauty could disguise the depths of despair I felt emanating from beneath her. From the tunnels and their cages. Just then a chill rocked my body, and I knew I could not let my thoughts wander so. To do so put me in danger — of being lulled to places in ways I could not afford to be.

A shadow cast itself across the horizon, as clouds collaborated to veil the sun. In an instant the breeze changed, and I thought how this abrupt weather shift seemed odd. My body so wanted to follow fearful impulses, but I directed my thoughts differently. Focusing on my breath, I eased myself into a peaceful vibration. And as I did so, the wind died and the clouds cleared, revealing once again the sun in all his glory.

Shaking my head, I reset my attention onto the task at hand: getting the boat docked. The marina had come into view, so I slowed the engines and guided her gently, until before long I was backing Red Lotus into the boat slip. Turning off the ignition, I smiled in self-satisfaction. It had been more than a thousand years, but some things you truly don't forget—captaining a sea vessel seemed to be one of them.

Once she was secured, I allowed myself to think Highest Light had already selected the best mode of transportation for me. Over and over I repeated to myself I would be provided for. I closed the boat door, entered the keyless entry's "forelysia" code, and a single beep let me know the lock had been set. Then I ambled toward the mainland. I hadn't gone far before I caught sight of a familiar face grinning up at me, from one of the many benches lining the dock.

"Well there you are, lassie!" Dehk hopped to his feet to embrace me.

"I'm so glad to see you, Dehk," I said as he held me away from him. I could feel him feeling into me, reading between the lines, noting my swollen eyes.

"It's all right, lass," he whispered, squeezing my shoulders. "He'll be back. And soon." I did my best to smile as he pried the laundry bag from one hand and a sack of trash from the other. "So I understand you may be needing some transportation, aye?"

"Aye. Any ideas?"

"You know you're always welcome to the horses, of course." He deposited the trash in a nearby receptacle before walking on with me. "But Alaric thought you might be needing something smaller."

"That sounds about right."

"Something like this?" He paused beside one of the dock's many benches. And there, parked by the railing, was the tiniest hovercraft imaginable.

"Yes," I laughed, nodding. "That's about exactly what I need. Is it a rental?"

"No, lass. It's Alaric's. Bought it a while back, and asked if I'd keep it for him at the barn for whenever he'd be in town." He scratched his chin, and I felt him trying to read between more lines. "Funny though. I've never seen him use it. But it sure is coming in handy for you now!"

"I'll say." I studied its slim profile. "She's the smallest one I've seen."

"Built for one, she is. Makes her very easy to navigate." Dehk replied. "Here's the ignition card." He handed me a thin crystalline device. "You'll want to go ahead and program her to recognize you."

"Of course." Taking the see-thru card he extended, I smiled at Dehk. "And is the code 'forelysia'?"

"Ha ha! Indeed it is!" He chortled as I typed the code into the device. "You sure do know your Alaric, child."

"I do, Dehk," I whispered, waving my palm across the card. It beeped, prompting me to slide my finger along the hoverdisk's touchpad. When I did, she whirred to life.

"What else are you needing from me, lass?"

I met his twinkling eyes, as an idea welled from within. "May I mind-message you around seven tonight? I'm sure everything will be fine. I should have heard from Alaric by then. But I'd really like to talk to you, especially if he is ... delayed."

"Of course, lassie," he whispered. "And if I haven't heard from you by the appointed hour, for some reason, some of my friends and I will come looking for you. Because you'll be at the palace, aye?"

"Aye."

"No worries, my dear." He tucked the laundry bag inside the ship's stowage compartment. "Is there anything else I can do before this evening?"

"Not that I can think of. But thank you so much. I can't even tell you how grateful I am."

"Remember, lassie. Anything that comes up for you, I'm just a mind-message away, aye?"

"Aye." I embraced him again before stepping onto the hoverdisk. And then I sped off, out over the open ocean, toward the selenite structure. Gifted with another magnificent view of the city, I realized how much I'd always loved flying such ships; they'd not changed much in the thousand-plus years since I'd navigated one. Higher and higher I took her, and she responded nimbly. It was mere minutes before I spotted my destination.

Settling the craft down near the dunes, I hurried through the sand. In my mind's ear, I could still hear the collaborative song between the mermaids and dolphins, and I was hopeful I'd find my friends in a better state today. As I entered the doorway, the smell of hot cacao and rich spices greeted me. The crew was busy filling plates, but as soon as I walked in, they hastened toward me.

"Hey, you," Hunter called out, taking me in his arms.

"Hey, yourself." I could feel his renewed vitality, and it filled me with hope. "I'm so glad you're on the mend! How are you feeling?"

"Much better. In fact, we're all much stronger today — thanks to you."

"El!" Ava rushed in to embrace me. "I'm so happy to see you! I think you'll be relieved to know how well we're doing."

"I am at that!"

"Elysia, dear." Kendrick kissed my cheek. He took my hands in his, and I noticed they no longer felt withered. "The sound healings are having quite a nice effect, I'm happy to report."

"I'm just so glad, Kendrick."

"Hey, kiddo."

"You look good, Will." I felt elated to see Will's dark circles had vanished. "Really good."

"But you're kinda pale," he observed, raising an eyebrow at me.

"Nothing a little something to eat won't fix." I touched his cheek then turned toward the table. "Who's joining me?" Even though I wasn't hungry at all, I knew some bone broth and hot cacao would be good for me.

Minutes later, we were all seated cross-legged on the sand. It was good to look around at my crewmates chatting and eating. Will cracked jokes just like old times. And every so often Ava squeezed my knee and smiled. I felt her trying to reassure me about Alaric. Just like Hunter was.

He sat across from me, and often I looked up to find his quiet eyes on mine. I sensed the calming energy he channeled. Not only could he read further into me than the others, but he was doing his best to ease my suffering, and it touched me deeply. I looked at him with all the gratitude in my heart, and he smiled just as Kendrick clinked his water glass with a spoon.

"All right crew," Kendrick said. "I know we're all enjoying the food and the company. And yes, El, we are very, very pleased to be graced by your presence." Everybody started cheering and whistling, and I couldn't help but laugh. "Yet in the midst of the merriment, I believe we should discuss the business at hand. Namely the dinner this evening. And how we need to approach it. Any thoughts?"

"Let's just go," Will shrugged. "I mean, if you can't run with the big dogs, you should keep your puppy butt on the porch, right?"

"I agree," Ava said. "I know I'm feeling so much better. I think it would be no problem spending the evening at the palace."

"I see no reason for us to bow out, either," Hunter added. "What do you think, El?"

For a moment I looked around at their expectant faces before answering. Perhaps more than any of them, I was aware how our essence-deprived bodies could fluctuate wildly in terms of available energy. But I didn't want to call their attention to that fact. Or diminish in any way the hope in their eyes. "Yes. I think we should go. And do our best to ground in more love while there."

"I'll drink to that," Will said, raising a mug of cacao.

"To grounding in love!" Hunter exclaimed. Hollering and whooping, we all lifted our mugs in the air.

After more food and cacao, we decided on a general strategy. They'd remain in the selenite structure as long as possible today, before retreating to their hotel rooms in preparation for the palace. After that, we'd meet in the lobby at half past six. The hotel had already secured a hoverdisk for them in the designated landing area, so their means of transportation was set. I told them I wanted to bring the smaller craft myself, as I wanted to keep my options open, depending on how events unfolded. Everyone nodded, and I was grateful nobody asked about Alaric. Once the plans were finalized I got up to go, and Hunter offered to walk me out.

"Is there anything I can do, El?" Hunter asked once we'd left the structure. "I feel the magnitude of what Alaric is facing, for all of us. And I can see what that's putting you through." I glanced at him as we trudged through sugary powder and was pleased his energy seemed normal, his posture as perfect as ever.

"There's really nothing any of us can do. Except maintain a hopeful frequency. But I appreciate you asking. More than you know."

"Hey." He reached for my arm, stopping me in the sand. "You don't have to be brave for me."

"I know," I whispered. "But I have to be brave for me."

"Elysia." He took me in his arms. "Please know I'm here for you."

"I do know that." Releasing him, I kissed his cheek. "I'll see you this evening."

I climbed aboard the craft, and it hummed to life. The hotel was in sight, and I barely got off the ground before it was time to land. An attendant was waiting, so I gave him the laundry bag and then watched him fly off. Afterward, I made my way back to the hotel room.

Entering the foyer, I tried not to think of how vacant the suite felt. I opened the back wall's multiple sliding glass doors, and the sound of the sea comforted me. Glancing at the buffet table, I noticed it was again filled with fresh food. I found a bowl of the dark colored berries, and popped a few in my mouth before heading for the hot spring's steaming relief.

Leaving my clothes on the bed, I descended a step at a time into the water's warmth. At my core, I'd been feeling alone and vulnerable, so I knew I just had to keep resetting a positive intention, make the best of things, and think only about how it was going to feel to have Alaric return to me—instead of dwelling on the emptiness.

I knew focusing on the problem never, ever brings about the solution. I also knew giving too much credence to what feels wrong in the world keeps derailing many humans' dreams, their happily ever afters. And I simply couldn't allow that to happen to me. To us. As I asked the water to comfort me, I kept telling myself over and over that things always work out for me. That Highest Light would provide a way. And soon.

THIRTY-TWO

It was nearly seven when we arrived at the palace. Hunter had flown the other hoverdisk and was next in line for the attendants. I'd pulled in behind him, doing my best to stay calm, although all I'd accomplished was a subdued state of shock. I hadn't heard from Alaric at the appointed hour of six. I'd used every ounce of my feeling capability to sense him, but my heart had remained silent, if not still, flitting about in such a way it made me lightheaded.

I kept refocusing my attention on "Plan B", trying not to imagine an eternity between then and midnight, and reminding myself of the more immediate relief of being able to mind-message Dehk at seven. I was looking forward to hearing his fatherly tone in my head. In the meantime, I kept praying to Highest Light, willing myself not to be consumed by the fear hungering for me.

After I watched Alaric's hoverdisk disappear beyond the rose gardens, I turned to find Hunter and the others waiting. As they'd been for the ball, the men were dressed in black. Ava and I had repeated our updos. Working with ringlets and pins seemed easier the second time, which was a blessing as we'd both dressed and done makeup and hair on our own. In the fading sunlight, I noticed again how much I loved Ava's grayish-purple gown, with its cap sleeves and lace detailing. I'd chosen a golden dress from among the evening attire Alaric had placed in the hotel suite's closet. The frock's silk body shimmered beneath a beaded overlay, which also wrapped its thin shoulder straps and scalloped hem. The beading made it heavy, which helped me feel more grounded. A matching stole added even more substance, and yet the color was a reminder to keep my thoughts light and bright — something I knew was absolutely crucial that evening.

As I joined the others, Hunter nodded approval, extending his arm. It made me think of us walking into the ball together just two nights ago. In some ways I couldn't believe how much had happened in the last 48 hours. And yet I knew I couldn't dwell on those thoughts, either. Taking a deep breath, I called upon my balanced queen.

Before I could fully channel her frequency, though, I gazed up at the palace entrance, and it gave me pause. Unlike the night of the ball, there was only the hue of red roses framing the doorway and painting its pillars. The sight sent a chill through me; so much of that ruby color splashed across the castle's five-story façade looked like spilled blood. I shook my head to clear the image, and I wondered if it was only my grisly imagination at work or if it was indeed some kind of ominous calling card from Gadeirus. Regardless, it was yet another thing I couldn't allow to capture my attention. Passing through the open doors, we entered a grand foyer teeming with guests. And filled—in every possible nook, around every available column, and along the entire perimeter—with red roses.

I smiled to myself. From within my centered depths, I decided I would choose to see each and every rose as a red lotus. I knew no matter what psychological warfare Gadeirus waged that evening, how I felt was ultimately my choice. And he could only affect me if I allowed him that power.

I took another breath, and in my mind's eye, I envisioned myself as a queen. Lifting my head, I grinned at each person we passed before noticing another curious sight. Just ahead was the ballroom, whose entryway was barricaded with stanchions and red velvet ropes. Gazing at Hunter, I saw he was peering at me with the same question in his eyes. Ava, Will, and Kendrick slowed their pace, turning to look at us.

"Wait here," Kendrick commanded. We watched as he marched over to where some workers were carrying what looked like bags of cement into the ballroom. One of the men saw him approaching, and I sensed Kendrick's sunny Gold Ray warmth putting the man at ease as he called out a greeting. For a few minutes, Kendrick conversed with the man. Then they locked forearms before Kendrick made his way back to where we were standing.

"Apparently, the castle has sustained structural damage," Kendrick explained. "The engineers are puzzled, as there's been no seismic activity or other easily observed reason as to why the castle's foundation has shifted, creating stress fractures throughout the marble flooring and pillars."

"I see," Hunter mused. The faintest smile cracked his lips. "No easily observed reason, huh?"

"That's correct." Kendrick scanned our faces. "We'd best look alert, crew. Even more than usual. Because they're going to be searching for not so easily observed reasons."

Pivoting, he led us down one of the hallways to the left of the grand foyer where intricately carved rosebuds opened along mahogany moldings. The gold ceiling stretched above us, high and rounded, while multiple chandeliers illuminated our path. As we walked, I found myself studying the floor. It was hard to tell at first. But once

I focused my attention, I spied cracks spidering out across the black marble. Again I glanced at Hunter. It was clear he'd noticed the same thing.

Near the hallway's end, we entered a colossal crimson room. Hundreds of round, ruby-draped tables bore matching napkin adornments and towering arrangements of roses. Attendants dressed in the brightest cherry courteously greeted each party, checking belongings and escorting guests to the appropriate tables. A line had formed, and as we waited I mind-messaged Dehk, using my dolphin sonar to scramble the signal for anyone who might try to listen. Both Ava and Kendrick had caught sight of ambassadors they recognized across the room, and so they excused themselves. Will turned toward Hunter and me, a bemused look in his eyes.

"So maybe it's me. But there's more red in here than all the kinds of stupid put together."

"It began at the entrance," Hunter murmured. "As Kendrick cautioned, we'd best be on our guard. Especially you, El." He glanced about the room. "I've been wondering where Jon and Tyrius are. I mind-messaged both of them back at the hotel, but no reply thus far."

"Any clue, El?" Will asked.

"None." I kept channeling the balanced queen to quell my heart's growing uneasiness. "My sense is we're being played. That Gadeirus is trying to foster feelings of fear and paranoia. So it wouldn't surprise me if he has somehow delayed Jon and Tyrius. And I would look for him to separate the rest of us before the evening gets underway."

"Divide and conquer," Will muttered.

"Yes. He's a bully, and bullies divide to conquer." I shook my head. "I'm afraid he's got a score to settle with me now as well."

"We'll all be watching your back, El." Hunter's voice was firm. "Even if we're seated at different tables, it makes no difference."

Before I could respond, it was our turn with an attendant. The young woman assisting us had black hair pulled into a ponytail and dark eyes. Hunter gave her our names, and her manner was pleasing as she scanned a crystal tabulator.

"Yes, sir. Each of you is on the guest list, although you are all seated at different tables." She smiled at Hunter. "Would you like me to check any items for you this evening?"

"Actually, we're still waiting on a couple of friends," he replied. "Can you tell me if Jonastus of Poseidia and Tyrius of the Great Central Sun region have arrived?"

"Just a moment, sir." She entered more data. "They have yet to register. But shall I go ahead and check any items or have you escorted to your seats?"

"Perhaps in a few minutes."

"Certainly, sir." She nodded before greeting the group behind us. Hunter led us to the side, where people stood in clusters conversing. I sensed him mind-messaging Kendrick and Ava. By the time we'd reached a suitable spot to convene, they'd returned.

"So they've seated us separately," Kendrick said.

"Yes," Hunter whispered. "And Jon and Tyrius aren't here. Nor have they responded to any of my mind messages."

"I see." Kendrick's ice-blue eyes bored into me. "I believe you're the most at risk, Elysia. Are you comfortable continuing as planned, even if we're all in different sections of the room?"

"Yes."

"All right," he replied. "We'll check in with each other on the hour at the beverage station, near the entrance. Casually and without fanfare. As for now, let them situate us wherever we've been assigned." And with that, Kendrick strode to the registration table, his white-blond hair shining like silver in the crystal lighting.

Turning toward the others, I observed Ava's calm countenance. She clutched my arm before she and Will walked over to wait behind Kendrick. Which left me with Hunter.

"I don't mean to overstep my bounds, El," he said, clasping my hands in his. "But I sense the pain you're not showing, and I know it has to do with Alaric. Will you please tell me what's going on?" For several moments I studied the floor's fine fissures before lifting my eyes to his.

"I appreciate your concern, Hunter. I've said nothing because I haven't wanted to worry you or any of the others," I whispered. "But Alaric was supposed to message me at six this evening, and he hasn't. So I'm doing my best to keep myself distracted and upbeat, until midnight, which is our 'Plan B' for making contact."

"Okay." He squeezed my palms. "So we're simply going to focus on having a good time this evening. Meeting and greeting and eating, all right?" I laughed as he released me. "It's going to be fine, El."

"You remember what Ava says 'fine' means to the humans, right?" I laughed again as he groaned.

"I could choose another word."

"No, I think that one's appropriate."

"Let's go find our place in that line again." He kissed my cheek. "And El?"

"Yes?"

"If anything at all seems unusual or makes you uncomfortable, I want you to message me immediately." I nodded, and we returned to the line. There were only a few groups ahead of us, as it appeared many guests had already been seated. Glimpsing a gilded clock near the entrance, I saw it was quarter past seven. And I realized I'd not heard from Dehk. A chill shivered me. Hunter's sharp eyes scanned me with concern.

"Are you cold?"

"It's just a momentary thing. It will pass." I smiled, doing my best energetically to reassure him. With all my focus, I breathed as a queen, letting her regal bearing fill me. Then one of the attendants motioned for us to approach. Hunter gave him our names, and the thin man with brown bangs began typing.

"Yes, sir. I see you've been assigned to a table on the western perimeter. And you, my lady —" Abruptly he paused, eyebrows arching before he recovered practiced politeness. "You'll be seated at the king's table." Smiling, he looked from Hunter to me. I felt him wondering if we were a couple, and if so why we would be seated separately. "Shall I check any belongings for you?"

Hunter and I shook our heads.

"Very well then. Let me have you escorted to your tables."

Hunter kissed my hand as a female attendant gestured for him to walk with her. Before I could see where he'd be sitting, a male attendant appeared at my side. Undoubtedly, Highest Light was not wasting any time this evening in bringing me to the wolf's lair.

Crossing the room, I felt eyes widening. I was sure most if not all the people here had watched me dance with Alaric two nights ago. I also heard whispering, and I sensed their thirst for gossip. Their overwhelming curiosity as to why the missionary was not on the prostitute's arm tonight.

Taking a deep breath, I held my head higher as I reminded myself to think only happy thoughts, no matter what. I was daydreaming of Alaric's caresses when the attendant delivered me to the room's most imposing setting. A trellis stretched high above the king's dais, with white columns barely discernible beneath all the red roses. Under different circumstances, I might have found the feature breathtaking. As it was, I felt I was being led to the gallows.

"Elysia!" Arianna's husky voice called out to me, as she rose from the chair opposite mine. "My dear, it's good to see you."

"And I'm most pleased to see you."

"I believe you'll be next to Gadeirus." She smiled as she held my hands, looking resplendent in a sage-colored dress with gold and diamond jewelry. "But I do hope to speak with you later, once the evening is underway."

"I would like that." She touched my arm before resuming her seat.

There were fewer faces this evening at the king's table, perhaps fifteen in all, yet every one of them had been sitting as his guest of honor two nights earlier. I offered my cheek or my hand as appropriate, allowing Gadeirus' entourage to welcome me to their privileged perch. One of the men held my chair as I sat down. I thanked him as he nodded, then he returned to his seat beside the four empty chairs to my left.

I was just about to make small talk with the wife of one of the king's close friends, when an orchestra on the opposite side of the room struck up a march. Everyone stood. As I got to my feet, Gadeirus entered the hall in a regal black surcoat and pants with gold trim. He was trailed by Desineus and two other members of his inner circle.

Gadeirus grinned and waved to thunderous applause. Once he reached the platform, he bowed to the crowd, which yielded more boisterous cheering and clapping. When he sat down, the orchestra settled into a waltz. Murmuring and quiet laughter arose in the background as we all slipped into our seats. Servants appeared with steaming soup bowls, and I felt the king's raven eyes upon me.

"My dearest Elysia." Reaching for my hand, he pressed his lips to my fingers. He lingered long enough for the gesture to be highly inappropriate—and for me to see his bloodshot eyes.

"Your Highness." I bowed my head, and was startled by his laughter.

"Please." He continued chuckling as he released my hand. "I believe we're way beyond such formalities, are we not?"

"If you say so." I was shocked by his appearance. His crown pinned disheveled curls beneath its weight. Fine white wisps frosted his bangs and temples, a contrast I'd not before noticed. Dark circles ballooned his eyes, and his complexion had tinged green.

"Yes," he whispered. "I say so." He brushed my cheek with icy fingers. "Please. Enjoy the soup, as I regale you with a thousand unimportant events of the day. Which you will then pretend is the most utterly fascinating verbiage you've ever heard." Dropping into my balanced queen, I stared at him. For a moment he met my gaze, and I could feel how he was torn, desiring to lose himself in a vibration that unsettled him. "What sorcery is this? That would render me speechless?"

"I'm merely listening," I replied. "Regale away, if it should please you."

"What would please me at the moment is a very short list. One that begins with you and ends with the finest champagne." He whispered to one of the servants, who hurried from the room. Then those eyes were leering at me. Black holes filled with malevolence. And mirth. "Yet I digress. I will spare you my loquacity. I would prefer to hear you speak about your whirlwind marriage to my dance instructor. Who is conspicuously absent, I see." He drew nearer. "Where is your precious Alaric?"

"Not everyone adores endless parties, Gadeirus. Certainly not Alaric." My voice held steady. "What more would you like me to tell you?" I continued to peer at him from my centered queen, though I braced myself. I sensed his drunkenness had numbed his manners if not his cruelty. And I could feel him trying to unhinge me.

"Everything, of course." Fingering dirty bangs, he ogled me. "But most especially if it has to do with the ecstatic coupling. The all-night lovemaking. Or the multiple climaxes, in a multitude of locations."

"It appears there's nothing I could divulge that you don't already know."

"The one thing I don't know is why." He leaned closer, the stench of alcohol rotting his breath. "I knew carnal passions burned in you. Frankly, it's part of your appeal. But why choose such a man-whore as your outlet? Especially when you could lie with a king, and have all of Poseidia at your fingertips."

"You wouldn't understand."

"I dare say I understand more of the heart than you do."

"Pray tell, then."

"No heart is without its shadow, Elysia." He raked me with his stare. "Not yours. Not your Alaric's. If you believe his lie that he never loved Charlaeus, then you are sadly mistaken."

"I believe some things last forever." I breathed myself deeper into my cave, as I could feel his words gutting my feeling sense.

"Nothing lasts forever!" He laughed as he nuzzled my cheek. "Nothing good."

"I'm sure that's been your experience."

"My experience has never been disproven," he whispered. "All matters of the heart involve compromise. And negotiation. Exemplifying how all relationships are merely — at their most basic levels — contracts."

"Why should your theories interest me?"

"Because our contract is such that I am willing to renegotiate its finer points." He kissed my ear, his cupid bow lips parting so his tongue could explore. "You give yourself to me, and in exchange I will restore not only your life, as I'd initially planned, but also the lives of your friends."

"Why would you choose me?" I pulled away to sip the soup. "I'm a hybrid being after all. I've no pure bloodlines to offer."

"Have I not made it clear I can overlook all of that?" He lifted my chin so I would see his scowl. "Is it not obvious I want you for my queen?"

"With you I'd say nothing is clear. Or obvious."

"Woman, I thought you said you were listening!" He slammed the table, rattling the stemware and everyone nearby. Awkward silence ensued, and I noticed even his henchmen fidgeted. He seized the spoon from my hand and hurled it to the floor. "I see I will have to teach you a thing or two about hearing me. And about showing proper respect." Just then the servant he'd sent away returned, pushing a cart of champagne bottles.

"Shall I pour for you, Your Highness?"

"By all means," he growled. Uncorking a bottle, she extended him the courtesy of smelling and tasting the offering. As he did so, his eyes restlessly searched mine before darting away — only to be drawn back to my gaze, which he could not hold. Once he nodded his approval, the servant poured for the table. I could feel Hunter and the rest of my crewmates on alert. I messaged them to meet me at the drink station. Then I emanated the Oneness Prayer from my depths as I channeled the queen through every pore, all the while trusting Highest Light was guiding and supporting me.

"Is everything to your liking, Your Highness?" The servant's voice was submissive. She met my eyes and her cheeks reddened.

"Yes, yes," he said, dismissing her. As she bowed and retreated, he again leaned toward me. "Almost everything is quite to my liking." From this close, I could smell not just the alcohol, but also something charred, suggesting he'd been smoking his hallucinogens prior to dinner. He shifted in his chair. "There's just this small matter of your impulsive marriage I need to attend to."

"Attend to?" I did my best to look bored as I observed those around the table. I realized everyone was eating in silence. Arianna gaped at me, her face radiating concern. All eyes except hers were either glued to their plates or else peeking at me uneasily. It was apparent everyone was avoiding altogether looking at Gadeirus.

"Yes. I could have it annulled." He studied me as a servant removed my soup bowl, replacing it with a salad while another worker wiped the floor.

"And what would the point be?" I crunched the crisp vegetables with a gusto I didn't feel, and yet I knew I needed fuel to sustain myself in this emotionally charged situation.

"So I could marry you, of course."

"You don't even know me."

"I know everything I need to know." He took my fork and put it down, turning me so he could clasp my hands. "I know you're the most beautiful woman I've ever laid eyes on, in spite of your bloodlines. I know you're highly sexed, with a body I covet. I know you're an exceptional dancer and would make an ideal hostess for the endless parties here." He nestled closer, a demonic grin searing his face. "I know I can have your essence restored, your wholeness reclaimed. Your life spared, and the lives of your friends. Returning your appetites and shaping your cravings so you will cleave only to me."

"You believe you possess such power?"

"I know I do."

"And you believe I would surrender myself to you?"

225

"I know you should." Again his fingers, cold as death, fondled my face. "It would be easier that way. Because one way or another, you shall be mine. To mold in the image of one worthy of Poseidia's riches. To teach in the ways of submitting to my lust and indeed all my wishes. As I can open up worlds of desire you've never dreamed possible, through the magic at my disposal."

"My, my. If you could only rid yourself of my smarts and self-esteem, you'd have your perfect queen." Taking a breath, I mind-messaged Hunter I was making my exit. "If you'll excuse me, I feel the need for intelligent conversation and uplifting company." He snatched my wrist as I rose.

"You can't just leave," he hissed. Grabbing a filled champagne flute, he shoved it into my hand. "Here. This will make you feel better." Defiantly I tossed the drink in his face.

"You're right. I do feel better." He sputtered and cursed, wiping his waistcoat as I set the glass down. I could feel everyone at the table struggling not to laugh as I walked away. Clutching my purse, I scanned the room for my friends, but there were hundreds of tables and thousands of guests. Again I mind-messaged them as I approached the beverage station. I also contacted Khrestes, hoping she might hear me even if my crewmates could not. Then I messaged Jon, knowing if anyone would be able to feel me, it would be him. After that, I put distress calls out to Dehk and Dara and Avalon and my hawk friend as well, sending them images of where I was located and telling them I was in danger.

Approaching the bar, I realized none of my friends was waiting. Panic wanted to grip me, but I insisted my body keep breathing. Moving deliberately, I walked toward the doorway—and saw eight guards lining its threshold. Weighing my options, I asked Highest Light for guidance as I ordered mineral water from one of the bartenders. When he placed a faceted goblet in front of me, I noticed him eyeing me curiously.

"Do I know you?"

"No, my lady." Dropping his gaze, he began to scour the already spotless counter between us.

"Are you sure? My name is Elysia." I channeled the balanced queen, willing him to look at me. Tentatively he raised blue eyes to mine. "You just seemed like you'd seen me before."

"It's nothing, really," he answered, and knowledge filled my being.

"What is your name?"

"Bolavius, my lady." He grinned, obviously pleased a pretty guest was being friendly. He had straight blond hair and a dimpled chin. "But you may call me Bo."

"All right, Bo. Perhaps you've seen my brother," I coaxed. "He's much taller than me, but he has my eyes."

"Aye, my lady. I've seen him."

"Just now?" I smiled, my heart in my eyes.

"Aye. Not 10 minutes ago."

"Did you see where he went?" I leaned closer, and he glanced around before scrubbing the counter once more.

"You didn't hear it from me, mind you," he whispered. "But the guards took him out of here."

"I see." I looked at him with all the intensity I felt. "I'm sure they will come for me as well, Bo. We're diplomats from Ahlaiele, and the powers that be here are upset by our humanitarian mission. Tell me, is there a back way out of this room?"

"No, my lady," he replied, and I felt him trying to think of how to help me. "There's not even a service elevator. We have to bring everything in and out through that one entrance."

"All right," I said. "Then could I please ask a favor of you?"

"Yes, my lady." He stared at me, his eyes dreamy.

"Do you know Lady Arianna? The king's sister?"

"Yes, my lady."

"If I'm taken from this room, please let her know — and ask her if she will come see me."

"Yes, my lady."

"I would also appreciate it if you could tell Kenaseus, who is on the diplomatic relations committee." My voice was quiet and even. "Do you know who Kenaseus is?"

"Aye, my lady."

"And would you please get word to him?"

"Aye. Of course."

"And if anyone else asks after me, please let them know what happened as well. To me and my brother. Will you do that for me, Bo?"

"Yes, my lady." Something from across the room caught his attention. He tore his gaze from mine, focusing instead on a non-existent spot on the counter. He rubbed the polished surface with vigor, before nervously glancing at me. "King's coming up behind you, on the left."

As I turned to face Gadeirus, I read the murderous intent in his eyes. If there'd been anything left of his genteel mask at the table, that false face had been washed away with champagne.

"That was unacceptable," he sneered. Before I could say anything, he seized my wrist and slapped on what looked like a heavy coiled bracelet. Looking down at the copper and gold band, I noted its fine silver wiring and embedded crystals. I glanced at Bo to see if he was watching. His blue eyes met mine before he busied himself with someone's drink.

Gadeirus' laughter brought my gaze back to his gloating face.

"Consider this a token of my love." I opened my mouth to speak, and found I could form no words. He giggled harder. "So much for me having to put up with your smarts. Or suffer your self-esteem." He leaned in close. "I said I would have to teach you a thing or two about hearing me. And about respect. Which will be much easier now that I don't have to listen to your insufferable mouth."

Once more those wintry fingers chilled my cheek, my neck, my shoulder. "Don't get any ideas about mind-messaging anyone, either. You are mute, my dear, in every sense of the word. And if you try to run or create a scene in any way, I can make this painful for you." To illustrate his point, he flicked his fingers toward the cuff, and agony stabbed my senses. I collapsed on the bar, my head in my hands, until he waved his palm over my wrist and the torment subsided. "So you can leave peacefully with me now. Or I will have the guards escort you. But either way, you're coming with me."

Calling on all the balanced queen energy I could channel, I smiled at Gadeirus. He flinched, his drunken eyes narrowing in confusion. I took note of the guards standing not 20 feet behind him, then I seated myself at the bar. The gilded clock above the entrance told me it was just after eight. Sipping mineral water, I felt Gadeirus' rage ready to explode as I settled my purse on my lap.

"Very well, then." He raised his hand, and four guards approached. "Bring her and follow me," he snapped. I took one more look at Bo, whose boyish face told me he would do everything possible to honor my requests, and then I was seized from the stool. I made it clear I wouldn't be walking of my own accord, thinking perhaps the sight of a guest being manhandled might raise eyebrows and questions. One of the guards whisked me into his arms. As he carried me from the room, nearby guests gawked and whispered.

I prayed to Highest Light, asking for guidance and strength as the guards followed where Gadeirus led. I kept reminding myself I was a queen, and if I could just stay in my true power, the bully would back down. As we moved along the corridor, in the direction of the foyer, I channeled into my surroundings the vibrations of hope and love with every ounce of intention I possessed. Perhaps the cuff had rendered me mute, but I was delighted to see it also helped me focus and direct Highest Light energies—almost as if I were wielding a healing wand from my wrist. I smiled to myself, appreciating the irony, as I funneled loving frequencies through the very weapon they'd devised to subdue me.

The few couples we passed in the entrance hall averted their eyes, as if they were used to ignoring whatever the king did. Gadeirus entered the elevator, shadowed by three of the guards and finally the one carrying me. As its crystal doors closed, I saw guests meandering about. Many of them threw a passing glance in my direction, but they continued admiring the flowers or the fountains, seemingly uncaring that such treachery was happening under their noses. I thought of how metaphorical it was, since all of Atlantis was poised to fall. And yet so many of the elite nobles were either completely oblivious or — even worse — unfeelingly uninterested.

My heart jumped as the elevator shot upward. In mere seconds, we disembarked on the fifth floor. The guards stood respectfully to the side as Gadeirus exited, then trailed his swift steps to the hallway's end. Slapping his hand across a keyless entry device, he threw open the room's double doors and marched inside. The guards followed, and then the one holding me set me down.

"That will be all," Gadeirus ordered, turning toward a decanter on a nearby table. He snatched two shot glasses from a stack beside a red spray of roses. The guards bowed and left. With a heavy clang, the doors sealed behind them, and if I'd been in the tunnels beneath the city I'm sure it couldn't have sounded more like the entrance to a prison cell swinging shut.

THIRTY-THREE

I watched as Gadeirus downed first one shot, then the other before glowering at me. His face was equal parts rage and lust as he approached. I kept reciting the Oneness Prayer, dropping into a deadly calm as I channeled Highest Light through the cuff. Leaning over me, his eyes sought mine, but as I stared at him he looked away. Softly he snickered, wrenching the crown from his head and hurling it onto a nearby bureau. "What witchery you possess, woman! That compels and repels in equal measure."

He ran quivering fingers through his bangs as he again studied my face. I felt him weighing and measuring and puzzling. And then he seized me by the shoulders. Roughly, he turned me toward a wall opposite the raised bed. He tilted my head, so I was staring up at the painting that had once captured a moment of bliss between Alaric and me.

"That gorgeous image of you is what started it all, my dear. This whole elaborate plan to bring you right where you are, in service to me," he whispered as his lips ravaged my neck. Breathing deeply from my balanced queen, I studied my face on the wall. In the painting I looked ecstatic, surrounded by a virtual sea of red lotus blossoms. I was dressed in a light gold gown, not unlike the one I was wearing. My engagement necklace and wedding ring were readily visible. It was easy to tell the male figure now rendered as Gadeirus was holding a posture belonging to Alaric.

Forcefully, Gadeirus spun me around, his mouth bruising mine. Already he was breathing hard, but I could feel his desire give way to frustration as my lips radiated nothing but queenly power. Panting, he recoiled as if my kiss had repulsed him. For a moment he held me away from him, his eyes enraged and bewildered by the energy with which I was engulfing him.

Abruptly he struck me, the back of his hand landing shy of my mouth. There was a sickening sound of flesh yielding to bone as my head lurched back. I felt him considering the cuff to induce even more pain, and then he began to cackle. It was the sound of a madman laughing. I was determined I'd allow neither my physical discomfort nor his howling to take me from my breath and my queen's energetic balance.

"Oh, I see," he hissed. "You need a little encouragement, is that it? Something to take the edge off? Put you in the mood?"

He released me, stumbling as he weaved his way to a bedside armoire. I prayed he would pass out before returning with whatever potion he sought. Flinging wide the cabinet's large double doors, he pilfered through a number of silk bags. While he was thus absorbed, I pried and pulled on the cuff.

It fit snugly, and a pulsing green light indicated its active engagement. As my fingers searched for any weakness or information that might prove helpful in releasing me, I kept channeling hope and love through the cuff's powerful laser-like structure. Moving a few steps back and forth, I grounded the room in Highest Light frequencies.

Several minutes passed, during which I was able to anchor a matrix of Highest Light within the wolf's den. Then beyond the bed, from outside a set of glass doors, I heard the hawk screeching. Her support was welcome as Gadeirus staggered toward me.

Dropping his treasures on a bureau beneath the painting, he brushed past me on his way to grabbing the decanter and more shot glasses from the foyer. He slammed the glassware onto the bureau when he returned. Then he whirled to face me, a crazed grin cracking his face.

"You're about to taste the finest—and strongest—liquor made here in Atlantis."

As he sloshed the plum-colored spirits into shot glasses, I wondered if I'd be in any shape to hear Alaric when he contacted me at midnight. Gadeirus bobbled the glasses toward me, only to spill them both onto the rose-motif rug at my feet. Screaming and cursing, he fumbled the vessels back onto the bureau, and I noticed the once-beautiful carpet had multiple purple stains.

Again he filled the glasses, though not as full as before. This time he clenched my wrist. Ramming one of the glasses into my hand, he seized the other vessel and clanged it against mine. "To the shaping and pruning of you, into a rose worthy of all Poseidia's bounty."

In one swallow he downed his drink. I only stared at him, my heart in my eyes, as I returned the untouched glass to the bureau. Once more he began guffawing. He couldn't look me in the eye though. Viciously his fingers twisted in my hair.

"Shall I make you, Elysia? Is that what you'd prefer? Brute force?" He clutched the shot glass and, whipping my head back, dumped its liquid fire into my mouth.

Turning my face from him, I was able to let most of the elixir run back out onto the carpet. The few drops I tasted were undeniably potent. I choked as the alcohol rushed straight to my head. Perhaps he was too drunk to realize most of the liquor had dribbled from my mouth. Or maybe the choking sound made him think I'd swallowed it all. Regardless, he seemed satisfied, as he didn't try to force any more of the spirits. Reaching for one of the silk bags, he removed some small disks, and I wondered what mind-altering effects the tiny buttons held.

"You're going to be begging for me once this little number takes hold." He chortled quietly, but no less maniacally. Popping a few of the disks himself, he then forced one between my lips. He clamped his hand over my mouth, still averting his eyes from mine. I knew holding steady within my queenly power was mightier than struggling against him so I set my intention Highest Light would prevail—no matter how things appeared.

It wasn't long before the disk dissolved. I could still hear him speaking, but his voice sounded remote and exaggerated at the same time, almost as if he were shouting to me from the far end of a tunnel. I felt like I could no longer hold my head up. Collapsing against him, I was aware he half-carried, half-dragged me up the platform steps before falling with me onto the bed.

Never one to think enough was enough, he grabbed a larger button and shoved it in my mouth. As that drug melted into my system, I realized I was about to lose consciousness. I didn't know if I would die or not, although in my weakened state, with half my essence, it seemed a likely scenario. But if I did, the only thing I wanted to be sure of was that I carried no anger or fear in my heart. I couldn't bear repeating the pattern from more than a thousand years ago, the one that had kept me hopelessly separated from my beloved.

With fading strength, I breathed in and out the Oneness Prayer, thinking only of Alaric's flesh fusing with mine as the hawk's cries echoed in the distance. If I died peacefully, in a pure vibration, then at least I could hope to look upon Alaric's face at some point, and I would remember how we'd always loved one other. From alpha to omega and back, through our coupled heart. It wasn't my happily ever after. But as I descended into darkness, it was enough.

About Jean Brannon

Jean Brannon is a licensed acupuncturist and author. Whether working with patients or the written word, Jean likes to use metaphysical and Eastern mysticism concepts as tools to help people become more self-empowered. Her dream is to give ancient wisdom and New Thought ideas a voice in popular culture. Born in West Virginia, Jean now lives in the metro Atlanta area with her two dogs, Rosey and Connell. To learn more, visit www.jeanbrannon.com.

Did you enjoy this book?

Please consider leaving a brief review for *Atlantis Writhing* on any online review platform.

Would you like to know about the latest Absolute Love Publishing releases? Join our newsletter on our website home page: www.absolutelovepublishing.com.

About Absolute Love Publishing

Absolute Love Publishing is an independent book publisher devoted to creating and publishing books that promote goodness in the world.

www.AbsoluteLovePublishing.com

Books by Absolute Love Publishing

Adult Fiction and Non-Fiction Books

The Chakra Secret: What Your Body Is Telling You, **a min-e-book™ by Michelle Hastie**
Do you believe there may be more to the body than meets the eye? Have you wondered why you run into the same physical issues over and over again? Maybe you are dealing with dis-eases or ailments and are ready to treat more than just the symptoms. Or perhaps you've simply wondered why you gain weight in your midsection while your friend gains weight in her hips? Get ready to understand how powerful energy centers in your body communicate messages from beyond the physical. Discover the root, energetic problems that are causing imbalances, and harness a universal power to create drastic changes in your happiness, your wellbeing, and your body with *The Chakra Secret: What Your Body Is Telling You,* a min-e-book™.

Finding Happiness with Migraines: a Do It Yourself Guide, **a min-e-book™ by Sarah Hackley**
Do you have monthly, weekly, or even daily migraines? Do you feel lonely or isolated, or like you are constantly worrying about the next impending migraine attack? Is the weight of living with migraine disease dampening your enjoyment of the "now"? Experience the happiness you crave with *Finding Happiness with Migraines: a Do It Yourself Guide,* a min-e-book™ by Sarah Hackley.

Discover how you can take charge of your body, your mind, your emotions, and your health by practicing simple, achievable steps that create a daily life filled with more joy, appreciation, and confidence. Sarah's Five Steps to Finding Happiness with Migraines provide an actionable path to a new, happier way of living with migraine disease. A few of the tools you'll learn: which yoga poses can help with a migraine attack, why you should throw away your daily migraine journal, how do-it-yourself therapy can create positive change, and techniques to connect with your body and intuition.

Have Your Cake and Be Happy, Too: A Joyful Approach to Weight Loss **by Michelle Hastie**
Have you tried every weight loss trick and diet out there only to still feel stuck with unwanted body fat? Are you ready to live joyfully and fully, in a body that stores only the amount of fat it needs? Then this

book is for you.

In *Have Your Cake and Be Happy, Too: A Joyful Approach to Weight Loss*, author Michelle Hastie uses her own research into nutrition and the psychology of weight loss to help you uncover the mindset you need to transition from fat storing to fat burning, without overly fancy or external tactics. No more strict regimens or unfulfilling meals. Just strong body awareness, deep mind-body connection, and positive results.

Don't change your diet or your exercise routine. Instead, pick up this book, and change your life.

Love Like God: Embracing Unconditional Love
In this groundbreaking compilation, well-known individuals from across the globe share stories of how they learned to release the conditions that block absolute love. Along with the insights of bestselling author Caroline A. Shearer, readers will be reminded of their natural state of love and will begin to envision a world without fear or judgement or pain. Along with Shearer's reflections and affirmations, experts, musicians, authors, professional athletes, and others shed light on the universal experiences of journeying the path of unconditional love.

Love Like God Companion Book
You've read the love-expanding essays from the luminaries of *Love Like God*. Now, take your love steps further with the *Love Like God Companion Book*. The Companion provides a positive, actionable pathway into a state of absolute love, enabling readers to further open their hearts at a pace that matches their experiences. This book features an expanded introduction, the Thoughts and Affirmations from *Love Like God*, plus all new "Love in Action Steps."

Mom Life: Perfection Pending by Meredith Ethington
Out-parented at PTA? Out-liked on social media? Wondering how your best friend from high school's kids are always color-coordinated, angelic, and beaming from every photo, while your kids look more like feral monkeys? It's okay. Imperfection is the new perfection! Join Meredith Ethington, "one of the funniest parents on Facebook," according to Today.com, as she relates encouraging stories of real-mom life in her debut parenting humor book, *Mom Life: Perfection Pending*.

Whether you're buried in piles of laundry, packing your 50th sack lunch for the week, or almost making it out the door in time for school, you'll laugh along with stories of what real-mom life is like—and realize that sometimes simply making it through the day is good enough. An uplifting yet real look at all that is expected of moms in the 21st century, *Mom Life: Perfection Pending* is so relatable you'll find yourself saying, "I guess I'm doing okay after all."

Preparing to Fly: Financial Freedom from Domestic Abuse by Sarah Hackley

Are financial worries keeping you stuck in an abusive or unhealthy relationship? Do you want to break free but don't know how to make it work financially? Take charge with *Preparing to Fly*, a personal finance book for women who want to escape the relationships that are holding them back.

Drawing on personal experiences and nearly a decade of financial expertise, Sarah Hackley walks readers step-by-step through empowering plans and tools: Learn how much money it will take to leave and how much you'll need to live on your own. Change the way you think about money to promote your independence. Bring control of your life back to where it belongs — with you. Break free and live in your own power, with *Preparing to Fly*. Additional tips for women with children, married women, pregnant women, the chronically ill, and more!

The Weight Loss Shift: Be More, Weigh Less by Michelle Hastie

The Weight Loss Shift: Be More, Weigh Less by Michelle Hastie helps those searching for their ideal bodies shift into a higher way of being, inviting the lasting weight they want — along with the life of their dreams! Skip the diets and the gimmicks, *The Weight Loss Shift* is a permanent weight loss solution. Based on science, psychology, and spirituality, Hastie helps readers discover their ideal way of being through detailed instructions and exercises, and then helps readers transform to living a life free from worry about weight — forever!

Would you like to love your body at any weight? Would you like to filter through others' body expectations to discover your own? Would you like to live at your ideal weight naturally, effortlessly, and happily? Then make the shift with *The Weight Loss Shift: Be More, Weigh Less!*

Where Is the Gift? Discovering the Blessing in Every Situation, a min-e-book™ by Caroline A. Shearer

Inside every challenge is a beautiful blessing waiting for us to unwrap it. All it takes is our choice to learn the lesson of the challenge! Are you in a situation that is challenging you? Are you struggling with finding the perfect blessing the universe is holding for you? This min-e-book™

will help you unwrap your blessings with more ease and grace, trust in the perfect manifestation of your life's challenges, and move through life with the smooth path your higher self intended. Make the choice: unwrap your gift today!

Women Will Save the World

Leading women across the nation celebrate the feminine nature through stories of collaboration, creativity, intuition, nurturing, strength, trailblazing, and wisdom in *Women Will Save the World*. Inspired by a quote from the Dalai Lama, bestselling author and Absolute Love Publishing Founder Caroline A. Shearer brings these inherent feminine qualities to the forefront, inviting a discussion of the impact women have on humanity and initiating the question: Will women save the world?

The Adventures of a Lightworker Series by Caroline A. Shearer

Dead End Date

Dead End Date is the first book in a metaphysical series about a woman's crusade to teach the world about love, one mystery and personal hang-up at a time. In a Bridget Jones meets New Age-style, *Dead End Date* introduces readers to Faith, a young woman whose dating disasters and personal angst have separated her from the reason she's on Earth. When she receives the shocking news that she is a lightworker and has one year to fulfill her life purpose, Faith embarks on her mission with zeal, tackling problems big and small—including the death of her blind date. Working with angels and psychic abilities and even the murder victim himself, Faith dives headfirst into a personal journey that will transform all those around her and, eventually, all those around the world.

The Highest Light Series by Jean Brannon

Atlantis Writhing

Atlantis is writhing. Chaos and greed have granted an obsessive new monarch enough power to destroy the world—and beyond. The only thing standing between King Gadeirus and intergalactic annihilation is Elysia and her fellow Light Ray missionaries. As time grows short, the missionaries work tirelessly to overcome the evil Lesser Light forces. When all options have been stripped away, a symbol long lost to antiquity surfaces just in time to inspire them to concoct one last desperate scheme.

Forbidden longings must be dealt with, too. Cravings Elysia must confront in the presence of hypnotic Alaric, a visiting dignitary with a scandalous past. But behind his seductive ways is a shocking secret—an unexpected key that may help Elysia unlock her potent power and wield it in the fight for the Highest Light.

The Raise Your Vibration Series by Caroline A. Shearer

Raise Your Vibration: Tips and Tools for a High-Frequency Life, **a min-e-book™**
Presenting mind-opening concepts and tips, *Raise Your Vibration: Tips and Tools for a High-Frequency Life,* a min-e-book™, opens the doorway to your highest and greatest good! This min-e-book™ demonstrates how every thought and every action affect our level of attraction, enabling us to attain what we truly want in life.

As beings of energy that give off and respond to vibration, it's important we understand the clarity, fullness, and happiness that come from living at a higher frequency. Divided into categories of mind, body, and spirit/soul, readers will learn practical steps they immediately can put into practice to resonate at a higher vibration and to further evolve their souls. A must-read primer for a higher existence! Are you ready for a high-frequency life?

Raise Your Financial Vibration: Tips and Tools to Embrace Your Infinite Spiritual Abundance, **a min-e-book™**
Are you ready to release the mind dramas that hold you back from your infinite spiritual abundance? Are you ready for a high-frequency financial life? Allow, embrace, and enjoy your infinite spiritual abundance and financial wealth today!

Absolute Love Publishing Creator Caroline A. Shearer explores simple steps and shifts in mindset that will help you receive the abundance you desire in *Raise Your Financial Vibration: Tips and Tools to Embrace Your Infinite Spiritual Abundance,* a min-e-book™. Learn how to release blocks to financial abundance, create thought patterns that will help you achieve a more desirable financial reality, and fully step into an abundant lifestyle by discovering the art of being abundant.

Raise Your Verbal Vibration: Create the Life You Want with Law of Attraction Language, **a min-e-book™**
Are the words you speak bringing you closer to the life you want? Or are your word choices inadvertently creating more difficulties? Discover words and phrases that are part of the Language of Light in Absolute Love Publishing Creator Caroline A. Shearer's latest in the Raise Your Vibration min-e-book™ series: *Raise Your Verbal Vibration:*

Create the Life You Want with Law of Attraction Language. Learn what common phrases and words may be holding you back, and utilize a list of high-vibration words that you can begin to incorporate into your vocabulary. Increase your verbal vibration today with this compelling addition to the Raise Your Vibration series!

Young Adult and Children's Books

Dear One, Be Kind by Jennifer Farnham
This beautiful children's book takes young children on a journey of harmony and empathy. Using rhyme and age-appropriate language and imagery, *Dear One, Be Kind* illustrates how children can embrace feelings of kindness and love for everyone they meet, even when others are seemingly hurtful. By revealing the unseen message behind common childhood experiences, the concept of empathy is introduced, along with a gentle knowledge of our interconnectedness and the belief that, through kindness, children have the power to change their world. Magically illustrated with a soothing and positive message, this book is a joy for children and parents alike!

Different by Janet McLaughlin
Twelve-year-old Izzy wants to be like everyone else, but she has a secret. She isn't weird or angry, like some of the kids at school think. Izzy has Tourette syndrome. Hiding outbursts and tics from her classmates is hard enough, but when a new girl arrives, Izzy's fear of losing her best friend makes Izzy's symptoms worse. And when she sees her crush act suspiciously, runaway thoughts take root inside of her. As the pressure builds and her world threatens to spin out of control, Izzy must face her fear and reveal her secret, whatever the costs.
Authentic and perceptive, *Different* shines a light on the delicate line of a child's hopes and fears and inspires us all to believe that perhaps we are not so different after all.

The Adima Chronicles by Steve Schatz

Adima Rising
For millennia, the evil Kroledutz have fed on the essence of humans and clashed in secret with the Adima, the light weavers of the universe. Now, with the balance of power shifting toward darkness, time is running out. Guided by a timeless Native American spirit, four teenagers from a small New Mexico town discover they have one month to awaken their inner power and save the world.

Rory, Tima, Billy, and James must solve four ancient challenges by the next full moon to awaken a mystical portal and become Adima. If they fail, the last threads of light will dissolve, and the universe will be lost forever. Can they put aside their fears and discover their true natures before it's too late?

Adima Returning

The Sacred Cliff is crumbling and with it the Adima way of life! Weakened by the absence of their beloved friend James, Rory, Tima, and Billy must battle time and unseen forces to unite the greatest powers of all dimensions in one goal. They must move the Sacred Cliff before it traps all Adima on Earth — and apart from the primal energy of the Spheres — forever!

Aided by a surprising and timeless maiden, the three light-weaving teens travel across the planes of existence to gain help from the magical creatures who guard the Adima's most powerful objects, the Olohos. There is only one path to success: convince the guardians to help. Fail and the Cliff dissolves, destroying the once-eternal Spheres and the interdimensional light weavers known as Adima.

Like the exciting adventures of *Adima Rising*, the second spellbinding book of The Adima Chronicles, *Adima Returning*, will have your senses reeling right up until its across-worlds climax. Will conscious creation and the bonds of friendship be enough to fight off destructive forces and save the world once again?

The Soul Sight Mysteries by Janet McLaughlin

Haunted Echo

Sun, fun, toes in the sand, and daydreams about her boyfriend back home. That's what teen psychic Zoey Christopher expects for her spring break on an exotic island. But from the moment she steps foot onto her best friend Becca's property, Zoey realizes the island has other plans: chilling drum beats, a shadowy ghost, and a mysterious voodoo doll.

Zoey has always seen visions of the future, but when she arrives at St. Anthony's Island to vacation among the jet set, she has her first encounter with a bona fide ghost. Forced to uncover the secret behind the girl's untimely death, Zoey quickly realizes that trying to solve the case will thrust her into mortal danger — and into the arms of a budding crush. Can Zoey put the tormented spirit's soul to rest without her own wild emotions haunting her?

Fireworks

Dreams aren't real. Psychic teen Zoey Christopher knows the difference between dreams and visions better than anyone, but ever since she and her best friend returned from spring vacation, Zoey's dreams have been warning her that Becca is in danger. But a dream isn't a vision — right?

Besides, Zoey has other things to worry about, like the new, cute boy in school. Dan obviously has something to hide, and he won't leave Zoey alone — even when it causes major problems with Josh, Zoey's boyfriend. Is it possible he knows her secret?

Then, one night, Becca doesn't answer any of Zoey's texts or calls. She doesn't answer the next morning either. When Zoey's worst fears come true, her only choice is to turn to Dan, whom she discovers has a gift different from her own but just as powerful. Is it fate? Will using their gifts together help them save Becca, or will the darkness win?

Discover what's real and what's just a dream in *Fireworks*, book two of the Soul Sight Mysteries!

Serafina Loves Science! by Cara Bartek

Cosmic Conundrum

In *Cosmic Conundrum*, sixth grader Serafina Sterling finds herself accepted into the Ivy League of space adventures for commercial astronauts, where she'll study with Jeronimo Musgrave, a famous and flamboyant scientist who brought jet-engine minivans to the suburbs. Unfortunately, Serafina also meets Ida Hammer, a 12-year-old superstar of science who has her own theorem, a Nobel-Prize-winning mother, impeccable fashion sense — *and* a million social media followers. Basically, she's everything Serafina's not. Or so Serafina thinks.

Even in an anti-gravity chamber, Serafina realizes surviving junior astronaut training will take more than just a thorough understanding of Newton's Laws. She'll have to conquer her fear of public speaking, stick to the rules, and overcome the antics of Ida. How will Serafina survive this cosmic conundrum?

Quantum Quagmire

Serafina suspects something is wrong when her best friend, Tori Copper, loses interest in their most cherished hobbies: bug hunting and pizza nights. When she learns Tori's parents are getting a divorce and that Tori's mom is moving away, Serafina vows to discover a scientific solution to a very personal problem so that Tori can be happy again. But will the scientific method, a clever plan, and a small army of arachnids be enough to reunite Tori's parents? When the situation goes haywire, Serafina realizes she has overlooked the smallest, most quantum of details. Will love be the one challenge science can't solve?

Join Serafina in another endearing adventure in book two of the Serafina Loves Science! series.

Connect with us and learn more about our books and upcoming releases at AbsoluteLovePublishing.com.

Made in United States
North Haven, CT
17 December 2023

45883110R00143